uine.

The Whitby Trilogy – Part 3:

Luke

Nov 2020

By John G Smith

Copyright © 2020 John G Smith
ISBN: 978-1-716-48778-1

Published by John G Smith 2020
thewhitbytrilogy.co.uk

9 781716 487781

*This book is dedicated to Amelia who helped
me so much, and she didn't even know it*

No author is an island. I express my gratitude to:-

*My wife Julia
Dave Robinson
Angus Macrae
Phil Holmes
Leigh Melvin
Steve Hewitt*

"You know Super, an old business friend of my
dad wanted me to know that *nubdy made big
dosh legal like*".

"Pearl didn't reply but thought, *yes young lady,
everything is all so marvellous but life will bite at
some stage, it always does*".

Luke

Character profile

Luke (born 1990) has driving ambition. Deep down he has a conscience which is well-guarded. Keen sportsman – plays squash. Confident. Wholehearted lover. A thinker and risk taker. Careful what he eats. Guile inherited from his great uncle Harold with the ability to use rather than need people and with a tendency to control. First class education. Likes quality. Exercises patience. Has his own gym in the Old Hall. Tall handsome man. Money orientated. Expert software engineer.

Pearl, now in her early forties, was born an only child into an upper middle class family. Her mother was killed in a car accident when she was 16, leaving her distraught. After public school and Oxford, she joined a national newspaper and rose to become sub-editor. Her career path was halted by her decision to nurse her father, a senior military man, who was suffering from a genetic disorder. She is tall and attractive, well-spoken and refined in her tastes. She has high morals and is always well dressed from independent boutiques. Her love of books led her to become a library assistant. She is an organised and no-nonsense lady.

Marcus was born in 1981, an only child to remote parents. He was introverted and didn't interact with other children until his late teens. He was exceptionally good at maths with a structured analytical mind. After gaining a Masters Degree he set up as a home-based stock market day trader. He has all the trappings of an affluent lifestyle: ground floor apartment in a fashionable part of north London, designer clothes and a high spec Maserati. A regular gym user, he is slim and has jet black hair. He has an independent spirit, enjoys stylish restaurants and quality wines. He would love to be a dad.

Kyaw (born 1996) is guided by Burmese principles of morality, notably courtship customs. She had a positive upbringing and is keen for her mother country to better itself. Femininity: alluring, teasing, drawing one in with Oriental magnetism. Kyaw was grief stricken at her father's passing. She has grace and charm and is imbued with the culture she was brought up with. Full of life, zest. Burmese student and friend of Pearl

Naing, born 1977 to Aung & Hlaing, who died when she was 10 years old. She is the granddaughter of Eugene and Chit, her grandmother with whom she spent much of her formative years. She was bright and extrovert as a child, graduated in Dentistry in Mandalay. Her love of travel brought her to England, where she joined a practice on the South Coast. She is forthright and not afraid to tell it how it is.

Alice, born 1982, was brought up in a nondescript part of Essex in a far from wealthy family. She describes herself as an "entry level copper in a man's world". She has long blond hair, almost down to her waist and legs to die for. Off duty she uses expensive perfume and has feverish lust: classically beautiful.

Aung is Naing's father and was married to Hlaing, now deceased. He was the only son of Eugene and Chit. He is a retired teacher and academic and lives north of Mandalay in Myanmar (Burma). He is viewed as a respected elder citizen with further contributions to make.

Prologue – the end of Pearl, the start of Luke

"In this job and after enough years, there are highs; of course there are. It's not all routine drudgery. It's not all dealing with a section of society that, being honest with ourselves, we'd rather not get involved with. When a villain has been sorted, when something precious has been returned to its owner, when you see an element of trust return, that is a high point. It makes it all worthwhile. And yet Alice, at times like this, I do despair. I lose faith in humanity. How does it work that a man as evil as this can destroy and destroy and himself stay unharmed, continue to live. And, what's more, into his ninth decade. Yes, when we have him behind bars it will be a high, but think of the cost in human suffering and how close he got to escaping completely. If the case hadn't been closed all those years ago, my illustrious predecessors may well have got the wrong man put away. Yes, they were competent coppers but lacking the science we have today. This Harold bloke would have won, just imagine that. He walks away with the family money, the family house and, I should think most important to him, the satisfaction of drawing down the final curtain on a younger brother he knew he couldn't match. He had bullied Eugene as a kid then snared him as an adult. And we have all stood by and allowed a serial poisoner to flourish. Alice, I needed to get that off my chest. You seem to be the only one I can talk to these days".

Alice remained silent but through those few words delivered by her boss with such feeling, she began to appreciate the weight of responsibility attached to the authority of his job. Superintendent Macrae was not the remote and blundering senior officer portrayed by crime series on TV. This cold case, that very nearly didn't happen, was very important to him. Had she realised from day one the confidence he must have had in her ability to uncover the truth? Has he felt the anguish of a predecessor needing passionately to right an injustice, only to have the rug pulled from underneath his feet? Has he countenanced that, after all this time and relating to the same Whitby case, he too might go to his grave with a tortured soul? And without a grandson Marcus to call on for redemption. All she could do was nod in a gesture of acceptance.

"I've the strongest possible feeling that time is of the essence. We have to strike quickly. Neil has three days to prepare our submission to the CPS and they are primed. I was serious about protection; the next seven days or so could be critical. Alice, I want you to text Pearl Bennett, no emails from this point. Ask her to call your personal mobile. Say we have a conference on the case this Saturday and it's important that she and her friend attend, feel sure you won't have to but apply whatever pressure is needed. Book a couple of rooms at Breadsall Priory. Make sure you spell out the bill is on us and that we'll cover all the travelling costs. Deal with this personally. I've already booked the training room from 2 as a further case review. No point in alerting the rest of the station. This sets your deadline. I intend to take a back seat; the floor is for you and Marcus. Provided the CPS is on side, the pre-dawn raid will be very soon".

Alice was looking directly at her boss. "What about this Luke guy?"

"Yes, you're right. Tell Pearl Bennett not to tip him off. Is he the one telling Harold what's going on or is it someone closer? The other thing we must bear in mind is that Luke Brown might face prosecution. Was he being used by his grandfather or was he an accomplice? OK, that's about it. Do you fancy a drink on the way home?" Alice rose from her chair.

"I won't if you don't mind. Best keep a clear head before starting on the theory report with Marcus".

Superintendent Macrae also left his chair and moving towards the door, turned back.

"Alice, I have worked out that you and Marcus are an item. I'm afraid it's obvious. Let me say how much I admire your approach to the job in hand. You have tried so hard to pretend he is just your assistant and got on with things the way you always do. Your secret, if it is one, is safe with me and once this lot is over, boy, will we have a party!"

*

Once the formal introductions were over, Superintendent Macrae was saying how pleased he was that Miss Pearl Bennett and Miss Naing had been able to join his team for this conference. He had asked DCI Alice Wallace, who had led the cold case review, to outline a theory of what happened back in the 1950's and at various times since. She would be assisted by Marcus Clarke, a special adviser. Addressing Pearl directly, he felt she should know that it was not Harold Whitby that got this review started. Indeed, as she will realise as the theory unfolds, that would be the last thing he would have wanted. In fact, it was Marcus here who got the ball rolling by carrying out the dying wish of his elderly relative. "You see Pearl (I want us all to be on first name terms this afternoon), the junior of the two officers who called on Mr Eugene Whitby after the severed arm had been found in the 1950's was Marcus's grandfather who, literally with his last breath, wanted the case solved. He had been instructed to drop all enquiries at the time". Pearl's response was simply, "Oh". "Alice tells me that she and Marcus will share this presentation. Everything is being recorded. I ask any of you to interrupt as you wish. The more we can flesh things out, the better. That's my bit done, over to you Alice".

"We start in the present time by asking this question. Why did Harold Whitby contest his brother Eugene's will?

We believe his motive was not to get the inheritance per se. The theme throughout this story is resentment. His objective was to get inside Pearl's head. She had no right to befriend his younger brother. He would send her on a wild goose chase; a journey to cast serious doubt on Eugene's character. At some point he would offer to withdraw his challenge. The condition of course would be a split of the inheritance. As I mentioned, not because he wanted the money but to establish his importance as the last Whitby standing. Someone who must not be ignored. Should Pearl refuse to divide the money or refer to her solicitor, he would make public an allegation that Eugene murdered his two brothers.

"There are three sources of evidence that directly link Harold Whitby to serious crime. We consider them rock-solid and, incidentally, so also does the CPS (sorry, Crown Prosecution Service). They are postage stamps, handwriting and recordings of his voice. I will hand over to Marcus to talk us through what we believe happened to and within this Whitby family and those unfortunate enough to be connected to it".

"Thank you Alice. Using potassium cyanide dissolved in tea with sweeteners, Harold Whitby is a serial poisoner. While there may have been earlier instances, we first detect the murder of an elder brother Jack. He was the black sheep of the family, returning from a commune of homosexuals to claim his share of the family wealth. Second was another brother Rob who knew of the demise of Jack and had to be silenced. Neither of the bodies was ever found. Had it not been for this resentment psyche that Alice referred to and especially given the passage of time, our man would have got away with it. But, he had to incriminate his brother. How would he do it? Well, why not fall back on the butchery skills that each Whitby brother possessed? He could sever an arm from one of the bodies and plant it where it was sure to be found with a link to Eugene. So, how could Harold be sure the body part would be found and not left to rot? Our thinking goes like this. We know he had contact with his sister Molly through circumstances that Alice will refer to later. In turn she was on good terms with her sister Mary (sorry if this sounds complicated). Mary was married to a farmer who had land close to Eugene's business premises. Farmers have dogs and dogs have a keen sense of smell – it's not difficult to work out. There were two elements to Harold's plan. He would plant an item taken from Rob on Eugene's premises. Then, to make absolutely sure of framing him, he would write anonymously to the police. Why did this scheme fail? Because the investigation into the missing body part was closed before any search took place. Yet, Marcus's grandfather (a detective sergeant at the time) kept the letter sent to the police amongst his personal papers, no doubt hoping the case would be reopened in the future. So, without either knowing it, Harold's deadly plan misfired and Eugene was saved.

"Alice, before you explain about the listening device, should I move on to attempts two and three to put Eugene Whitby in serious trouble?"

"Yes and please try to speak more slowly. As you say, it's all somewhat complicated, especially with the different family members".

"OK – slapped wrist. (*Pearl smiled to herself. Had she been hasty in getting annoyed at his manner when he barged into her cottage with the policeman? Adviser – what sort of title is that? Who is this man? Actually she quite liked him. So does this DCI Wallace judging by the looks she keeps giving him*). This second aspect of our theory has no evidence to back it. Taken in isolation, it would amount to very little. Unlike the accusing letter I talked about before, there is no postage stamp to fit into Harold's set and also unlike episode three that I will come onto, there is no handwriting to prove he was the sender of a letter. What we do have is the record of a car mechanic's sudden death one month after a fatal car crash in 1957.

"Fanciful as it might seem, Alice and I have developed a theory. Somewhere in the vastness of the internet there is what I will call a closed-user-group of stamp collectors and dealers. And, I suspect it is hosted on the dark web. Now, here is a rhetorical question. In our review, have we come across anyone with the technical ability to set up such a user group? I'll answer that question. Yes, one Luke Brown. The great nephew of Harold Whitby is a computer expert. He runs his own computer business and tutors students in IT. If Harold asked for his special contacts to be hidden away, Luke could do it and not necessarily be suspicious of a motive. We now know that there can be big money in trading rare postage stamps: fertile ground for secrecy one might say. I must add that, to date, such a group hasn't been uncovered, but the backroom techies are working on it". Marcus looked at Alice.

"Should I finish off this bit?"

"Yes of course – you did most of the work".

Harold contacted a fellow stamp geek living somewhere in the North Devon area. By trade this person was a car mechanic. I want to break off just to say how indebted we are to Pearl for all the papers she handed to us. I have been told to stick to hard evidence and not to let any form of emotion enter into our work but I have learnt on this project just how hard that is. I know Pearl is a very sincere person and her friendship with Eugene was as spontaneous as it was genuine. True unselfish friendship is a very rare commodity and, until recently, something that has eluded me. Understanding the circumstances as I believe I do, if I had been creaking old Eugene, my stash of gold would have gone to her too". Marcus looked directly at Pearl and she had the most strange experience, something like the thump from a mild electric shock. What is happening? "Sorry Alice, got a bit carried away – another slapped wrist! The thing is, there is nothing in those notes or indeed in the other paperwork we examined in Eugene Whitby's bungalow, that casts any light on what caused the steering on his in-laws' car to fail. So, as pure speculation, this is what we think happened. Harold asks his fellow philatelist to tamper with the car and it worked. The car crashes and kills both occupants. Probably, the idea was for an item belonging to the car or the occupants to be planted on Paul, Eugene's nephew and business associate. Remember that Paul is Garry as mentioned in the note handed to Pearl at the graveside. As with the first attempt to implicate Eugene in a murder, why did it fail? Who knows? Almost certainly, we are back to postage stamps. Did the Devon accomplice get greedy over the trade of a rare stamp or did Harold renege on a deal? Why didn't Harold write to the police with his accusation as before? My guess is he got cocky. He thought the police were already onto Eugene re the two murders and now, a short time later, was at it again. Now they will pounce. But they didn't". Superintendent rose to his feet.

"We'll take a break at this point. Pearl, I know this is a lot to take in. You look a little flushed. Let's take a breath of air before Marcus and Alice complete their hypothesis".

"We move forward some twenty years to events that occurred in 1977. Dorothy, Eugene's wife and business partner, travels to North Devon to pay her respects – to mourn again. She takes a footpath that her parents trod all those years before. But forgetting to pack her insulin needles, she dies alone on a hillside. At the time it was a mystery and has remained so. Was it a mistake or a planned suicide? OK, this is partly supposition but it is also hard evidence backed. Amongst my grandfather's papers was a letter written to the police accusing (you might say for the boring umpteenth time) Eugene of murder. The writer was dismissed as a crank". Pearl interrupted.

"My God". Naing said.

"Whoever's God, yes".

"Harold, and we know it was written by him due to the handwriting expert's report, says the needles were switched for ones filled with a placebo and that this was Eugene's fifth murder. What we now surmise is that Harold was telling the authorities what he himself had done, or probably, what he had got someone else to do. And the latter theory could well stack up since our sleuths Pearl and Miss Naing found the record of a sudden death in the locality soon afterwards - you might think following the pattern of twenty years before. This time it was of a professional person who just happened to be a stamp collector. The coroner returned an open verdict due to there being no known cause of death. What this second philatelist did to deserve his gift of tea and sweetener, is anyone's guess.

"That just about ends my part of the theory so I will hand over to Alice who has concentrated on the mystery of why money was invested by Eugene Whitby offshore for the benefit of his sister Molly". Alice left her chair and moved to the whiteboard.

"I'll stand for the rest of the story, it helps me concentrate and I need to point to a few of my notes. My curiosity was aroused by what at first seemed an innocuous short note in one of Eugene Whitby's files. He records a visit from Harold and in the context of the great fuss (as he called it) made by his wife Dorothy. He placates her first with what was almost certainly a lie and secondly a firm statement of fact that really struck home to me. He says Harold congratulated the supermarket for selling fresh meat, thus restoring the family reputation as butchers. I disbelieve that. But then says she is not to worry because Harold will never visit again. How could he be so sure? Like Marcus's rhetorical question earlier, I'll answer that myself. It was because Eugene had agreed to pay money into a Jersey based bank. Why did he agree to do so? Almost certainly in response to a threat. Harold had already buried a body part of their brother Rob and had told the police where to find it. If Eugene refused to pay, Rob's gold watch would be found in a place only Eugene was linked to. It would be an anonymous tip off. We know he did send a letter and it referred to the gold watch. Presumably it hadn't actually been planted at the time of Harold's visit.

"Here we have the mind of a very cunning man. He double-banks every step he takes. Whether Eugene bought the entire threat we do not know, but certainly it was enough for him to agree. We have to remember that two Whitby men are missing and the police have already been to see him. His business is taking off and his reputation is high. There is however one imponderable. Eugene knew that his brother Harold was a murderer or had deeds done at his behest. Did he ever suspect his involvement in the car crash or his wife's demise? He didn't record any such thought either at the time or later. Perhaps preservation of the family's good name was always paramount and his nephew Adrian referred to his secrecy. The irony of course is that both catastrophic events increased, ultimately, Eugene's wealth. That Harold's resentment increased over the years, ultimately led to Eugene's death".

Alice moved closer to the whiteboard and pointed to a name. "Why is Molly to receive funds paid secretly for so many years? The answer is blackmail. Molly is making Harold pay for his crime. What she never knew was that this debt is passed to Eugene, a brother she actually likes but keeps her distance from, for fear of revealing the family secret. What does Molly know? At this point her grandson Luke Brown enters our story. Working to our instruction, he hands over some personal effects of his late grandmother including electronic and related items kept in memory of her late husband. Our conclusion is that a listening bug was planted by her in Harold's cottage and the receiver and storage devices were probably within a vehicle parked outside. She sought restitution for the Whitby girls being cut out of the family fortune and her husband had the technical skill to trap Harold.

"From what has been retrieved, we have a spoken confession to the poisoning of the two brothers". As before, Pearl interrupted spontaneously.

"My God".

"Yes and there's something else that really does beggar belief. Our clever adviser here (she looked at Marcus and Pearl gave a knowing kind of glance in Naing's direction) has decided that the words recorded were not spoken by Harold to a human being but to his pet parrot. A background screech that the audio scientists thought might be of a motorbike applying its breaks was actually the parrot doing whatever parrots do. To them the bike theory made sense because later there is what is described as a berrum, berrum noise". Marcus shot up from his chair.

"Alice, say that again – exactly the way you pronounced the sound".

"Berrum, berrum". There was complete silence in the room for what seemed an eternity. Marcus held his head in his hands.

"Christ, I have been so stupid, idiot, idiot. Why didn't I hear it that way before? I just knew there had to be a reason why the way that Harold guy spoke kept running through my head. That dialect. It concertinas proper words and it knocks off the ending. That was no motorbike. It was the damn parrot again. It was mimicking. Harold had told his Polly what he intended to do. Berry um, berry um. In plain English BURY THEM". Macrae jumped to his feet.

"Pearl is right – it really is My God. That bloody bloke has done just that. Somewhere in his garden we are going to find two skeletons".

*

Pearl was saying that it was really quite sweet. "It's not that unusual for two female friends to share a hotel room, is it?" Naing poured a dry sherry from the decanter into each of the two small wine glasses, handed one to her friend and took a sip.

"No and it's a shame because we can't really release the other room without the keen detectives detecting something! Still, I expect the boss man has a whopping expense budget and anyway, who knows, we may fall out. After the events of today, nothing from now on will surprise me". The girls settled in the two armchairs to enjoy the welcome drink: there was a long pause, eventually broken by Pearl.

"I expect you're thinking along the same lines as me. This guy Harold. One reads about such people in novels involving barely believable plot lines and of course, throughout history, there have been notorious poisoners but to uncover one over sixty years since he started his murderous deeds must surely come close to being unique. But more than that, it would never have come to light if an old man hadn't walked into my library asking questions on travel that he could so easily have found answers to himself. He wanted someone to talk to and I must have seen something of my daddy in him. Life can take so many unfathomable twists and turns, can't it?"

"Were it not so Pearl we wouldn't be sitting in this bedroom; in this posh place. Me, thousands of miles from home and you a couple of hundred, but yet glued together for better or worse. This man who we now know is a killer, what honed his personality? Born, almost a hundred years ago, into a huge family of butchers, and a misfit. From what I have learnt he refused, right from an early age, to toe the line. He did not kowtow to his father. He did not slaughter as instructed. He slaughtered when he wanted to and for his own reason. His introversion acquiesced with postage stamps: first a hobby, then a living. But all the time, he harboured a hatred that centred on a younger brother. One who would conform. One who returned from the big wide world a hero. One who found a beautiful and connected wife and who started a business that would go from strength to strength. That is, until he gets his comeuppance. One day they will find out which of the lads was the clever one. Just a question of being patient. Biding one's time as you English say. Pearl, let's get showered and take that resplendent dining room by storm. Let's see if the food is as good as they claim. As a starter, I might ask for Mohinga, what do you think?"

*

Alice and Marcus were tucked up in their favourite place, bed. Alice had been saying that she felt this had been the greatest weekend ever for sheer release. Soon it would be all over.

"My adorable gorgeous girlfriend, how soon?"

"This exercise is a very rare event and only the top brass have the details – I am OK with that. Darling, it is imminent. There cannot be the slightest possibility of him slipping through our net. Actually, the cottage has been under constant observation since your berry um, berry um". Alice propped herself on her elbow and looked down at him. "Clever, smartarse Mr. Clarke". Two hours passed.

"Alice, I want to be serious. It is agreed and there is no going back. OK, there will be the celebration at the station party and obviously, I'll be invited. If not, you will be shackled to this bed and Macrae can take all the credit the DCI is indisposed." Alice giggled. "He can tell your lot we're engaged and are shortly to marry. Then I whisk you off in the Maserati to be salaciously ensconced in my secret Tufnell Park pad".

"Oh Marcus, you say the most wonderful things".

"Now we get down to business, I mean, not that business, our future. I know what you said before but definitely take the new job. They need you, you need the buzz. Anyway, I can't be distracted from my trading screens. At least, not until baby No 1 arrives. Just think of the extra pension based on your whopping new salary"

"Pension, pension. How dare you talk of my old age? I am young, fit and able. Look, I'll show you".

*

The raid was at dawn. The battering ram wasn't needed; the door was unlocked. Just a push and it swung open. Harold Whitby was sitting in a bamboo rocking chair, his right hand holding a walking stick. In the air was a faint smell of almonds. On a side-table was a small china teapot and a single cup. All four walls of the room were covered, floor to ceiling, with shelves. Empty shelves. He was dead. The police officer who had entered the cottage through the unlocked back door spoke first. "There's been a fire in the garden. Even in this half-light I could see bits of paper everywhere". Alice recalled, *Marcus said this room was full of stamp albums, rows and rows of them. Looks like he's destroyed the lot. Must have been thousands of pounds worth of stamps. He couldn't even let anyone else benefit from a lifetime's work.*

"Nothing more we can do here: a job for the white-coat brigade. All that planning, what a waste of time. Neil, you stay here. Wait for the forensics to appear. Secure the site and the contractors are due at 10. Don't let them out of your sight. They know the drill but you make sure. I'm told that each of those apple trees will have a tap root. They are to work slowly and carefully. If possible we want the skeletons intact. Hang on, something's set that parrot off. Neil, is it talking? What's it saying?

Not sure, that damn accent. Sounds a bit like, *won't get me, silly sod, stupid bugger"*.

*

The bar staff had their instructions. No alcohol to be served before Superintendent Macrae has said his piece. "I'll start with an apology (collective groan). Sorry to have dragged you all to this remote and rugged wilderness of Wessington (slight titter) but DCI Wallace absolutely insisted and one thing I've learned over the past six months is never to cross her (a few guffaws). As compensation, I have allocated the whole of my remaining expenses budget for the year to financing a free bar until the beer runs out (loud cheers). The reason we are here is to celebrate a successful conclusion to the force's first cold case review. I realise that only a few of you knew exactly what was going on, as opposed to the story we let out, but it was essential to avoid any possibility of leaks (silence). The fact is, and I put my hand up in expressing grave doubts about its initiation, the team headed by Alice has solved the murder of two local men back in the 1950's (more cheers). Not only has justice been served but also an accusation made against a wholly innocent man has been disproved (mild applause). This success is not going unrewarded. Alice is being promoted although sadly she will be leaving to join the Met. (some groans). DC Neil Collett is promoted to DS and is staying with us. I want to be the first to congratulate him (loud applause). Now for some really happy news and once you have a full glass, this must be the first toast. A certain Marcus Clarke brought this cold case to us and I know you have all become accustomed to his cheery face about the station and at one time or another begged for a ride in his banger (loud cheers). He and our lovely Alice met on this case, became an item as they say these days and are to marry (great cheers and much banging on the table). Both Alice and Marcus are soft

Southerners so why they have chosen to hold their nuptials in harsh and darkest Derbyshire is a mystery, except that a little bird whispered that they had their first date in this very pub (more loud cheers and banging on the table). Well, what are you all waiting for, let's party!"

The party was in full swing when Macrae asked Alice if he could have a private word outside. He shouted over to Marcus who was struggling to escape the attention of three WPC's, "Want to borrow her for a couple of minutes, no need to worry. Alice, I really am so very pleased the way things have turned out. You've been the best No 1 I've ever had. I've downed a few drinks but that's when the truth comes out doesn't it? If you get any problems down in London, you know with the smart alecs, give me a bell. Just two things and you can rescue your man. First, Luke Brown. I'm not sure about him. The CPS say the case against him is not strong enough. But, you know, the old copper snout. He delivered that first note to Pearl Bennett, he set up Harold Whitby's computer trading and the dark website we found of the stamp collectors' database. Our security have found no trace of a mole at the station, so who tipped the villain off? When down in the smoke, just keep an eye out. He's got work not just here but in Australia and Burma. Just a word to the wise. Secondly, the legal eagles say the challenge to the will of Eugene Whitby is null and void. A murderer can't benefit from his crime. Email that firm in Brighton and let them know. Alice, give me a peck on the cheek. I'll miss you."

*

Pearl was saying it felt so much like the *Last Supper*. While they were all too conscious of the events bringing them together this evening, what the future held was an unknown quantity. So, time to take stock. For herself, the long-promised book beckoned. If this whole experience did not have the making of a cracking novel, then Charles Dickens never existed. She had the skeleton (oh dear, poor choice of word!) of characters for the plot and now new ones will appear.

*

It was as if the morning of 7th May 2016 heralded the start of summer. There was no cloud. The sky was deepest blue and the song thrush, bursting his speckled breast with the most complicated combination of notes, was as appreciative as any guest now leaving through the lichgate of Holy Trinity Church, Brackenfield. Did his potential mate, perched on the topmost branch of the horse chestnut tree standing a few yards to the right of the imposing oak door of the Horse & Jockey, harbour any doubts after the long damp spring? Who knows?

Superintendent Macrae was extremely honoured to be principal guest at the wedding breakfast. He recalled one lunchtime glancing out of his office window and seeing a beautiful blonde lady passing her hand slowly and almost lovingly over the bonnet of a Maserati in the front carpark. He had thought to himself *Ah, beauty and the beast.* How could he have known that the beast was about to drag his best officer away from the wilds of darkest Derbyshire?

The guests, most still holding a drink, mingled and merged into small groups on the lawn outside the pub. Marcus left his bride and strolled over to Pearl. He placed his hand on her left elbow and guided her slowly away towards the oak tree. "Pearl, there is something devastatingly scientific I want to say to you".

"Really?"

"Yes. The day I intruded into your private world and unwittingly upset you, I noticed you went to the window to find your spirit self. Am I right, the robin?"

"Yes".

"Pearl did you know that little bird survives by observing the laws of quantum mechanics?"

"No, but the way you put it, I wish I had". They looked at each other and smiled. Pearl turned to face him. "Marcus did you know that Naing and I are a couple?" There was a pause.

"No Pearl I didn't but if that is how it is, I'm happy for you. The one thing I have learnt since meeting Alice is that we all need someone. We might go for long periods and think we don't, but we do". Pearl reached for Marcus's hand.

"Naing and I want a child. Will you do that for me?"

Saturday 23rd September 2017

The two elderly women were walking towards the church. One had lost her husband recently and the other had never married but always believed she would. Having been friends since school days, they had heard of a big wedding and wanted to see the bride.

The wedding guests were already mingling on the lawn following the service and the photographer was busily organising groups. They were in luck. The bride was in this group. Her dress was pure white and she had a white carnation in her hair or, viewed at this distance, it could have been some sort of daisy. The four ladies looked so alike that the elder one must surely be the mother and the other two, younger sisters. Each held a bouquet of brightly coloured flowers. Their smiles were dazzling. One of the women watching from the perimeter fence sighed deeply.

Just to the right of the group being photographed stood two other ladies. One was dressed in bright yellow with matching coloured flowers in her hair, the other wore a pale blue suit and was holding a baby. They guessed four months old, perhaps five. A tall man approached. He stooped slightly, took the young child and held it in his arms. He rocked the infant gently and started to talk to the lady in blue. Her husband they supposed. What they had missed a few minutes earlier was this handsome man talking urgently on his mobile phone. There was a terrorist incident on the South Bank and his wife had left.

Now being manoeuvred into the photographer's sights was an old man in a wheelchair. He had two medals pinned to his jacket lapel. Pushing the wheelchair was a big man with broad shoulders and a ruddy complexion. He was leaning forward and talking to the old man and pointing to other guests.

A young man dressed in a very smart charcoal grey suit emerged from the porch. One of the two ladies thought he walked with a slight swagger. Now at his bride's side, he gestured to the gathering *watch this* and with a teasing manner drew her veil down over her face. After a few seconds he slowly raised the veil and kissed her full on the lips. The couple embraced. The photographer looked up from his camera tripod and the guests started to clap.

The woman onlooker who had sighed a few moments earlier said to her friend, "All these posh people gathered together for a wonderful wedding and not one of them knows what tomorrow will bring. Life is strange isn't it?"

The Gathering

One

They say all babies look the same. How silly. Every mother knows her baby: she could pick him out from a batch of a hundred, all born on the same day. How do you think a mother puffin picks out her chick when returning from a day's fishing at sea? Instinctive isn't it? Anyway, he's not a baby any more. His features are set. The pout of the lower lip. The stern stare. Wasn't he born with a mass of jet-black hair? Obviously he's Marcus Mark 2. Obviously. Of course, we couldn't call him that. It was a typical piece of Naing inspiration. "What a test of those little lungs. What an outcry. What a tumult". Next day she came back with the name and I had no say in it. None at all. A sort of unspoken - you got the baby - I got the name. Tristan. And that was it.

Did we take the right decision? If it had been the artificial route, would I now think well, it's been a success and I can give all my feelings to Tristan. No different in principle to the injections against yellow fever when travelling with Daddy. I mean, that was to prevent something horrid happening. This was to make something wonderful happen. Instead, we went into that hotel bedroom and did it and I can't get that night out of my head. What's more, Marcus and Alice were newly-weds and Naing and I couldn't do it ourselves, could we? That's why I asked Marcus to give me a baby. No other reason. I felt nothing for him as a man. Daddy would have understood, Naing does. It's just that when I look at Tristan, like now, having his afternoon sleep, lying in that most uncomfortable-looking position of face down, head buried in the pillow and bottom in the air, I get these pangs. I still have this picture of Marcus cradling Tristan in his arms at

Kyaw and Luke's wedding, as if it was the most natural thing in the world. Well, of course, it was. Except it wasn't. More than two years ago, yet it seems like this afternoon. I must get Tristan's tea ready.

I ought to do some research. After all, there are mountains of academic studies on every conceivable (how did that word enter my head?) subject under the sun. I can't be the first person to feel this way, yet I don't want to know what some amorphous body concluded. This is me: it's private. I have to work it out for myself. And I know why I'm jittery. Marcus is calling again this afternoon. Just happens to be passing by and wants to drop off a small gift for Tristan, again. Of course, Naing will be here later. She always comes to the cottage on Saturday evenings. Our little menage-a-trois, when it should be a conventional quartet. But apparently Alice is on special duties again. We've drifted into this routine of walking on the sea front with Tristan in his pushchair, but he soon wants to get out and hold our hands. It's his little game. He knows he'll soon be picked up by Marcus. Two-and-a-half years old and already dictating what's happening. I suppose, in a way, binding me and Marcus together.

Didn't think I would, but actually I've got interested in what Marcus does. It started with him throwing down a sort of challenge. "Pearl, as a lady of letters – and I want to talk about that sometime – I suppose you wouldn't be interested in how I made some money this week? Shame in a way especially as Alice's world is very different and, as she says, she mustn't be distracted by the risks she knows I take. So, I'm still the lone ranger, even after all that has happened". As he must have known from the start, this was an open invitation: one I was going to accept.

The Saturday afternoon promenades were timed perfectly because he could describe his Friday 4.30pm closing positions and work backwards to explain why each had been opened. Like he said, I didn't need to get swamped in technical jargon. Apparently, the stock market day trade strike price gave either a closing profit or loss. I realised this was exciting stuff. After a while I could hardly wait for the next update. And then came what he called his "Maserati Moment". I'd never seen him so elated. He kept throwing Tristan in the air and catching him to squeals of delight.

Marcus removed his left hand from the pushchair and placed it gently on Pearl's shoulder. As he'd intended, they stopped walking and he turned to face her "Pearl, there is something I'm bursting to tell you. I knew it was going to happen and it did, it really did. All this doomsayer rubbish of the bearded leftist grabbing power or at best a hung parliament. It was always going to be a Tory landslide. All the marginal-seat polls said so, all my candlestick charts said so. I was certain. Alice accused me of being too confident, something about the Met. preparing for street riots. I could have done sterling or the Footsie 250 tracker or a composite and, in the event, they did put on a few percentage points. But the UK house builder I'd watched all summer and autumn was yelling so loud from each screen, it couldn't be ignored. Pearl, between you and me and that squawking seagull, and for God's sake don't let on to Alice, my last trade just before Thursday close of play was £250,000 on Taylor Wimpey. By five past eight on Friday I was out. After trading costs I cleared £36,000. Whoopee, I can almost smell the leather on that next Maserati. Look, let's pop in here as usual. This time I'll get you a proper coffee, not that bland black Americano stuff you always ask for".

Their luck was in, the corner table with its clear view of the sea was available. Pearl used her best pleading voice. "Marcus, I'm pleased for you, really I am but no you can't get him a sticky bun. He's not old enough and anyway I don't want him getting fat. I want a slim fit little man - someone who'll grow up to be like you. Sorry, sorry, shouldn't have said that. Look, he's asleep. It's not surprising, he must be exhausted after being thrown about all afternoon. Marcus, let's take this chance to have a proper talk. I'm bored stiff hearing of your latest stroke of financial genius. Tell me, what's all this about me being a lady of letters?"

"Listen Miss higher-echelon graduate of the English language: Miss posh newspaper assistant editor or whatever you once were, the Tristan sleep-deprived nights are history and I know perfectly well that Naing takes over during every spare minute she has. So, no more excuses. You must start plotting the Whitby Saga and I insist on helping with the structure and, actually, here is my first bit of mentoring. Pearl, will you stop staring at those cakes and listen. You are in a theatre, fourth row back, near the centre with a perfect view. The story unfolds. It's complicated and before the final curtain many actors will take part. In fact, you are one of the actors although not appearing for a while. Think clearly. It's like a dream, absurd things happen but at the time they seem real, very real. In the opening scene, two men and a boy alight from a butcher's van in a farmyard. It's dark and eerie: dodgy things are afoot. O.K. it's over to you. Get those creative juices flowing". *Pearl trembled slightly, did it show?*

*

Superintendent Alice Clarke was not worried. Why should she be? Not at all. It was just that here she was standing alone a few yards along Victoria Embankment from the imposing sign NEW SCOTLAND YARD. The neo-classical Curtis Green Building seemed unfriendly, even remote as if to deny she had walked out of its portals only a few minutes earlier. Her official car would pull up and, with any luck, she'd be home within half an hour. No, she wasn't worried. Still, the homecoming wasn't quite what it used to be and even at around 10 p.m. on this Saturday night, Marcus might not be there. It was always the traffic. The A23 on the stretch out of Brighton was often choked, especially with the shoppers going home. He'd texted an hour ago saying he'd intended setting off in the late afternoon but Naing had arrived earlier than expected and they'd persuaded him to stay for supper. Anyway, he knew she wouldn't mind. Her being wrapped up in that fraud case and knowing how he loved reading the bedtime story to Tristan. Pinocchio again!

It was a good thing really. After all, Marcus was Tristan's biological father and it was lovely seeing his eyes light up whenever the little boy's name was mentioned. Even more so when that next gift arrived, courtesy of Amazon. Of course, Alice and Pearl were very different people. Well, sexuality must come into it, but maybe it was more to do with their different backgrounds. Alice wasn't jealous just a bit put out by the way things had developed. In the first flush of their lovemaking she'd been aching to have his baby. Well, they'd agreed to it and it was all so spontaneous she sometimes wondered why she hadn't become pregnant: Pearl had, straight away. But then the London job, the move into Tufnell Park. She supposed the good life, posh restaurants, West End theatres, really getting to know each other, meeting the families. All so whirlwind. But really was it more to do with taking this senior job and not wanting to let Bill Macrae - her old boss – down? Plus, Marcus being so deep into his charts and saying he'd lost six months on the cold case up North. Actually, she was a bit worried. God, after the day she'd had, this bloody traffic. She needed a drink. She needed Marcus. She needed him like crazy.

*

It took six months for Pearl and Naing to accept that their original aspiration, at least on timing, had been naïve in the extreme. Deciding to set up a public benefit charity was one thing, getting it off the ground was quite another. It hadn't helped that each had been self-sufficient. The committee thing had come into play. At one meeting Naing had interrupted the chat with, "Now I understand why some wag has claimed that a camel was a horse designed by committee". It was true: every member had a view and each initial thought branched into divergent paths. In the end it was decided that Pearl alone would draft a submission to the Charity Commission. After all, it was her money, her restitution, her debt (as she saw it) to Eugene.

The name of the charity would stay as the acronym Dotcom (Deed of trust children of Myanmar). Aung would chair the panel and, as creation of the trust evolved, Luke Brown and Marcus Clarke would be invited to join Pearl, Naing and Kyaw as trustees. There was a perceived good reason for their inclusion: Luke's computer skills and Marcus's knowledge of the stock market.

Pearl was intent on drawing on her editorial experience. There would be no flowery language and no padding. Cut to the chase. She was clear on what she wanted. The charitable purpose, written as the Objects Clause of the governing document, was education. The charitable achievement would be providing finance to enable selected children of Myanmar to benefit from a secondary education, otherwise unaffordable. Special emphasis would be on a command of spoken and written English. This objective would be attained by searching schools in and around Mandalay. Overseas university placement, prioritising the UK, would be favoured. With Pearl's initial seed corn capital of £1m, Dotcom was launched.

Following the registration of Dotcom, Pearl and Naing had a celebratory meal at the *Flying Mackerel* and, walking to Naing's flat afterwards, exhaled what in later years they would refer to fondly as their "collective sigh of relief". Yet, Pearl was thinking *done but not done. Some, as yet unknown, future youth of Myanmar will help that poor country take its rightful place amongst the Asian Tiger economies. I know dear Eugene would be pleased. But it's not enough. He never knew what happened to his wartime sweetheart Chit. He never knew she got back home safely and that he had a child and a grandchild. Marcus was right, I have to write the story. But there is more, it nags at me. Think. Where is that piece of ground that Chit worked on, where she laid to die? Does Naing actually own it through her wider family? If not, can I buy it? Can that ground be dedicated to Chit's memory? Is placing a plaque in the local Pagoda allowed?* Pearl turned to Naing. "Think I might FaceTime your dad tomorrow. As well as starting our Dotcom searches, I've thought of another little job he might consider doing for me.

*

It was just after 10pm on Saturday 25th November 2017 and Pearl must have been nodding off in front of the log fire when the alarm went off. *Silly me, that's no fire alarm, whatever is it?* The landline was blasting – demanding to be answered. *Who on earth is that?*

"Pearl it's me, Adrian. Oh, sorry, didn't realise it's got this late. Were you asleep?

"No, no, of course not. How nice to hear from you Adrian, you know you can call me anytime, actually you woke me from a weird dream. Everything was lovely. I was pushing Tristan in his pram along the front and out of nowhere appeared young Luke: without a word, he tried to take the pram off me and just as I was about to scream for help, some sort of alarm went off. After a few seconds I realised the 'phone was ringing and, thank God, it was you – what a relief. No, always happy to hear from you. Naing went home about an hour ago and Tristan is fast asleep in his cot, I must have dropped off as well. Sorry, nattering on, what fabulous news have you got for me?"

"Well, funny you should say that, but not fabulous at all, quite the opposite. Had a call from Billy's sister earlier this evening. She rang to say Billy died earlier today. She was weepy but I gather his body was found on High Borrans. Must have set off for his usual climb and snuffed it. It's hard to take in really, I mean it's only, what, a couple of months since I was pushing his wheelchair at Kyaw and Luke's wedding. Apart from his legs giving him gyp that particular day he seemed in good fettle and certainly hadn't lost his thirst for a pint or two. He was old of course, in fact his sister said he'd 'ave been ninety in a week's time. Tell you what Pearl, he'd have been proud to have beaten Eugene by a couple of years. I'll get to the funeral whenever it is and should I represent you? You mustn't even think of going all the way to Kendal, especially not with that young 'un in tow".

"That's really sad Adrian. He was a dear man and I really enjoyed our trip up there to talk about Eugene. Yes, please do mention me. Honestly, and assuming someone's going to talk about his life, I don't think I could've listened to the eulogy. Bound to include Burma and all that and I'd be at Eugene's graveside again. Selfish I know but that's how it is I'm afraid".

"Pearl, don't worry. I quite understand. As before, we're going to have to pull together as these events unfold. This won't be the last time the past will come back to haunt us, I feel it in my bones. Oh, and by the way, there's a couple of other things I want to chew over with you. Is it better if I ring another time?"

"Not at all Adrian, carry on. I'm wide awake now and anyway rude awakenings are something I've got used to over the past months. Instead of attending to my little horror, what's better than listening to your dulcet tones?"

"Well, stop me whenever you want because in some ways the subject I need to open up will, as you put it earlier, place you at Eugene's graveside. It's about that scoundrel Harold. You see, it occurred to me that with all of us putting past events to the back of our minds, and especially as all the suspicions about Eugene turned out to be unfounded (as we knew they would be), one development has been overlooked".

"Really?".

"Yes. In a nutshell, what happened to Harold's money? Let me ask you straight out Pearl, have you ever thought about that? Don't answer, I'll rabbit on assuming you haven't. In my amateurish way I've been looking into the legal bit. First, did any of his wealth come from his victims? Well, as far as anyone knew and will ever know, it didn't. It's important to establish this since under a rule known as forfeiture, a murderer cannot benefit from his crimes. So, as far as I can see, the money was rightfully his to leave as he wished.

"So then I thought about who was entitled to inherit the rascal's pile of gold. Well, astonishingly, I discovered that there are no legal provisions in the UK which would prevent a murderer from leaving money to his blameless offspring. Of course, Harold had no offspring but, on the other hand, he didn't die without making a will, which could have really complicated things. As we know he had a great nephew. His validated will left all his money to that person. So, Luke Brown who married your student friend Kyaw two months ago became, in September 2016, a very wealthy man".

"I must say Adrian, this is all news to me. I'm really surprised Kyaw hasn't said anything".

"That's probably because she doesn't know. Been thinking a lot about young Luke. Doing my bit of research into the inheritance thing made me wonder if he actually was blameless in terms of being able to receive Harold's fortune. But, I suppose, he must have passed whatever tests the solicitor handling the estate applied. OK, he was brought up under the wing of his great uncle and, as I told you a couple of years ago, was indebted to him (quite deliberately on Harold's part of course) until his university days were over. Perhaps afterwards as well, if he knew of his inheritance. We know from the forensic tests after Harold was found dead that Luke set up the stamp collectors' database used for online trading, but that hardly puts him in the frame as a partner-in-crime, so to speak. Anyway, I suppose questioning his role in a moral sense is no doubt quite different from what is unlawful when it comes to inheritance. And, this sort of ground must have been raked over because Marcus told me (probably shouldn't have done as it would have come from Alice) that an opinion was sought by the police on whether young Luke had been an accomplice to Harold's ill-gotten gains. Obviously, it gained no traction at the time".

"Adrian, I'm taken aback by what you're telling me, especially querying whether Kyaw knows about what her husband inherited from that evil Harold. In fact, it's shaken me. I'll find out, one way or another. As you probably know, I was really upset when Naing and I found that Luke, at the behest of his great uncle, had wheedled his way into Kyaw's affections. But he relented and chose her over Harold. Now you've sown doubt in my mind about his sincerity. By the way, how much are we talking about?"

"Just over £2 million"

"What! I'd absolutely no idea. How on earth did he make that sort of money? Right, well, that's convinced me that Kyaw doesn't know. She would have told me in a flash, I'm certain."

"Pearl, where have they been since the wedding?"

"They're just back after six or seven weeks on their honeymoon. I say honeymoon, and no doubt the first few days in London were, but from the gist of Kyaw's texts, it's been a lot of travelling and Luke making business contacts. The first leg of what I gather has been a world tour was Perth. They stayed in a lovely big house which, apparently, he inherited from his Aunt Petula whom he first visited nine years ago when he was eighteen. Kyaw said she'd had plenty of time to visit the sites because Luke spent most days visiting banks and some of their larger customers. The evenings were lovely with the two of them going to top restaurants. It seems the seafood was second only to that served in the Hotel By The Red Canal in Mandalay. Lucky girl. If I remember correctly, they had intended to fly to Myanmar from Perth but Luke had got on so well with the business side of things that they went first to Sydney and then to a couple of cities in China en-route to her home country.

"I was so pleased that Kyaw had seen her mother and sisters much sooner than she expected after the wedding and another bonus was that Naing's father Aung took Luke to some big-wig conference where all the good and mighty of the city had gathered. In fact, they delayed their return for a week or so while Luke visited a few companies and the university where he once delivered a paper on Artificial Intelligence or something of the sort".

"Pearl, I'm pleased I disturbed your slumbers. We should catch up more often. In fact it's time you bought me lunch at The George again. Look, one other thing. Is Kyaw intending to stay in the UK permanently with her go-getting husband?"

"Yes, I believe so. Luke has promised her a visit back home whenever she likes and, oh, I nearly forgot, he's done some sort of property deal. A large house called The Old Hall is being restored. Before you called, I was mystified on how he'd financed it. That's now become clear. The most recent text from Kyaw talks of a big graduation party and we're all invited – once their mansion is finished of course. You know Adrian, after all we've been through and as they say, all's well that ends well".

"Hmm. I'll hold judgement on that. Good night Pearl and God Bless".

*

Pondering on life. Was it looming retirement that brought it on? It had seemed such a good idea when the Rotary Club and the County Council joined forces to create the Millennium Memorial Gardens. The consensus amongst the writers to the local paper thought, whilst a bit late, better late than never; an attempt to heal the scars. There was never any question of building on the land where the cottage once stood or in the grounds of the old apple orchard. But then you get stopped in your tracks. Will the evil of the past inevitably seep through to the today?

Police Superintendent Bill Macrae had intended to drive past - but he couldn't. What had been beautiful only two months ago was now tainted. Three winos were draped over the oak bench carved in dedication to the residents of the village. Discarded needles lay by the path winding around the newly planted Eucalyptus and a syringe had been thrown into a Peace rose. *Some bloody peace, more like a war zone.* He could arrest them and take them back to the station, but what's the point? Could it really be that Harold's spirit was here; would never leave? He even caused those fully mature Laxton Superb apple trees to be uprooted. Of course, his men didn't recognise the variety of apple or appreciate how long the 20ft high examples of prime English orchard had stood there. But the tree-man from the council did, and verbalised his stupendous knowledge even as the skeletons were exhumed. Supercilious sod. Bill Macrae felt his anger welling up. He had to leave.

Back at Derbyshire Police HQ, a still agitated Superintendent Macrae sent a message downstairs for Sergeant Collett to come to his office before signing off.

"Neil, that damned Whitby double murder is in my head again. Did you keep in touch with Marcus Clarke? I remember you wanting to".

"Yes, Super, why?"

"It's just that before my former 2 IC left to join the Met, in fact before Alice married Marcus, I mentioned my doubts about the great nephew Luke. You know, bad blood flowing down and all that. Between you and me, a bit of a trade-off really. If she needed anyone leant on down there, to let me know and if I wanted an inside track on what young Luke was up to, she and Marcus would call on their friendship with Pearl Bennett to quiz her ex-student friend Kyaw on Luke's activities. I should have guessed Alice would handle anything the city bobbies threw at her and so peace has reigned. Can't really call in a debt that doesn't exist, can I? So, I was wondering. Could you, maybe, invite yourself down to their pad on some pretext? Old time's sake, a couple of beers recalling happy memories of the cold case review, advice on investing the huge dosh you're now pulling in. I don't know, use your noddle. But see if Alice has any bad feeling about what Luke might be doing. You know the drill. Walking in that bloody memorial garden today got the old nostrils twitching. I'll cover your tracks if the DI gets awkward".

"OK Super, will do"

Two

For Kyaw it was wonderful. Buddha approved. The Mandalay Palace was built for her alone. If only her father hadn't died. He would have been so proud. How far she had travelled. How high she had flown. Because of the elongated honeymoon, it was seven weeks before she could actually speak to Pearl and then her first words were, "It must have been on the second leg of our flight to Perth before I emerged from a daze. Honestly Pearl, I was just in a whirl. My sweetheart Luke has been so loving, so gentle with me - I am the luckiest girl in the world and it's all down to you. If you hadn't asked for my help in tracing the relatives of Eugene's wartime girlfriend, I'd probably be a trainee English teacher back home. Now look at me. A world traveller, the wife of a wonderful man and so looking forward to living in a huge country house that Luke has bought for us".

"Kyaw, can Luke spare you for a few days? Come down to the cottage. We can have a proper talk like we used to. You'll be amazed how much Tristan has grown. He's chattering away and generally running riot. Anyway, you'll need to practise nappy changing and knowing what baby food to buy and a hundred and one other things! Sorry Kyaw, only joking, but please come to see us. Naing will be bursting to tell you about her promotion and we can't wait to hear about this fantastic honeymoon and your new life back in England. Try and make a weekend. Marcus calls most Saturday afternoons and I'm sure we'll all get on famously. It'll be like old times but without that horrid cold case business".

Kyaw had been a bit taken aback. They hadn't fallen out over it or anything like that, it was just that while Luke wanted her to stay friendly with Pearl, of course he did, the top priority was for her to oversee work on the Old Hall. It mustn't get off to a bad start: surely she understood that. The girlie catch-up could wait a couple of months. But Kyaw was also hearing the last words of her father. That he had passed through into the spirit world made her resolution stronger. She had to stand up for herself. In the West, she was anyone's equal. Pearl had already sent the travel tickets via the train app. They were meeting at St Pancras and taking Tristan to London Zoo in Regents Park. Luke shrugged his shoulders and went to his office feeling dejected. There was much catching up to do.

Tristan was having his afternoon sleep and Pearl was all for taking tea in the garden, but after Kyaw said she hadn't felt warm since arriving back, they opted for the sitting-room instead. During the morning Pearl had rehearsed in her head how to open the subject. It was important to strike the right balance between being interested but not pushy. After all, there would be oodles of time to suss out if Adrian's niggles about Luke had any merit. "Now then my worldly-travelled friend with the handsome, super-techie husband. You with the superlative English degree to complement the oriental charm, let's leave all the boring holiday stuff until Naing arrives. I want to say something that's been on my mind. It's just in case I can help without anyone else knowing. Tell me, do I have to worry about how you and Luke are coping, money wise? I mean, looks like our plan to go into the detective business is a non-starter unless you apply for a teaching post or something. Please, don't get me wrong. Mustn't interfere but I am your Western World Mother".

"Oh Pearl, you are such a kind person. Thank you for being concerned for me but no we are what Luke calls *nicely placed.* Not sure myself what that means but he didn't hold back on anything we wanted to do while travelling and as you know from my text message, he has bought this large house for us and eventually *our family football team* (I had to ask my friend from uni. what he meant by that – seems I'll need that baby training you mentioned). The Old Hall stands in its own grounds".

"Coming from your own lips and being the worrier I am, what a relief. And Kyaw, I think Naing's father may have found our first child to help, through the charity we set up. Dear Eugene would have been so pleased. Luke's IT practice must be going well considering how little time he's had".

"Yes, well, he's very clever working with computers. His prof. told me *he can virtually make them talk.* I'm still learning of course. Trying to catch up. I didn't realise at first but he managed to combine our honeymoon with building what he calls his *worldwide network.* One evening we were sitting on the veranda watching the sun go down and I think he'd had a few more beers than normal but anyway he started to talk really seriously about his plans. He intends to open up a second line to add to his software business. Do you know anything about sending money abroad Pearl?"

"No, afraid not".

"Neither did I, but I'm starting to understand the sort of broad principles involved. Do you need to check on Tristan? We can talk about this anytime"

"Kyaw, when he wakes, believe me, we'll know. Carry on, this is fascinating".

"He said the idea came into his head years ago when he visited his Aunt Petula in Australia. He'd worked out how much money was lost simply changing English pounds into Australian dollars. What's more, he said that as an eighteen-year-old, it was as if he'd been turned over by a pickpocket. Money just disappeared. That was despite his Great Uncle Harold insisting he chose a travel company that displayed a *no commission* sign. He asked himself where, no, not where, but *how* the money disappeared. He knows now that the answer is what is called *the spread* which apparently is the difference between the rate of exchange when selling English pounds and buying Australian dollars. Pearl, doesn't it seem odd to sell and then buy money when it's money itself we're dealing with? Luke told me not to think I was being stupid in trying to work out how your money is taken without you even realising it. It took ages for him to understand what was going on. That's how he got his big idea.

"Like all big ideas, the first thing you hit are the snags. If hurdles didn't exist then everyone would be jumping on the bandwagon. Sorry Pearl, I'm beginning to sound like Luke already. Anyway, Luke said while he realised how easy it was to make money just by handling the stuff, one had to be a large business and well established like a bank, a well-known travel agent or even a specialist money-changing outfit, in order for people to trust you with their cash. So, for a young go-getter like himself, it was a no-no. But then he wondered if there was another way to handle money and cream a bit off the top without the owner really caring or understanding what's going on. Pearl, he said it was his Eureka moment and his brain started to whirl. Honestly, the way he spoke and the way he looked at me, I felt so excited and of course he knew I was getting aroused and that soon we would be heading indoors. I had another glass of wine and he grabbed another tinny.

"For a while I thought I was listening to your Marcus, oh sorry again Pearl, I mean Alice's Marcus, not my Luke. He started to talk about his second idea. I was having to concentrate really hard. Apparently, the point was if money can disappear while being changed, it can while being transferred. Simple as that. Then, a related thought. A small mark-up on a small amount equals a small profit. A small mark-up on a large amount leads to a large profit. When are large amounts of money transferred abroad? That's a rhetorical question Pearl because my Luke had the answer.

It's when people are buying and selling property abroad and also when they are moving abroad or coming to this country and have to convert all their cash.

"There's more. Luke told me that since he first had the idea, he's been studying the most likely places for overseas property and people movements. He reckons his timing will be perfect because of last year's Brexit Referendum. Needless to say, our trip to Australia and then China was about making contacts there, but now he also sees potential in Europe. He says the decision to leave Europe has unsettled a lot of people in a position to return to their homeland. If they don't take that drastic step, they will probably move large sums of money back home. By getting statistics on the number of EU nationals living in the UK he discovered that the second largest group after Poland were from the Republic of Ireland and, after ignoring those from Romania and Portugal, the next two were from Italy and France. So Pearl, my Luke has what he called his hit list; the five countries to which large sums of money will be sent from the UK. He intends to become a foreign exchange broker specialising in just two types of transaction between the UK and his five selected overseas countries. After he'd told me all this, there was quite a long interlude". Kyaw giggled. Pearl did not.

"Look Kyaw it's been a long day and drinking coffee so late is a bad thing, or so they say, but who cares? It was really great to see you and Naing getting on so well again, although what you two were nattering on about in that strange language of yours I don't know, and what with Tristan playing to the crowd, I wasn't offended you cut me out – honestly".

"We didn't cut you out, silly, she was just asking how my mother and sisters were coping and I was interested in how Aung was finding his new role. Anyway, it's your own fault, you should make an effort to learn some basic Burmese". Pearl didn't reply but thought, *yes young lady, everything is all so marvellous but life will bite at some stage, it always does. Me, learn Burmese with Tristan, Naing, Marcus and his bullying me into writing that first chapter. I don't think so.*

"Since you told me about Luke's big idea, I've been thinking. I mean, going into a new business area and a very specialised one by the sound of it, must be risky and aren't there well-established big players there already?"

"You know Pearl, I realise there is so much to learn about the commercial world. I wish I'd asked those questions but my Luke must have gone into all that. I remember him saying that there was always a market for a new player and especially with foreign exchange because the type of people he'd be dealing with, were very cost conscious. Their bank, for example, would quote a transfer cost up to four percent more than the rate they charge when borrowing from each other. As a broker, that add-on cost would most likely be nearer one percent and a special computer program he's written will highlight the rates of all the brokers and in real time. Automatically, his cost quote will beat the best and so he's sure to pick up business. Oh, and something else he's mentioned more than once. Apparently, there's no compensation scheme if a broker goes bust. He thinks that's important because the client will use his service knowing the risk. It means they will believe his business to be financially sound and perfectly legitimate. All the documents accessible online will show that it is".

"Sounds amazing Kyaw but how do you fit into all this?"

"Oh yes, well it's really exciting. I'm going to be the Chief Executive Officer and, as he puts it, *front the business.* As backed up by all the documents and information he will put online, he says who will doubt the sincerity of a young whizz-kid hitting the block? My face, if not exactly launching a thousand ships, will launch a thousand money transfers!

You know Pearl, my Luke has such a wonderful way with words - ("with my computer skills and your looks and personality, how can we go wrong?"). After all the travelling, the physical side and all that sort of thing, I can't wait to get started on our first big venture. But first I have to plan all we need for the office set-up at the Old Hall. Oh, and Luke is giving me some shares in the new company. He says he's not sure how many yet but I'm definitely going to own part of the brokerage.

"There's one other thing that I'm supposed to keep secret but I can tell you can't I? I know you will keep it to yourself. I don't want you worrying about whether we can succeed or not so this will put your mind at rest. You see Pearl, we're not actually going to transfer any money abroad. Luke has thought of what he calls *a unique selling point* and it's all to do with timing. He says if Amazon can do it, so can we. Guess what? The money is going to be available at the receiving end within one hour. He said to me "will that shake up the stuffy brokers or what? Do clients really want what they're offered as inducement now, the gimmicky vouchers or cash back? No. They want to see their money deposited safely and in the blink of an eye".

"I can see that but how on earth will it work?"

"I have to admit Pearl, I don't understand myself but it's something to do with what he called *peer-to-peer* and please don't quote me on this – in fact please don't tell anyone. Luke got quite serious about this bit of his business plan – it's because the money a client wants to send abroad is not the same money deposited abroad. There is a pot of money already held abroad and so it's a simple step to allocate the right amount to the sender. Of course, the client doesn't know that – they don't need to. The important thing is that the money is where the client wants it to be and quickly at low cost".

"Well, it sounds very clever and I really hope it works out. Come on Kyaw, time for bed. In no time at all, a certain little man will be knocking on your bedroom door."

Oh dear Kyaw, what are you getting involved in: I wonder if I should call Adrian?

*

Naing had intended to take Tristan in his pushchair to the marina but Sunday 10th December 2017 had dawned bitterly cold. A strong South Easterly was threatening to bring a scattering of snow across the promenade. Instead, he seemed perfectly happy to hunt through the box of toys she had collected over the past year and ignored completely the call of bye-bye from Kyaw and the wave from Pearl as they set off for the short walk to Brighton Railway Station. The 11.05 to London Bridge was delayed by forty-five minutes so what better excuse to retrace their steps to Café Coho. Although Pearl went through the motions of sharing Kyaw's concern about making the connection from St Pancras to Nottingham, secretly she was rather pleased to have the extra time. Anyway Kyaw had an open ticket and there were later trains heading North. Luckily, few of Brighton's coffee addicts had ventured out on this winter morning and the girls had two of those great comfy chairs to themselves. Pearl took a deep breath.

"Darling Kyaw, now we're alone again, I want to ask you something. If you'd rather not say, that's fine, but sometimes I can't help being the concerned Mother in this foreign land where, even now, things must be so different for you. The thing is, when you were talking last night I remember a couple of references to Luke as a physical partner, if I can put it as delicately as possible"

"Pearl, ask away. I'm no longer a snowflake, even though Brighton will probably welcome a few of those this morning".

"Well, I wanted to ask if he is treating you properly in that way"

"Yes, yes, he is a loving husband and has been very gentle with me. In fact – no I won't enlarge on that side of things. He had a girlfriend before me you know but I was a virgin when we married. I promised myself that at least one of our customs would be kept and that's why I love him so much. He said from the first time we dated he would respect what I wanted, and he did. My Luke will never do anything to hurt me – I am sure of that".

"What a relief. We will never speak about this again. Kyaw, there is something I want to ask you which is connected in a strange sort of way. It is important to me. Do you know how Tristan came into this life?"

"Pearl you won't let me miss my train will you? I, well we, assumed you and Naing came to an arrangement of some sort. Honestly Pearl, I am worldly-wise now. Your relationship doesn't bother me in the slightest and what a blessing - isn't he just wonderful?"

"You won't miss your train, I promise. We'll leave in five minutes. I know I'm old enough to be your mother but I would like your advice. It's this matter of experience – kind of thing. At your age, well, much older actually, I didn't have any boyfriends. There didn't seem to be time what with my job, helping with my daddy's work and then trying my best to look after him when he was ill. And, I don't know, I've thought about it a lot lately, I never had the urge, so to speak. But then, Naing came along and it just happened. It wasn't planned, it just happened. Hard to explain really but then we thought how nice it would be if we could have a child. But how? Naing did the research and we agreed it all seemed so clinical, so scientific somehow. You know, not natural.

Anyway, I thought of Marcus. Somehow he got through to me at that briefing in the police station. It was weird because when he came to the cottage with that policeman who was trying to find evidence to pin the murders on dear Eugene, I took an instant dislike to him. He came over all arrogant and condescending and it ended with me, more or less, throwing them both out. So, when he pretty much alone worked the Harold thing out, I realised the earlier upset was me being silly. He had been asked to get under my skin. He disliked what happened as much as I had. Kyaw, I know I'm not making much sense and you are keen to get back home, but what I am trying to say, woman to woman as it were, is that he fathered Tristan in a natural way and although I try not to, I have feelings for him. I mean, he's happily married and Naing and I adore each other, so we can all carry on being good friends. Except the way he plays with Tristan and makes corny excuses to call by to see him, I find myself feeling kind of strange. Anyway, come on, let's get you on that train. No doubt there will be a welcoming party at the other end".

A tall handsome man was standing a few yards behind the turnstiles at Nottingham Midland station. He was holding a large placard displaying the words *Welcome home darling Kyaw* and she rushed into his open arms and wept uncontrollably. "Darling Luke, I will never leave you again, never, ever. That train was so cold. Get me warm, please get me warm". As Kyaw climbed into the front seat of the car, she said "I've got some news, you'll never believe what I've found out".

Three

It was just after four o'clock on Friday afternoon when Marcus's private mobile rang. His immediate reaction was not to answer it. This was the worst possible time. *Doesn't whoever it is know I have to close these positions? I'm well up on the week. Better answer the damn thing, suppose it could be Alice. Hmm, fat chance of that, when was the last time she called during the day? Best I can hope for is a text saying she'll be late home again.*

"Marcus! It's Neil from the Derbyshire police, your old cold case colleague, have you got a minute?"

"Of course Neil, great to hear from you. To what do I owe the pleasure?"

"Well, we said we'd keep in touch. I know, I know - my fault, it's been best part of eighteen months. Marcus, short notice but I'm off this weekend and meeting up with an old mate who lives somewhere near Brighton for a few beers tomorrow night. Bit of a cheek but I wondered if there's any chance of meeting up somewhere near your place this evening on my way through. Nothing like a nosy copper to push his luck but don't suppose you and Alice have a spare bed, just for tonight I mean?"

"Hey, that's a great idea. I'll give you the postcode and you can park under the building, we have a spare slot. Never quite know when Alice will be home but we can have a drink first and she can join us for a meal. Let me know when you are close. Hey Neil, got to ring off, the next hour for me is vital to make the next half million".

"As you can see Neil, this is the Tufnell Park/Highgate patch, note that I still remember some of your lingo. I mean, it wouldn't be called a patch down here, we're in a desirable part of North London don't you know. But, I'll tell you what, I do miss your Derbyshire villages, that gritty steeliness sort of thing. You might not believe this but we've often talked about moving back. Makes no difference to my job where we are but, as you know, Alice is heading up the fraud side of the Met. and that had to come first. Actually, between you and me, I wish we'd stayed up there. She must have had a good chance of taking over when Macrae retires, don't you think? Sometimes it pays to be patient. Just think back to that Harold guy. Didn't exactly rush things did he? And, let's face it, damn nearly got away with his murderous ways. Anyway Neil, it's great to see you again and we're walking to the Lord Palmerston. It's not glitzy like some around here, in fact it's kind of Victorian with an open fire and leather armchairs. Just the place for a Police Sergeant from up North to feel at home".

Marcus was just about to drain his second pint when the text came through. Alice would be thirty minutes, no more, promise darling. He knew he had to tell Neil before she arrived, it was simply a matter of how. Neil was back with pint number three.

"Neil, something I wanted to fill you in on before Alice arrives. It'll save any embarrassment should the subject come up when the three of us are together. Not sure whether you already know, but you remember our star guest detectives Pearl and Naing, well fact is, they're an item. But that's not the half of it. They have a baby, a handsome little chap they've named Tristan. And Neil, better take a good swig of that pint, I fathered him with Pearl".

"Well, thanks for telling me. No good pretending I'm shocked. In my line of business you come across all sorts. And it just shows what a pretty useless detective sergeant I am. Should have worked it out when I saw you holding a baby at Kyaw and Luke's wedding. Now I think about it, chatting together you did seem quite close. You might say, just like a married couple. Actually, now your news is sinking in, I am a bit surprised. How is Alice taking it? Why did she agree to it? Well, before you answer that question is Pearl still in touch with Kyaw since marrying Lucky Luke?"

"Oh yes, in fact Kyaw came down to see Pearl only a few days after she got back from the honeymoon, a somewhat extended honeymoon I should add".

"Obviously, you still know what Pearl's life is about then".

"God yes. To tell you the truth I can't keep away. Any excuse and I'm off to Brighton to change his nappy. In fact, most Saturday afternoons".

"Would that include tomorrow?"

"Well yes unless Alice pulls me in another direction which is most unlikely. She works most Saturdays due to this big fraud thing going on".

"Do you think I could tag along? It's just that this mate of mine is some sort of lecturer at the University of Sussex and he's got a place not far from Brighton. I'm not expected until Saturday evening. Suppose I'll have to soak up some more of this insipid Southern beer. He's a real ale fan. Don't know how I manage to pick 'em really – thought you would be a gin & tonic merchant by now. Once again I'm wrong about you".

"Neil, Pearl will be delighted to see you again and even more important, I can show off my little boy. Between you and me, ah, look, my lovely wife has just come in – no more on this subject – I wish I could give Pearl another child".

*

Sergeant Neil Collett was telling his Super that, on the whole, it had gone quite well. Driving around London was a drag but having to get to Brighton there was no option. "How they ever get any work done down there defeats me; must be all by remote while they sit in another traffic jam. And everywhere is so noisy, how do they think? Before we talk about our Lucky Luke, you'll be really pleased to hear your ex No 2 and flashy Marcus have got it made – and how. What they're pulling in between them heaven knows, but he seems to be working the stock market, or whatever he does, as well as we reckoned when he first appeared on the scene. His latest Maserati has a higher spec. than that first gleaming monster. Add that to Alice's salary, well you'll know what she's on, plus the London weighting of course. Adds up to a bob or two, plus the years building up on the pension which, I might add, Alice is very aware of. And yet. Well, you know me. Ever the philosopher. Every coin has two sides. For every plus comes a minus, sooner or later. Something is not quite right and I suspect it's to do with the lady I've started to think of as Perfect Pearl".

"Unusually for you Neil, we're a bit off track, but go on".

"Start with this. Marcus is not a drinker. OK he pretends to be but in my opinion he is merely trying to be one of the lads. Actually, his brain's in a league some of us can only dream about. We should remember he was a lone-wolf bachelor for a long time before our Alice knocked him sideways. He's incredibly disciplined. I see it this way. Chart-crazy, maths-genius loner suddenly lands a blonde goddess with brains, but they are spending a lot of time apart and it's mainly due to her job.

"The thing is this though, something quite outside his experience happens. He wakes one morning holding a baby boy – how come? He is blown away. The charts and his lady are starting to drift into the background. Only slightly, but still it's happening. Just three things I'll mention, but they're more than enough. No 1. He made sure I didn't mention Pearl once Alice arrived at the pub on the Friday night. Why not?

They're all in this together. Touchy subject you can bet. No 2. He went to bed while Alice and I stayed chatting. Yes, about the job, boring for him but she said he often went first and that's when he texts Pearl to check how the little lad has been. No 3 and the most important. I have seen Marcus and Pearl and Tristan all together. If it was a case of *here's my seed, get it inside you and good night* then I'm a Dutchman. As you well know Super, I'm Derbyshire born and bred. Not too strong in arm and not too weak in head, as they say".

"Right, we uncover a little threesome complication, so what?"

"You asked me to sniff around and that's what I've done. Alice wasn't just a good copper, we all liked her. I think we should keep an eye on things. As I said, that Marcus is a clever bugger. Anyway, whatever Pearl gets out of Kyaw about Lucky Luke will reach Marcus. I'm certain of it. And, Super, me and Marcus are drinking pals aren't we? I can hold it, he can't".

"Point taken. Tell me about young Luke".

"In my view we have it made and it's simply because Pearl and Kyaw are really good friends and I'll eat my hat if that ever changes. In fact, they're like mother and daughter. Kyaw has told Pearl about Lucky Luke's new business venture. I didn't need to ask any questions, surreptitiously or otherwise. She had been delighted to have a visit from Kyaw so soon after the honeymoon and so, carrying on to relate how her newly-married friend had fallen on her feet, came out quite naturally. It seems he's developed software to enable large sums of money to be transferred abroad very quickly. Just how that's achieved is his big idea and to be kept under wraps, although I got the impression Kyaw actually told Pearl how it could be done. Anyway, our genius has built contacts in Australia and other countries that didn't get mentioned. You know Super, an old business friend of my dad wanted me to know that "nubdy made big dosh legal like". I've always remembered that saying and it entered my head as we were walking past Brighton Pier with its signage inviting all and sundry to enter and play the gaming machines. Will Lucky Luke's customers be gambling? It made me wonder. He's already restoring some sort of Mansion House and so must see the prospect of big money pouring in.

"One other thing. Alice was very cagey about what she was working on. In a nutshell, I learned nothing, but Marcus, after a couple of pints, told me she was heading a fraud unit. Maybe Super, you know what's going on down at the Met but it might be an idea to tip Alice off about Lucky Luke's activities".

"Good work Neil and of course Alice would never discuss trivial details of a case such as this with Marcus. Between me, thee and she, we might have a little fun with this one".

"And Super here's me never knowing you were a poet".

"Push off back to your desk – get some proper work done".

Neil had sixteen emails in his inbox. It was the one listed as "Yesterday" and timed at 21.35 from "Pearl Bennett" that caught his eye.

From: pearl.bennett@tiggy.co.uk
To: neil.collett@derbyshire.police
Subject Kyaw

Hi Neil,

Lovely to see you again and so glad you had time to pop in with Marcus. Like old times except of course I'm much more worldly-wise now! And a mother too, were you very surprised? Nice of you to ask if I thought Kyaw was coping OK with her new English life. You seemed a little anxious that Luke might be trying to run before he could walk and was she strong enough to caution him not to overreach on the money side of things. I was touched by your concern and actually I've been worried along the same lines. New country, new husband, somewhat isolated and not just from her mother and sisters but also from me and Naing, at any rate on a day-to-day basis. I will keep a motherly eye on her as best I can . Regarding money, although I suspect Kyaw may not know, Adrian told me that Luke inherited a small fortune from his Great Uncle Harold. That will explain the international nature of the honeymoon and, I suppose, the house purchase. So you see, from a financial angle the young couple will be fine.

Neil, what I really wanted to say and hope you don't think I'm being silly but it would please me very much if you were able to meet Marcus occasionally now contact has resumed. OK, he's successful at what he does and he now has Alice to share his life but actually, he finds it hard to make friends. He confides in me quite often and I know he hopes you two will stay friends. Why not tootle down here on a regular basis? The prospect of the old team of you, Marcus, me, Naing and even possibly Kyaw all putting our heads together again gives me goose bumps. All we need is another mystery to solve – hopefully not a cold case one next time!

My very best wishes, Pearl. Oh and PS, remember me to the big boss.

Sergeant Neil Collett leaned back in his chair. He read the email again and this time more slowly. *The Governor hasn't been in this job a long time for nothing. Crafty bugger.*

Pearl looked in on Tristan. He was fast asleep with his left leg on top of the duvet. She put his leg back under the covers and tucked him in. She bent and kissed his cheek and stayed looking down at her wonderful son for a full minute. *I made him. I made him. That's my son.*

There was a young man. Although Pearl couldn't make out his features, it was Luke. He seemed to be conducting an orchestra except his baton wasn't leading the musicians but pointing straight ahead. A young Asian girl was playing the lead violin but not reading the music. Instead, she was looking directly at the conductor and smiling. It was a confident smile as if she knew this piece of music by heart. Behind Luke was a suitcase which had burst open and its contents were strewn over the floor. Pearl strained her eyes trying to make out the currency but she couldn't. It was just stacks and stacks of paper money. No-one seemed bothered that a fortune lay at the conductor's feet. He carried on pointing his baton and the lady violinist carried on playing and smiling. A young boy walked from the wings. Pearl guessed he was about five years old. He was dressed very smartly in a light-grey school uniform and wore his cap a little tilted to one side. He was holding the hand of a little girl in a bright yellow dress. Hand-in-hand they walked past the conductor and headed straight for the edge of the stage with its steep drop into the orchestra pit. Pearl yelled at them to stop. No-one else seemed to notice. The conductor carried on pointing his baton, the lady violinist carried on playing and smiling. Just as the little boy and girl reached the edge, they turned to face Pearl and waved goodbye. Pearl was frantic, she yelled and screamed at the top of her voice but nothing changed. The children turned away and started to walk again...

Pearl woke with a start. She was sweating profusely. She rushed into Tristan's bedroom. He was still fast asleep with both legs covered. She dropped to her knees and clung onto the edge of his little bed. She was shaking uncontrollably.

Four

Ever since he'd started writing computer code Luke had been a fan of *open source*. Apple had perfected the hardware which gave computer programmers the opportunity to write applications that merged seamlessly with the operating system. This was the key move to achieve mass international take-up. He thought of it as *you play ball with me and I'll play ball with you, everyone's a winner.* That's why he had no time for secrets. As his American colleagues would say "Let it all hang out man, you find my faults and I'll find yours". As he saw it, that was the fault in the old email from Pearl Bennett he was re-reading *"While I cannot prevent it, I hope you will not mention this to your Great Uncle Harold".* Why ever not for God's sake? Just because he asked me to hand a note to you at Eugene's graveside doesn't mean he shouldn't know you've asked to meet in Nottingham. He's over ninety years old. He lives alone. Actually, he aches to find out what's going on outside his cottage walls, especially if it's connected to the family. Though why our meeting is connected, I fail to see. OK, I have agreed to stop using Kyaw to find out what Pearl and her friend Naing are up to because I think they are right. If Great Uncle Eugene chose to leave his money to Pearl, so be it, why shouldn't he? Anyway, I never understood why Harold challenged the will. What did he hope to gain, especially at his great age?

Just as he had no truck with secrets, Luke couldn't understand the current fashion for genealogy. As far as he was concerned, the past was the past - today was all that mattered. He intended to make a fortune and make Kyaw the happiest girl in the world. It was because of Kyaw that he had agreed to help her friend Pearl who was, it seemed, the latest victim of the family tree vortex. So, at Pearl's request he went to see his dad and got hold of some papers left by his grandma Molly. It would be interesting to check if she'd found them useful and wouldn't his grandad Jack have been flabbergasted comparing the electronic bits he'd left behind with today's chips? He must remember to ask Pearl if she sent them to a museum. None of this would interest his great uncle but he did tell him about adding a couple of names to their stamp collectors' database. It never failed to amaze Luke how interested the old man had been in the cloud-based information store. He wrote down the two names and said that Neil Collett would be the fifteenth policeman on the file.

*

Had he expected a response from Yadanabon University? Did it really matter one way or the other? After all, things were moving along brilliantly. His decision to offer his software package by licence rather than risk release of the software source code was paying off. Revenue was increasing gradually month my month. True, Kyaw had reassured him that a passive audience and an absence of questions was quite normal. But still, the absence of any vocal enthusiasm was disappointing. Then a whole month after delivering his lecture "Artificial Intelligence" on 31st January 2016, an email arrived from the Rector. It began by quoting verbatim one assertion made in his talk, "*My personal view is that as a development of computer science, the advance of Artificial Intelligence is unstoppable and when one sees a photograph of a Western Government minister talking to a robot, that proves it*".

The Rector described the profound effect his lecture had had on the engineering students and how gradually his paper had found traction amongst the university's wider academic community. He felt that an *"AI Initiative"* could be the step-change they had been seeking for some time. He understood the potentially sensitive and guarded nature of work in this area and that consequently a case would be made for establishing a discrete unit within the engineering faculty. Coincidentally, the university had, within the last six months, formulated a *One Hundred Talents Plan* designed specifically to recruit overseas' researchers. Each selected *talent* would be a strategic scientist on the university's payroll. If Mr Luke Brown was interested in taking a position of strategic scientist, would he kindly submit a paper suggesting one specific aspect of AI that he recommended the university pursue.

To Luke the content of this email was more exciting than winning the lottery, which would have been impossible anyway since he never bought a ticket. Great Uncle Harold had driven the message home years ago "Tha dusna pay voluntary tax lad, tha leaves it tu mugs". As usual, sound advice from the old man. It was not the prospect of a post as overseas' researcher nor any payment attached that ignited Luke's imagination, but rather the opportunity to instigate a ground-breaking study away from the UK. A place where, as he now appreciated following his visit, meritocracy ruled by definition, each tiny step would be a leap forward and success would be appreciated and valued. But, best of all, the country to benefit was Myanmar, birthplace of his new girlfriend. Kyaw would be so proud of him: he had to put Yadanabon University on the world stage. And, if he was patient, there was a chance he could profit from whatever developed. As his Great Uncle Harold had advised, "tek thi tym lad, all cums good in end."

*

Luke felt so sure about the future. Miraculously, it had all worked out for the best and it was just a question of timing.

Most importantly he had to be fair to Kyaw. He could push hard but it wouldn't be right. Once again, he saw Kyaw's mother and sisters waving them off. That haunted look on smiling faces. He had to do the right thing, he just had to. His left hand belonged to Kyaw but his right searched the iPhone calendar. Before he'd time to plan, there it was, staring back. The plane was scheduled to land at 7.30 am 9th February 2016 Shrove Tuesday.

First out of the school gates, running as fast as his legs would go. Grandma Molly with the pancake mixture ready to pour in the pan. What did he want on top, syrup, sugar or lemon juice? Oh, that smell, that taste. At first it was always syrup but, as the years passed, he preferred dipping into the sugar bowl until by that last visit (was it really five years since she died?) he was squeezing the half lemon. She had been such a wonderful grandma. Without her, no pocket money and no Great Uncle Harold to visit on Saturday mornings. With no Great Uncle Harold, no encouragement to study, no knowledge of postage stamps, no trip to Australia, no paid-for university and no inheritance to look forward to. Those two generations of Whitby looked after their own, he saw that now. Kyaw tugged his arm gently and turned to face him "Luke, this is our happy time but you look sad, what are you thinking about?"

"Kyaw darling, I'm not sad honestly, just thinking of the past. Me and my daydreaming. We'll be landing in two hours so should we make a plan? We agreed to stand by your custom of dating for a year before we marry and I realise you'll be surprised by this, but now we are sure of each other, perhaps it should be a little longer. Finishing your degree at Nottingham takes us to the summer of 2017. I want you to have the best possible chance of getting a first or at worst a 2:1. We can wait until the early Autumn; you concentrating on your studies while I bag more clients to secure our future. I'd feel very happy if we can honour your family in that way".

Luke reached over and kissed his beautiful girlfriend who had tears in her eyes. The plane might have hit a spot of hot air turbulence but two seats were unaffected. A young couple, very much in love, journeyed smoothly to the future.

*

Paper prepared by Luke Brown MSc (Nottingham UK) for Dr Maung Maung Naing, Rector Yadanabon, University, Myanmar

Subject: A route into Artificial Intelligence

Many aspects of human endeavour are being researched for the application of Artificial Intelligence (AI) concepts and technology. A by no means exhaustive list would be:-

- Transportation
- Health
- Education
- Financial inclusion
- Agriculture
- Climate change
- Care for the elderly
- Help for the disabled

The breadth of attention being paid to applying AI technology can be appreciated by the attendance recently in Central London of over 100 companies to a "Tech for Good" awards ceremony.

Having spent four weeks researching which specific area would be best addressed by Yadanabon students, the following factors prevailed:-

The limitation of finance (compared to the huge American digital platforms).

The restrictions imposed by limited computer power.

The relatively modest knowledge base within the Engineering Faculty.

An aspiration to make a positive contribution to mankind (not prestige).

An end product capable of development by other faculties within Yadanabon.

Having considered the development stage of each of the eight categories listed above (bearing in mind the point made in my paper dated 31st January 2016 that once mainstream, a category, for example voice recognition, is no longer considered AI) the most appropriate is *Health*. Once the software has been created, the knock-on benefit would favour your Mechanical Engineering (robotics) and Medical (surgical) departments. It is no coincidence or secret that leading NHS (National Health Service) hospitals in the UK are passing deep-mined data to, for example, the USA technology giant Google to create medical diagnostic algorithms.

Technically, there are two contrasting paths taken in AI. One is generally referred to as *"rules based"*. An example would be driverless cars (red light = stop, green light = go, here's a cycle lane = look for a cyclist and so on). The other path is *"machine learning"*. Examples are computer image recognition, speech synthesis and the mastering of games such as GO and CHESS. Of these two approaches, the second is recommended. Scientists working in this area refer to "cases and connections" and the buzz phrase is being part of the "fourth industrial revolution".

If the generality of this paper finds favour, a one-to-one discussion on a specific application is favoured to ensure confidentiality and security.

Luke Brown 31st March 2016

Luke didn't really care whether his second paper to Yadanabon University struck a chord or not. He did have a specific AI application in mind but he was only prepared to discuss it face-to-face with the Rector back in Myanmar. He saw medium to long-term potential whether it was picked up over there or not. Right now his priorities were to keep his promise to Kyaw by limiting their time together to what they decided to call the *Sacrosanct Saturdays* and promoting his *Risk Management* software application. She accepted he might need to visit his two clients in Australia to demonstrate his latest version and, of course, she wasn't concerned he would contact his ex-girlfriend over there. That was the past.

Just as his grandma had asked him to, when he was six years old, Luke used to collect a paper from the local newsagent each Thursday to give to Great Uncle Harold on the Saturday morning. Not that Luke had any interest in what the local rag had to say but he was touched by how his great uncle devoured each page of the Great Sutton Advertiser - almost as if his life depended on it. That's why it was such a surprise. Staring back at him with no modicum of decency, no thought for his feelings, "Local philatelist Harold Whitby found dead – neighbour shocked".

The report said that the (unnamed) neighbour was leaving her house just after dawn to walk her dog when a police car pulled up outside his cottage and two officers walked up the path. After pushing open the front door they simply walked in. "As if they knew it wasn't locked, yet Harold always locked his door". Less than half-an-hour later, an ambulance arrived and she saw a stretcher being loaded.

By mid-morning she heard workmen in the back garden and, peering out of her bedroom window, she saw them digging up the orchard. Asked by our reporter for a statement, PC Neil Collett confirmed that an elderly man had been found dead.

Luke hadn't expected to be put through to Neil. There's always some reason a named officer is unavailable. In fact, any policeman, they're just invisible. When was the last time anyone around here even saw one? When was the last time a minor crime was even investigated? But he was connected. "Hi Luke, look, before you say anything, I was coming around to see you this evening. It's been one of those days and bloody bad luck on timing all round. Your relative was only found yesterday and some nosy-parker neighbour went to the Advertiser's office before we knew what was happening. Of course, it had to be the night they went to press. Didn't check with us, just blasted it all over the front page and bingo, here we are".

"Well, are they right. Was it Great Uncle Harold?"

"Yes and I'm sorry you got to know through that damn paper. A man from somewhere nearby, Pincton I think he said, phoned to say he'd been trying to ring the old man for three days with no answer. Seems Harold had some postage stamps for him or something of the sort. We sent in a patrol car that happened to be nearby. We have to wait for the medical report but everything points to a peaceful end".

"What's all this about digging up the garden?"

"I wouldn't call it digging exactly, you know the press. If there's going to be a body, might as well dress things up a bit. Routine; checking for footprints or signs of intruders, that sort of thing. I'll let you know when the formalities have been dealt with. I expect you'll want to arrange a funeral. Is there anyone else we should notify?"

Six months later Luke Brown learned the truth. By then he didn't care. He had his memories and he had the money.

He also had an invitation from the Rector of Yadanabon University.

Five

Very slowly and on a Sunday Morning Marcus entered the real world. He had left the dream world of a pillow fight with Tristan but he wanted to go back, he wanted to cling on. He was happy, happier than he'd ever been. They were pounding each other. At first Marcus had the upper hand, Tristan was trapped in the corner of the sofa but somehow he broke free and pummelled his dad with blow after blow and Marcus was about to surrender when it all disappeared. He tried so hard to get back to the fight but it had gone and through bleary eyes he peered at the clock on the bedside table – 9.25. In his growing consciousness he began to recall what happened.

A smash on the M23 had caused a huge tailback and added over an hour to his journey home. It was almost ten o'clock when he swung the Maserati through the security gate and drove down to the private car park. The late hour meant that for once Alice was home first. On entering the hall she rushed to greet him. All she could whisper was "Darling Marcus thank God you're safe, I've heard the travel news and been so worried". She wore the little red dress that always aroused him and her blonde hair flowed freely almost reaching her waist. He recognised her perfume from the first time they'd made love. There was a bottle of Prosecco on the lounge table but it would remain unopened until the early hours. Alice's feverish lust; God, what a night. And there she lay, so classically beautiful. Her hair was tousled and bunched around her flushed cheeks. He slipped out of bed to make tea and toast, just like in their Derbyshire cottage. *We've only been married just over three years but we're drifting apart. She knows it, I know it. Christ Almighty, it mustn't happen. I'll pretend everything's normal, as it should be. We'll go out for brunch and be as close as we used to be. This afternoon, we'll be back in bed. I'm not letting my gorgeous wife slip away – no way!*

"Alice, sweetheart, I've made plans which you'll go along with, won't you? Any hesitation and I'll email your resignation to that Commander guy".

"Marcus, you brute, are you bullying me? Are you trying to control my life – at last?"

"Absolutely, and you know me, the research was thorough and everything's fixed".

"Go on then, bore me to distraction. Bore me, what am I saying? You're just so damn sexy, I don't know what I'm doing. I've got that ache again, it's driving me mad".

"It's all true, come here a minute. Right, so here are your orders, you out-of-control floozy. Next Friday you leave that New Ireland Yard, or whatever it's called at one o'clock on the dot and come home to me – you understand Madam? Home to me. I'll whisk you off to where it all started. To where we were in paradise. Yes, you've guessed Derbyshire, but not that grubby old cottage in Brackenfield, instead we'll slum it at The Cavendish on the Chatsworth Estate. If you prove you're worth it, I might ask for an upgrade. And, you needn't try to wheedle your way into my affections again because there's more to come".

"Oh no, not more"

"Yes. I have a plan to prise you from that standard bedroom. I was thinking of the night we had after the hike from Castleton to Moneyash, and to test whether my beautiful wife is still up to it, we're going on an even harder plod. We'll walk Curbar and Froggatt Edge. Back at the car, provided you're not too exhausted, I might drop the front seats".

"My Marcus, for a man of numbers and charts and those candlestick things, you say the most wonderful things.

What about me absconding on Thursday, make an extra night of it?"

Luke

It was late on Saturday night and Alice and Marcus were taking coffee in the lounge of The Cavendish. The walk had been harder than expected and after a wonderful dinner, they were tired but happy - content in each other's company. All the other diners had either left the hotel or gone to bed. The second-time-around honeymooners sat close together in front of the log fire. Marcus took a deep breath.

"Alice, I wanted us to come away; you to forget your job and me to leave that damn office. Just lately I've been feeling so bad about myself. But, after the way you welcomed me home last week, it proves we're as strong as ever. I'd better come clean. I'd better confess".

Alice straightened up and withdrew one hand from his. "For goodness sake Marcus, what have you done?"

"Darling Alice, that's just the point – it's what I haven't done, thank God. Alice please give me your hand, I need you to hold onto me, now more than ever. It's about Pearl. And, before you ask, I haven't been with her or anything like that. The thing is, I've been building myself up to asking whether you'd agree to me giving Tristan a little sister but after we found each other again and sitting here with you now, I realise how disloyal that thought was. What I did was a one-off to help Pearl and Naing. Pearl must be getting to that age when she can't have another baby anyway. It would be best all round if I stopped visiting Brighton. Can't hide the fact it'll be hard because I think the world of my little man. It's just that sometimes, especially when I first arrive, he seems so alone in that playpen. I was an only child and perhaps would have grown up more extrovert if I'd had a brother or sister. I mean, I try to be a proper daddy to him but the distance, the circumstances and everything. Perhaps there should have been a clean break from the start".

There was a long silence. Marcus was studying the pattern on the carpet, he feared looking at her. Alice suddenly jumped off the sofa and straddled her husband. She kissed him passionately. She didn't care if anyone was looking, let them see what they wanted. She nibbled his ear and whispered in a deep throaty voice, "Do to Pearl whatever you want. You're my man and I'll never, ever, let you go. Take me to bed, Christ I'm gagging for it. You said all that to bring me on again, didn't you? Crafty, sod".

*

There had been a whole flurry of correspondence to the Brighton Argus. It was rare for praise to be heaped on Brighton & Hove District Council but, with a couple of exceptions, readers were pleased with the decision, some sent in *thank you* emails. Pearl and Naing had been amused by one of the dissenting voices who thought there was no need for a toddler play area because seventy-five percent of residents were over eighty. But here it was. The prospective developer had been told to pack his bags and Tristan was happily bouncing on a miniature trampoline. Sitting next to Naing on one of the benches, Pearl appeared pensive and Naing was expecting further collaboration on how the first chapter of "Eugene", about the machinations of a dysfunctional family, her intended novel, would be plotted – but no.

"Naing, have you noticed that each mother here is supervising two children? And look how competitive those children are".

"I can see what you're getting at Pearl but an only child can develop an independent spirit, think of Marcus for example".

"That's true but they can become pretty spoilt too especially if their every need is provided for and their every whim satisfied, like Tristan for example. Strange you should mention Marcus because he was saying only last night, can't remember how it came up exactly, how lonely he'd been at Primary school and only started to make friends at around A-

Level time and really only then due to a common interest in maths".

"He's still calling you in the evening then?"

"Not every day, suppose three or four times a week. It depends on whether Alice is back from work".

"Why does he still ring so often? What do you find to discuss?"

"Oh, nothing intellectual, he just asks what sort of day we've had and, honestly Naing, he's only interested in how Tristan is. Even if our little boy has had a bump or something, I don't tell Marcus since I'm sure he'd come charging down. Think I must have been looking at the little ones playing on all this marvellous new equipment through new eyes due to something he said".

"And what was that?"

"It was an aside really, a sort of joke. With all the pranks we get up to on Saturday afternoons like Marcus throwing Tristan into the pool to land with a great splash amongst the other kids, he was sure our little man would not be lonely at infant school. His dad never took him to the pool as a toddler or later. He didn't have a chance to play with other children. Which, of course, led to him asking me".

"Sorry, asking you what?"

"To be absolutely sure Tristan won't be lonely, why don't we make another one?"

"Oh".

There was a long silence after which Naing rose from the park bench and walked over to the sand pit where Tristan was playing at filling his little bucket, emptying out the contents and then refilling to start all over again. She spoke to him, held his hand and together they walked to the far end of the play area. She lifted him into the swing bucket and started to push. After a while she moved to the front and stood so his legs crashed into her. Tristan screeched with laughter; it was great fun.

As they walked back to the car Naing said, "Pearl, we can have a proper discussion about whether we want a second child and if so, whether I sell my flat and we all live together, how we work the finances and that sort of thing. But it makes me feel sick to think of you and Marcus having intercourse again. If we did go ahead, it would have to be by artificial means and I'm not even sure the donor should be Marcus. I sometimes worry that you two are getting too close. I know you're older than him and I know he has a beautiful wife who has a successful career and that they enjoy a wonderful lifestyle. But I've seen the way he looks at you. And I don't want him near you any more … other than necessary for Tristan.

Six

"My most beautiful and adorable Kyaw, I need to apologise in advance for having to tell you something that I realise will really upset you. Sorry, sorry, don't look so mournful, stop casting those eyes downward, I'm only joking. Seriously though, you'll have to survive next week without our usual Thursday afternoon study session. Before you burst into tears, I'll explain".

Kyaw snuggled even closer, she half knew what was coming from hints dropped over the summer.

"Since about late April, actually just after your twentieth birthday party, I have been exchanging emails with the PA to the Rector of Yadanadon. I haven't mentioned it much because, to be fair, I honestly thought it would all fall apart and at one stage I even wondered if I was being pumped for information so that the university could proceed without me. In the event, and as I'm sure you could have told me from the start, the Rector and his staff have been as good as their word. Of course, I have been very careful not to divulge any precise detail of what I have in mind so perhaps they had little choice. Anyway, I'm off to Mandalay again".

"Luke, sweetheart, just as you did when promising to abide by the courtship custom of my homeland, I'm in two minds. I want you to be accepted as one of their strategic scientists under the *One Hundred Talents Plan* you mentioned, of course I do, and I hope it somehow helps Myanmar *to be put on the world stage* just as you described. But I'll miss you terribly".

"Darling Kyaw, I'll miss you too. Can I last one week without seeing you? The answer is, I have to. The way I see it, we are sure of each other. Two people so in love often have to spend time away from each other. Over the next few years, and especially after your degree, we are going to build an international business. Inevitably that will mean spending time apart, and it will be worth it, I promise. The other thing I've had in mind during the exchange of emails is making sure I'm contracted to return to Mandalay at least once each quarter, and you'll be with me. As an ex-student who has made good in the Western World, how can they refuse? All flights, hotel accommodation and meals on expenses, just think of that. While I work, you'll be with your mum and sisters. A perfect arrangement all round. Wish me luck in pulling it off. Oh, that reminds me, would one of your sisters act as an interpreter for me?"

"I expect so. I'll text Garma and Hla and ask"

"If both of them are willing then, as an important Western businessman, I claim the right to choose. Tell me Kyaw what does each name mean?"

"My sister Garma is named after the Goddess of dance and Hla means beautiful".

"Well, my heart probably won't survive a second beautiful sister so if there's a choice I'll go for Garma. Since I can't dance a step, she won't feel uncomfortable".

"Mr Luke Brown, I must say you don't lack confidence do you? One more sarcastic remark about my family and I'll instruct Garma to mis-translate the technical aspects of your contract (which you might not be offered anyway) so my old university holds all the cards and you end up working for nothing".

"Point taken my delicate Burmese snowflake. From this second on I'll tread very carefully and treat every oriental person with the greatest respect: after all, we don't want to miss out on this ground-breaking, world-shattering opportunity do we? Oh, Kyaw I almost forgot. Would it be in order, I mean, would it be courteous if I met Naing's father Mr Aung again while in Mandalay? We seemed to hit it off when Pearl brought him to my squash club last year and since he's the chair of the Dotcom charity that Pearl and Naing have asked me to join as a trustee, I'd like to understand what work has been done so far".

"Luke, I'm so disappointed with you. Shortly after we first met, one of your chat-up lines was using audio tapes to learn the basics of my language. How could you have forgotten so soon? One thing you'd better do is take those tapes for the flight. There is no Mr Aung. He is "U" Aung and an adult female is "Daw". It must help if you get the basics right. Also, think about the students you'll talk to; the girl is "Ma" and the boy "Ko or Maung". The sooner I go with you, the better".

Kyaw reached for his hand. "And the sooner you cuddle me, the better".

Hand-in-hand, a young couple walked out of the Thai restaurant. Within seconds they were lost in the darkness.

*

In the exchange of emails it had been suggested by the Rector's personal assistant that his visit should be scheduled for the first week of November for two reasons. First, the new intake of students would have settled in and secondly the wet season would have ended and the cool dry months begun (Luke had to smile at this seasonal advantage. As he'd experienced in the past, a Myanmar *cool* was not exactly a UK East Midlands *cool)*. Even so, he applauded the consideration behind the timing suggestion and reckoned it could only bode well for the geniality of the discussions to come.

Another pleasant surprise (although looking back on it a few years later it shouldn't have been) was the use of the latest technology by the Rector's office to confirm his travel and accommodation arrangements. It all came zipping into his smartphone. The flight tickets; Saturday 5th November (shame but nowadays Bonfire Night had all but disappeared in favour of the American influenced Halloween. Unless he was watching the fireworks with Kyaw by his side, what was the point anyway?) Heathrow 21.35 hours Thai Airlines to Bangkok arriving 16.00 hours Sunday 6th November 2016. Depart Monday 9.55 hours Thai Smile to Mandalay arriving 11.20 hours. Accommodation: Bangkok Marriott Hotel The Surawongse. In Mandalay, no hotel would be needed since a Yadanadon University student room would be available. Open tickets for return. To be met by official car at Mandalay airport and taken directly to the campus. Flight fares and hotel room paid in advance. Expenses to be recorded and reimbursed by the university. Luke was very impressed. The Rector and his senior staff meant business. Good, so did he.

During the long flight Luke indulged in what he increasingly regarded as the one true luxury of life: thinking. So much progress had been made to get this far and he mustn't mess up. Technical stuff was fine. He could hold his own in that arena but a little voice inside his head was telling him that success or failure would turn on how cleverly he played things and he supposed that meant his skill at tactics. He had some experience with gaining and holding his *risk management* clients and he understood only too well that it was less to do with demonstrating the software application than how he handled himself. He had to pick up and feed off the vibrations coming from the other side of the table. But that experience came from working with UK and Australian based buyers. OK, he'd been to Myanmar before and he'd quizzed Kyaw as much as he could, but still, the University staff would hold the high ground. He needed a plan to level the playing field.

However cautiously, however subtly, Luke's big idea was to skew each step in a developing discourse to his advantage. To achieve this, his mindset would be not as a seller who is forced to give ground to clinch the deal, but as a buyer having the upper hand. The University had to sell him their need for a leapfrog in a line of applied technology. He might bite on that need or then again he might not. So how would he achieve this apparent reversal of role? The answer came after his third beer in the bar of the Bangkok Marriott. He would not divulge the specific application of the software and robotics until a contract had been signed. Not promised but signed and approved, including any re-drafting, by his UK-based lawyer. And, crucially, the contract must contain a clause giving him access to the source code of the latest software version and the opportunity to suggest changes before final release. This opportunity to *fine tune* the release would ensure adherence to international standards and enhance the University's reputation for high quality work.

As a quid pro quo, Luke's company would contract not to sell the developed algorithms to any third party.

Luke opened his laptop and started to type, he must get his ideas down. He fired off an email to his UK solicitor and a none too delicate text to Kyaw (would it get through?). Dare he try a glass of the local rum with his meal? Best not: stick to beer. He would need a clear head for tomorrow.

*

Pearl was surprised when Marcus knocked on the cottage door.

"You must have absolutely flown. That "thirty minutes away" was actually twenty minutes".

"Well, believe it or not, there are no points on the licence now so I figured why not, and the A23 was traffic free anyway. Pearl, I know you're hopeless at dates but it's an important anniversary so I had to get here pronto".

"Sorry, what anniversary?"

"Tristan is exactly two years and three months old today. Do I have to jog your memory about everything? It is Saturday 20th July 2019. Twenty-seven months ago something happened that changed our lives for ever".

"Well yes but I wouldn't call it an anniversary exactly".

"To me it is and staring at the *Negretti & Zambra London Victorian Carved Barometer* the air pressure is rising and so the cloud is drifting way, The Sun Is Gonna Shine and things are warming up. Let's get to the park – where is the little scamp anyway?"

Because of the premium on parking at this time of year, they took Pearl's Ford Fiesta and found a space on the road running past the park railings.

"Marcus, we're in luck because I wanted us to sit on this bench rather than down the other end and then explain why and tell you what's happened".

"Oh dear Pearl, I can see now you have your sad face on. I've been flippant since I arrived, I'm sorry. Tell me what's wrong and I'll sort it out - promise".

"It's not really something that can be sorted. I'll start at the beginning but we'll have to keep an eye on Tristan, that other small boy often starts throwing sand and I have to rush over before any gets in his eyes. Well, it must have been about three months ago, the week before Tristan's party, which if you remember Naing couldn't make. We sat on this bench and I told her about your phone call, you know, when you asked if we (Naing and I that is) wanted another child. I'm afraid her reaction was pretty much instantaneous. She said no, definitely not, especially if we did it the natural way, like with Tristan. To be fair, she promised to think about me getting pregnant via artificial means, although she was not happy with you being the donor. I'm afraid my reaction to that was immediate, instinctive I suppose. I wouldn't want two children each with a different father. One thing I would never be is promiscuous".

Pearl reached for Marcus's hand and held it tightly.

"I'm sorry to drag you into this Marcus but I need someone to hold onto, going through a difficult patch and all that. It's my fault, I shouldn't have broached the subject but honestly I didn't expect that response. I mean she was OK before and she's really taken to Tristan so why not a brother or sister?"

"Pearl, would you mind if I kissed you very gently on the cheek – well I'm going to anyway and think on this, if you scream in this place I'll be locked up in minutes and what will Tristan make of me being carried off in a police car?"

Marcus looked at Pearl, their eyes met and both smiled. The atmosphere changed, things had changed. Hand-in-hand they walked over to the sand pit. Marcus grabbed Tristan from behind and winged him onto his shoulder. He started to run bumping the little boy up and down. Tristan loved it and was screaming with excitement. Pearl ran after them trying to catch up.

By six o'clock they were back at the cottage. It was now very warm (26c according to the clock on the garden wall now in shade) and Pearl carried a tray of tea and ginger biscuits into the garden. Tristan was rummaging in his toy box which Marcus, as commanded, had carried outside.

"Marcus there's something else. Might as well tell you everything before you zoom off. Since that incident in the park, things between me and Naing have not been the same. It took a while for me to realise but small things started to add up. She used to come over every Saturday evening, arriving just after you'd left, but it became every two weeks and now, well, actually, Tristan hasn't seen her for over three weeks. Apart from everything else, it's a shame because she had started to teach him a few Myanmar words. And, I suppose you might as well know, she hasn't stayed over since the *park bench chat* as I think of it. Things have obviously been going on in the background and now I know what. Yesterday, I received an email from her. Can you imagine how I felt? Marcus, an email from my partner – not a phone call, not a text but a cold carefully worded email. In a nutshell, she's returning home to Mandalay. Clearly, her father Aung has been involved for some time and with his help, contacts I suppose, she is considering setting up her own practice over there. I must have hurt her very badly, I mean she's only just been made senior dental surgeon".

Marcus looked at Pearl, searching her eyes, looking for a signal. She could feel it. He walked over to Tristan, picked him up and placed him on the miniature trampoline. The little boy bounced and bounced. Pearl was thinking *our little man's in toddler heaven. But where am I, where?* She walked over to Marcus.

"Marcus could you possibly stay for an hour after Tristan's gone to bed? Naing's decision has knocked me for six. I'd really appreciate your take on what we're going to do, I mean you, me, our little boy and of course Alice".

"Oh, damn it Pearl, I can't, not today. Alice is, for once, not at work as such. Senior management training course or something. As always with these things a so-called full day ends at four-thirtyish and we've booked our favourite restaurant for eight. Thinking about the traffic out there I'll probably be in trouble for being late. Look, Tristan's playing happily and we've known each other long enough so let's sort things out now. I have to square with you. Being the sort of guy I am, head full of numbers, never very good at making friends, analytical by nature really, well, human nature has never been my strong suit. I seem able to work most things out except what makes people tick, especially those of the female gender. But that doesn't apply to you. I know you too well. I can sense what's going through your head. That first moment I upset you with that policeman, barging in on your privacy, your grief. I can't tell you how unnerved it made me. Me, the ultimate cold fish and us being on opposite sides. I've often wondered since, if that's how all good things start. Just look at Tristan. Isn't he a miracle?"

"Marcus, please give me a hug. Nobody's looking, I don't care if they are".

Pearl gave a deep sigh. The few seconds that passed seemed like hours. When Pearl broke away, she was weeping quietly.

"Dear Pearl, I don't know what to do. I mentioned my problem understanding people. Suppose I'll have to come straight out with it. Why are you a lesbian? Why did you take Naing as a partner? When we made our little boy, was that the first time you'd been with a man?"

"Why am I trembling on such a warm afternoon? Father Marcus, it's confession time. Taking the last question first, the answer is yes. Why? I can't explain. It must be to do with having a low sex drive or something, mustn't it? Thinking back to the private school and the university college, both for girls only, I didn't have any feelings that way although the activity was all around. The Fleet Street jobs. Wonder if it started then, I mean I grew to hate and I really mean hate certain men. Chauvinist Pigs was the term at the time. And they were. After that I was my daddy's escort at the important Military and Home Office functions and caring for him during his long illness. I never thought about men in a sexual way, he was the only one in my life, always was after my mummy was killed so tragically in a car accident. Some sort of reverse Oedipus Complex perhaps. Another thing is, I can't remember ever feeling lonely. Not even after he died. I got my little job at the library and then of course met dear Eugene and, well, you know the rest. But Marcus, ever since Tristan was born, I have been lonely. For the first time since dear Eugene passed away I am missing someone. Deep down I ache for company. I never used to".

"Pearl, I understand all that and it's not a million miles from my background. I was in my own little bubble until

Alice came along. And, you know, confession time as you say, why hasn't she got pregnant? During our early days, our relationship was very passionate and she was going to give up her career. Lots of babies would come along. For some reason it never happened and now she's really senior in the Met. and involved in things I'm sworn to secrecy on, little ones interfering with our wonderful life seems more like hope than expectation – at any rate on my part. At times it's like she can't wait to get back to her office, it's like a magnet and of course magnets have both the power of attraction but also if the poles are not aligned repulsion. Right, that's off my chest so now tell me, why Naing?"

"It started the night we celebrated after I told her she was dear Eugene's granddaughter. Neither of us drink much but that evening we did and somehow ended up in bed together. After that it just carried on. As you know, we haven't lived together or shared finances or other domestic things. I have to say Naing has grown very fond of Tristan (she named him you know) and that she can leave him behind is, to me, the most surprising aspect of her decision".

"Pearl, I really do have to get home but I need to know, when we made love, did you have any sexual feelings for me".

"Oh God yes, I thought I would explode".

Seven

Kyaw had obviously contacted Aung because his message to Luke was to grab a taxi and visit him on the outskirts of Madaya. His home was only 39 kms North of Mandalay using National Highway 31 and so he would arrive in about 30 minutes. Perfect. Luke needed a break from the talks and getting out of town to see U Aung was just the excuse he needed. Kyaw had explained the position in society that a retired teacher and academic would enjoy and had done her best to describe his house. Even so, Luke's curiosity about what lay beyond the urban sprawl was awoken. He opened his laptop and searched under *A traditional Burmese house* and up popped the website of the *World Monument Fund:-*

Elevated above ground on a structure of sturdy teak wood, with bamboo walls and a thatched roof, the farmhouse building type is the embodiment of a centuries-long building culture in Myanmar. Such farmhouses once abounded in Burmese villages throughout the central plains of Myanmar and around the Irrawaddy River delta. Under successive kingdoms, dwellings in Myanmar were subject to sumptuary laws ensuring that building height, materials, and construction techniques were consistent with a person's status in society. The end of monarchy and the colonial period saw the end of sumptuary restrictions on building, allowing for grander houses to be built using teak, a material that had once been restricted to monastic architecture alone. Drawing on a tradition of wood joinery and carving, farmhouses were built on sturdy posts, supporting a broad platform and a sparsely furnished main level. A covered staircase gave access from below, while the space beneath the house provided shelter for livestock and a place to store agricultural tools. Roofs were built of thatch, which always represented the risk of fire, and were increasingly replaced with corrugated zinc after the nineteenth century.

Today, even as agriculture continues to underpin Myanmar's economy, many farmhouse owners are opting to replace their homes with modern buildings that allow for a higher level of comfort. Old farmhouses are sold as their historic building materials, especially teak wood, continue to command a high price in the market—so much so that teak has formed the basis for illegal trade throughout Southeast Asia. But while these changes are plainly visible, little research has taken place on the mechanisms that are driving them, and little documentation of the disappearing farmhouses exists in libraries and archives.

Luke smiled to himself "the end of sumptuary restrictions". He loved it: exactly the principle he and Kyaw would work to after buying their love nest and turning it into a Anglo/Burmese mansion.

"Certainly Luke we can discuss the charity and how you can help but first the purpose of your visit intrigues me, precisely what is this great leap into a technological future we are about to take? As you English say, I am all ears".

"Earlier this year I presented two papers to the university on the common theme of Artificial Intelligence. For reasons I still do not quite understand, the ideas put forward have gained traction. At any rate there was sufficient interest to ask me back after my first visit. So far this week I have been explaining why I believe the Health sector should be chosen for developing an application".

"Why that particular sector with so much in the news about a wide range of other potential applications? Yadanabon doesn't even have a medical school does it?"

"Actually I'm not sure, but what I picked up was the Rector's aspiration for making a positive contribution to mankind. Oh, and please understand, I'm not advocating medical research, although it was reading about the spread of viruses that gave me an idea. In trying to think through how an AI application might have helped prevent the spread of, well, any of the more recent ones such as HIV/AIDS, Bird flu H7N9, Ebola, MERS or SARS, I couldn't see any amount of clever software supplanting the laboratory assistant and the test tube. Nevertheless, the health sector as a fertile ground for AI kept nagging at me and then I came across this TV programme, one of those fly-on-the-wall films, where one is taken inside an operating theatre to see all the gory goings on. Then it hit me. I thought, this is so inefficient. I mean, obviously these surgeons are highly skilled and know exactly what instruments to use and so on but even so there are pre-determined steps here. First, I assume, diagnosis from symptoms or scans, followed by precise location of the affected body part before the physical removal and closure of the wound. Well, each of those steps can be subjected to computer command.

"When I spoke like this to the head of the computer faculty, she referred to my paper recommending the *machine learning* as opposed to the *rules based* path. In fact she proffered the view that if a computer can learn to play GO and

CHESS and beat the number one in the world at both, it can certainly locate and remove a tumour. You know Aung, when thinking about extraordinary human brain power, AI has been around longer than is generally accepted. Garry Kasparov, the chess grandmaster and often considered the best chess player that ever lived, was beaten by IBM's Deep Blue computer back in 1997. He's on record as describing the game as like playing against a god. The great man is now warning the world that AI will render most human professions worthless. Here's another quote I learnt by heart:- for several decades we have been training people to act like computers, and now we are complaining that these jobs are in danger. Of course they are in danger. Sorry to stress my point at the risk of boring you but Kasparov also says that only 4% of jobs in the US needed human creativity and so 96% were likely to be replaced by AI.

"Most people could never aspire to the brain power of Kasparov but, as a small contribution, here is a prediction – in less than four years from now, there will be a checkout-free grocery shop. It will work by tracking what shoppers put in their basket and they will be charged by a computer app afterwards. Remember Aung, when you are the head of a world-leading charity devoted to educating the non-privileged child, you heard it first from me!"

"My goodness, I can tell what young Kyaw sees in you, or should I say has learnt from you. And I thought intellect in the young Westerner was dead!"

"Strange you mention dead but I mustn't go further. My brilliant idea cannot be leaked until the contract is sealed, signed and delivered. Oh that reminds me, and I hope you don't mind, but I mentioned you to the Rector and he seemed impressed that we were acquainted; even more so after learning of my intention to marry one of his students who is now on an international year in the UK. U Aung - sorry I know you asked me to drop the "U" but I find it difficult given your seniority - would you consider contacting him to lend your support to my involvement with his university? It might just tip the scales in my direction and, of course, further your claim to be the chairman of my new company. Best ignore my little joke but if you could put in a good word, I would be grateful".

"Luke, I think you and I will get along just fine. As with the charity, I can see the need for a mature-in-years chairman to keep a young upstart on the straight and narrow. Ah, the charity, let's talk about that. It's early days but Pearl and my daughter Naing have seen to all the formalities and for my part I've visited the local schools and delivered the message. By the end of this academic year, we should have our first student to support and if that goes well I'm confident that through my contacts over here we will get more sponsors to add to Pearl's most generous seed corn funding. After our meeting today I believe that your coming on board will be a big plus. Your technical skills and Marcus's financial talents will play a major part in the expansion of Dotcom. I sometimes wonder if that charming lady Pearl envisaged the scale I have in mind. I thought my contribution to Myanmar was over but this opportunity has given me a new lease of life. I am full of admiration for Pearl you know. She didn't need to put a million pounds of her inheritance towards helping our children. She respected my father Eugene and having discovered my mother Chit's letter had been concealed from him, wanted to put things right. I've vowed to build on her generosity and I don't just mean of money but more importantly of spirit".

"Aung, could we meet at the university during my next visit assuming my proposal is accepted of course? Before I leave there are a couple of things I'd like to pick your brains on. Sorry, that's probably an expression you're unfamiliar with - I seem obsessed with the human body. What I mean is, I would appreciate your opinion on two things".

"Fire away young man, you might be surprised how much colloquial English I'm familiar with. My mother's studies later in life left me quite a legacy".

"Once the charity is up and running, and I need about another year to get my *risk management* business fully established, I could take a few of the bursary students as internees. I would envisage offering free accommodation and on-the-job training assuming the charity funded the travelling and living expenses. I know Kyaw would be delighted to take them under her wing and I'll bet your daughter Naing gets involved in the cultural exchange too. Anyway, see what you think and obviously how both of our activities turn out. Secondly, Kyaw and I plan to marry in September next year once her studies are over and I intend to find out if she can then apply for dual Myanmar/British citizenship. After thinking along those lines, I then wondered whether, in say a few years' time, I might qualify for dual status. Any advice on that possibility would be appreciated".

*

"Only mad dogs and Englishmen … and all that". The morning plenary session had ended and the afternoon discussion would result in a decision. Luke had done all he could and the lunchtime and afternoon would be, at last, free time. Kyaw's younger sister Garma had offered to stay with him "as your official tourist guide to add to my C.V. as a Myanmar translator" which was sweet of her but he wanted to be alone. She was so like Kyaw – so delicate, so charming – her work for him had been professional in the extreme and yet these Myanmar ladies had something about them. He couldn't quite fathom what they possessed: a femininity somehow even beyond that of his ex-girlfriend Siobhan. It wasn't sexy as such but more alluring, teasing, drawing one in. He had to be careful. He thought of when he visited Kyaw at the family apartment on his previous visit. The reserved grief of her father's passing. How her mother had detected the silent signals between her eldest daughter and himself. He must be respectful. The correct word was careful.

The taxi dropped Luke off at the entrance to the Southern covered stairway. During his climb to the 735 ft summit of Mandalay Hill, he was not cognizant of the pagodas and monasteries, nor did he take note of the burgundy-coloured robes adorning the quietly-spoken monks and, unlike all other visitors to this world famous landmark, he paid no attention to the yellowish-white Thanaka cream painted circles on the ladies faces. Luke was miles away. His grandmother's pocket money was safely tucked away as he unlatched the small gate before walking up the garden path leading to his great uncle Harold's cottage. He was hungry and the red painted biscuit tin would be sitting on the kitchen table. "Tha takes as many as tha likes – got em in special like". Luke paused to look at the vast plane far below; if there was a boundless display of paddy fields stretching to the horizon, he didn't notice.

It makes my blood boil. They think I believe that cock-and-bull story from that copper Neil. A phone call from a fellow stamp collector, a police car that happened to be passing by at the time. Do they think I'm stupid? We'll see who's stupid. History will repeat itself. Just like Great Uncle Harold, it's me against the rest of them. Kyaw was trying hard to resist when she spoke and what she said stopped me in my tracks. I had to listen, some things are more important than sex and I can wait, it's in my interest to hold off. Who knows what other secrets might be spilled now I understand the channel. It makes wonderful symmetry; an elegant algorithm. Neil the humble copper looks up to super-sleuth Alice now married to Maserati Man. In turn, Marcus, resulting from the so-called cold case success, is friendly with posh high-class lady Pearl. And guess who Pearl is extremely friendly with? That's right, my delicious Kyaw. Obviously, this would have been the communication route used when asking me, shortly before his death, to stop doing little jobs for the old man. So, if that lot used me to further their ends, I can do the same from now on. What's wrong with that? Kyaw will tell me if the police start poking around my activities and equally I can avoid getting her involved in anything I don't want them knowing about. What Kyaw picked up was that the police had opened a case going back to the 1950's when two of my great uncle's brothers disappeared. She even said they proved Harold was a serial murderer. What rubbish, what proof? After all this time – absolute tosh. They even tried to implicate me – Oh, I see, because I did his computer stuff, because I drove him to Great Uncle Eugene's a couple of times! As Harold would have put it, "tha lives in cloud-cuckoo land". His lessons were not in vain. I'll be a self-made loner too; they won't pin anything on me either. Think I'll chat up Hla this evening – see if I can make Garma jealous.

The meeting was convened for five pm. Luke and Garma were led into a large room offset from the Rector's office. What surprised Luke was its formality with no obvious concession to Myanmar's culture or traditions except, Luke noticed, for the chairs which were edged in black wood (ebony?) with a latticed seat (raffia?) and curved back rest; admiring them presented Luke with the perfect opening comment. Garma spoke his words and smiled and the Rector and his four senior academics returned the compliment with a slight bow of the head. Luke felt positive, all would be well.

The Rector explained that, after due consideration, the university had agreed to establish an Artificial Intelligence Unit and he was invited to be their external consultant. The three-day delay, which he apologized for, was due solely to a clause in the contract allowing release to Mr Luke Brown of the source code but after several redrafted exchanges between the legal people, final wording has been agreed. The university would own the intellectual property rights to any developed application and Mr Luke Brown would not be allowed to pass associated algorithms to any third party. Yadanabon University, recognizing the experience and skill drawn upon, would pay a monthly retainer fee and all expenses incurred in returning to the campus each quarter to supervise progress and schedule the next phase of work. Although the university couldn't at this time accede to Mr Luke Brown's request to own 10% of any company formed to exploit the commercial potential of the Artificial Intelligence Unit if, as expected, a new Myanmar Company Law was passed next year (2017), this request would be granted.

The university's legal representative explained that the most significant change in the law was likely to be the introduction of a new definition of a foreign company. Under the existing 1914 act, a locally incorporated entity with any foreign shareholding is considered a foreign company in Myanmar. The new legal definition was expected to allow new companies to have up to 35% of their shares held by foreign nationals before being considered a foreign company. This would enable a foreign investor, such as Mr Luke Brown, to partake in business activities that were previously restricted to companies with 100% of shares held by Myanmar citizens. The Rector added that it was the business community that had pressed for this change and it was important to prove their case that a foreign shareholder would be motivated to help boost Myanmar's economy.

The legal documents were passed between the Rector and Luke for signature and counter-signature. The room was awash with smiling faces and bowed heads. Luke signalled to Garma that it was time to leave but the Rector asked them to stay.

"Mr Luke Brown, on behalf of Yadanabon University I welcome you as a senior colleague to our academic staff. At the outset of our discussions you mentioned having a specific application that our new AI Unit would work on. Now is the time to enlighten us".

"I want to build a database of donors and matched recipients. I want to build robots that, by remote command, extract body parts from deceased humans".

Eight

"Marcus, would you mind taking Tristan to the park this afternoon while I stay here? I'd like a couple of hours to finish off some work and hopefully we can then go through it together once he's gone to bed – you did say you could go home a little later this evening didn't you? I hope you'll be pleased with what I've done".

"Pearl, those two little words coming from you "hope" and "pleased", if only they were set in a different context. Quite aside from that, dare I hope and be pleased you've started the novel?"

"Now you've gone and spoilt my surprise, but yes. Well, not exactly. Buzz off and please don't fill him up with ice cream and fizzy drink this time".

"OK, and off to the sandpit we go, but just before leaving and to boost your confidence, I'll enlighten you on a piece of painstaking research I've done"

"Really?"

"Yes, it's about literary genre. Well, perhaps not genre exactly but let's say categories. No, that's not right either, I mean degrees of difficulty. Apparently, an autobiographical work is easy since it relies on memory, diaries and other personal jottings. Next come biographies, which, while once a product of a thousand hours in the British Library and the like, are now much easier courtesy of Google and the other search engines. But novels are different. They require creativity and that Pearl is what you're in for. OK, you had your talks with Eugene and his papers have been returned by the police but they are only pointers to a full scale novel. You have to use your imagination. I mean, you can hardly knock out 120,000 words from memory and just his sparse notes.

With that in mind, we men will venture forth to find the see-saw while you wrestle with the jigsaw of ideas. Oh, one last thing – nearly forgot – I've decided on your pen name. Though I say so myself, it is rather brilliant. You will write as Stay Bennett".

Marcus hadn't even finished Chapter 1 of Pinocchio when Tristan stopped wriggling. He was perfectly still; fast asleep. On the sitting room table were a couple of sheets of typed A4. Pearl called from the kitchen, "Marcus I'm making coffee and as I can't bear to watch your reaction to my meagre effort, I'll stay here until you call".

Marcus started to read;

Eugene is the last of 13 children born to a family of master butchers. Two themes permeate the novel. Personal regret and the corrupting influence of a perceived need to preserve the family's business reputation.

After a brief reprise of the killing of one son during the invasion of Singapore by the Japanese army in February 1942, the story starts with twelve-year-old Eugene accompanying two of his older brothers to slaughter a cow at a local farm. The meat is destined for the war-time black market; business that will make the family financially but ultimately break it with potentially disastrous consequences.

Shortly after VE day and his 18th birthday, Eugene is called up. HMS Devonshire is en-route to Australia but his troop is disembarked at Bombay destined for Burma; first Rangoon, then Mandalay. He contracts a tropical disease and is nursed back to health by a young Burmese girl "Chit". They fall in love. She is smuggled with the troop as it moves overland via the Death Railway route first to Bangkok, then down the Malaysian peninsula to Singapore. Eugene is forced into a decision. Either marry the girl, face court martial and a possible death sentence or return to the UK. He takes the latter course. His lifelong regret. There is a letter that could have changed his life but it is concealed and not found until many years later.

Eugene expects to re-join the family business but two brothers have wrested it from their now ailing father. He is taken in hand by another of his older brothers "Frank" and opens a grocery store with help from a young girl he starts courting, "Dorothy".

There are family tragedies. One older brother commits suicide and the young husband of his sister is killed in a major coal-mining accident.

Frank is an entrepreneur. He has little schemes while still at school and gets into building restoration before being an early pioneer in the manufacture of potato crisps. Then, he is inculcated in local council planning corruption and makes a fortune from the post-war boon in building council houses. He is assisted in both ventures by a Mrs Robinson figure "Mrs Lazenby" and through her the seeds of his ultimate destruction are sown. Booze and gambling feature.

Eugene marries Dorothy and together they are amongst the first to open supermarkets. Her affluent parents have a fatal car accident for which there is no adequate explanation. Over time the supermarkets are very successful but the marriage starts to crumble over finance (Dorothy's refusal to invest her inherited wealth), the absence of children and Dorothy's declining health.

One of Eugene's older brothers is "Harold". He is, throughout, a shadowy figure. Another, "Jack" turns out to be homosexual and a third, "Rob" has connived with Harold to defraud the father of his business wealth. There are two suspected murders but no bodies are found except an identifiable body part. Eugene comes under suspicion.

As an old man, Eugene meets by apparent chance a beautiful and elegant young lady called "Pearl". She helps with research into his family tree and the two become firm friends and confidants. It transpires that both her late father and grandfather were senior military men and by chance the grandfather was Eugene's commanding officer in the Far East and it was he who forced the decision on Chit. Pearl's interesting and in parts tragic life-story is revealed.

Pearl decides to visit Mandalay in the hope of finding Chit or her descendants. She is successful with the latter and returns to give the good news to Eugene. He had died a few days earlier. Her distress is compounded by the content of an airmail letter Eugene had found amongst the contents of his late wife's papers. He had not told Pearl of this.

A mysterious old man attends the graveside at Eugene's funeral. It could be Harold. Pearl is handed a letter which she reads later. It purports to be from Harold and the contents give a devastating twist to all that Pearl has learned from Eugene. Who does she believe? Her dear departed friend Eugene or the shadowy Harold? – if it was Harold.

Pearl appeared with two mugs of coffee. She looked pensive.

"Marcus, please don't say anything, not yet. After the events of today, with our little Tristan safely tucked in bed, after letting you read my synopsis of what I now know will be my first novel, I feel quite emotional. Look, I'm going to have a glass of wine, having to drive home, I know you can't join me".

"Pearl, I didn't dare mention this before, but it's been on my mind ever since I arrived. I could stay the night if you wanted me to".

"Oh!"

There was a long pause. Pearl and Marcus looked at each other. She reached for his hand. The room was silent; if tenderness spoke, neither heard its words. After what seemed an eternity, Pearl spoke.

"What about Alice?"

"She's in Brussels, some European take on a large fraud case or something of the sort. It was her idea. Said she knew I wanted to stay with you for a night and would I meet her off the flight on Sunday afternoon. Oh God Pearl, I so want us to give Tristan a sister. Your idea of a glass of wine sounds wonderful".

Nine

It was an Indian Summer gone mad. Everyone thought so. The temperature in the early afternoon of Thursday 18th September 2014 peaked at 77 degrees Fahrenheit. By pure coincidence that was the day Luke took a call from his Great Uncle Harold. "Luke lad, pop rownd early afternoon, tek car for spin, somat important to do and havin afternoon tea with old Fred Salmon".

The Old Hall was sited on the Nottinghamshire/ Derbyshire border. In fact, a stream flowing through the middle of the large lawn was the county border. Fred Salmon, the owner, had been at school with Harold and the two had stayed friends. Mr Salmon was explaining to Luke that the shade in this far corner of the garden came from a Mulberry tree believed to be as old as the Hall itself and so dating from about 1690. The history lesson, so familiar to Harold, would inevitably follow but his calculation was that it would be worth it. As usual, Harold had a plan. Fred Salmon was saying that the local squire was registered on the title deeds as the original owner of the Old Hall together with all the land and farmsteads in the locality including Red Roof Farm where his friend Harold's sister had lived. An earlier house on the same site as the Old Hall belonged to the Earl of Sheffield and it is possible for a building to have been there since Norman times when the village of Newton was recorded in the Domesday Book.

Not for the first time, Luke could only marvel at the enigma that surely was his great uncle. Never had this place been mentioned and now, walking stiffly to join them was a maid wearing a pure white and immaculately pressed apron. She was carrying a silver tray with an ornate tea pot with matching cups and tea plates. Placed regally - a huge home-made cake. It was like a scene from a Sunday evening TV period drama. Luke was thinking that one day, he would have a place like this. If old money can live in elegant luxury, then so can new. They'll see. After taking tea and cake they strolled in the grounds and Mr Salmon pointed out three graves of a Mr Downing and his two wives. Their host chuckled – yes, two wives. The vicar of the day refused to inter the Downings in the church yard because of Mr Downing's adultery. He had married his wife's sister whilst his wife was still alive, although very ill and expected to die. Dear, dear, the Good Lord would be cross – he laughed once more. Luke looked at his elder relative and smiled. Harold returned a steely stare. Luke knew what that meant – "keep thi mouth shut, there's a job afoot".

Fred Salmon hadn't finished. "My family have been in residence since the early nineteen hundreds, and the son of an earlier generation became Sir John who at one time was the first Air Marshall of the R.A.F. His brother, who was a naval officer, was killed in the First World War and had a military funeral in these grounds. For my part on Friday nights, I used to fetch the men from the George & Dragon to listen to the late news to see how our lads were getting on. That was during the Second World War".

Luke looked on as the two old men wandered off to the far end of the orchard. He had a strange feeling. Gratitude for one, orderly respect for the other; a creeping sadness for both as they neared the end of their line. What hard times they'd lived through. How many of their kind had not survived beyond their early twenties? The War Memorial on the village green was filled with names, but there was no Harold Whitby and no Fred Salmon name to fade away slowly as weather and time took their toll. What were they discussing? He'd wheedle it out of his great uncle.

Wheedling wasn't necessary. As Luke caressed the purring Jaguar homeward, out it came. "It be all fixed Luke lad". Luke was finding it hard to concentrate on both driving the car and deciphering the Old Saxon English (as he thought of it). But, in essence and of course no surprise to Luke, wily Harold had a predetermined purpose for the pleasant afternoon visit to his old friend. Had Luke noticed the brick buildings joined on to the back of the Old Hall? No, probably not – too busy day-dreaming as usual. The office wing had been built in the early seventies to get Fred's son started as an architect.

Was history about to repeat itself? At the cost of a new stamp album and "a few stamps – nice to luk at but worth nowt" for Fred's grandchild Harold had done a deal. Luke could use the premises for a year, rent free. But, the lad was to understand, he'd get no more help. "Tha's on thee own". He wouldn't succeed in business if he was feather-bedded. Harold had forged his own path away from the family and now Luke must prove his metal too and should note that an ounce of forethought was worth a pound of after. Think it all through before starting. Make a plan; write it down. Don't be afraid to borrow money. Only set on the best people and pay them full whack, "tha pays peanuts, tha gets monkeys". A business must be built on a solid foundation. "Harold will see thee rite – all in gud tym lad, all in gud tym".

*

Luke came across the term *Risk Management* by pure chance. To gain his Masters, he wanted his thesis to be based on a suite of software programs capable of creating a new business that presented a formidable barrier to entry. After much research and consulting his tutor, the idea of limiting exposure to price volatility in commodities took hold. If he could reduce the risk of holding financial instruments such as derivatives, a well-marketed proprietary package could be a winner. The users of such instruments such as investment banks and hedge funds had the financial motivation to pay. A minute shaving of risk could produce huge marginal savings.

Having graduated, Luke's plan was to understand thoroughly the workings of Futures/Forwards, Options and Swaps which derive their value based on the value of something else, for example an index or an underlying asset such as a commodity. He would learn that these derivatives are used to hedge and speculate in the market. A Futures is an obligation to pay or receive money. He thought of an example. As the summer season approaches, the owner of a sweet shop takes the view that the price of sugar is going to increase due to a demand and supply mismatch of sugarcane. Now, suppose he and a third party (counterparty) get into a futures contract. It might mean he has to pay that counterparty a certain amount (say £100) at the end of six months for 50 Kgs of sugar. He has hedged his risk of a rise in the price of sugar. For its part, the third party will have to deliver 50 kgs of sugar at the set price that was decided on day one, even though the actual price of sugar might be the same, less or more than £100.

As Luke got deeper into the management of derivatives using software, he devoted more and more time to Options which are more aggressive to trade than Futures. This is because they offer a higher leverage in trading than regular stocks. Options are a right, but not an obligation, to buy or sell a certain product. This means a trader has an option to trade at a certain price that is not necessarily the final amount. Options are regarded as *tricky* and that is what appealed to the young man.

Offering a start date of Monday 5nd January 2015 would give Luke bags of time to get the offices ready, or so he thought. But a non-practical man is soon out of his depth and a local firm of jobbing builders can treat this minor task as a *hospital job,* an expression unfamiliar to a computer geek but one which would lead to a few sleepless nights and no little frustration. As a middle-aged gnarled-featured pot-bellied foreman enlightened the maestro, "if tha thinks any others will take on a half-done job – think again lad". As a furious Luke said to his first potential employee. "It's not as if there's much to do. Three internal walls to knock out to create open plan, re-plaster the walls, slap a coat of paint on, totally re-wire and liaise with BT to bring in broadband. They're making a mountain out of a molehill, the business ought to be called *Bodge-it & Scram,* they're ripping me off. Think I'm stupid do they? Just wait till the final bill wants paying. Just wait till the rusty nails mysteriously appear on the drive as they finally leave. There is more than one way to be ripped off". Eric had a deep-throated cackling laugh. It was the first time Luke had heard it.

Fortunately, Luke found a way to offset the idle-time expense of the cowboy builders. Furniture. Absolutely no point in buying new, even specially designed and equipped computer consoles. Cheap second-hand stuff abounded. He puzzled on the why of it and concluded that young entrepreneurs like himself set off with ideas and enthusiasm but no financial nous and went bust in the blink of an eye. Here was a lesson to be learnt. He needed a bean-counter and not a lapdog either, more a bloodhound. Someone not afraid to keep him in check. The answer was an outsider prepared to walk away if his or her advice was ignored. Blindingly obvious when one thinks about it and yet presumably not heeded by the sellers of second-hand office furniture. How to find this money-bully? Luke decided to talk to the business management people back at uni. - perhaps they knew someone.

Eric was the first employee; Luke knew him as the most efficient programmer amongst his fellow students in the third year. That he hadn't landed a full-time job was down to just one thing, although no prospective employer had mentioned it. Eric had impaired vision. In fact, as he had confided to Luke after they had reviewed each other's work in the final module, more impaired than he cared to admit. He was almost blind in one eye and had severely restricted vision in the other. That's why his head tilted to one side and was held close to the keyboard when working intently; a practice that disturbed those he presented to. Luke didn't give a jot. Like the Peregrine Falcon on the university tower swooping on an unwary pigeon, so Luke homed in on Eric by asking what salary he expected. Without hesitation that figure was agreed and so the fulcrum of Risk Management was installed. After shaking hands to cement the first employee engagement and selfishly to hear that cackle of a laugh, Luke asked Eric not to crash through the office doors as newly hung by a cowboy joiner. "Best poke them with your white stick before entering".

Who better to find an assistant for Eric than the man himself? For years to come, Luke marvelled at this astute move. Delegation and motivation in one move; superb. Eric recruited Murray another ex-fellow student who had found a permanent position but disliked his boss. Eric had a superb boss and so for Murray to join the new company was a no-brainer. There was to be one other member of the founding team and who most definitely must be selected personally by Luke. From his internship with a large software house in London, Luke had learned one vital lesson. A software application is sold by demonstration. The potential buyer mentally assesses two key aspects. First, *does the functionality meet my need?* The demonstrator knows that against a standard of one hundred percent, it does not. The skill lies in highlighting the unique aspects of the application and soft-pedalling on the gaps that, now understood, can be addressed in the beta version to be released shortly. Secondly, *is the demonstrator a sex bomb?* In a tiny minority of instances the key decision maker will be female and in such cases Luke will demonstrate the magnificence of the application. But, in the main, it will be a man who decides. Therefore, Luke's business needed a lady possessed of natural charms such as long slender legs. This is where Becky came in.

Luke spotted Becky in the main dining hall. It would have been hard not to. She was tall. He guessed a shade under six feet, a brunette and very slim. Yet, it wasn't her appearance but more her mannerisms that held his attention. Standing in the queue she somehow looked out of place. Being a little older than the other students, did she display a sense of haughtiness? (*It's not that I want to be here, it's that I have to be*).

With the confidence of one about to be awarded a First, Luke made straight for the vacant chair next to the ravishing lady. It ought to have been embarrassing, she with a pie-of-the-day and chips and he with nothing, but it wasn't. She seemed to accept as quite normal that a man would crash into her space.

After a few more *accidental* lunchtime's sharing of a table, Luke got the story he was after. Becky wouldn't accept his invitation to meet later for a drink, not because she found him unattractive but due to the small matter of her being married. Her husband had some sort of health problem which she preferred not to talk about but, if Luke heard correctly, it didn't prevent him playing golf three or four times a week and off a low handicap. And, no, she wasn't into software, her aim was to become a technical writer. To help pay the rent, she moonlighted for a couple of local companies writing systems manuals.

"So, from the write-up you can demonstrate that the application is exactly as specified, find the bugs and so on?"

"Yes, exactly".

"Look Becky, here's my card. Once you've finished your course, contact me. I have a position that will suit you down to the ground and you can keep on with the part-time work, the more experience, the better. One thing though, will you be OK with overseas travel?"

*

Although suggested, Luke hadn't expected his three staff to turn up at the new offices by nine o'clock on Monday 5th January. The past few years at uni. had taught him that timings among the budding computer community was haphazard at best. But he was wrong. Here they were, Eric, Murray, Becky and himself all somewhat bewildered and trying to take in the surroundings. Shiny near-new desks, spotless computer monitors, miles of cabling and walls adorned with an eclectic mix of sketches and paintings purloined by Luke from undisclosed sources. Becky broke the ice by saying it had gone (the ice that was) with a milder temperature of 4.5c. Murray offered to make coffee and the brain-storming began.

Three months later and cosseted in the George & Dragon, Eric rose from the drinks table and made his longest ever speech. "Our team has, in the last ninety days, created more innovative technology than witnessed in the entire history of IT". Murray felt the need to respond. "Sit down Eric, stop making a fool of yourself and also stop drinking from my beer mug as well as your own". It was a wonderful and heartfelt celebration of Becky's final clearance of their new suite of Risk Management programs branded as *London Wall*. She rose from her chair and moved to where Eric now sat.

"Gentlemen, this decrepit old soul has been complaining that he can't see enough of my legs". She lifted her skirt some twelve inches higher, possibly more. Luke felt himself overheat and Murray, with his impeccable sense of timing, fell off his chair.

Once calm was restored and Luke had fetched a further round of drinks, he cleared his throat with an exaggerated cough signalling the need for attention.

"Next week I have to take a couple of days off having promised to take an elderly relative down to somewhere near Brighton to see his brother. It's hard to believe but between them they've clocked up one hundred and eighty years on this planet. That is approximately one hundred and fifty-five years more than I'll last if Becky carries on with her drunken antics. Seriously, Eric's in charge while I'm away and I'll support any decision he takes, so no squabbling in the ranks. Ok, we smirked at Eric's little speech but he made a good point. We're on our way and I want to back that up. We need the income flow from renting our systems but when it arrives, I intend to pay you a bonus. The way each of you has buckled down since January has exceeded my wildest dreams; God knows how many hours we've put in without a single grouse from anyone. Becky and Murray, I'll let you into a little secret. A couple of weeks ago I returned to the office, couldn't sleep for thinking about that Option 3a bug. It was just after two and Eric was still here with his head even lower than usual over his keyboard. I promised not to let on but it's hard to keep quiet over something like that. Look guys, I've made another decision. Each of you will be receiving a five percent share of the business. It may not sound much and maybe I can increase it later but if London Wall really takes off, I want you to benefit from more than just salary and bonuses.

"I don't want any thanks, just to get the second suite finished and bug free. Oh, and this relative is hinting he'll want taking down South again in a few weeks. Don't know why but I need to keep him happy. If it wasn't for old Harold we wouldn't be in these offices; come to that, I'd be riddled with debt and have no wheels. Now I've softened you up, here's the crunch. In July I'm off to Australia for the month and I'll need Becky for the first two weeks. Can't remember whether you know but it's been my regular trip since I was eighteen. I visit an aunt in Perth and she's quite well connected. The thing is, she's got me an appointment with the top two banks. Both of the derivative variants must be ready by then. Guys, this is the big one. If I can sell to them, we're running on gas. If we pull it off, Becky is free to sock it to the big boys back here. Come on, we can do it".

Ten

It was a mandatory instruction from Becky *"Old Hall, London Wall suite"* the opening salutation when answering the land line. It might seem pretentious at first but soon would morph into standard vernacular; posh but not over-the-top, professional but not intimidating. Portrayed image meant everything, especially with a start-up. Becky became the company standard bearer, no dissension.

Between April and July 2015, the open-plan office situated to the rear and in the shadow of the Old Hall witnessed frenetic and occasionally fraught activity. Computer applications were specified, programmed, tested to destruction, re-programmed, re-tested, peer reviewed, described under the online *help* icon and reduced to writing as a user manual. In the secondary application, actual derivative usage was tested against known outcomes. Becky demonstrated the vanilla application to the critical audience of Eric, Murray and Luke. Bugs were identified, isolated and fixed. Red-eyed late evening sessions were commonplace. Animated liquid sessions in the George & Dragon became weekly events. The locals had seen and heard nothing like it. A collective noun emerged as *Salmon's Crazy Coots* (plus a rude version as the evening wore on). Undaunted, the team pressed on.

Luke and Becky were on the second leg of the Etihad Airways flight, Abu Dhabi to Melbourne and he was saying that if they could wind the clock forward two or three years, a direct flight to Perth would save loads of time, if not money. Of course, by then, shedloads of cash would be flowing and the first-class airfare would be just another business expense along with a luxury hotel room instead of sponging off his aunt Petula.

"Luke I know you told me before but my head was full of that Options stuff and it didn't really sink in. How is it you have an aunt in Perth?"

"My grandmother was part of a huge family of thirteen children. I know – unbelievable! Anyway, a brother was killed in the war leaving a baby behind. That baby was my aunt Petula who was taken to Australia as part of the Ten Pound Pom programme. She is now seventy-four and I've visited her every year since 2008, paid for by my great uncle – you know, the one I took down to Brighton a couple of times recently. Don't get me wrong. When I said we'd stay in a posh hotel in years to come, it doesn't imply slumming it on this trip, because my aunt has a lovely house and we'll be very comfortable. You two will get on very well. Like you she is a very smart and classy lady".

For the first time on this long-haul flight, Becky reached for Luke's hand and gave it a squeeze. "I'll nip to the back – a beer for you, wine for me".

It was on the final leg across Southern Australia that Luke explained his plan.

"Becky, I want you to know that what you've introduced to the office in the last six months hasn't gone unnoticed. For example how we should answer the 'phone and what to wear when meeting potential clients. Then designing the logo and such. To be honest, not my bag at all but it has created the right image as a quality software house. I know because more than one outsider has mentioned it. What I'm thinking is, if we pull in the two banks down here and feed off the success with the four we've targeted in London, I'm going to promote you to Director of Sales and Marketing. It will fit perfectly with your demonstration skills and if we progress that far, I'm going to increase your share of the business to ten percent but please don't mention that to Eric or Murray. The thing is, I've had a first get-together with an outsider who might become a sort of sounding-board. Initially, I was thinking of just financial advice but after that first chat, help with strategy would be useful. For example, she was saying I must build the business on solid foundations. Apparently, like anything new, it is vital to understand the basic principles of management. By the time she left, I was wondering if I should have taken an MBA.

"The thing that hit home was her advice to distinguish between technical competence and management. So, if I'm getting this right, take the example of Eric and Murray. They are technically excellent but I mustn't confuse that with higher level work. Build the software engineers up within their competence, you know, bags of moral boosting, top whack salaries and such but never fall into the trap of assuming that skill in one area will transfer to another. It might of course but it's not worth experimenting until a business is well established. What I'm trying to get over to you Becky is that your role will be different to the boys. I want you fronting London Wall and whatever comes after it. If you have any spare time in Perth, start thinking about what our marketing plan should cover over the first two years. I hope you'll stay with me on this.

"Let's try and get some shut-eye before we touch down. Oh, and by the way, although Australia is in the grip of mid-winter, I anticipate the pilot announcing the temperature in Perth as 27c. Won't that be great? I hope you packed your bikini".

It was the evening of day four and the trio had returned to what Becky described as *the best eating place ever,* prompting Aunt Petula to say "don't be too hasty sweetie, as Luke well knows, there's a few more to try yet". It was just after eight and the place was heaving. At the *Oyster Bar Elizabeth Quay* they each had a platter of the house signature dish – *six plump oysters au naturel presented on crushed ice.*

"I'm not sure you two limeys should be partaking of this delicacy. You, young Becky with a husband on the other side of the world and Luke not seeing the beautiful Siobhan this time - or will he?"

Becky slipped the first oyster down with a generous slurp of sauvignon blanc. She gazed at the swelling ocean and expressed the view that there was something about this city, this climate and ice-cold oysters. Apparently, as she was packing up the computer equipment after the demonstration at the National Australian Bank, the tall blonde guy they'd been pitching to, flipped his card into her laptop case. He had crossed out the official stuff and over-written a mobile number. Would they mind if she didn't join them tomorrow night?

After Perth, Luke presented to both Macquarie Bank and Westpac in Sydney and Becky started her rounds in the City of London.

For Luke, 2015 couldn't get better. Yet it did. In late September while queuing to pay for his salad, he spotted Kyaw.

*

It was not something Luke normally did but on the morning of Saturday 22nd October 2016 he was back in the office. He had to finish the proposal and get it to the Mandarin translator before midday, a self-imposed deadline he missed by over an hour. The Chinese guys were smarter than he'd anticipated and he had to prove that the formula would work and, more importantly, explain how. After getting the paper off and to clear his head, Luke strolled to the far end of the garden to join old Fred Salmon who sat in the shade reading a newspaper.

"Hello young man, been putting more hours in? Surely you can take some time off, come and sit down". For a while neither man spoke, both marvelling at the wonderful display of the dahlia border and fascinated by the bees hard at work collecting the pollen. Then, after placing his folded newspaper on the table, Fred used his walking stick as a lever to turn and face Luke.

"How time flies. I was thinking before you came over that it's just two years since we sat here with Harold and he bribed me with a few packets of rubbish stamps into letting you have the offices for a year rent-free. Not that I regretted it for one minute. It's been great having my old place buzzing again and, hey Luke lad, that Becky of yours - what a bobby-dazzler. If only I'd been a few years younger, none of you lot would've stood a chance. Oh dear, getting old is no joke, everything shrivels up and some days my mind goes blank and yet that September day when Harold was here, I remember the temperature gauge was up at 77 and, can you believe, it's reading 63 today".

"Strange but I was also thinking about that afternoon when I brought him here and about the postage stamps you mentioned. How old is your grandson now?"

"Oh, thirteen I think, and growing up fast".

"I was about that age when Harold got me into stamps. Next time you see him, ask if he wants any help. I can put his collection online, he'll know what I mean. More than that, if he's really keen I can put him in touch with dealers and other collectors. You probably know from talking to Harold, there's a living in stamps if you learn enough. In fact, if he's only half as cunning as my great uncle, he won't lack for pocket-money. Tell him to come and see me next time he's here. Oh, nearly forgot, there's something I've been meaning to ask you. Because the business I set up here is going well, we're bursting at the seams for space. I'd hate to move from the Old Hall, it's such a lovely spot, so I was wondering if there was any possibility we could take over some space in the Hall itself. If it worked out and you weren't too inconvenienced, I had another idea. Would you consider selling the whole place to me? Your life-long friend, my great uncle, left me his money and he'd have been delighted if I used it and became Lord of the Manor!"

Mr Fred Salmon, now in his ninety-fourth year, chuckled.

"Nice thought lad and it would certainly solve some of my inheritance issues but I was born here and the old bones must rest here along with my ancestors".

"Oh, well, I don't see that as a problem. Break my heart too if you left. No, no, I should have explained better. Between you, me, and that Mulberry Tree, I plan to marry my girlfriend next year and if I was able to buy the Hall, no doubt the young lady will ask for a few internal alterations before we move into our love nest. Don't get me wrong, I'd never allow the character and original features of the Hall to be changed. But, if we got a proper firm in, you know, one that specializes in restoring period houses, we could carve out a nice flat for you. For a small discount off the asking price, you would still have a place of your own and rent free".

"My dear young man, you really are a chip off the old block. Let me think about it. We'll talk about this next time we meet in the garden. Cost you a peck on the cheek of that girlfriend of yours".

"That's fine, no rush at all. Next month I'm off to Myanmar, or Burma to you. Suppose you got fed up with Harold's tales about his brother Eugene being posted out there in 1945?"

"Sorry, Luke lad you've lost me there. Never knew he had a brother by that name".

Eleven

Luke didn't always see eye-to-eye with his business consultant. In fact, there had been times over the past two-and-a-half years when they seemed to be tearing each other apart. But this was not one of them. She was right; he knew it instinctively. What better day? 1st January 2018 and time to take stock. She posed two simple questions. First, how did you get to where you are now and secondly where are you heading. Luke mentally added a third, what leverage do I have?

*

Kyaw was really surprised. Luke had actually suggested it. "Why don't you pop down to see Pearl again and spend the New Year with her? After all, it will have been Tristan's first Christmas and the celebrations are bound to spill over. Naing will be joining in and after what you told me, how can Marcus keep away?" She was thinking that Luke must be softening up and could it be due to Pearl's baby – was he expecting her to come back wanting one herself? Something must have happened since early December when he was quite annoyed that she'd insisted on seeing them. However, within the hour the train was booked.

How he'd longed for it; being alone. Office closed, parties over. She had made it sound so attractive – *a cold compress to the head, a clean sheet of paper, absolute silence, personal time and space.* "Luke, no communications in or out, you have reached a crossroads, stop and think – where am I heading?"

Luke's first heading on his metaphorical clean sheet of paper was *London Wall.* The Risk Management suite of programs had developed from his first business idea. The venture was highly profitable and would remain the mainstay of his income. Looking back on those first six months of 2015, he had taken a tremendous gamble. True, he had set out with no debts but neither had he any capital to speak of and yet he'd ploughed ahead by recruiting his three key staff. Could he even afford to pay them?

If only they'd known the trip to Perth had drained his business loan. One lesson he'd learnt, and it could so easily have been terminal, was the need for a generous dollop of luck. The sheer arrogance of believing that a bank on the far side of the world would buy into an unproven product: and to manage their money market exposure at that! But, as it turned out, the timing was perfect. The new regulations pretty much insisted on managing swap and options risks in a clear and unambiguous way. The Becky help button way, the Becky documented way. And Becky herself. A completely unexpected turn-up. What she did God only knows but the next morning he signed the letter of intent.

The momentum had built from that first success in Perth. The rival bank was not to be outdone and neither were the two *biggies* in Sydney. Becky in her splendid element was fabulous to behold as one-by-one the London investment banks came on board. As the monthly rental income grew, so it gave Eric his head and by the end of December he had a team of eight software engineers including Murray.

January 2016 witnessed the step-by-step implementation of Becky's marketing plan. The first phase was headed *Get ourselves known* and involved joining national trade associations, attending trade fairs and included an initial foray into digital advertising targeted specifically at investment banks and hedge fund managers. Luke soon realised that he was not best suited to this promotional activity and consequently was playing second fiddle to her. Paradoxically this worked well. The tall well- groomed presenter was soon accepted as the face of the business while he tagged along as the geeky expert.

Luke often wondered about "my husband", whom he hadn't met, not even at their social gatherings which admittedly were invariably held at the George & Dragon. Perhaps for an accomplished golfer, the pub was not quite his scene. Becky still remained an enigma. There were men, he was sure of it. But who and what type, he had no idea. Was "my husband" a front? While riding the crest of a wave, no point in endangering the surfboard (aunt Petula would love that metaphor).

2016 – what a roller-coaster of a year that was! He had lost his great uncle, wonderful man. Where would he be now if not for him. Making a young lad do something he'd rather not, can pay huge dividends. Why was he made to visit a grumpy old man who lived like a hermit, when kicking a ball with friends would have been more fun? But grandma had been right all along, he learnt loads, even though at times struggling to understand what the guy was saying.

Then the wedding of that police woman Alice to city-kid Marcus, all smiles, knocking back the bubbly and hadn't they been so clever? The old guy was a murderer? Got proof have you? I know what he'd have said. "Kiss me arse yu av, silly sods, stupid buggers". Conned me into helping their little scheme. They were all at it, plotting behind my back. The two love birds plus classy Pearl, sniffy Naing and even my darling wife in some minor way. Well, they're all going to pay, swear on Great Uncle Harold's ashes. Swines. Oh yes, and to compound the intrigue Kyaw finds out that Marcus fathered Pearl's baby. Unbelievable, you couldn't make it up.

By September the rentals from London Wall were climbing steeply. The consultant's spreadsheet showed that provided there was no further increase in the payroll and overheads, the business loan would be paid off within the next six months. But, as she pointed out, some leakage of licence fees was inevitable and so resilience of the present risk management modules, and the roll-out of those planned, was crucial. Luke handed a copy of the report to Eric and Becky with his hand-written note on the front – *bonus? dividend?* On Tuesday 20th the cheque from the solicitors dealing with the estate of Great Uncle Harold arrived. As advised, he passed it to *Tisley Great Invest* the wealth managers. Her note read, *Tell them you want low to medium risk and Luke, as regards a solid investment, see what Fred Salmon thinks about selling the whole place to you - Hall, grounds, office block, the lot. No rush, gently does it. Attached is my fee invoice for the last quarter.*

Rounding off an extremely good two years was the signing of his consultancy contract with Yadanabon University. In his heart of hearts, Luke hadn't expected this success. Sure, they'd pay for a couple of visits, absorb the ideas in his two AI papers, suck him dry on the latest developments in the UK and throw him overboard. But no, his involvement now stretched years ahead and he had a sneaking anticipation of learning as much from their research and development as they took from him. Well, hadn't that been his underlying idea all along? Certainly a few nice trips to Myanmar, a most welcome retention fee, a chance to make Kyaw jealous with his attention to her sisters, were not to be sneezed at, but these were bit parts in the grand scheme of things. Robotics to remove human body parts by remote control – there was a fortune to be made – he just had to work out how.

Aung had played a key part in securing the AI deal, Luke was sure of it. In some way, influence had been brought to bear. Could it have anything to do with the Dotcom charity? Aung intended to be chairman of a substantial organisation. He'd made that very clear. Could the Rector foresee kudos from association? Interesting - something to keep an eye on. Luckily, Luke was a trustee of Dotcom so he'd bottom it when the time was right. Perhaps the part that Aung might have played was instrumental in Luke's share of the new company being increased. Once the lawyers had finished their drafting, Luke was astonished to read he'd been awarded 15% of the equity. Whether Aung had pulled strings or not, he had absolutely come good on his promise to send the first student on the international internship programme. To date they had taken three, and didn't they work hard? Didn't they learn fast? The problem Luke had was prising them from Eric at the end of their secondment.

What had the consultant called 2017? Yes, that was it. The year of consolidation. The prospect didn't sound too exciting, but then it wasn't supposed to. The plan boiled down to holding his ground and moving forward steadily. "Not in your nature but vital. Split the software team. Eric's staff to concentrate on new development, Murray's side to maintain the installed systems. Becky should spend less time on pitching to potential clients and more on finding out what the opposition is up to and what the next set of regulations are likely to be. In other words, less direct sales and more market analysis. The mantra for this year should be London Wall Cutting Edge – You Saw It Here First".

Luke had appreciated the logic of the case and while it cut across his basic instinct of pushing forward at all speed, it did make sense to stabilize what they had achieved. And there was another factor. Big things were happening outside the office. Things wrapped up in one short word, Kyaw. He had promised to respect her culture and so they had not made love and their relationship was not helped by Kyaw's close friendship with the imperious, and seemingly untouchable Pearl. Does the female of the species actually get broody? How would he know, but after the elegant lady gave birth, his girlfriend had changed. Yes she needed to finish her course and yes she was determined to get a good degree but more important than either she wanted to get married. "Luke, how are we going to stay this way until September?"

Luke became tense. At first he couldn't decide why. The business was under control: there was no discernible problem with the staff and yet something was playing on his mind. The more he thought about it the more he came to one conclusion – zip – it had gone. The early thrill, the risk, the battles with his external adviser, the frenetic sessions in the pub after work. Little by little office life had normalized. He had been warned it would happen but still he didn't like it. Then, as with so many key events in his life, the solution came from left field, out of the blue. And it was blue cloudless skies that now beckoned him. The Australia National Bank claimed to have found a bug that Eric said didn't exist. He couldn't issue a patch for a perfectly sound piece of code. Emails of a disparaging tone were escalating. Luke needed to sort things out plus, coincidentally, Westpac were interested in migrating the systems installed in Sydney to their Perth branch. He decided to return to Perth, and this time alone.

They were in the same seafood restaurant as two years earlier and about to order the oysters when Aunt Petula told him. "Luke, I'm dying".

The *Oyster Bar, Elizabeth Quay* had been bustling with activity on this balmy evening. Friends were greeting friends as they moved to and fro, chairs scraped along the lap-board floor, a couple at the next table were ogling a lobster and somewhere in the far corner a fizzy wine cork popped. But that was before. Now the place was empty, silent and cold. Luke couldn't speak. Rising from his chair he stood behind his aunt and held her head in his hands. Tears rolled down his cheeks, he couldn't stop them and he didn't care. He wasn't in Perth anymore but on the doorstep at home and a stranger in uniform was saying something about an old man being found dead and asking if he was a relative.

Petula was saying that really it was so strange. She actually felt fine but the brain tumour was inoperable and she had six weeks, maybe less. She had savings and had left some to her old university and some to a lifelong friend but whatever remained plus her lovely house was to be Luke's. Of course she couldn't insist, but her wish was that he didn't sell it but kept it in memory of the *Aussie Whitby's*. It had been hard for her mother in the early days but unlike many of the other Ten Pound Poms she'd stuck it out and made a good life for her daughter. For a Whitby to have a small piece of Australian real estate would be nice, she would like that.

"Luke, you are marrying your girlfriend later this year. I'm so glad you'll be settling down and I wish you both all the happiness in the world but I want to ask a personal question. What went wrong with your Aussia girlfriend Siobhan?"

"I just can't take this in - you look fine to me. However did you get a tumour? Oh I know you can't answer that question but the medics must be wrong. It does happen you know. Our computers are like that. One minute perfect and then they go bonkers. Oh God, why do we have to live so far apart? Well actually I've just answered my own question. Being apart, that's the thing. I couldn't move over here while Harold was alive and Siobhan wouldn't come back to the UK. I met Kyaw and Siobhan is now living with some guy, just how things turned out really. As you know , I did see her last time and we're meeting again tomorrow night in that hotel I stayed at during my first visit nine years ago. Shouldn't be telling you this but we're like two magnets, can't keep our hands off each other. I don't know what else to say. If, one day, I do own your wonderful home, which won't be for years to come, and if things don't work out back home, I'd put money on living in Australia. If I did, Siobhan and I will be together again, I just know. Thanks for asking and by the way, it's all your fault for egging me on that first time - surfing lessons you said".

The text message arrived two months later. *Ms Petula Caruana died peacefully at 10 am – Alexander Quay hospice.*

Luke left the office asking not to be contacted over the weekend and drove to the memorial gardens. He needed to talk to his Great Uncle Harold.

*

Was Midsummer's Day the 21st or the 24th of June? Luke couldn't remember. But, whatever, he would always remember the 21st of June 2017. That was the day a handwritten note appeared on his desk. It was from Fred Salmon and if Luke was still interested, he could buy the Old Hall. There was no need to get an estate agent involved. The place had been valued and if the idea of carving out an area for him to live was still open, then they could do a deal on the price. One second after reading, Luke was texting Kyaw. *We've got the Hall. Come over. Bring a bottle.*

Luke was saying to Eric, "Christ Almighty, it's hardly brain surgery. They were instructed in June and completion of the Old Hall, after God knows how many missed dates, is now scheduled for Friday, 25th August. We all know about the Friday afternoon scams; keep an eye on it for me, we've got Barclays coming in and I need to be with Becky".

Saturday 23rd September was his wedding day: he could hardly forget since it was Kyaw's sole preoccupation and topic of conversation. To be fair, he had been a willing participant in the planning, but that was before the events of March, May and June. Now his enthusiasm had drained, the best approach was to let Kyaw and her friends just get on with it. In fact, no, he mustn't think that way. He was happy and anyway he needed Kyaw.

In every conceivable way, the wedding was perfect. Everyone said so and he was genuinely delighted to see Kyaw's family once more – especially Garma. Other guests, such as the crew he'd become entangled with back in 2015 – Pearl, Naing and Marcus – he viewed more with interest than enthusiasm. And, that little incident outside the church when Marcus took the baby from Pearl, why had it needed Kyaw months later to point the finger at him as the father? In hindsight, it was obvious. But then, most things are.

Sex with Kyaw was fantastic. He'd had no inkling of her release. Asian girls are different, and how! Making love with her had been the perfect antidote to the eternal round of business meetings set up by Becky. And the travel was exhausting, Perth, again, but sadly with no Aunt Petula to take charge, then Sydney and China and finally Myanmar. How had he done it? But still, it had paid off handsomely with Becky signing up the Bank of China within a few weeks of his return.

It was at the Christmas party that Becky expressed the business position perfectly. Undoing the top button of her blouse she announced, "Now guys we can really let rip". Murray's chair wobbled.

Of course and aside from Kyaw, who had been sworn to secrecy, they knew nothing of the money transfer idea.

*

Time for coffee, but with no Murray (the established coffee purveyor) Luke made it himself. Now for the consultant's questions.

First, I have to understand how I reached this point in my life. Surely, there are two sub-sets to this question. First, in a personal sense, and secondly in a business sense. OK, so personal. Fortunately, I was made to visit a great uncle who, in my early years taught me the value of patience, guile, common sense and the ability to use rather than need people. I had a first-class education and chose a work skill in great demand while being my own boss "tha gives orders, not teks um from uthers". I chose my staff for their technical competence being unconcerned if they were better than me. I learnt the rules of sex at an early enough age to prevent me making mistakes later. Finally, I was left a fortune which boosted my self-confidence.

With business, I was very, very lucky in choosing a market sector (finance) that is both highly paid and secretive and by developing software applications that have a high barrier to entry and are driven by ever increasing regulation. From a young age I had the opportunity to travel which fortuitously sat well with the international nature of my products. Mine is not a hard-sell, capital-purchase business. Licence fees appear reasonable compared to reward. But, highly profitable.

Next, I have to decide where I want to be. It may seem strange but I think of the negative. I don't want to be an *also ran*. I got into the market just as the financial regulatory authority was baring its teeth. Edging against risk is gaining momentum with every month that passes and given the prestigious clients on board, my business must continue to grow rapidly. But not at the expense of quality. Becky's team must not outrun Eric's and ensuring that will be my top priority. In addition, having just one business is, to coin a phrase, *risky*. Swaps, options, in fact all financial instruments could be outlawed. Who knows? I have my two other ideas and each might, in time, develop into a substantial business. The work in Myanmar has a chance of commercial exploitation and my share of the company could become very valuable especially if I find a way to use the robotics over here. The contract ties my hands somewhat but one never knows – clever lawyers and all that. The second idea of instant money transfer has huge potential. Just needs more thought and maybe my consultant can earn her corn at last.

Where do I want to be personally? Kyaw must act as *Lady of the Manor,* she will be perfect for the part. I will keep her so busy that thoughts of trips back home become a distant memory. Of course, I must continue to visit Yadanabon University to advise and check on progress. Likewise Perth and Sydney. Siobhan was asking if there would be enough business in Australia to justify opening an office in either city. She said "Remember big man, I have a degree in Business Administration".

That will do for now, the squash court's booked for eight twenty and I'll thrash that little runt Roger if it kills me. Oh, hang on, must make that secret list and hide it on the dark web:-.

Leverage

Eric	My most important employee. Keep increasing his salary and bonus. Dangle carrot of dividends. If he needs medical help, I will pay for private treatment
Murray	Gradually bring to same level and terms as Eric. He needs a woman – can I help?
Becky	Vital to future of London Wall. Tie her in with a three-year service agreement. Like her higher share stake, tell her to keep it secret. Find out what her *man thing* is. NB – she is "director of", not yet real director
Kyaw	Build her position in local community, lunch with the ladies, dinner parties etc. Formally appoint her CEO of money transfer side and get her heavily involved in day-to-day stuff. No travel except with me. I'm to be nice to Garma when in Myanmar and she will send videos etc to Kyaw
Siobhan	Keep satisfied whenever and wherever possible. To rent my property in Perth? Head up Australian office? Trip to London? Hidden communication line

Aung	Keep close to. Support his position as chairman of Dotcom, encourage liaison with Uni. rector. Suggest London Wall recruitment of his better students. Mention Pearl's beautiful baby! Naing must be proud? Gradually sow seeds of doubt re Marcus
Alice	Meet in London for old-times-sake chat?
Marcus	Needs more thought

Luke looked at the time - Christ, better dash.

Twelve

"I'm really surprised by this traffic, can't even remember there being four lanes never mind each one being choked. Looking at the satnav, what's the chance half this lot peels off at junction 28 and heads for that Outlet place? OK, 14th December 2019, Christmas shopping and all that, but what is it they haven't got for God's sake? I thought we all bought personal services these days. Which reminds me Alice darling, what personal service can I render you when we eventually arrive at Breadsall Priory".

"Sorry, missed that"

"Oh, never mind. Are you excited to be returning to one of our old haunts?"

"Yes, I suppose so. It seems a long time ago now".

"It's only just over four years since I first encountered your breathtaking looks and blinding intellect".

"Marcus, just concentrate on your driving and get us there in one piece".

*

"Darling, I thought we'd agreed to bring only our personal mobiles and leave the work ones behind".

"So?"

"Well, that's your police one isn't it? It must be, it just pinged and there's some sort of official looking crest and "From Brendan" at the top".

"Damn, sorry, my fault".

"Who's Brendan?"

"Marcus, you know perfectly well who he is, I mentioned him the other night".

"I don't remember that name".

"That's probably because, as per usual, the computer screen was more interesting than my voice".

"Alice darling, that's not fair, and let's not start bickering again. We promised ourselves a lovely weekend at Kyaw's graduation party. Sorry, who did you say Brendan is?"

"I'll tell you again and please try to take it in this time. I went over to Brussels and he heads the European side of the fraud team. It was the weekend you stayed with Pearl".

"Ah yes, that was the Saturday I couldn't get hold of you. I even contacted the hotel reception but you hadn't checked in, eventually I gave up".

"Well Marcus, let's face it, you probably had other things on your mind and the drinks party did go on a bit. Look sweetheart, I know things between us haven't been brilliant lately. Ring down for a bottle of fizz while I get showered; there'll be time for a cuddle before the taxi arrives won't there?"

"OK, please be quick"

"Christ Marcus it's huge, where did that come from? Phew ...... how does she compare with me?"

"Well now, let me see".

"Marcus, seriously, do we have to go? Can't we just stay here and get room service – to go with your service!"

"Alice, darling, you really can be a naughty girl. We'll have to delay a bit, as your lads used to say – I'm knackered. I promised Pearl; we don't have to stay late. Kyaw wants to get the old gang together".

"Who exactly?"

"Well, because Pearl wanted to meet them again, your two ex-colleagues from the Derbyshire force, Neil and big-wig Macrae and an uncle of Luke called Adrian who met Kyaw off the plane when she first arrived from Myanmar. Not sure who else we'll know but it'll be interesting to chat with some of Luke's employees. My source of intelligence, (note, oh high-flying Met. officer, how your lingo has permeated my vocabulary) known in some circles as the Pearl/Kyaw link, hints at an Old Hall and outbuildings swarming with whizz kids and weirdos. My task will be to ply a geek with booze to loosen a tongue. What are they up to we ask ourselves. Come to that, what is this blonde bombshell up to? I've a feeling the lady really does want to stay in bed".

"This is a command from on high – stop talking".

*

"Marcus, use your Uber app to pick us up at 11, we must be back here as early as politely possible, service must be resumed by midnight. I was thinking, it's over two years since Kyaw graduated, why take so long to have a party?"

"I asked Pearl about that. Apparently, Kyaw and Luke have been so incredibly busy that the graduation celebration just took a back seat. After the wedding in September 2017, he whisked her off on a sort of world tour honeymoon although, from what Pearl could gather, it was as much a business trip as anything else. And then during the next year and presumably most of this they've concentrated on their two businesses".

"Two? I though he was into risk management, whatever that is".

"Well, yes, and other than their friends, the people milling around will work on that side but there is also this secret thing that only Kyaw knows about".

"Marcus, my big hunk of a man, has sex addled your brain? You talk in riddles; thick wife here is asking herself a) how can it be secret if hubby is aware and b) what secret thing?"

"During the heated passion of the honeymoon, Luke let slip that he intended to get into the money transfer game. He then asked his bride to keep shtum. Well, you know what ladies can be like, she told Pearl who in turn told me".

"Yes of course, wife not so thick after all. Bill Macrae sent an email, but that must be two years ago. What a tangled web we weave. I'll bet that you whispered to Neil who, obviously, passed the info to his boss. Bill suggested I keep an eye out. Been nothing since, so I presumed it had died a death. Hmm, suddenly I have a spark of interest in the graduation party. This senior Metropolitan Police Officer is asking herself if such an activity actually exists and if so where its staff are located".

"Unless Kyaw lives in a fantasy world, it absolutely exists because Pearl said that Luke has some sort of consultant involved who had shown Kyaw a spreadsheet forecasting a profit only just short of what the main business was making. The only other thing I picked up was that Kyaw is the Chief Executive Officer and might even own the business, but Pearl wasn't sure about the share-holding part since Kyaw was a bit vague herself. Staff? Location? No idea. Over to you. One thing I would add is that transferring money can be very lucrative because it's all about buy and sell exchange rates. There are also sizeable pitfalls. I shorted a Travelex stock last year and did very well".

Very little surprised Alice. It was part of the price paid for her time at New Scotland Yard. But this did. "My God Marcus, how did he get a place like this? I'd absolutely no idea, had you? Coming down that driveway I thought of the Derbyshire stately homes we visited, Haddon, Hardwick and Chatsworth and while it's not on that scale it is pretty impressive. Those hints you've been dropping; I feel that cold-case buzz coming back. We need to take a look at Luke. Amazing, he's still in his twenties isn't he? Look down there, it's absolutely huge".

"I know, it's all natural, I can't help it."

"No, silly. I mean the marquee. This is disappointing, we're not entering the Old Hall itself then, I was hoping for a sneaky poke around before the melee. Looks like we walk through that archway leading to the grounds and the big tent".

"Correct, those orange lanterns might be a clue".

"Marcus, don't start. This is our lovey-dovey weekend, remember. As it is I'm going to lose you for a couple of hours. Don't forget Mr Uber-man and our midnight date".

Alice and Marcus accepted a glass of champagne from the girl in the black & white Longyi dress. Marcus placed his arm around Alice's waist and they melted into the crowd to find Kyaw, graduation girl.

*

Luke was one of the first to spot Alice and Marcus and took it as a cue to disappear for a while - *let the liquid refreshment take hold before I make a move* – time to rescue Becky.

"Becky, I can see you're wondering why the Myanmar ladies make those jerky movements in the traditional dance. Drawing on my immense knowledge of that far off land, I can tell you with infinite confidence that they mimic a puppet. Interesting isn't it? Bring your drink. Let's move to where it's a bit quieter, I want to have a chat, can't seem to find time in the office these days. So, no escort again? I'm beginning to think that hubby is a figment of your imagination, although the least distraction at work, the better. But seriously, just wanted to say I've got a bit of legal work going on which I hope won't be a waste of effort. I would be over the moon if you'd sign a service agreement. The draft is for three years but, like the other clauses, we can discuss the length that suits us both. Thing is, I want to tie you into London Wall. Now we have the technical platform in place, I see you as the key employee. Funnily enough, the insurance linked to the agreement refers to you as a *keyman*. Ever since I first spotted you, anyone less like a *man* I have yet to encounter".

"Luke, on the basis that Kyaw is not looking, may I give you a peck on the cheek?"

"What a surprise! Tell you what, I'll get a clause to that effect added to the agreement. Becky, in a year or so, I can see you running the company. I've a couple of other irons in the fire and the risk business will be safe in your hands. Murray is already trailing you like a lapdog and I'll make sure Eric is on board. Anyway, we'll pour over the agreement when the lawyer eventually coughs up. Look we'd better join the rest before tongues start wagging. Oh, one other thing, I want to ask a little favour, just between you and me. I'm going to introduce you to that tall blonde woman – look over near the bar talking to Kyaw – ask her about her job, where she works, any tittle-tattle like that but then move away and leave her with me. That's not the favour. The job I want doing is this. Her name is Alice, lives in London and is something senior in the police. I want her mobiles hacked".

"Hello Alice, Kyaw and I are really pleased you could make her party especially as you must be so busy. Seems a long time since I was asked to help with that cold case and I still have the press cuttings announcing your success. It certainly put the Derbyshire force on the map and I suppose helped your career. Successful ladies have really come into their own lately and I want to introduce you to another. This is Becky, officially my number two but actually in the heat of the battle for new clients, I'm her assistant. You two have a chat and I'll nip to the bar and pick up two more glasses of fizz. Must keep the ladies lubricated".

"Alice, you and Becky would get on well, she's my star employee but now I've got you to myself, and this is not a few glasses of wine talking, I want to congratulate you on your promotion to the Met. Honestly, I'd no idea you were so senior until bumping into Neil just now. I pretended to tick him off for being somewhat economical with the truth about the circumstances of my Great Uncle Harold's death which is nearly four years ago. Anyway, as he explained, PR and all that. Before Marcus drags you away, I can see him hovering about, wondered whether we could meet in London sometime. I'm down there a lot these days talking to clients and the like. I'll treat you to lunch, assuming that's not regarded as a bribe, and perhaps you can update me on the latest fraud activity – always willing to learn new tricks. Sorry, only joking".

"That's OK my Lord Of The Manor, no offence taken. When we do meet, and yes why not, I'll arrange for the room to be bugged and then via a cunningly disguised series of questions unearth the dastardly deeds that brought you the fabulous wealth on show here tonight".

"Just so Commissioner and by the time our liquid lunch is over what's the betting you'll ask to join my growing empire?"

"Luke, I really do want to thank you and Kyaw for inviting me and Marcus to the party and to congratulate you on acquiring such a wonderful old building. In view of what happened during that cold case review, we were surprised to be asked but I'm pleased we came. I need to join Marcus now but a word to the wise. It could be that our friendly chat has drawn a future battle line. We'll be leaving shortly".

"Safe journey home Alice – yes it could be".

*

"Hi Pearl, just seeing you again brings back so many memories. When you walked into my squash club, wow, must be four years ago now – this is the gospel truth - I thought to myself *so this is what the aristocracy look like.* I'm not joking. I felt like a naughty schoolboy being summoned to the headmistress's office".

Luke

"Luke, my protégé's dashing beau, flattery will get you everywhere, but yes I recall that meeting so well and, never mind me, I think you really were in awe of Aung, such a charming man".

"You're right there, Naing's father – haven't spotted her yet".

"Oh, didn't Kyaw mention, she's returned to Myanmar".

"No she didn't - when? No, I mean why? Sorry Pearl, I mean, I thought she was your partner, I thought she had a senior position as a dentist or something like that. Did you fall out? What on earth happened? Why am I going on? It's none of my business but Kyaw always came back from Brighton saying you and Naing were very happy and loving parents to, Tristan isn't it?"

"We didn't fall out as you put it, just didn't see eye-to-eye. It's no secret. I wanted a playmate for my little boy and we didn't share the same thoughts on how to make that happen - if you see what I mean. And then, well, it was just a coincidence really, Aung was getting more and more serious about our Dotcom charity and Naing was worried he'd drift back into full-time work mode. Anyway, the two events seem to tip her over the edge and she resigned and left. I'm still coming to terms with what happened and Tristan keeps asking where she is which doesn't help. FaceTime's been good, they see and talk to each other once a week. It's rather sweet really, she talks to him as if he's an adult and not a two-and-a-half-year-old. He knows all about her new dental practice and how she's helping her father with the charity".

"Amazing isn't it? One drifts through life and out of the blue someone bowls a googly and wham, all change. Thanks for filling me in Pearl, you didn't need to and I appreciate how hard it must have been but listen, to me you look absolutely wonderful, positively blooming. If Kyaw and I can do anything to help, and I mean anything, you'll let us know.

I'll refresh your drink, is that sparkling water? Think I'll need time to recover from this shock, well two shocks really. Naing going home and then working for the charity. Do you think it's time we had a trustee meeting? After all, the full board of trustees are supposed to approve senior staff appointments. Oh, nearly forgot. Kyaw showed me a picture of Tristan. You must be so proud, what a handsome little chap. Jet black hair and so serious looking. I was trying to think who he reminded me of".

*

Becky had been disappointed at the headline her tame journalist had conjured up in covering the graduation party. The idea she'd floated was of local boy made good but instead it read "Lincolnshire Squire Descends On Derbyshire Pile". She realised her mistake had been ordering the cask of real ale which, destined for Eric's boys, had obviously been commandeered by the guy in tweeds and the impressionable journalist. And, although he hadn't said so directly, she realised now that Luke didn't exactly enjoy being cornered by a slightly intoxicated giant of a ruddy-faced man called Adrian.

"Luke lad, got you at last. Seen you fluttering about like a butterfly on a hot summer's day but be still for a few minutes. I want to congratulate you. Not, like I'm sure the rest have been doing on capturing such a beautiful wife, acquiring this magnificent mansion, not even on building what seems to be a very successful business. I take those things as read, given your background and the breeding you've had. No, I salute your provision of this excellent beer; assumed I'd be stuck with namby-pamby white wine – virgin's water I call it."

"Uncle Adrian, are you a bit drunk?"

"Good God lad no. Just wanted you to know I'm still alive and kicking and aware of all's that's gone before".

"Oh really, like what?"

"Harold of course. All those years and never a mention of the Salmon family. Crafty old sod – still, that was Harold and lucky Luke gets two paydays. First the money from the dodgy stamp deals and then, no doubt, priming old man Salmon to get you this place. One good thing though, Harold didn't inherit from uncle Eugene, although I expect he tried hard enough".

"What you're drinking is bitter beer. I heard you get plastered every Saturday night with your farming cronies so I got hold of a cask of the same stuff. I thought *suit his nature – bitter as hell".*

"Luke lad, I don't want to humiliate you in front of this lot so I'll resist the temptation to knock your block off. I only came here to see Kyaw again, let's square with each other, we're unlikely to meet again. Harold took you under his wing and as far as I can see kept you there for too long. I admired Eugene who Harold resented and so the bad blood flowed and will continue to flow until the Whitby clan dies out. Your dad Terry was my closest cousin in age but we never got on, so any contact between you and me was pretty much doomed from the start. One last thing before I push off. Like Harold, I know you harbour resentment. Eugene's left his money to an outsider, Pearl. You don't need it or any part of it, so I'm telling you straight - leave that lovely lady alone".

"Goodnight uncle Adrian and safe journey back to darkest Lincolnshire. Oh, and keep a wary eye in case a thug is lurking behind a stone pillar as you stumble home on a Saturday night".

*

Marcus turned from the bar and she'd gone. He wasn't surprised, it seemed to be happening a lot these days. One second Alice would be at his side and then effect *her disappearing act.* Before he could decide whether to head for the food counter or wait for the queue to subside he felt a tap on his shoulder. "Excuse me, are you Marcus?" The speaker was a few inches shorter than himself and, on first impression, looked a bit vacant and out of place. He wore trainers, jeans and a grey woollen jumper that had seen better days, but his most stand-out feature was a mop of unruly brown hair and a face dominated by thick lens glasses. "Sorry to butt in but I've been talking to a lady in a blue dress, I think her name was Pearl, who suggested I dig you out because of a common work interest, financial stuff. She said you were a genius at buying and selling shares. I'm Eric and head the programming team for Luke".

"Hi Eric, I'm no genius. As the lead software engineer you'll know this computer game is all about detail, precision and let's face it sheer hard grind. You'll be ahead of me. You write the stuff, I'm just a user".

"A modest man speaks. I like that. Between you and me there is a lack of it here at times. I break my balls, often into the early hours, only for Miss Perfect to laud it over the bugs she finds. My eyesight might be poor but it's good enough to capture the low-cut red dress over to my left. Still, I'm paid well and our code must function, we keep pulling the punters in".

"It's risk management that pays for the party?"

"Correct. Swaps, options and other hedging stuff. Are you with one of the big trading houses then?"

"No, I work alone – Footsie 250 mainly. In recent years I've tended to specialise in shorting. You'll understand the personal risks I take but I close my positions at the end of each week to mitigate. Mind you, I did have a big fright last week."

"I say Marcus, and perhaps it's this free booze that's talking, but could you slip me a tip now and again".

"I could if you're prepared to lose your stake. I don't always get it right, my candlesticks have been known to topple over. Sure, let me think about it but I wouldn't get you into margins, it would be a straight stock loan. Tell you what, send me one of your option screens, see if I can fathom what's exciting the clients, perhaps it's time I thought about managing my risks! Quid pro quo sort of thing".

"Done, and thanks Marcus. I want to get another pint before that cask runs out. There's a big ruddy-faced guy who seems to think it's his exclusive property. Earlier I was matching him pint for pint but gave up, he's out of my league".

*

Alice bided her time. Her chance came as the star of the evening moved away from the troupe of dancing girls. "Kyaw, I want to thank you for the invitation to your wonderful party, so much must have gone into its planning. I was thinking about my graduation celebration but can't remember much except it wasn't on this grand scale. Do try a sip of this cocktail, it's not too strong, I've had it made specially for you. It's called a Pegu and originated in a club not far from Rangoon, sorry I mean Yangon, gin-based of course, the senior Brits' tipple of the time. See what you make of it. I don't recall meeting before but our lives are connected in a weird sort of way".

"Really? Hmm, it's delicious, thank you for thinking about my homeland".

"I'm married to Marcus who's still in touch with your friend Pearl who he met on a police case a few years ago. Your Luke also helped with the enquiry. Complicated isn't it? Boring stuff but I did so want to thank you personally for a lovely evening. I mustn't keep you from your friends, it's just that we might have one other thing in common and possibly you can help me".

"Oops, haven't got the hang of sipping, hope I won't regret drinking it too quickly. Of course we'll help, how?"

"It's only a small thing really but at Scotland Yard there's an enquiry, just routine at present, into sums of money leaving the country without using the banking system. Since it's not something we've dealt with before I wondered if you'd mind introducing me to the consultant that I gather advises on this sort of thing".

"'I'm afraid she couldn't make it tonight, prior engagement, but I can ask Luke to get her details to you".

"That would be wonderful Kyaw and here he comes now. Did you realise the graduate has to make a speech? Looks like you're destined for the stage".

*

Kyaw was signalling to Pearl to join her; it was a way of trying to resist being steered towards the far end of the marquee but she was losing ground as Luke simultaneously was proclaiming, "make way for the graduation girl, speech, speech", echoes of which resonated from those realising what was happening. Kyaw's complaint of "I haven't written anything, Pearl help me, Pearl help" were destined to fail and now she stood as the reluctant hero, standing on the small stage, alone save for a microphone. But not for long. A tall lady dressed in a long blue dress was voicing "excuse me, excuse me" as she moved through the partygoers and stepped onto the stage to join Kyaw. She took her hand, made a motion indicating a deep breath and slowly counted to five. Releasing her hand, Pearl turned to Kyaw and made a gesture showing her two open palms that indicated it was time to start.

Luke

"My English is not perfect. If I say the wrong words or they leave my mouth in the wrong order, please to excuse me. Were it not for my friend Pearl (she took hold of Pearl's hand) I would not be here. There would be no graduation from an English university and no party. Where would I have been? I would be teaching English at a school in Mandalay in central Myanmar. Most of our guests know my story but for those who do not, my adult life has been shaped by this lady, my best friend Pearl. Four years ago I was a university student in Mandalay when chosen to help Pearl trace a relative of an old man who lived in Southern England. My job was very small, merely an interpreter. I thought, if all English people are like Pearl, it must be a wonderful country to visit. Kyaw took a deep breath and smiled (there was loud applause and from the far corner of the marquee, came a piercing whistle). My university was linked to one here in Nottingham and with the encouragement of Pearl I applied to spend one year as an overseas student. I would then return home with better English. But two big things happened. First, Pearl gave me a home and took me to many beautiful places including the Island of Jersey and asked me to help her solve a mystery. Then I met my darling husband Luke and together we have built our business. That is the end of my speech but I want to thank all of you for listening and coming to my party. I wish you could all have met my mother and two sisters but as my darling Luke said, it is a long way for them to travel and it can be cold in an English winter. I hope you liked the Myanmar dancers and waitresses in their traditional costume".

There was loud applause and this time a lot of whistles and before Kyaw and Pearl could leave the stage a man with a slightly bowed head pushed his way to the front and, ignoring the step, jumped to join them. He was not dressed smartly; there was a moment of unease and the sole security guard started to move forward but Luke held his arm in restraint. The intruder took the microphone.

"My name is Eric and I'm the senior software engineer working for Luke and Kyaw's business. This is all wrong (amongst the guests there was a palpable if silent nervousness). Kyaw is thanking us for being English, for giving her an English education, for being befriended by an English lady and for being taken as a wife by an English entrepreneur. Wrong, wrong and wrong again. It is we who should be thanking her. How did battered old England come to deserve the presence of the most beautiful young lady I have ever seen? My sight is poor but it's good enough to recognise grace and charm and oriental magnetism. If I had spotted Kyaw before that bloke Luke, he would have had no chance. Of course, we can all dream. She was never going to choose me over him, was she? I think Eric's a bit drunk, I think he should get off the stage".

Never before had there been noise in a marquee like it. Pandemonium. Was there anyone who didn't want to fetch Eric a drink?

*

Alice needed the ladies room. The facilities were in the Old Hall and having visited earlier in the evening, she knew where to go except it wasn't down this corridor. She was about to retrace her steps when she saw them. The girl had her back to the panelled wall and the man was standing very close with one hand resting on the wall about her head, Alice couldn't see his other hand.

At the second attempt she found the powder room. There was a large gilt-framed mirror above the wash basin. Her reflection was gradually being replaced by that of the couple in the corridor. She could see now that the girl wore a yellow dress, just a little of which was visible hitched round her waist. It was clear now that the man had ginger hair. Alice had drunk a glass of wine too many but now she realised who they were – Kyaw and that software guy Murray.

The image disappeared but another one took its place. It was shimmering slightly but even so there was no doubt. Marcus was standing close to Pearl. He had his right hand resting on her shoulder and they seemed in deep conversation. At this angle Alice could make out a small bump under the blue dress. Earlier she'd overheard Pearl answering a question from Kyaw, "sixteen weeks". The image remained but it was more than shimmering, rather, swimming around. A waitress appeared at the door. "Are you Alice? Your husband says please hurry the taxi's arrived. Oh I'm sorry you're crying, are you OK, can I help?"

"It's nothing, I get sad sometimes seeing people having a good time, enjoying the moment and not thinking too much about the future. Tell him I'll be a couple of minutes, just need to fix my face".

Thirteen

"Look at this spread Alice, what luxury, we should take Sunday breakfast in a posh hotel more often. That muesli fruity stuff we have every morning back home is healthy but let's be honest, it does get a bit boring after the first thousand servings – and look here, that's black pudding isn't it? Hadn't even heard of that until I ventured into darkest Derbyshire".

"Marcus darling, while you were in the gym I did some texting and please don't be mad but I want to change our plans a bit".

"Go on then, you want a divorce".

"No, silly. But what I do want is to spend an extra night here, I mean, on my own. Of course you need to be in your office tomorrow morning but I'd like a few hours with Neil and Bill at their HQ down the road in Ripley. They'll send a car and take me to the station later. From what we learnt at the do last night, I suspect he's transferring money using unconventional routes. Luke is up to no good, I'm sure of it".

"Oh Alice, does it have to be now? Surely, if he's been dabbling for two years, an extra day or so won't matter will it? I was thinking of a late lunch or early dinner on the way back – finish the weekend off nicely".

"It's just that being so close to my old base and wanting to set up a surveillance, it makes sense. I'll make it up to you tomorrow night, promise. Marcus, listen, I need to whisper, you know when we first got together I told you of my great ache, real physical ache, well it's back. You huge brute of a man, when you set me off, I can't get enough".

"Well, if you put it like that, suppose I can last out for one night. I'll get two more eggs, they've just brought a new lot in. What's the thinking?"

Luke

"Two years ago when you mentioned Kyaw telling Pearl of Luke's idea of rapid money transfer – peer-to-peer it would be – the premise was one-off occasions of large sums and secondly flows between the UK and specific countries. Some of the countries referred to were in the EU because he felt wealthy individuals would send their ill-gotten gains back to France, or wherever, and likewise expats' dosh would return to the UK. I'll bet that with all the Brexit dithering and Parliamentary defeats and general uncertainty, those flows didn't materialise because the rich set sat on their hands. But we've learned he's active and so which countries? Let's have a guess. Here's three for starters. One, China - because he's picked up banks there for the risk management side; two, Australia - ditto bank business and he has a property there and three would be Myanmar, home to little wifey and we know he has contacts with a university in Mandalay".

"Hmm, well I'll give you this my sexy Alice with her wonderland, you've certainly used that party to advantage".

"Indeed, and there's more my good beau. I stumbled, just about literally, on a weakness in the Luke empire armour".

"Are you inferring a little tipsiness".

"I'll ignore that facetious remark and, what's that on your plate, I thought you never ate sausages? Anyway, before we left, I set off for the ladies and somehow in that baronial pile I missed a turning and guess what, spotted Kyaw and that ginger-haired Murray guy in a clinch. If that isn't worth a bit of inside info at some stage, my name's not Alice".

"Right, well hear this oh super sleuth and, by the way, I never eat sausages due to their fat content so like last night you must be seeing things. At one point during the evening Pearl sent Eric, the guy who jumped onto the stage, to chat to me. She was right in thinking we'd have IT stuff in common but that's about all on the technical front. Anyway I didn't see it coming but he asked for a share tip. The thing is Alice, another term for what they're into is derivative trading, I know a bit about it although I didn't let on. In exchange for making a quick buck for him I asked to see one of his finished screen shots. Incredibly, he agreed. Also, if we're seeking vulnerability, he assumed I'd sympathise with a programmer's antipathy towards the bug-finder. In their case the glamorous Becky. He'd jump at the chance to score points over her.

"But Marcus, it would be a mistake to get carried away. Luke is a smart kid and if he's ducking and diving on peer-to-peer money transfer, he'd want to ensure the risk management side was absolutely kosher".

"OK, I hear what you say, should we have coffee in the lounge before I push off? You know Alice, after last night's events, I'm starting to get those Whitby cold case goose bumps again. You dig into money transfer and I'll try to unravel what Eric and co. are up to. The Alice & Marcus team swing into action again!"

"Marcus darling, I'm sure you knew but I wasn't really looking forward to this weekend. We seem to spend so much time apart, my fault of course – the job taking over – and niggles creeping in when there's no need, but being with you here and delving into a few things, has made such a difference and it's started me thinking again"

"Go on".

"You remember the *Harold* investigation, could it be that Luke carries a strain of evil handed down from his great uncle? Take for instance Kyaw's speech. There was that throw-away line about her mother and sisters' absence; one could interpret that as a plea for help. Is she being controlled? Control leads to manipulation. Then, on a different front altogether, why would she be made boss of the money transfer business? It doesn't make sense. And what's he up to at the university in Mandalay? Something quite different could be going on there. I wonder if our best route is asking Pearl to tease information from Kyaw. By the way, how did Pearl get to the party?"

"Actually I don't know and I feel bad about arriving at the Old Hall after Tristan had been put to bed, I'd promised to read him a story. She could have driven or come by train. I'll find out and see if a lift to London would help but Alice, are you thinking that Pearl could get Kyaw to open up?"

"Yes".

*

Luke called a meeting. It was more of an event than it sounded since a physical get-together was an anathema to him; inefficient waste of time. Microsoft Teams was the preferred option, but this was different - he called it a de-briefing. There was just the three of them, himself, Becky and Eric. He explained that of course the graduation party was for Kyaw and wasn't she the star? The centre of attention – just as intended. Even so, he had to admit that letting a couple of years pass had been deliberate. He had to have the business established before they could party and also there were some family issues that he guessed would only surface once he had established himself. Luke wanted Becky and Eric to know that way back in the 1950's two members of his family went missing and the authorities still kept a file open. His father and grandfather had both said it was a centuries old procedure known as *tracing the money* and some of the old family wealth had passed down, hence the presence of three outsiders last Saturday.

"It's ironic really, Kyaw wanted both Pearl and her police colleagues from the past to be invited. I mean, in the round it doesn't matter a jot except I want my top two executives to make sure everything we do is above board. No offering bribes, no dishing out fancy presents. The last thing we need is to give them any excuse to dig into our affairs. My gorgeous wife Kyaw I love dearly and wouldn't change a thing but she is an innocent walking abroad".

Becky rose from her chair to fetch the coffee but before reaching the machine turned to face Luke, "I'm confused and getting a bit irritated. Why on earth would either of us want to risk the reputation of the company? We manage risk don't we? Come on Luke, there are three adults in this room, what is it you're trying to say? Who are these *outsiders* anyway?"

"Right, I'll roll both questions into one. Years ago, my family included a murderer. If it can be proved that money I inherited was not rightfully mine, I'm in the shit and I put all that cash into this business. The most senior of that trio was the blonde I introduced you to. To me, she is a very dangerous woman because she's into fraud, fraud is money and we earn our crust from those that manage it. Also, I happen to know she makes frequent trips to Brussels and Becky, that's on the next page of your marketing plan, isn't it? You're doing a little job for me – remember?

"Next down is the guy they referred to as Bill. Quite apt since he's the police superintendent responsible for this patch. I need any problems with him like a hole in the head. Third was the tall lanky bloke called Neil who works for Bill. I know him from the squash club and he's no PC Plod I can tell you that".

"Sorry Luke, jumped in with two big feet as usual, here's your coffee, am I forgiven?"

Luke took the cup, walked to the whiteboard and placed his chair closer to Eric. "I saw you talking to the guy who's married to top cop Alice. Was he digging at all?"

"No, not really, but it's interesting after what you've said because it was Pearl who suggested I chat to him. I feel in the middle of a spy thriller. It all seemed natural enough, she knew I was a software engineer and assumed I'd be on familiar ground with her friend Marcus because he made a living buying and selling shares. Fair enough; to be honest I was bored. I nearly went back to the office, there's a piece of code I'm really struggling with. In the event he's quite a nice chap and that wife of his, wow! I'd no idea she was a senior cop".

"Yes Eric, fine, but when I walked past you were both pretty absorbed and I don't think it was debating the specific gravity of the ale".

"Good God no, he's no beer drinker, pretty clued up on white wine I'd say. I asked for a share tip, that's when it got serious".

"Great, good man; I knew you wouldn't let the side down. How did he react".

"Sweet as a nut. Mind you he specialises in shorting so it involves taking out loan stock and waiting for the price to drop and of course to make any real money on a one-off I'd need to invest a fairly large sum and hope the share price drops. The thing is though, Pearl told me he's right more often than not and she also dropped out that he owns a top-of-the-range Maserati and lives in a nice apartment in Tufnell Park, North London. Tell you what, I think she might be a bit keen on him".

"Eric, this gets better and better. Hold him to it. Never mind about the cost, we can discuss that when Becky's not listening – unless she wants in too! Now let me guess. He wanted something in return?"

"Yes, one of my option screens, though Christ knows why."

"Fabulous, fabulous. If we reach that point, you and Becky can doctor it. We'll give the buggers a run for their money. Sorry Becky, I realise you won't have heard language like that before. It was a favourite of my old great uncle. Don't I wish he was still here to savour this? Listen Eric, Becky and I have just one thing to say about your drunken speech in praise of my sweetheart Kyaw. Fantabuloso! Come on, pub calls, and it's on me tonight".

It was in the pub that Luke broke the news. As soon as New Year was over, actually on 4th January, he was going back to Aussie. After his second pint, and as gently as he could, Luke told Eric that this time he was asking Becky to take charge so both of them would have experienced running the business. He planned to stay for a month and had promised Kyaw the trip, but having thought about all the goings on at her party, had changed his mind and now felt she should stay and organise the next phase of restoration. If he could win two more clients in either Perth or Sydney, the consultant's figures justified a base over there. The clincher had been to use his property in Perth rather than rent an expensive office in the city. In fact, the savings paid for an office manager and whilst over there he intended to interview a potential employee. If the lady he had in mind proved suitable, perhaps she could be trained to demonstrate the modules and at that point, Becky would probably have to go out again.

It was nearly midnight when Luke arrived back from the pub. Kyaw was lying on the chaise-longue in her see-through nightie with an expression he knew so well. He was about to kiss her when she said, "Oh Luke, I forgot to mention that Alice asked for details of the consultant".

"Sorry sweetie pie. Why? How did she know we used one?"

"I'm not sure but she's running some sort of money transfer fraud thing and thought our experience might help".

Luke straightened his back and stepped away from his wife. "And how does she know we have a business of that kind?"

*

On a Sunday evening the farming fraternity don't frequent the Old Coaching Inn at Maxey St James, but Adrian does; not the bar but the somewhat posher lounge. He and the Lodge's Grand Master usually had something to chew over.

"Sam, here's your pint. A favour. Have a quiet word with the Blackwell Lodge. A young upstart named Luke Brown. He owns, or at any rate lives in, the Old Hall. Little runt has threatened me. See what they've got on him and put out some soundings in our Lodge. Who might he use around here for a bit of rough stuff? Bitter east wind tonight, fancy a snifter?"

The Happening (three years later)

One

Kyaw found it within seconds, she was so thrilled. Luke was late coming down for breakfast but she had to FaceTime her mother and sisters straight away.

At last night's ceremony held at the Nottingham Conference Centre, Mr. Luke Brown was awarded the prestigious title "East Midlands Entrepreneur Of The Year" and will now go forward to the national final held later this year in London. Asked by our media reporter Jessica Lowe to what he attributed his success, Mr. Brown was quick to praise the skill and hard word of his staff. "It is one thing to have an idea for a business but quite another to find the people who can make your dream a reality". The chair of the judges said they had been particularly impressed that a local business had broken into a market hitherto dominated by City of London software houses and had won international clients.

"Kyaw darling, just coffee for me, can't face eating after last night. What a surprise when *London Wall* was called out and to think that Becky will have flashed the pictures all around the world by now. To be honest I don't remember much after that but was I dreaming or did you whisper in the taxi that you thought you might be pregnant?"

"Luke, you don't look too good, should I get a couple of aspirins? Yes, I did say that. I've missed my period twice now but haven't been to see anyone".

"But didn't we agree to wait another year?"

"You know I was told to switch to the morning-after pill, could I have forgotten to take one – I don't know – sorry".

Luke got up and went to stand behind Kyaw, wrapping his arms around her shoulders.

"Sweetie pie, don't be sorry. It's wonderful news; just a shock I suppose. It's my fault as much as yours, still can't get enough of my oriental lady! Not at my best this morning. Look, when a proper test confirms you're pregnant we'll have some planning to do but two things we'll need to factor in. Your trip back home will have to be postponed and I'd better spend longer than I thought in Perth next month to make sure the office out there can stand on its own two feet. Our top priority now must be the patter of little feet in the Old Hall".

"Darling Luke, you're such a wonderful husband, always looking after me. I love you so much".

"Kyaw, I'd better have a session in the gym, clear my head. I might need to go out later this morning, there're a few staff problems to be sorted before the office opens on Monday. Why don't you have a good long FaceTime with your mum and sisters, see what they think about coming over later in the year. Tell you what, make one of your special dishes for this evening, I'll definitely be back by six".

Luke left the breakfast room and climbed the main staircase, turned left and walked along the long corridor to his private office and gym. One piece of equipment was uppermost in his mind. He put on the boxing gloves, glanced at the framed picture of his Great Uncle Harold and hit the punchbag over and over with all his strength. Damn, damn, bugger it, bugger it. On and on he punched till the sweat rolled into his eyes but his head had cleared, he was thinking fast. Breathing heavily, he sat on the lounger and grabbed his mobile. He scrolled down to "Becky" and texted. *Don't yell back at me – not about last night – know it's Sunday and what we agreed. Can you make a quick lunch – alone – name a place.*

They went straight to a table at the far end of the restaurant, this early the Teversal Inn was quiet. The waitress brought a bottle of the New Zealand Sauvignon Blanc Oyster Bay, "Not quite our Perth tipple but it'll have to do. I want you back there next month, time you met the office manager and the three of us got down to Melbourne and pulled that one that's playing hard to get. Becky, I'll come straight to the point, Kyaw's pregnant – God know's how – thought she understood my timing plans but something's gone wrong. I'll have to accelerate things. Me, tied to domesticity, can you believe it?"

"Well, congratulations I suppose and no I can't see you tied down. Take a deep slurp and tell me why I've been dragged to this dump".

"Becky, what I want to say, and I guess last night's success and booze will help, is that since day one when you, me and Eric got together we've done well. In fact, by any standard, bloody well. Yes, we worked hard and by God we've had more than our share of good luck – even so, we've ridden the surf without coming off the board. Now, as that consultant woman keeps drilling into me, we must be ultra careful. I want *London Wall* structured properly for the medium to long term and I want *Rapidmoneyex.com* ramped as a milch cow for a short-term kill. Thirdly, I want Eric shielded from the world".

"Go on Lord and Master, I can see more than one bottle of this plonk being needed and how to get back to our respective pads – Mr. Uber I suppose".

"Indeed, get it down you and here we go. Your Service Agreement expires next month. I want to renew it for five years not three. You will not be director of sales and marketing but chief executive officer. I will slide upstairs as non-executive chairman".

"You, non-executive – pull the other one".

"I'll ignore that remark. Seriously, it'll be your baby. Lean on and learn from the consultant, she's good. Now, if you accept my deal, we must talk about Eric. I know full well there's ill will. He does all the work and you take all the glory, sort of thing. Obviously, putting you in charge has potential to make things worse. So listen carefully, treat him with kid gloves. What Eric wants, Eric gets, or so he must always think. And Becky, this is serious, I know his eyesight is deteriorating. We pay for whatever is available. If you disagree, leave the table now and I'll find someone else to run the business".

"Luke, I'm with you one hundred percent. Without Eric none of us would be here, I understand perfectly, I'll flash my legs any time, although he's not quite Murray!"

"Good, good – waiter, another please. Now let's get down to the serious stuff; the money transfer side. You saw the figures last week, it's making as much bottom line as London Wall but of course in a different way. Our risk management brings in the regular rental income but with the money transfer we must keep finding new punters. Granted you're doing that and logically there's no reason why it shouldn't continue. One might expect that when a group of overseas' individuals stop sending their funds here, whether quite legit or to be cleaned up, another takes their place. Similarly, the other way. Remember the migration of the clique from the UK to the supposedly safer haven of Australia at the height of the Covid-19 epidemic. When that was all over and the stats. came out, what happened? They came back and re-purchased the posh pads in Belgravia or wherever.

"What I want to get over is that you and Eric agreed to help me use London Wall to effect my definition of peer-to-peer. Of course it was not the accepted definition of paring a willing party in one country with a willing party in another. That would be a practical impossibility and cost the earth to set up anyway. As you know our party-to-counterparty is done within the risk management system and therefore can be pretty much instantaneous. That is our USP and Christ how you've sold it, I've been so impressed. I say Becky, you rated this place a dump and I poured scorn on the wine but actually we're doing OK. Those six oysters went down a treat, should we share a lobster? The reason I want to up the pace is fear of attack. I've picked up on the grapevine that the big money-transfer guys in London have put their heads together and worked out we're not actually finding a willing recipient. I mean, losing so much business, they were always going to go for us at some point. If you were on their side, seeing us make so much on low margins, you'd be bloody mad. Well, they are".

"Luke, what's our main weakness? I'll work on it".

"It's all about the two intermediaries we have to use. One is just about defendable but the other is, to put it mildly, dodgy. Let's not discuss it now, it'll spoil my lemon mousse, not to mention whatever mess you ordered but the set-up was devised originally by the consultant as a little experiment just to see if it worked. Of course it has, and how - but could we somehow make it legit? Let's get some coffee - fancy a short? Becky, there's something else the consultant set up and this is why you must cosy up to Eric. *Rapidmoneyex.com* is constituted such that the profit can be taken out as cash in the most tax efficient way. It has preference shares carrying a seven-and-a-half percent coupon which means it pays that figure on the nominal value of the share before any dividend is declared on the ordinary shares. Not only that, the shares are cumulative so that the money due builds up if not paid out and we haven't taken any funds so far. One other thing, this class of shares is convertible to ordinary ones should we decide to in the future. I'm telling you this because although all the preference shares are in my name, my intention is to transfer a quarter to each of you, leaving me with half. Then, on one fine day soon, four year's dividends will be paid and the thing is Becky I'm told the income is taxable at between fifteen and twenty percent. Bingo! Can't remember if I ever told you but the consultant worked her magic on the rest of the company set-up. Kyaw has fifty-one percent of the ordinary shares so technically it's her business. However, the Articles of Association requires three-quarters of the ordinary shareholders to approve a special resolution to make board appointments and the like. She is the sole director. I used a registrar as company secretary and they are the company's registered address".

"Good God Luke, you need to win awards and get Kyaw pregnant more often. Will I fix the third-party issue? You bet I will".

"Becky, have another one of those, I'll get us home somehow. Before we get carried away, I see an attack from another quarter which, actually, I'm more scared of. It goes by the name of Alice, the blonde I introduced you to at Kyaw's party. She and I clashed, oh, must be seven years ago now and then again at that accursed party. She led that murder enquiry I told you about and will stop at nothing to bring me/us down; I know it. And she'll be urged on by Marcus since true to his word, he has given Eric a few share tips which, apart from one, came good and made us a bob or two. By now the shares wizard will have realised our screen shots on London Wall got him absolutely nowhere. Hacking her phone, have we got anything?"

"Yes, I was going to tell you tomorrow. It's taken a while and been difficult. Actually, in the end, I had to pay someone special. The bill will be on my expenses this month, you won't recognise the name".

"Go on"

"The lady is having an affair. He's called Brendan, Irish and something big in Brussels".

"Bloody hell Becky, how have you held that back?"

"Well, you kept rabbiting on about this business rubbish, hadn't the heart to butt in".

"Christ! Of course, she's a smartarse. When the time comes, she'll deny everything and have a feasible cock-and-bull story for Flash-Harry Marcus of Maserati fame".

"Probably, but I've some lovely pictures. Pure art really – naked lady, entangled couple – that sort of thing".

"Becky, I know what you like doing, never been there myself. Should we retire to your place?"

Two

As she opened the front door of Mrs Tiggy Winkle Cottage, Pearl's instinct was to rush forward, but she didn't. "Marcus, how lovely to see you, and so pleased you could both make it. Where is Alice, she has come hasn't she?"

"Yes of course, she'll be here in a second, still in the car sending a text to a work colleague or something of the sort. By the way, if you pick up an atmosphere, don't worry it'll soon pass".

"Is it about me and the children?"

"No not at all, just a difference of opinion on whether we stayed in a hotel tonight, she wants to get back home and I prefer tomorrow. She's right really, there's still only one flight to Brussels on a Sunday morning and it's an easy journey from our pad. Amazing isn't it, nearly three years on and still the airlines operate a skeleton service. That Covid–19, what a legacy".

"Come inside out of that cold wind, leave the door ajar for Alice – Tristan, Mandy, look who's arrived".

Tristan had been sitting on the living- room carpet opening his presents but jumped up and rushed to Marcus who swung him high in the air, "Happy birthday Tristan, six years old today, who wants to see what's in my bag?"

Pearl was as excited as her son, "Marcus don't drop him, be careful. All morning he's being asking when you'd arrive, didn't seem bothered about his friends, expect it's because he sees them every day. Come into the kitchen, two of the mothers are helping but it's still chaos, did I mention you're in charge of the games? Mandy's got the sulks and feels a bit left out, you have got a gift for her haven't you?

Make yourself at home, I'll nip outside and drag Alice off her phone, we could do with another pair of hands in the kitchen".

Before Pearl opened the door, Marcus moved to her side and took her hands in his. "Pearl, I want you to know, there is no-one in your cottage more pleased to be here than me. All week I've been counting the days. We should have arrived hours ago but Alice has been fiddling with her face for ages and try as I might, just can't get her off that phone. You'd think being as senior as she is, there'd be cover at the weekend but this move to the Brussels Bureau of Interpol seems to be all consuming. See if you have more success than me in introducing my dear wife to this world. I'll get Mandy laughing, you'll see, I've brought a jack-in-the-box, didn't realise they were still around but I found this site *toysyouplayedwith.com*, rather neat don't you think?"

*

Mandy had fallen asleep the instant her head hit the pillow and Marcus was upstairs reading Pinocchio for the umpteenth time to a little boy determined to stay awake as long as possible. Pearl and Alice sat at the living room table sipping coffee. For a while neither spoke. Pearl was noticeably tired, seemingly in a trance. *So long ago, so much has happened since I sat here being asked what papers I had belonging to dear Eugene. Two men, complete strangers, what right did they have to intrude? And yet, looking back, it was the start. The start of a long, long adventure; Kyaw, Naing, Aung, Neil and the real hero, Marcus. How I hated him, then grew to admire him and finally invited him into my world. The father of my children. They adore him. Their first words on waking tomorrow are certain to be, "where is daddy?" "He had to go away again, he'll be back soon".*

"Pearl, you look done in, your eyes look sore, the smoke from the candles I expect. As soon as Marcus comes down, we'll be off and leave you in peace. To think only six of Tristan's friends here and yet the work you put into the party, I wouldn't know where to start. And the noise, the excitement, where does their energy come from? It's a world I know nothing of, should I be pleased? Should I be sad? Please don't answer that. While we're alone, I want to ask you a question but don't answer if you feel uncomfortable. I've been trying to work it out after something Marcus once said. Were you forty-four when you had Mandy? I mean, not being that much younger than you, I have a personal interest in things biological".

"Yes, left it a bit late in life you might say".

"It's just that, well, I've been looking it up. A woman of that age has only a three in one hundred chance of conceiving. Not only that, and ignoring special treatment, the chance of it happening as a one-off event are practically zero. So I was wondering …"

"Alice, I've just been so very lucky, Mandy is such a cutie isn't she? Oh God, don't cry – I didn't think. Stupid insensitive me, daddy would have been very cross had he known how silly I've been. Come with me, Marcus mustn't see you like this".

When Marcus came downstairs, the living room was empty. He had an inkling that some confidences were being exchanged: he took a decision.

"Darling Alice, as master of our household, I have taken an executive decision. We are not returning to dreary north London tonight. I have, at enormous expense, secured a sea-view room at The Grand Hotel. Scouts honour, I promise to get you to Heathrow for your flight tomorrow morning. In addition, I shall, this very instant, dump the car at said hotel, returning here by cab loaded with wine of multivarious colours for our evening's delectation".

"Oh Marcus, you're such an overpowering bully. Pearl and I accept the proposition on the basis that your action is pronto and not to slam the door on leaving and wake the children. You know Pearl, that man, the father of your children, can be so irritating at times. But he's a lovely guy really, let's wave him off".

*

Alice was reminiscing, philosophising really. She wondered whether things had really improved over the years. Perhaps one positive aspect of the coronavirus tragedy in the Spring of 2020 was making people take stock of their lives. Start to re-evaluate what was important, what really mattered. They could survive without the latest model of car, the luxury cruise, seeking out the latest restaurant with its award-winning chef. Growing up in a nondescript part of Essex in a far from wealthy family, slumming it in rented uni. digs, being an entry-level copper in a man's world. But, one handled things as they came along, didn't seem any great need for the so-called good things of life. Take this meal that Pearl has so lovingly served, cheese and biscuits, the left-over party cake – what more did they need to end a perfect day? Why had it taken over three years for the three of them to come together again? She supposed the only link to the past now was young Kyaw.

Pearl agreed. "Young children show the way and have an unnerving habit of bringing one down to earth with a bump. Impervious to their surroundings, they just want to be loved and be happy. Simple things to desire, somewhere along the line mankind has lost its way. Grab, grab, faster and faster. You mentioned Kyaw – not sure she is happy"

"Come on girls, it can't be all that bad. Pearl, what's this about Kyaw".

"Oh, I don't know. When she first came over here, she was so full of life, so eager to learn, so grateful for the chance to polish her English – so wanting to integrate I suppose. But now that zest seems to have gone. Not that I see much of her apart from FaceTime chats every two weeks or so. It's exactly what you were saying Alice. She's married to a handsome and very successful businessman, lives in a wonderful house set in its own grounds, money apparently no object. On the face of it everything's perfect, and yet I wonder if she misses her mum and sisters and the culture she was brought up in? Couldn't blame her for that but I think she's lost her freedom. A bird in a gilded cage – something like that".

Marcus put down his glass, rose and walked a few paces to stare at the bookcase. Without turning he said, "Are you thinking what I'm thinking, Luke Brown is a control freak?" Alice reached to refresh their drinks, "It might not be as strong as that, maybe he just wants to shield her from harm, trophy wife to be kept close – that sort of thing. Tell you one thing we've picked up though. If he didn't hold a grudge before, he does now". Pearl shuddered.

"Against Kyaw?"

"No, sorry, I'm switching relations. Against his uncle Adrian. Don't know whether you saw them talking at the graduation party, anyway, no love lost there, that's for sure. I'll explain. The Masonic Lodge. That secretive organisation that a few from the police ranks, including the Derbyshire force, decide to join for whatever reason. After Luke's business award, someone proposed him for the local Masons. His application sailed through the interview panel but when put to the membership ballot, he got blackballed, or whatever they call it. A member, and I'm not saying it was a copper, expressed doubts about his character and suggested a delay of twelve months. Obviously an innuendo of needing time to look into something. Not only that, a senior member of the Lodge took a call from a counterpart in another Lodge who also had reservations. Outcome, application refused. A rare occurrence I am told and which set off rumblings in local business circles. Our intelligence is that Mr Luke Brown was slipped the location of the foreign Lodge. It was close to where his uncle lives". For a second time in minutes, Pearl felt uneasy.

"Alice, do I take it that the police are still keeping an eye on Luke? I wouldn't want to say anything out of place and of course it's none of my business but can't we just let sleeping dogs lie? It was all such a long time ago. Suppose I'm a bit concerned for Kyaw. I hope she'll not get dragged into anything bad again, that would be so unfair. I mean, if we think she is being controlled in some way, surely we can put our heads together and do something about it?"

"I do understand your concern for Kyaw , really I do, and anyway this is not the time and place to go into detail, but our interest is not so much the business he is now lauded for but a second one involving transferring money between countries. Don't get me wrong, it might be perfectly OK but, in certain quarters, the speed with which large sums get from one place to another is arousing suspicion. Obviously, the players in this market have a self-interest in tripping him up but even so, I have a few people looking into his affairs. Why do I mention this? Well, it's because, technically, Kyaw owns the business. He's had it set up such that she is the majority owner of the ordinary share capital and on the formal documents lodged with Companies House she is the sole named director. Now, of course, he might just think it's a sensible arrangement, i.e. he owns the risk management business and his wife the second business. What's wrong with that? Perhaps nothing unless of course there's something not quite right with one of the businesses. So, I would say any move we make is more likely to protect Kyaw than the opposite".

Once again Marcus took a stroll towards the bookcase, "Pearl there's something else. It cropped up by pure chance; a bit like (if you remember) when I came across the key to my grandad's private box of papers before the cold case review got underway back in 2015. At Kyaw's graduation party, Luke's top programmer, the guy who gave a little speech in her honour, approached me for a share tip. In exchange he promised to pass on a screen shot from the risk management side. I worked out that the shot, and a few others sent since, had been doctored, no doubt to throw me off the scent. Had I wanted to use the software to hedge the risk on one of my short positions, I'd have been in a mess. In fact, without going into technicalities, I would have been in a continuous loop – getting nowhere fast. OK, stupid me for asking for something he was never going to provide. The question is, did he think if he gave me the real stuff I'd pick up something not quite kosher? What he overlooked was my ability to decompile the code. Two things are happening. First, there is interaction with third parties unrelated to potential clients and secondly they're undertaking what we in the trade refer to as rapid trading. I've no idea what that first thing is about but on the second I suspect they're using the money they get hold of in the second business (actually Kyaw's business as Alice has described) to make money on the open market before it zooms off to wherever. As you'd expect, I've passed my thoughts to Alice's team".

Pearl sighed and said she'd fetch something special to cheer them all up. She returned from the kitchen with a tin of biscuits and a fancy-shaped bottle. "Seems such a shame to put a damper on the evening with my friend Kyaw possibly tied to a rogue. I do hope it's all much ado about nothing and that she remains lady of the manor, a role I saw as suiting her well. Roll on lots of charitable works, a respected position in society and bouncing babies galore. Right, you two, may I present my end-of-evening treat. My very special ginger biscuits are kept in memory of dear Eugene and this golden liquid reminds me of when Naing and I first became friends. I'll lighten up the proceedings by passing on my own two pieces of intelligence. Kyaw is doing a spot of matchmaking.

Apparently, Luke mentioned that the number two programmer, Murray, was in dire need of a girlfriend and so she put him in touch with her sister and persuaded Luke to agree to Murray making the next trip to Myanmar". Alice took a sip of the whisky and interrupted.

"Interesting; will that little diversion from the work-a-day life have meant Kyaw and Murray getting together at times, FaceTime chats and so on?"

"I should think so, she certainly seems to know quite a bit about him. Let me press on before I lose my train of thought. Last week after Naing spoke to Tristan on FaceTime, she told me that Aung had been invited to Yadanabon University by the rector to see a prototype robot created by the Artificial Intelligence Unit. What it has been created to do is a closely guarded secret, but the rector was extremely pleased with the advice and guidance provided by Luke. In fact he couldn't praise the collaboration enough. When I mentioned this to Kyaw yesterday, she appeared to know little or nothing about what Luke was helping with although she recalled him saying whilst they were on their honeymoon that he was expecting to get more out of the work in Myanmar than just his retention fee. It struck me that keeping something from one's partner for over five years is a little odd especially with him being held in such high regard in her own country. Whatever one might think of Luke Brown, he can certainly keep a secret and also it would seem bide his time. I recall we three thinking the same sort of thing about that horrid Harold man. What do you make of my Burmese fire water? Here, have another tot". Alice stood up and looked directly at Pearl.

"Pearl, we really must be leaving. Is it in order for Marcus to take a peek at your sleeping angels, I know he is dying to but doesn't like to ask. And, Marcus darling, do take ten minutes over it, I have a couple of favours to ask Pearl and they are not for your ears. Depending on what she feels, I'll mention it later.

"So Pearl, I had this idea, what if I plant in Marcus's mind the prospect of him finding a pad down here? It would have so many advantages including spending more time with Tristan and Mandy and staying a few days rather than rushing back to London on a Saturday night. I know he would love that and if my suggestion finds favour, you could help him look around tomorrow. I can get a cab to Heathrow, honestly the expenses over in Europe are so generous. The other thing I wondered was, will Naing ever come back to the UK do you think?"

Three

The captain came onto the PA system to say they would touch down in exactly one hour's time at twelve noon, just five minutes over schedule. The weather in Perth was typical for late autumn with a light sea breeze and a ground temperature of 22c. He hoped they'd had a comfortable flight and would not hesitate to choose the Qantas Dreamliner in the near future. Even though this was Luke's fifteenth annual visit, he struggled with the time differential. By noon, Perth time, and give or take ten minutes, a whole twenty-four hours had passed since leaving Heathrow. Still, what an improvement. Even with the one-stop flights, his best time had been twenty hours and this non-stop had covered the nine-thousand miles in under seventeen.

When he wasn't asleep, or pretending to be, Luke had to endure the chatter of one of Her Majesty's Foreign Office staff. Such an important guy who'd been everywhere and done everything. Last year after sorting some diplomatic tangle in Singapore, he'd taken the direct flight to Newark, New Jersey. Of course, one gets blase about hopping around the world, even if that is currently the longest non-stop flight at eighteen-and-a-half hours. Luke made a mental note to e-mail the Foreign Office in London outlining his companionable flight experience and sharing their desire to put this gentleman on the longest possible non-stop flights. Perhaps they would agree with him that non-stop ought to mean what it said on the tin.

Wondering if constricted boredom could be tweaked to good effect, Luke pumped the travelling genius for some useful information. Take, for example, a UK entrepreneur building a business in Australia. Could such a successful businessman apply for permanent residency in that country? A long and tedious answer could be summarised as – how successful? An investment of A$ 1.5m degree of success. With this level of monetary faith in the country, the applicant could apply for a Permanent Resident Investor Visa after having lived in Australia for at least two of the past four years and of course already holding a Business Skills Provisional Visa. Was Luke correct in thinking that sum was equivalent to £.75m sterling? Just so, until the UK is taken over by the Chinese! *(not just boring but a smart-arse to boot).*

The taxi pulled up outside the property left to him by his aunt Petula. The splendid four-square detached house looked magnificent in the early afternoon sunshine not least with its new imposing frosted glass and matt steel front door. To the left, a brass plaque inscribed *London Wall (Australia) Pty Ltd. Registered office 17, Patterdale Road, Rockingham, Perth, Western Australia.* A small notice to the right read *Please ring and enter.* Luke did so. The entrance hall had been converted into a reception area. A young lady sat at the desk on which, for the avoidance of doubt, was a sign *Reception.* "Good afternoon Mr Luke Brown, I trust you had a good flight. Please turn the door sign to closed – thank you". Siobhan rose from her seat and moved away from the desk. Apart from a bright-red G-String and colour-matched high heels she was, from the waist down, naked. "Please follow me through this door and up the stairs, one or two things have been waiting for you".

*

Luke glanced at his watch, two-ten am. He was wide awake. He knew he would be, it was always the same after the long-haul flight, he'd feel drowsy by about seven and zonked out all day and for two or three days afterwards. Lying next to him, Siobhan looked so beautiful and docile. Every ounce of that Tiger had drained away. Just like the first time on Cottesloe Beach, she'd straddled him, teased him, made him wait. But only for so long; they'd gone mad, crazy mad. Out of mind, out of body. Siobhan and Luke, two worlds to collide, two appetites to satiate.

Her scent, her body, her everything. It feels so absolutely right, it is right. Why didn't I come back after uni? Ten years slogging my guts out, building two businesses that are probably as fickle as hell. Sacrificing myself at the high altar of what exactly, wealth? position? What would Harold have said? "Tha settles darn, tha nows thi station lad". How do I get out? What can I raise? Half of what I inherited is still tucked away, mortgage the Old Hall to the hilt, rape London Wall (UK) Ltd for maximum divis, get the preference divis out of Rapidmoney and start making the robots pay.

Luke fell into a restless sleep. The plane was rocking from side to side, it only steadied after the announcer said there'd be one hour before the sun went down. A large elderly man was pressing the service button demanding more beer, while a stewardess was rolling a barrel down the aisle and from an attached tube was trying to fill his pint pot but kept missing; beer flowed everywhere and two small children wearing wellington boots were splashing in the puddles. From the seat behind, a blonde woman reached over dangling a pair of handcuffs and he tried to get out of his seat but the seat belt was stuck so he pulled and pulled and .....

Siobhan was standing by the bed gently pressing his shoulder. "Lukey, wake up, you've been rolling around and pulled the sheet off me, what's the matter?"

"I don't know, I was wide awake and then had a terrible dream, I was trapped in this plane with two adversaries from the past and – oh, it doesn't matter. Siobhan, please come back to bed. I need to hold you, I need to talk to you".

"Lukey, honey, it's four-thirty, can't it wait?"

"No, I have to sort things out; you have to help me".

162

"Come here, idiot. Of course, I'll do anything".

"Siobhan, you have a lover, I'm married, I live on the other side of the world but I want to be here with you. I'm thirty-three – is it possible for us to have children? How long have I got to sort things out in the UK? You'll wait for me won't you?"

"Lukey, slow down, steady on, let's take it one step at a time. You're jet-lagged and I've worn you out. We'll take our decisions right now, no more poncing around. For Christ's sake hold me like you mean it. That's better. Lukey, I'll wait as long as it takes but if we're gonna have kids I'd rather not watch 'em playing on the beach from my wheelchair. Tell you what, we should be living together in this house in two year's time. For better, for worse, as they say. Let's get some sleep. Oysters on the quay at lunchtime – my treat but I'll stick it on expenses, visiting dignitary".

*

"Siobhan, that was a lovely lunch and how I needed those oysters, eaten how you taught me - *au naturel* – just as we were back then, eighteen years old, met by pure chance, free as a bird and what a bird you were, still are. I Luke Brown am a very lucky man. It's such a beautiful day, let's walk, talk and plan".

Anyone watching the lovers strolling hand-in-hand past the Dolphin Swim and along the Esplanade, would never imagine that these two people who meet just once a year were about to take life-changing decisions. Deception, betrayal and death. But that was for tomorrow, lovers' confidences were of today.

"Siobhan, sweetheart, from today we communicate only on the dark web. Any leak will be pretty hard to deal with. Let's talk first about your guy, how will you handle him?"

"Well, I was hoping we'd discuss this during your visit and have been thinking about it quite a lot. Clancy's a nice guy, not the sharpest knife in the box but he's well settled in the environmental charity he works for. Christ knows what they hope to achieve, I thought these recurring viruses had sorted all that polluting stuff out. Let me say what he's good at and how he might fit in. In a word, selling. Clancy can rabbit the skin off a Koala".

Luke laughed out loud. He pulled her to him and they kissed. "I can't think what's coming next".

"OK, well this charity outfit seems a bit slack to me, he's able to take time off whenever he likes. Becky arrives next week, right? Let's suppose she trains him to talk London Wall. Obviously not to demonstrate, he's a bit behind the eight-ball for that but he loves to travel and I'd sweet talk him into selling on commission only. So, he keeps his cushy job but travels and softens up the next potential client for us. Actually, if Becky thinks I'm good enough, I'll run through the applications and do the clinching. We might even team up and really get stuck into the big boys in Sydney. By the way, our trip to Melbourne is fixed for the week after next with Becky. What do you think Lukey?"

"Brilliant, absolutely brilliant. Keeping Clancy that close, he won't suspect a thing and if it doesn't work, all it's cost is a few expenses. What will he do when I come to live here?"

"Oh, he'll be fine. Aside from rabbiting on, he does have one other talent but that's none of your bloody business".

Luke laughed again. They paused under a eucalyptus tree.

"You're so good for me. Can't remember when I last laughed, can't remember when I last felt so happy. Where is Clancy now? Not hiding behind that next tree is he?"

"God knows. Probably cuddling some Sheila on one of those yachts out there. Clancy's easy, what about Kyaw, your betrothed?"

"Oh Siobhan, it's so difficult and no-one's fault but mine. I will find a way, I promise. How on earth did she get pregnant? I know, you sexy beast, it's a silly question but she's so disciplined about taking her pill. After her problem she had to switch to the *morning after* one but even so, how come she forgot unless she wanted to deceive me, but that's not in Kyaw's nature. She'll be fine financially, I've set in motion cleaning up the money-transfer side and, as I mentioned, technically she owns it and at some point I'll put my preference shares in her name. But with a toddler and all her social circle and me having done a bunk, I just don't know. My guess is she'll go back to her mother and sisters although Pearl, who I've told you all about, will fight her corner and I suppose Kyaw might move nearer to her. Thinking about it now, it might influence things if Naing was back in the UK. Yes, I might try and work on that".

"Lukey, look over there, that's a boat trip to Garden Island, let's run".

"You see Siobhan, I can't take a boat to an offshore island from the Old Hall. One can take a sodding bus to a dump called Mansfield – that's about it. Tell you what, if we see a dolphin, I'll give you a multiple tonight and Lukey always keeps his promises. Going back to my dear wife, something interesting came from left-field, as the American's say. I've got this programmer called Murray who's got the hots for Becky, every time she takes a bow he practically comes in his trousers. She's out of his league but for a laugh I suggested to Kyaw she put him in touch with her sister, thinking, well, give him a trip to Myanmar and see what happens. She picked up on the idea and to give him half a chance, she's coaching him on the local customs, teaching him a few Burmese words, that sort of thing. Becky told me they've been seeing a lot of each other while I've been away, which is good. He's one friend she'll have when I scarper.

"On the plane coming over I was thinking about how my Australian company was set up. It appeared sensible at the time but it won't do for our future. My advisers will have to be involved. Somehow, its business as a subsidiary of London Wall (UK) Ltd will have to be disbanded in favour of a wholly-owned Australian company. Until I get my permanent residency, maybe it will have to be owned by you. The consultant I use back home has been looking into the feasibility of opening offices in Singapore to cover the Far East side and here in Sydney. She thinks it makes financial sense for the Pacific Area clients to operate out of Sydney rather than Perth. If Becky and her team continue to pick up international banks and investment houses, then No 17, Patterdale Road could become our registered holding company base for everything outside the UK. In theory, why shouldn't it control any clients we pick up in Europe too.? After all, the UK idiots decided to cut themselves afloat from the EU. The more I turn that over in my mind, the more elegant it becomes. I'll sell the UK risk side to Becky and Eric and leave the money transfer company to Kyaw".

"Lukey, let's go home – sorry I mean back to the office – I need to lie down, my head hurts. Well, I need to lie down anyway".

*

The instant she was greeted at Perth Airport Becky could tell. She tried not to show it and smiled inwardly. She absolutely knew they were an item. Siobhan spoke first.

"Becky, my new boss, welcome back to Perth. Lukey said you were tall and he wasn't wrong. Follow me, it's this way, we're stopping off at my secret place – the best Aussie sparkling in town. Leave him to drag your case, there's so much I want to talk about".

"Right ladies, let's settle in this corner. If I know anything about service in Australia, that waiter will have a second bottle on the table before you can say Crocodile Dundee. Don't worry about falling asleep Becky, we'll get you to the hotel safely and tuck you in bed. You have the whole of tomorrow to relax and recover from the flight but I do want to explain the way I see things panning out during your visit.

"First, let's talk about Siobhan's role. Oh, and by the way, she'll pop to your hotel tomorrow and go over her background. I'm familiar with it and don't need to be there. As you know, she's on trial as our office manager and you need to decide if we make it a permanent appointment. The question is, and to hell with the office and admin, can she become our *Australian Becky?*. I have to be confident we show off our modules to the best effect. Take as long as you need to put her through the demo. paces. This business is a long way from base and we have to be sure it's in good hands.

"Right, so we have three potential clients in town. If you decide she's up to it, I want you taking the first bank with Siobhan as observer but then you two swap roles for the second presentation. Remember Becky, she's on your payroll. I'm sure Siobhan won't mind me saying this but I have to be sure she's up to the job. Now, assuming she is, there's a second interview I want you to do. She has a boyfriend who, apparently, is a bit laid-back and has a soft job with plenty of spare time. She tells me he can talk the hind leg off a donkey. What you have to decide is, can he soften up a potential client? He'd be on commission only and we could consider letting him work the Sydney market if you deem it safe to let him loose. Obviously, we can't afford him, or anyone else for that matter, spoiling our pitch. If he is worth setting on, he could possibly come with us to Melbourne next week.

Siobhan, I think I've mentioned it before but this is the plus side of being in Australia. Back home, I'd have to ask for a second bottle but true to form here it comes right on cue. It must be instinctive; guy with two beautiful Sheilas requires much nourishment". Siobhan spoke directly to Becky.

"The big boss – doesn't lack confidence does he?"

"Sipping bubbly with you two, what peacock wouldn't be displaying? Becky that reminds me, tomorrow evening can we three meet for dinner, I'll like to know how your day went, there's a lot riding on it". Becky hesitated before answering.

"Actually Luke, can we make it the following evening? I've promised to meet that guy who invited me out last time. Given his firm has really come good, I felt obligated, plus he wants to bring along a mate who apparently heads a financial consultancy. If we get on OK, he'll introduce me to some of his clients". Luke lifted his glass and for a few seconds stared at the rising bubbles.

"Absolutely".

*

Luke entered the concourse of Mandalay International Airport and immediately felt his pulse quicken. Someone in the waiting crowd was holding aloft a board *Mr Luke Brown*. Not until he'd rounded the barrier could he make out who it was. Beaming a smile and moving quickly to greet him was Garma. "We're so thrilled with the news, so pleased you could break your journey home to see us". In an instant she was giving him an enormous bearhug. Had he imagined it or beneath that thin silk dress, could he feel her heart beating?

There had been an accident on the perimeter road and their taxi had been stuck in traffic for over thirty minutes before they were finally released onto Expressway AH1 for the thirty-seven kilometer journey to the city. Luke was saying that being met at the airport had been such a lovely surprise and looking at Garma how overdressed he felt. How could he have overlooked the need to change into his lightweight clothes? It was warm in Perth but twenty-three degrees hardly prepared one for a typical Myanmar afternoon. Garma smiled and with a slight nod of the head he now recalled so fondly, said he looked pretty cool to her but would he like to choose a few items in the bazaar after he'd checked in?

"That would be lovely Garma but actually I'd prefer to have an ice-cold beer in the hotel bar, will you join me after I've freshened up?"

Early that evening, Luke was explaining to Garma that after a long-haul flight he had learned from experience to take the next day off before any business meetings. He thought of his work as a battle ground and as such needed time to relax before confronting the enemy, although of course the university Rector was an exception to the rule. He'd become a very good friend. Would Garma be available to act as his interpreter again? The meeting the day after tomorrow was very important and there must be no misunderstanding on the detail of any agreement reached. Luke stressed that part of the discussion would be of a confidential nature and he relied on her discretion. If she could just treat the event as a job, adding to her experience, helping her appreciate how business works, that kind of thing. Would she like another cocktail? It looked so delicious, he might try one himself.

"Garma, I would like to treat you and your mother and sister to a day out tomorrow. I was doing a bit of research on the plane coming over. I suppose you'll have done it before but can we take a river cruise south? Let me just pause and you can tell me if I've memorised this correctly and see how rubbish my pronunciation is. From *Sagaing Lay Kyun Man Aung Jetty* to Yandabo, the pottery village. I'd like to choose a present for Kyaw". Garma swung her legs on the bar stool to face Luke directly.

"Luke that was very good, you really should keep on learning our language. Your pronunciation makes our language sound very attractive. Of course we can come, we would all love it, I'll make a booking".

"You flatter me, everyone knows we English are rubbish at foreign languages. But listen, this will knock you out. I happen to know that Irrawaddy is Sanskrit for Elephant River. Now that has impressed you, admit it. Garma go steady with that cocktail, it's got quite a kick you know. Look, before I fall asleep on this bar stool, let me explain what I want to do on this trip. First, we will discuss progress on the Artificial Intelligence work with the Rector of Yadanabon University and, by the way, this could be my last consultancy advice as they have made incredible progress. I will see a demonstration of an actual functioning robot but I'm not sure if they'll let you be present due to it all being shrouded in secrecy. You see Garma this work has enormous commercial potential and the Rector will either want to float off their own company or sell the patents to an outsider organisation. He won't take any risks, so you might have to stay in the dark. But, afterwards you must definitely be by my side. I have a proposition for him and my thoughts must be explained very precisely.

"Let's order one more of these rather special drinks, what does the barman use to make this orange colour? Anyway no matter, it slips down very well especially after God knows how long a flight from Perth, almost lost the will to live. What was I saying, oh yes, my itinerary. The day after our uni. meeting I want to see U Aung again. His English is impeccable but even so can you come with me? What's that gorgeous perfume you're wearing – must take some back for Kyaw. Have you decided on a career after your course is over? You know, the charity he chairs is now a major organisation, we have monthly progress meetings on Zoom and his daughter Naing is one of the senior executives. Between you and me, I have a sneaking feeling she might want to return to the UK. If that happened, would you be interested in a senior position in Dotcom? Have I ever told you how like Kyaw you are? We should send her a video of all four of us on the boat tomorrow, she would like that".

*

The meeting started promptly at ten o'clock in the Rector's office and after the opening pleasantries his two advisers took turns to explain that the trials had gone well, as would be demonstrated later in the laboratory. Obviously, a dummy would be used on this occasion. Once certain official hurdles had been overcome, the plan was to commence live operation within the next three months. He expressed a view that without the advice and close attention of Mr Luke Brown throughout, this project would not have been conceived, least of all brought to what they all believed would be a satisfactory conclusion. The advisers then left the office to set up the demonstration.

The Rector confirmed that their conversation was not being recorded and, as far as Luke could tell from his basic knowledge of their language, Garma was asked not to take notes. The university had decided to form a company to exploit the commercial potential of *in vivo* kidney transplant and a draft of the formation documents showing Mr Luke Brown's shareholding would be sent to his solicitor within the next fourteen days. Standing to leave and with a slight bow, he indicated his intention to lead them from the office. Luke also rose to his feet and spoke to Garma.

"Please ask the Rector if we can continue the meeting for a few more minutes as I have a proposition he may be interested in".

The Rector indicated he was pleased to continue and Luke spoke slowly to Garma giving sufficient time for the translation.

"I've had an idea that might be of interest to the Rector. Our original agreement was that whilst I would have access to the Artificial Intelligence source code in order to assess progress and suggest amendments, I did not have any ownership rights over the developing applications and must not pass the work to any third party".

The Rector whilst looking a little taken aback, merely nodded. Luke continued.

"Without in any way disturbing our agreement, would the Rector look favourably on Luke's team back in the UK examining the possibility of adapting the final application so that the robot performs a different type of *in vivo* operation? If this worked, he had in mind licensing the production of the robotics to an existing UK manufacturer who in turn would exploit its commercial application".

Luke paused and spoke directly to Garma.

"Garma, please explain this next part as carefully as you can using your own phraseology and take your time, there's no rush but I want the Rector to understand the innuendo. Please explain that now the Covid-19 virus has finally been eradicated, no expense will be spared anywhere in the world to save lives during the terrible period between the next viral infection and developing a vaccine. It is reasonable to assume that, once again, the vulnerability to humans will be respiratory. Garma, then pause slightly for effect and continue saying that the big breakthrough in that period before a vaccine comes on the market will be the ability to quickly and efficiently transplant one or even both lungs. Our robots will be programmed to do just that. I appreciate that his staff will be engaged fully in the kidney transplant project. As a result, and so as not to complicate work schedules and to assure security, perhaps it would be advisable to keep the idea to themselves. Once the costs of developing the software are covered, my proposal is to share the licence fee income fifty-fifty. If he agrees with my proposal and by using the facility of one of my other businesses, I can arrange for his share of the income to be transferred to any bank account of his choosing. Then, please pause and say finally that I anticipate over time this figure will be substantial".

Luke sat back in his chair whilst Garma spoke to the Rector.

Once again the head of the university rose from his chair and, in perfect English, spoke directly to Luke. "I agree with your proposition. There is to be no paperwork and please do whatever is needed to see that the young lady is properly looked after".

*

Luke was telling Garma that after the successful meeting with the Rector he felt confident enough to order the taxi himself and ask to be taken the thirty-nine kilometers on National Highway 31 to Madaya. If they found themselves being driven South she was allowed to intervene and explain that the Englishman was too dim to master even the basics of their language. Garma giggled. *She is so like Kyaw, it could almost be her.* Aung was in the garden sitting in the shade of a Mango tree and welcomed them like long lost heroes and immediately signalled the maid to bring tea. He was delighted to learn that the project at Yadanabon had every chance of success and mentioned that he and the Rector met on a regular basis to discuss the work of the Dotcom charity.

It was a beautifully warm and sultry afternoon and the conversation ranged far and wide not least since Aung took a keen interest in UK affairs and particularly the economic struggle to recover the ground lost due to the devastating consequences of the viral epidemic three years before. Luke felt at ease with the old man and listened patiently. Time was on his side and then came the opportunity. Aung was saying that at Pearl's request he had been looking into the ownership of the piece of land once worked by his mother's family. She was enquiring about the possibility of erecting some form of memorial to Chit and thereby indirectly to her late friend Eugene.

"Aung, I want to thank you for agreeing at our last Zoom meeting of the trustees of the charity to start reimbursing the salary and living costs of the internees working in my UK business. As was mentioned, it ought to be possible soon to move the best students onto a postgraduate scheme under the control of my senior software engineer. Oh, and when you mentioned Pearl, it reminded me to ask about Naing. I do hope her work is satisfying especially as it must seem such a big change from practising her dentistry skills. Actually, and through the UK grapevine, I heard a whisper that she might return to the UK. Apparently, Pearl told Kyaw that the senior partner at her old practice was retiring and he'd made a tentative enquiry about her coming back to replace him. Obviously, you'd be sad to lose her but I'm told she misses the children terribly. Aung, after that most unfortunate spat we had about Naing's appointment in the charity not being properly ratified by the full board of trustees, would you support a proposal from me to replace her with Garma? Of course, that could only happen if Naing returns to the UK.

Four

Marcus was wrong on both counts. He assumed they'd pop into the hotel bar for a nightcap but Alice said that while he was welcome to have one, she would go to their room. Secondly, he felt certain they would make love but Alice knew she shouldn't have drunk Pearl's whisky, she never touched spirits and what with the journey tomorrow and preparation for the evening conference with the head of the bureau, she needed her sleep. Breakfast wasn't a roaring success either; the room service was late and the scrambled egg too sloppy and barely warm. The taxi arrived at five to ten and she was gone.

Back at Pearl's cottage, Marcus entered a war zone. Tristan had been accused of hiding Mandy's *Snuggles* - which he hadn't, and she had accidentally trodden on his paper model. Within seconds he and Mandy were searching for the soft toy and then he and Tristan set about making a new model. Order restored, he accepted an Americano from Pearl and they left the battle ground for the temporary peace of the kitchen.

"Marcus, are you and Alice OK? I know it's not really my business but when you two left last night, I could feel a bit of tension in the air - similar to when you arrived. Sorry if I sound prissy but if it's about me and the children, don't you think we ought to have a serious talk. As Daddy used to say *there's always a way round these things* and with him, there was".

"Honestly Pearl, it's nothing to do with you, well, I suppose it might be slightly, I mean it must be strange for Alice seeing me so at ease with children that are not hers. Then again, thousands of couples are in the same position and they must go through rough patches for all sorts of reasons. Anyway, we've survived our downers before and we will this time. It must be said that I'm not the easiest person to live with. Should a born loner like me have got married in the first place? Fridays can be stressful to put it mildly, I close my positions either in or out of the money. When it's the latter, I get mad with myself though fortunately Alice is never around. Invariably we meet later in the pub or restaurant and pretend we've both had a good day. Take it from me Pearl, a fun night out and dining at the latest eatery sounds great but it soon wears thin. Put another way, it can't compete with reading Pinocchio to Tristan or tucking Mandy in".

"Yes I understand that but Marcus you two were one of the happiest couples any of us had ever known. It was like a scene from a Hollywood romance, a dashing beau, a beautiful and successful wife, riding into the sunset. Not a dry eye in the house. Come on, whilst it's still quiet out there, tell me more".

"Hmm, not easy to pin down. Alice is now forty-one; we have no children and although that was a conscious decision early on, we have tried pretty conscientiously since, if you get my drift. But aside from that, we've had this dream of retiring early and travelling. In Alice's case that added up to rapid promotion to reach a very high salary level, so that the resultant pension meant our retirement lifestyle would be pretty much unchanged. In fact, and perhaps because I just plodded on with my charts regardless, she seems to be obsessed. Why otherwise accept a secondment to Brussels when we had what most people would regard as an idyllic life in London. I can feel myself getting wound up, let's drop the subject. Did I mention I've put myself on a four-day week? Well, I reckoned there's never much trading on a Monday so why not take it off, after all I'm alone in the week these days and it's high time I put my mind to something new. Monday is my new *out of skin day.* You're impressed, I can tell".

"Marcus, I will be genuinely impressed the first time you show me your oil on canvas "Sunset Over Hampstead" or "David As A Youth" hewn out of granite".

"Ah, so the posh lady comes over all *Primrose Hill Set*. Right, well now I'll get my own back. Once those rascals have gone to bed and if you invite me for supper (I'm staying at the Grand again tonight) I'll explain how my newfound creativity has been released. But first, this idea Alice had. This afternoon why don't we all go window shopping among the Estate Agents in Brighton, see if Tristan can pick out a nice place from which he and I can rush down to the sea leaving the girls panting in our wake? Pearl before you answer, that reminds me, did Naing sell her place down here before she went back to Burma?"

"Yes, let's do that. Even if ultimately you find an apartment through an online portal, the children will love choosing a picture from the window displays. Naing, no, she rented it out which perhaps should have told me something. There is a possibility she will come back from Myanmar – did you know that?"

*

"You know Pearl, one doesn't need drink, fine food or artificially induced and supposedly erudite conversation to escape the humdrum of life. I've had a wonderful day today, going out with you and the children, holding their hand, wondering at their concentration in selecting my next place to live. They don't get wrapped up in the why of things, they're just in the here and now and accepting that which is. It made me think that in growing up and being jostled by events, somehow that beautiful simplicity has been lost, and it's a shame. Coming home, having tea, going through the bedtime routine, falling asleep in their safe place. Just wonderful really. Wonderful. Having said all that, let's have a glass of wine to round off the day, I'll leave the car here and get a cab to the hotel".

"Marcus, while in no way wishing to burst your balloon, I ought to mention that there are days when bringing up two little ones is not exactly a bed of roses. No, forget I said that, it feels wrong – I shouldn't be saying this but I want you to know – I've had a lovely day too. It was bad enough when Naing went away, but how I'd handle Tristan if you left, I dread to think. Anyway, leaving the self-congratulatory mood, what has your creative side produced? Let me guess, you've bought a potter's wheel".

"Absolutely not. All my creativity is centred on you".

"Indeed".

"Sorry, I didn't put that very well. No, I'm referring to your writing skills. I've been through the draft you sent and honestly I couldn't put it down. I want to make a few suggestions and actually on the first read-through I wasn't taken with the start point but after more thought, I now see that a piece of instant drama can be key to drawing the reader in. Now, Pearl, brace yourself for a shock. Remember showing me your synopsis of Eugene before actually starting. Well, I've done one for book two on the basis that you left your readers with a big unanswered question: namely was Eugene a good or a bad man. My suggestion within the synopsis is of course just one route you could take.

"The other thing is that I don't think you, or rather we, should attempt to publish at this stage. My research concludes that the chances of finding a literary agent prepared to take you on are, to put it mildly, slim. Believe me, not because of the story or quality of writing or anything particularly literate but you're not a film star or Premier League footballer are you? Perhaps too cynical but why waste time and money when Eugene is crying out for a sequel".

"So, my scholarly manager, you've prepared a blueprint".

"I have and not only that I want you to read it now while I fix us a drink and take my time checking on Tristan and Mandy. I won't be offended if on my return it lies in tatters on the floor".

Marcus went to his car and returned with three sheets of A4 which, very gingerly and pretending to shield his eyes, he handed to Pearl.

"Oh, and by the way, my suggested name for the book and its principal character, is not you. Remember what I said originally, you are Stay Bennett. She with the vivid imagination". Marcus left the room and Pearl started to read.

A synopsis

Pearl in mourning for Eugene. Her decision to disprove Harold's suspicions. Note left for Pearl by E. relating visit of Harold with tea and sweeteners. Introduce Marcus (grandson of Sup. Clarke). Harold driven back from Brighton by Luke (grandson of Molly) after surprise visit to Eugene. Harold blames Eugene. History of Marcus, his career choice. How he makes money.

Pearl ponders on Eugene's motive for her visit to Burma. Pearl suspicion grows. Wonders if Harold's visit contributed to Eugene's death. Pearl meets Naing.

Harold as a stamp collector. Harold as "user" of people. Marcus researches cold case. Case is opened. Naing telephones her father and tells him of his lineage.

Harold contests the will. Aung writes, piecing together what happened to Chit. Kyaw arrives in UK. Secret payments to Jersey, Pearl and Kyaw to go there.

Marcus finds key to box of papers. DI Wallace explains progress on cold case review. Marcus tells of his findings. Pearl and Kyaw discover secret payments.

Luke's bonding with Harold. He researches "Ten Pound Poms". Travels to Perth and meets his Aunt. He returns with file of papers.

Kyaw researches war veteran records. Pearl brings Adrian up to date on Jersey money. Doubts about Adrian creep in.

Marcus has date with Alice. Marcus reads his grandad's notes on the 1956 case: of the theory he and his boss had formed.

Luke accidentally meets Kyaw. Luke makes connection prompted by Harold. PC Neil is stamp collector and knows of Harold's reputation as philatelist. Alice researches watermarks on stamps.

Pearl puts case for prosecution, psychopathic? The theory of murder and Eugene's mistake. Further theory re murder of Dot's parents. Naing challenges prosecution theory. Pearl is frightened.

Luke and Harold plot against Kyaw: turn her against Pearl. Luke is falling for Kyaw.

Alice plans stage 1 of review, Neil & Marcus together. They visit Pearl and she hands over important documents. Neil finds letter from H. with distinctive stamp. Alice suspects Harold.

Aung is child of Eugene and Chit. Plan is Luke to access HW's computer. Get database of collectors to police. Super tells of Alice's promotion and she tells of her theory of HW being serial cyanide poisoner.

Luke goes to Myanmar to present paper on Artificial Intelligence to students. Pearl and Naing's theory of poisoning. Macrae outlines plan.

Why Harold's plan misfired. How Dorothy was murdered. Theory of why Eugene paid money to Jersey. Molly's blackmail via bugs. The dawn raid. The parrot speaks. Pearl's proposition.

*

Marcus returned to the living room carrying a tray which he placed on the table. It held two glasses of white wine and a plate of ginger biscuits. He straightened his back and bowed his head slightly in a humble pose. He pointed to the door and made as if to leave.

"Sit down, silly. Marcus, I'm almost lost for words. You must have spent hours and hours on this, not only deciding what actually happened but how. I got lost in places but the most impressive aspect was sequencing events into what seem to be self-contained chapters. Are you really serious about me using it to tell a full story?"

"Of course I am. You can't leave your readers dangling in mid-air. We have to get to the bottom of it, for better or worse. Seriously Pearl, if you have a go, I'd like to try my hand at editing. I don't mean structurally but, well, perhaps giving a bit of advice on how some of the male characters might think, how they would express themselves and react to things. For example, a fair bit of policing has rubbed off from Alice, and my research experience might come in handy.

Apart from all that, what better excuse for popping in more often to check on progress?"

"Marcus, are you serious about finding a place down here?"

"Let me ask you a rider. If I came back tomorrow morning before going home, would you be happy if I took Tristan to school?"

"What a stupid question. Yes".

"In that case, I'm deadly serious. I want to spend more time with Tristan and Mandy. Remember, I don't work on Mondays so I could stay over on Sunday evenings now and again".

"Marcus, putting my writing and your fondness for our children aside and while we have some time together, have you any idea what's going on in the East Midlands? Daddy always used to say I'd be worried if I had nothing to worry about, but I've become increasingly anxious about whatever Kyaw's got wrapped up in. Did you find out any more about that money-transfer business she ostensibly heads? Before answering that, don't you think it really odd that the moment she tells Luke she could be pregnant, he zips off to Australia? I appreciate he's got business over there but surely one of his staff could have gone. I mean to say, your wife says she's having your baby and you respond something on the lines of, nice to know dear but it won't change my plans. I ask you Marcus, did you fly off to distant parts when I gave you my news? No, Marcus, don't come any closer, I'm trying very hard".

"Yes, you're right. I know a bit more about what he's doing but it's far from a complete picture. Bear in mind Pearl that I can't describe this without getting technical because the use of financial techniques is precisely how it works. Let's start with the premise that Luke is one very smart cookie. His successful risk management business is living proof. He is definitely using a financial instrument called a CFD – it stands for a Contract For Difference – which is an agreement between an investor and a CFD broker to exchange the difference in value of a financial product between the time the contract opens and closes. At this point Pearl, you need to take a deep slurp of your wine.

"The prerequisite is that a shell company exists on the UK AIM market. I say shell because it doesn't actually do anything. There is a second *market maker* company, let's call it Dodgy (UK) Ltd. At present, I do not know the name of either the shell company or the one I've styled as Dodgy. Actually, they could both be controlled by Luke or one of his mates. Luke would have his own risk management office in Myanmar.

"Take a hypothetical case. A man living in the UK wants to transfer a large sum of money to Myanmar. Perhaps he wants to invest in a Burmese company under the new and looser regulations or he has a contact there prepared to hold his funds before onward shipment. He uses Luke's - sorry Kyaw's - company because speed is of the essence and he'd quite like to pay less than the four percent commission charged by a bank or traditional money transfer firm.

"What happens is this. Step one; the Myanmar office places a buy CFD order on Dodgy (UK) Ltd using his risk management CFD broker. Step two; using the money lodged for transfer, he places orders on Dodgy causing the quoted price to rise. Step three: since the Myanmar CFD is in profit (in the money as the trade calls it), the position is closed just like I close my short positions each Friday afternoon. Voila! The profit – that is the difference between the opening and closing contract price – is now in Myanmar. Depending on the amount of profit made and of course the total to be transferred, opening and closing positions may occur many times. This presents no problem since they will happen in rapid succession and be automated until the computer recognises the total sum has flowed across. One other thing that seems to happen is the placing of many small but timely sell orders at computer generated prices to ensure there is sufficient liquidity for the trades to be met and the price can be seen to move up".

"Marcus, I can't understand any of that but what interests me is how you've worked it out. I mean surely if you discovered the methodology, why haven't the other players in the market done likewise and stifled his competitive edge?"

"Because the underlying software and associated computer screens are kept very secure. It is imperative that no competitor gets anywhere near them. You see Pearl, the risk management business has developed computer modules that are sold on licence to help the customer, well, literally manage risk. What I am trying to say is it's the customer who is trading. But here we have Luke's own business trading, that's what made me suspicious. Plus, the use of CFD's which are not in the risk management package".

"OK I sort of get that but how do you know?"

"Recently, the share tips I've sent Eric have come good. This seems to have stimulated him to be more adventurous in what he's passed to me or maybe he's become a bit sloppy. Then again, he could be showing off a bit, techie to techie sort of thing. Honestly, I don't know but whatever, I spotted rapid dealings in CFD's with the same counterparty and took it from there".

"Marcus, my head's spinning, let me grab another bottle, I've got one somewhere. I suppose this is a naïve question, but is all this legal?"

"Not naïve at all, it's a very good question. Basically, there's nothing inherently dishonest about being smart and there's been lots of examples of what might be termed financial engineering becoming standard practice over time. However, buying a share, for example, with the sole purpose of increasing its price and then selling at a profit, might be considered market manipulation. Also, this so-called Dodgy company will have a sponsor to oversee its business and market makers to facilitate trades. If these third parties are fake, well, over to the lawyers. The short answer to your question Pearl is, I don't know. I must say, this is a very acceptable wine, our dissection of Mr Luke Brown isn't spoiling it one bit.

"Talking of wine, here's something you'll find amusing. You remember Neil the policeman I came to see you with on the cold case enquiry, well he's now become a big mate – at any rate he keeps telling me he has. He knows I prefer wine and so he tries to get me half-cut on real ale. There's always some reason for him to pop down and stay over on a Saturday night and it usually starts with a couple of pints in my local The Lord Palmerston. There is of course only one reason for his visits. After all, he and I have nothing in common except the cold case experience of eight years ago. He's under orders from that Macrae guy to find out what Luke is up to. It's so damn obvious it's pathetic: I see you, you are friends with Kyaw and she, in strict confidence, spills the beans on hubby. It's not working of course, simply because Luke has twigged too and he tells her precisely nothing. However and since I can hold my drink, it's working in reverse".

"This gets better and better, go on".

"I know what the Derbyshire force is up to and I know how Alice is involved. The thing is that she, before going to Brussels, raised the issue of fraud with her old boss Macrae. He, needless to say, would like nothing more than to feel the collar of our Luke. As a result, the Old Hall we were invited to for Kyaw's party, is under continuous surveillance. I wouldn't go as far as saying there's a phone tap but certainly all comings and goings are monitored. Without wanting to sound arrogant, I believe the only way to catch Luke is by playing him at his own game, i.e. proving that some of his dealings are technically dodgy. Luke Brown is too smart to be caught using old fashioned policing methods. Pearl, one other thing while I'm still on my soapbox, if Kyaw is being set up by being named as the sole director in the money transfer business, there is such a thing as shadow directors. These are people who actually control the running of a business even if not named. So if, in this highly technical-based business, things are not as they should be, I would envisage Kyaw being exonerated in favour of the technical experts. But, I'm no lawyer or student of the various company acts. My point is, don't worry about her. She has a good friend in you and I certainly wouldn't stand by and see her damaged".

"Thanks Marcus, my white knight for a second time. After what you said about Neil, here comes my late-night confession. It's more likely his visits are triggered not by Macrae but by MacBennett. Probably me being silly, but after you two got on so well on the cold-case, when he came to see you in London and you brought him down here, I did sort of suggest he might make a habit of it".

"Why?"

"Marcus, I often think of you being alone in N7. I suppose it's because of the one-man-against-the-world nature of daytrading you've explained to me and knowing that Alice is very often not with you. Also, I sometimes wonder if you regret that your children live sixty miles away. Thinking back, after Mummy was killed, I spent so many hours alone in my room at school and later at university. Then, during Daddy's last few years, I was mentally if not physically alone again. It was only meeting dear Eugene that made me realise there are other people out there".

"Darling Pearl, Uber man will be here in ten minutes. The world won't suddenly stop spinning if we have a hug, will it? I find leaving you so very hard. You're right about finding a property through the online portals but even so there's really no substitute for knowing the patch and keeping one's ear to the ground. Can you have a proper search along the seafront, I suppose west of Brighton, but no further than Shoreham. I don't need much of a place. The main attribute must be no more than a three-minute dash to the sea for me, Mandy and Tristan. Needless to say, we don't want any bossy mother holding us back, spoiling our fun".

"Marcus, stop, your taxi's here, you have to go. Don't forget to phone Alice, she'll be missing you and eager to hear how your day went".

"Yes, of course, I'll do it from the taxi or the hotel room although recently by this time in the evening, I've not been able to get through. Alice says her days are so exhausting that she often turns her gadgets off and just flops. See you in the morning".

John G Smith

Business interests of Luke Brown BSc(Hons)

Company name	Business	Equity	Senior management	Head office	Branch office
London Wall (UK) Ltd	Risk management	Luke 85% Becky 10% Eric 5%	Chairman Luke, CEO Becky	The Old Hall	None
London Wall (Australia) Pty Ltd	Risk management	Luke 100%	Chairman Luke, GM Siobhan	Perth	Sydney Singapore Brussels
Rapidmoneyex.com	Global money tx	Kyaw 51% Luke 49%	Chairman Luke, CEO Kyaw	The Old Hall	Various
Myanmar (Robotics) MCA Inc	in vivo Kidney tsp	Y. Uni 85% Luke 15%	Not disclosed	Mandalay	Nay Pyi Taw
LB Robotics (UK) Ltd	in vivo Lung tsp	Luke 100%	Chairman Luke	The Old Hall	None

Five

Kyaw wondered if Luke might succeed where she had failed. Old Fred Salmon was a very proud man and her suggestion of home help had met with stoical refusal. Could Luke persuade the increasingly frail ex-owner of the Old Hall to accept some degree of social care? Also, why doesn't his grandson James come to see him anymore? Instinctively, Luke shied away from what he regarded as domestic trivia but Kyaw's worry gave him an idea. "Ask Fred how I can contact James – you do it as your good nature always comes shining through. It's high time that young man assumed responsibility for his benefactor, then leave it with me, I'll sort it".

It was a few minutes after ten on a cloudless and already warm June morning when James Salmon pressed the Old Hall bell. Kyaw greeted him with a slight bow of her head and led him down the oak-panelled hall to Luke's private office. She thanked him for coming and hoped his talk with Luke would go well. Leaving his desk and beckoning James to join him on one of the sofa seats, Luke was about to speak but James got in first. "Hi Luke, haven't you come good in grandad's old place, this super office and seeing you sitting at that huge desk like the chairman of a multinational combine? Wow – really impressive, oh and just to say I can't stay long, the squash court's booked for eleven forty. Did you know I've just moved up into your box, so I'll soon have the pleasure of knocking you off your pedestal".

Luke ignored the banter and started to pour coffee from the cafetiere. "James, I want to thank you for the invitation to your twenty-first. Unfortunately, neither of us can make it but *coming of age,* as they used to say in the old days, is important and should be marked. When you were thirteen, the year before we moved here, my great uncle gave you some postage stamps hoping it would get you interested in collecting. Now I'm telling you this is strict confidence. Before he died he destroyed his life's work as a professional philatelist. Except he didn't".

"Sorry Luke, you've lost me".

"I'll spell it out. My Great Uncle Harold made a fortune from postage stamps. He was a wily bird right to the end especially where money was concerned". Luke smiled. "He'd say, w*hy shud taxman get slug of me best bits, they'll tek plenty from me cash pile as tis.* So, about six months before he passed on, he gave his special stamps to me. Now James, I'm going to hand you a few sets. If you've kept up the hobby my advice is hang on to them for a few years, there's a ready market. But, if you want to sell, go ahead. I'll not give you a valuation today but put it this way, you'll leave uni. with no debts, have a nice little runner to impress the girls and after putting a deposit on your first pad, still have a few quid over. There is however one condition".

"Go on".

"I have a favour to ask".

"I'm listening".

"I have an uncle who's messed me about. I want him taken down a peg or two". Luke returned to his desk, pulled open a drawer and handed James a photo.

"This was taken a few years ago but I doubt he's changed much and here's his car registration. In Stamford, Lincolnshire there's a very old coaching inn called The King William. On the second Thursday of each month, this guy meets his cronies for some sort of old boys' get together. Meeting at around eight, they leave at throwing out time, half-cut. I want one of the tyres on his Chelsea Tractor knifed. Now listen up James, this is not to be done by you personally, you get a mate, and he needs to be well covered – cameras are everywhere. With a bit of luck the flat won't be noticed until he's driven a few yards and if he's full of booze, he might be stupid enough to get the police out and then get nicked for drink and drive. Mind you, the local clan will no doubt cover it up. Whatever, it's the hassle I'm aiming for and two or three other little events will follow, for example, he's devoted to his lovely big dog that might tuck into some meat that's a bit off".

"Crikey Luke you've really got it in for him. Sounds easy enough – how much did you say the stamps are worth?"

"James, if you're going to make the squash court, it's time you went, I'll walk to the end of the drive with you. Ah yes, squash. Let me tell you that the only reason I've slipped down the ladder to the box you've just entered is my time away travelling when I couldn't get a game. Here's the challenge. If you take more than two points off me in any one game, I'll slip an extra stamp in the envelope. Shake on it. By the way, almost forgot, Kyaw tells me your grandad's getting quite frail now and refusing to accept any help. So, I have a second proposition for you. If anything, and certainly in a year or two's time, you might consider it superior to our first little arrangement. His living quarters are nicely tucked away overlooking the garden and are completely self-contained. After he's passed on, we're happy for you to treat them as your own, at any rate let's say for five years or so. No need to bother with any paperwork. A fit and handsome guy like you must surely have a loving girlfriend and between you and me I'll slip a few choice films in a wall safe that's in there. As we get to know each other better, you'll learn there's always a condition to accompany my good nature and here it is. Until your grandad is no more, or has to enter a home, you'll visit him every weekend and stay at least a couple of hours; persuade him to let the social services come in to check things out and decide what help he needs. You will regard this as a firm commitment. One last thing, after each visit make a point of updating Kyaw. She worries about him and I need to put her mind at rest especially at this time, she's sixteen weeks pregnant - could you tell? Well, thanks for popping in, have a good sweat".

*

Luke wasn't into meetings, if one added up all the cumulative time spent from each attendee, the lack of productivity was appalling. The online platforms improved time utilisation if executives were scattered, but his team were not and the inability to pick up nuances of feelings far outweighed any time savings. Aside from that, his capacity to fix outcomes ahead of discussion was constrained severely. Raising a hand in one's image box to catch the attention of the leader was so incredibly childish, in fact it took him back to school days and his natural instinct to rail against authority. Had it not been for the constant demands of a progress report from Great Uncle Harold, God knows where he would have ended up. No top of the class, no qualifications at all and absolutely no university. But this was different. The two-year time horizon agreed with Siobhan meant he had to set his priorities, decide on a roadmap to specific outcomes and, most important of all, cost the resources to get there. That's why he was meeting the consultant in her office, away from prying eyes and with no distractions.

The consultant placed a spreadsheet on the table and suggested to Luke that it should form the basis of this discussion on future strategy. Luke was genuinely taken aback perhaps because he had developed his business interests on an ad hoc basis albeit discussing each move with her in advance. The way the business interests were laid out made him appear a titan of industry, which he knew he wasn't. Still, he was impressed: he felt his chest swell slightly. The consultant suggested that he talked through each of the five strands to his activity and together they could brainstorm where the business was heading and decide what action to take. As ideas emerged, she would make notes on the laptop. Luke studied the first line of the spreadsheet and started to talk.

"As they say, the first time is always the best and stays with you for ever".

"Luke this meeting is deadly serious, you're not down at the pub bantering with the lads now".

"Sorry, sorry, you have my full attention. What I mean is London Wall (UK) Ltd was a first foray into the business world and I regard it as my true love to be supported whatever else might be around".

"Right, stop there. That's the first mistake of the morning. Feelings and sentimentality – out with both. How you got started is irrelevant. It's today and tomorrow we're here to discuss. Here's an example: I gave advice to a huge combine in the Far East called *Horse and Carriage Pte Ltd* - they assembled jet engines. You see, the owners never forgot their heritage but how they'd moved on! That first business might remain your mainstay, but it might not. Luke, that's what this session is all about. Now, let's discuss where we're at with LW UK"

"So be it, my esteemed adviser. By the way, you're in a bloody awful mood this morning, did he kick you out of bed? I'll start, jump in whenever. That, so far, we've not lost a single client is no fluke. Eric is top notch, his code sticks and with responsibility for modifications, Murray is equally on the ball. Just as important is that once Becky has gone through our whole suite of applications, the decision makers, invariably of the male gender, want her back. So, retention has not been a problem and even accepting that she has broadened our client base, I regard this ability to hold what we gain as fundamental to the business success. There is the issue of extending the geographical base beyond the UK and I'd welcome your view on that. The way I've thought it through is that for better or worse we left the EU and yet for all the political bluster at the time, London remains the main financial hub of the world, with the possible exception of New York and Hong Kong. The decision to hold our nerve and concentrate Becky and her team on establishing a firm foothold amongst the City of London investment bankers has proved a wise one".

"OK that's good and the figures support your thinking. Before we move on, what about America and Hong Kong?"

"If you'll forgive my choice of language, it's a sodding mess. We are well out of it. Who'd have thought those over the pond could descend so swiftly into a load of Charlies? Blinded by their world of technological innovation, what didn't they see coming? I'll answer my own question. Covid-19, Covid-20, racial riots and the Chinese usurping of just about everything they'd invented. I tell you, if we had gone for that office base in New York, we'd be sitting here deciding how to handle my creditors and how to pacify a weeping Kyaw. As regards Hong Kong, I mentioned the mighty Chinese empire, need I go on? I'll say this, it validates the point you made in the early days. Most sports matches are won because the opponent makes mistakes, not because of one's own blinding winners. My competitors can have the USA and Hong Kong and good luck to them".

"Let's move on. You texted about an exit strategy. So soon?"

"I'm thinking about two years. I want my money out while still young and fit enough to enjoy it and if practically possible I see Becky and Eric buying me out. If LW is worth more than they can finance, well at least their shares will set them up for life. Plus, I'm not stupid enough to believe that some products won't hit the market to our detriment. I'd like you to take this as your next job. Under various scenarios of growth and profitability, what will the company be worth in two years' time? Draft the terms of reference yourself, I trust you, we've worked together long enough".

"You know Luke, when we were first introduced, I never imagined this young whippersnapper becoming my most important client. I value your faith in my advice and appreciate how you've taken my criticisms on board. My plea is that you keep those feet anchored to the ground. I have a feeling we'll look back on today and mark it an important step in achieving your ambitions. Let's turn to Australia".

"As you know, we have five clients currently and having just returned from Perth, I'm full of enthusiasm and, believe me, it's not misplaced. Becky thinks the temporary member of staff will make the grade and so she'll be appointed General Manager. More importantly, she has what it takes to demonstrate our systems. Moreover, we seem to have the embryo of a sales team. Becky seems to have impressed some important guys in Perth and made a promising start in Sydney. I intend to keep sending her out, certainly for a couple of years. But, here I go again, there's a job for you on the legal set-up. My feeling is that our business needs to be a wholly-owned Australian one. They're surprisingly parochial out there. Can you sort it?"

"I'll take a look. Let's talk about the envisaged branch network run from Perth. Yes, Sydney is the big city and an obvious choice and there's no harm in keeping the registered office in Perth but as regards it controlling overseas' branches, well, take me through your logic".

"I see Singapore as the hub for the Far East. Its financial reputation is sound and we see more and more bank and investment house migration from Hong Kong due to the influence of China which, no matter what sanctions are applied, is hellbent on gaining absolute control. Switching our Bank of China client from the UK to Singapore would, on its own, pay for setting up an office".

"Luke, I think you're right and also Australia has to keep China sweet because of its dependence on the export of its minerals. Running any business you gain on the Chinese mainland out of Singapore or even Perth would make sense. And you're correct in that we can't own a Chinese company and so this structure is strategically sound. But, I don't see why one would want a branch in Europe (Brussels) run via the Perth set-up – not exactly close are they?"

"Perhaps my strategic thinking is now running ahead of yours. Seriously though, geography is irrelevant to the risk management game plus I'd better come clean on a longer-term scheme that just might make sense. Remember for the UK side, I've this dream of offloading in about two years' time. Well, accepting that the number of clients we win in Australia itself will be limited, I see no reason why the Perth office shouldn't administer our business in both the Far East and Europe".

"Fine if, I suspect, a bit fanciful but that doesn't answer my question about Europe".

"It is a bit *on-a-wing-and-a-prayer* as my great uncle used to say but I want to get to Brussels soon to see that Alice woman. As you know she's had the coppers snooping around our offices and I intend to find out why but the real reason is to get Becky to demo. a few banks. If we can pick up EU-centric clients in due course then why not run the licence fees out of Aussie? Is that where my - sorry our, future lies? I'm not exactly a stranger to the West Coast. Considering the staggering fees some consultants charge, one would think at least coffee could be supplied when VIPs enter their hallowed portals. A couple of chocolate biscuits wouldn't go amiss either".

"Sorry Luke, I find these sessions with you so intense that everything else goes out of my head - I'll ring. It will of course go on my bill as expenses! Right, we move onto my favourite business, the money transfer. It was of course my recommendation, but even so, making it work in practice using the risk management software has been, well I have to say, quite brilliant. Inserting a nominal market-maker and broker into the cycle of what otherwise is a normal monetary transaction has actually worked as I thought it ought to. But you mentioned having cold feet. Why?"

"Well it's these bloody stupid bureaucratic watchdog types; pity they've nothing more productive to do. That Alice woman I referred to earlier seems to have her knife into me. Why can't she leave the past behind? They had success on solving an old crime and it's gone to their heads. If she was just an ordinary Dick I wouldn't care a toss; them against me – only one winner there. I make dosh for the UK economy. I ask you what contribution do they make? Not content with heading up a large fraud unit at the Met. she's got seconded to Interpol in Brussels. Hell has no fury like – not a woman scorned exactly but one thwarted. She more or less came straight out with it. Anyway, you know me, not exactly one to sit back while one of her backroom boys finds a lead. I've asked Becky to put things on a proper footing".

"How?"

"It's up to her, she's motivated enough now I've passed a slug of the preference shares over. There's probably a couple of options, either we set up two pukka companies or form an alliance with two existing ones. The first would attract the scrutiny of the regulatory sods and the second cut our profit margin. Neither is attractive but let's see what she suggests. Actually, you'd better have a session with her since either way will add to our costs and affect your profit forecast".

"OK and Luke while cleaning things up a bit, we really should get Kyaw to do some actual work to justify her salary".

"I know but it's tricky. I can't let her into what Eric and Becky are doing, it would pass to Pearl and whizz round the grapevine in seconds. Wonder if I could get Becky to start her off building a database of potential customers, perhaps ones we definitely don't want, so if it leaks it won't matter. If only I could get Alice, Marcus and the lot of them off my back".

"Cheer up, I'll ring for coffee and sandwiches; we'll move onto the healthcare side this afternoon".

"Fine, I need a break. Oh, first though, an update for you. I've had those false doorbells fitted so we can see who's lurking around the Old Hall and pick up any sounds and I also had a few installed in the old man's flat. He's getting quite weak now and if he falls or anything, Kyaw will see it on the control monitor. Did I mention telling his grandson he could use the place for a few years once Fred has passed on? I might get him to do a few jobs once he's settled in. History repeats itself – years ago I ran errands for my Great Uncle Harold, looking back it did me the world of good. While you're fixing lunch I'll just nip outside and get my daily update from the Perth office".

"Isn't it late at night there?"

"Yes, but our new GM likes to fill me in before she retires, or more likely finishes her beer on the quayside; touching isn't it?"

The consultant was surprised how long Luke took to FaceTime his manager in Australia. Things must be going really well for them to talk this length of time. Still, her fee clock was ticking away nicely. Yet she couldn't help wondering how far this gravy train was travelling. Ah, here he comes now and looking very pleased with himself.

"Luke, were the sandwiches OK? I had the smoked salmon brought in specially. Obviously what you have in Burma is beyond my brief but I have a few questions to keep you on your toes".

"Fire away and yes the salmon went down a treat. I'm really lucky to have the oriental dishes prepared by Kyaw but on occasions it's great to eat some real food. Oops, shouldn't have said that – sorry wife".

"Has anyone ever mentioned that you can be a real bastard at times? Oops, shouldn't have said that – sorry top client. Luke, I've now got my serious hat on. When will you have some idea what your fifteen percent of the robot business might be worth? I ask because of tax since with dividends from that company added to your consultancy fees, there might be a case for keeping some money over there. Secondly, the new rules allow up to thirty-five percent foreign ownership. Try levering your stake up a bit".

"Good point. I'll ask Kyaw's sister Garma to look into the tax position and now I think about it, she's met U Aung who's friendly with the University Rector. Perhaps Aung will make a case for me, especially now we're taking more students through his charity. You don't miss much do you? Don't answer that. I'll lead on the UK robotics idea. You'll think I've finally flipped but what about this for a forecast: Luke says his company which licences a system that uses robots to extract and transplant in vivo a human lung by remote control, will make him very rich. I'm pleased to get that off my chest (no pun intended). Now, the caveats. It will be expensive in terms of software development hours and risky because the business model assumes an existing competent manufacturer will not only agree to produce the robotics, but is willing and able to persuade the NHS to purchase the kit. Nevertheless, I have all the source code needed to make specific modifications of kidneys to lungs and I'm minded to pull Murray off London Wall to head up a Robotics team. I'm told he spends time with Kyaw when I'm away and this will be a kind of thank you. Although whether my gratitude will be reciprocated is open to doubt once he learns what's involved".

"Luke, are you really onto something that good?"

"You know the ways of business, some you win and some you don't, but yes. In five years' time you'll dine out as the consultant who pushed a young man who won a local award into being a national entrepreneurial star. And won't the plods hang their heads in shame?

"Meantime, here's a metaphor for you. Can you see the Burmese maids closing the window shutters and do you know why? It's because they sense a gathering storm long before it arrives.

"I have to go. Got a session with Becky this evening. Here's a key code to a 12P network, put your notes there and extract the action points with an estimate of your time and fee. Destroy that word document".

*

Adrian was thinking it was a long time since he'd had such a good evening. What a surprise and they'd kept it under their hats until nearly throwing out time. An oil on canvas of the famous stallion *Grey Stamfordian* by the local artist Miles Cromford. He hadn't even realised he'd been chairman of the *John Stoppard Charity* for twenty-five years and it wasn't as if there was much work involved: just to agree what proportion of the annual rent to pay out and how much to give to each *deserving poor of the parish.* One last round before the bell and out he stepped into the stormy night. If that bitterly east wind didn't sober him up, then nothing would. Out of the back door, turn sharp left and up the old brick steps, steady man – didn't there used to be a handrail, must have dropped off and with the picture under his left arm – hmm, a bit tricky - he must remember to have a word with Jack, needs fixing. He turned right along the garden path, nodded politely to the three-hundred-year-old Mulberry tree and walked under the stone arch to reach the rear car park. Driving down the side of The King William he sensed something was wrong with the old bus. It would be the cross wind and he was in luck, the traffic lights were on green and he turned left onto High Street. Ten minutes and he'd be home to that roaring log fire and his nightcap. Halfway across the bridge which spanned the swollen River Welland the Land

Rover Discovery swerved to the right and into the path of a *Lincs Fresh* lorry which unceremoniously pushed the intruder over the stone wall. The Discovery plunged into the fast-flowing river. Adrian was aware of a spinning sensation before his head hit the driver-side window. Blackness.

Six

Tristan was so excited. That the ten minutes to midday train from London was running eight minutes late didn't help Pearl calm him down. Jumping up and down, holding her left hand and then her right, trying to edge closer to the platform to peer down the track, she was wishing she'd left him with a friend. Not that Mandy showed the slightest interest in events, due to Pearl's second regret of buying an ice-cream that was far too big and melting far quicker than Mandy could cope with. What should have been a joyful occasion was turning into a nightmare not helped by the jostling of Brighton residents here to greet the early season tourists. Pearl was thinking that it was always the same, the person you're here to meet is never the first off the train or even the second or the third. Why was she so nervous? Tristan was doing his best to pull her arm out of its socket. Then, he was gone, racing up the platform dodging each person in his path with a skill that belied his six years. He unceremoniously threw himself into the arms of the lady in the yellow dress. The lady who had tears streaming down her cheeks; Naing was back.

By the time Naing had extricated herself from the young boy, straightened her dress and wiped her eyes Pearl was standing by her side complete with pushchair boasting a little girl covered in pink ice-cream. They hugged but Pearl had more of a *glad you have arrived safely* feeling than one of *you should never have gone away, God how I've missed you.* But there was no time to reflect, Tristan was holding onto Naing's hand as if life depended on it, Mandy was trying her best to escape the containing straps of her pushchair and somehow two suitcases had to be pulled along. No onlooker could possibly have guessed how two nearing-middle-age ladies with two young children came to be leaving Brighton railway station on this July summer's day. Even less, what lay in store.

For Mandy, nothing had changed: just another lady helping her fill the plastic buckets with sand. It was different for Tristan whose questions centred on how Naing had stepped out of the *talking screen* to be *really here*. Naing had described in detail her first flight in the aeroplane to Bangkok and then the second much longer one to the big city of London, before coming on the train that he, Mummy and Mandy had waited for. Tristan still held her hand as if to prove she couldn't possibly be the face on the phone each Saturday morning. In fact, it took finishing a one-hundred piece jigsaw and her help with two pages of his colouring book, to finally convince him she was actually there. Eventually, an hour or so after his normal time, the little boy fell asleep while still holding Naing's hand. Perhaps it was the lack of sleep on the bumpy flight from Bangkok, perhaps the sight of his beautiful innocent face, perhaps the sheer emotion of a return to where she had been so happy. Who knows, but she stayed rooted to the chair by his bedside and very quietly let the tears flow.

As discreetly as possible, Pearl had watched Naing and Tristan all afternoon. She understood; something that only a few months ago could never have happened, in fact had. That is why she waited patiently in the garden for Naing to come down from the bedroom and join her. The heat of the day had been replaced by a warm and balmy evening. The white wine rested regally in its ice-sleeve at the centre of the bamboo table and for a few minutes both ladies sat in silence. Pearl poured the wine and with her forefinger gently tapped the tabletop.

"Because this was your parting gift, I hunted it out to welcome you home. Naing, if you harboured any worries that Tristan had missed you, well, from the moment you stepped off that train, he must have swept all doubts aside and with absolutely no prompting from me. With only a couple of weeks before your flat is ready, you could have stayed here, there was no need to use Airbnb".

"Pearl, I know, but we need space to sort ourselves out. I've had loads of time to think things through and I just feel that getting involved again or at any rate so soon after my return would be a mistake. Please agree, it is so important to me".

"Of course I agree. You need time to get settled in and take over the dentist practice and, well, you can see how I'm fixed. But, none of that hides the fact that I'm very pleased you're back. I don't know how you've managed but I've not found what I would call a proper friend since you left and it hasn't helped that Kyaw has become increasingly remote. In fact – oh well never mind, we can talk about that once you're up and running".

"I want to talk about Kyaw. She's one of the main reasons I decided to come back; remember it was the two of us that persuaded her to give Luke a second chance after that horrid business with his great uncle and now I worry we made a bad mistake".

"Well, I know for sure she hasn't left the Old Hall for some time now but, to be fair, she says it's only because there's so much work to do and not just looking after their home, she's taken on a big project concerning one of the businesses. I suppose that's why she doesn't travel with him anymore, then again, it's really none of my business. Have you been in direct contact with her?"

"Yes Pearl I have and just speaking in our native tongue has revealed a few things. Listen to this; she told me that the reason she was surprised at getting pregnant had nothing to do with forgetting to take her morning-after pill but because she couldn't remember the last time they had made what she called *proper love*. If that doesn't set alarm bells ringing, then I don't know what does. Another thing, which I expect you already know, is that her mother isn't coming over for the birth. And, note this Pearl, Kyaw definitely wanted her mother to be here. She told me it was the same with her graduation party when Luke thought a visit at a later date would suit her mother better. As you can guess, she didn't visit at all and it sounds to me like it won't happen this time either. Something is not right and I intend to find out what. Once settled, I'm going to pay her a surprise visit. If Kyaw doesn't know I'm coming, then he won't either".

"I can't believe I'm saying this but be careful. I feel increasingly that Luke might have inherited some of that Whitby bad blood. Oh dear, I do hope not. I wonder if I could come with you. Hmm, it would have to be a weekend so I could ask Marcus to stay over with the children. Perhaps it's the effect of this second glass of wine but I'm starting to feel a chill run down my spine – it's not the evening air either. I was only saying to Marcus last week how odd it was that no sooner had Luke learned of the forthcoming baby than he whizzed off to Australia".

"Well, let's hope we're both wrong. Tell me, how is Marcus?"

"Having signed the lease on an apartment down on the Brighton front, he's as my daddy would have said, *like a cat with two tails*".

"He'll be around a lot more now then? Have you two …..?"

"No, of course not, silly. I told you how it would be before you left. Naing, listen, I don't want to talk about it. The past is the past. I have my two lovely children and for the first time in my life I feel fulfilled and even happier now you're back. With a great deal of help from Marcus, my first novel is finished and I've made a start on the second. Daddy would have been proud of me - I feel sure of that. Look, I'll get a taxi. Why don't you leave the two big bags here and we three will nip them over to your b&b tomorrow morning? Tristan and Mandy would love to see where you're staying. Oh, one other bit of news. It seems that when we were all involved in that cold case, Neil, the policeman, approached Marcus about becoming an adviser of some sort. Since then they have become friends and he's mentioned it again. I think Marcus might take some sort of role. If he does, what's the betting they ask him to look into what Luke is up to – I don't know, it's just a feeling. Good old Uber, he says ten minutes".

"Thanks Pearl, well here's something we can talk about in the morning. No sooner had I resigned from my job with the dotcom charity than Kyaw's younger sister, Garma, replaced me. And guess who fixed that? Luke of course. That man seems to straddle the world, well, the parts we know anyway. I think he caught Aung on the defensive, pointing out that my job wasn't agreed by all the trustees so *quid pro quo* as they say, I want Garma in. But Pearl, this Luke guy should not underestimate my father. He's coming over to call a full face-to-face meeting of the trustees and he intends to take a careful look at what the charity students are actually working on in Luke's risk management business. I say that because one has told Aung she's involved in modifying money transfer software - that is quite different from what she was supposed to be doing".

"Ah, your car is here. I wonder if somehow we can time things so that you, me and Aung can meet Luke sooner rather than later. I mean, have a trustee meeting but support Aung if necessary and find out if Kyaw does have a problem. Have a good sleep and see you tomorrow".

*

A visit by Luke to Becky's office was rare. He believed in delegation and she liked to do things her own way. But here he was and absorbed by the wall charts.

"I have to say Becky that when we first met at Uni. and I learned of your specialisation as a software technical writer, never in my wildest dreams did I see this flair for marketing, though of course you marketed yourself pretty well".

"Flatterer – carry on my esteemed boss".

"This graph of the growing client base and monthly revenue from London Wall says it all, if a picture paints a thousand words and all that – not to mention if a face could launch a thousand ships – overlaying the Australian side is just a brilliant idea – Christ, it's almost caught up".

"You're in a good mood this morning, must be Kyaw's expanding waistline and thoughts of a son and heir".

"Becky, have you had a session with the consultant?"

"Yesterday, just about to put a note on the dark web. It didn't take long. We agreed to form an alliance with an existing broker and market maker and work under their names. In fact she's doing it, hope that's OK with you, her firm has contacts it seems. Once the terms are negotiated she'll re-work the profit spreadsheet. We might have to increase our commission on money transfer to pull the cost back but we can discuss that once we get that far. You are right, it does need doing, one of my guys is sure we've had at least one bogus player. Of course our security stopped the transaction but someone out there is having a poke around. Oh, and just to add to your morning's joy, I think we might have found our manufacturer for the robotics. Bit of a fluke really. I was reading the report of the official inquiry into the COVID 20 response and …"

"Sorry, you were what? Just because you're now a Chief Executive Officer, doesn't mean you're obligated to read Government reports!"

"Well, you know Mr Brown, my mind hovers over such a wide range of topics. No, seriously, there was a reason. I wanted to find out who was rated best performer in producing mechanical ventilators. The fluke arose since it was Dobsons and they're down the road on the Chesterfield industrial estate. The chief executive is interested and when we have our software ready he's agreed to make a prototype. Actually, Luke, I know him but that's between you and me".

"Seems to me we should have met earlier, just think if I'd married you, then together we would have conquered the world, still, we are doing that anyway. Becky, I actually visited your inner sanctuary for a reason. Look, I realise how busy you are but this is something you can offload if you like. I want to arrange an awayday or whatever it's called. One day should do but a mixture of serious stuff and a treat. For some reason I was thinking about Windsor so we can maybe take in a river trip or perhaps visit the Great Park. I've had this strategy meeting with the consultant and she's agreed to make a presentation. Timing would be middle to late August and obviously it'll have to fit in with summer holiday commitments. So, we two plus Eric, Murray, the consultant obviously and whoever you get to make the arrangements. Actually, you need to nominate a second in command and bring him or her along. Oh, nearly forgot, we ought really to invite Siobhan. Sod the cost and anyway she can come with us to Brussels and learn how you pull in new clients. After all, if Europe is to come under Perth, it makes perfect sense for her to learn the patch. Must go, got a conference call to Bank of Singapore at ten our time."

*

"Hi Luke, it's Aung speaking. I'm in a taxi queue at East Midlands Airport, sorry I couldn't alert you before but I've had trouble with the paperwork at Bangkok airport, throwback to the virus apparently and up to the last minute I wasn't sure they'd let me board. Anyway, I'm here and staying at the Priory for a few days. I want to talk to my students, discuss your charges and speak to a few local universities about their postgraduate positions. Oh, and while here, I'll call a meeting of the charity trustees. Naing's coming to see Kyaw so I can book a small conference room at the hotel and it's possible she may have Pearl with her if Marcus can babysit. Of course that will rule him out but we can FaceTime if any contentious issues crop up".

"Aung, hang on a minute".

"Sorry Luke, my taxi's here, I'll call you tomorrow".

*

Kyaw was wondering if there was some natural law stating that life could never be perfect. There was always an element that came along to spoil things. After the honeymoon Luke had found their wonderful home and given her loads of money to spend on just the sort of furniture she wanted. And of course, they had agreed to take two or three years to build the two businesses before starting a family. And what had happened? She had become pregnant. It wasn't a disaster. Back home in Burma, a well-connected girl of her age would have had several babies by now, and although Luke pretended to be pleased, she knew he saw it as a setback. He had ideas which became plans and those plans always worked out. He was very successful that way and she was so proud of him. Did he consider her pregnancy as his first failure? Whatever, since last February all his attention and energy had centred on the business. He was still her Luke of course but with working so hard they spent little time together.

And now this second upset. Luke might not be around much but he had made sure she was very comfortable. This garden furniture for example, bamboo to make her feel at home with the super-padded cushions, and insisting her friends visited whenever they wanted. And the weather; the forecasters were saying it might be a record for the number of sunshine hours – all through July and now the first two weeks in August. However, the weather was one thing, the atmosphere quite another and all because of that meeting of the charity trustees. Naing had told her all about it. Luke had been so aggressive; it had taken them by surprise. And, without telling them in advance, he'd entered the room with another person who he introduced as his consultant who was there simply as an observer. Apparently, the meeting got off to a bad start with Luke saying he had major reservations with the main item on the agenda. This concerned greater diversity of company internship which he interpreted as meaning that Aung wanted to send Burmese students to businesses other than his own. Aung reprimanded him for jumping ahead and proceeded to read his report under Agenda Item No 1 *Student progress London Wall*.

Naing said her father wasn't criticising the quality of work being undertaken but its application. The contract stipulated risk management for a good reason. In particular, the Rector of Yadanabon University saw this discipline as part of a nascent financial service industry. Luke knew this perfectly well. Hadn't Aung personally introduced him to potential clients of the software application? In his one-to-one interview with each student it was clear that their project assignments had changed. Some were recoding part of a money-transfer application whilst others were part of a robotics team. In response Luke accepted that some of the wording in the contract needed updating but U Aung (Naing realised her father had noted the more formal name and was displeased) should appreciate the wider experience gained by the internees. In relation to the Rector, he advised her father to confer with him. He might find the Rector's reaction to be at variance with U Aung. Naing thought the tension then increased partly because the so-called consultant observer was typing at speed on her laptop, notwithstanding Aung's glances in her direction, and partly after her father expressed surprise at the increasing costs borne by the charity. He had failed to reconcile the salary element of that cost with the pay each student actually received.

Pearl told Kyaw that in her opinion Luke's attitude did not arise from Aung's criticism which, in fact, he'd handled well, but because he'd been taken by surprise. He hadn't known that Aung was arriving or that she and Naing had planned to visit. It was obvious to her that normally Luke had his world under tight control but this time he'd been caught on the hop.

Kyaw's thoughts were interrupted; her best friend Samantha had arrived and was crossing the lawn.

"Kyaw, don't even think of getting up and thank goodness you've seen sense at last and stayed in the shade, I must say, propped up with all those padded cushions, you really are the *Lady of the Manor* which is just how it should be. I looked at the forecast before popping over and now we're in mid-August apparently this is the seventh week of pretty much cloudless skies. At least that shower earlier this morning has freshened things up a bit. I thought I told you to stay put".

"Sam, thanks for coming over, my mind wanders a bit when I'm left alone for too long, I need to move and there's a tea-tray ready in the conservatory – just need to boil the kettle and I made a sponge cake this morning, back in a minute".

Once the excitement had died down Kyaw freely admitted to her friend that it had been her own silly fault. Carrying the tray with both hands and stepping down from the conservatory onto the grass which was still damp, she slipped and fell. Sam sprang from her lounger and sprinted to her friend's side.

"Oh God Kyaw are you alright? I should have fetched the tea myself, what was I thinking? Let me help you, grab my arm". "Thanks Sam, there must have been a wet patch that I didn't see. No need to worry, I'm a bit shaken that's all. I can walk back to the seat, not helpless, no damage done. I've still four weeks to go and they did say I should take plenty of exercise but I guess that didn't include falling flat on my face".

"Kyaw, never mind all that, lie on the sunbed and put your feet on this cushion. That's an order and stay there for half an hour. I'll go and clear up the tea things, looks like one of the cups is broken. We'll start all over again and this time, I'll do the honours. In a luxurious abode such as The Old Hall, there must be a spare cup somewhere. Good job Luke isn't around, I'd probably be marched off the estate. My heart's racing, next time you pull that trick, give me five minutes notice to get prepared".

*

Kyaw awoke with a start, - *what was that* – she turned on the bedside light and looked at the small alarm clock, 2.27 a.m. She had an unusual feeling in her stomach, *must have been the baby moving, it's much too early for anything else.* At this advanced stage of her pregnancy, Kyaw knew her sleep was important. She turned off the light but couldn't get comfortable. On several occasions she must have dozed off but something she had not experienced before, was happening. By 6.00 a.m. she'd made up her mind. She rang Luke. The reason for a delay in pickup must be due to calling a wrong number since she thought she heard a high pitch sound but no, Luke answered.

"Kyaw sweetheart, it can't possibly be the baby, it's not due for four weeks, you know that and of course you want me with you but today's the conference with all my top people and I have a full schedule. Look, remember what the midwife suggested if you got too uncomfortable; take a couple of Paracetamol. Sorry, but I really must go, still have some preparation to do". Kyaw heard the noise on the line again and then it went dead.

By 8 a.m. Kyaw was in pain similar to cramp-like period pains and then backache. She started to panic and rang Luke again. His mobile rang and rang but there was no pickup. She was finding it hard to think straight. Then she decided.

"Pearl, what should I do? I'm feeling desperate".

"Kyaw, the most important thing is you must stay calm, it sounds to me as if you're actually in labour although very early, have you had an accident of any sort, no, don't answer that, it's not important. Right, listen, ring the midwife straight away and I'll get hold of Naing, she'll definitely come up".

Having spoken to Pearl and knowing Naing would arrive during the day, Kyaw felt less worried and it helped when the midwife started asking questions that she could answer. *Had her waters broken – no, did she have backache – yes, feeling nauseous – yes, stomach cramps – yes.* "Kyaw, for the baby's sake as well as your own, you must try to stay calm. You are early but it's not unusual. Get a friend to take you to the hospital and I'll text them.

Within half an hour Samantha arrived and together they prepared the overnight bag. Sam swore under her breath at the morning traffic, she was thinking *is this due to that fall yesterday, I'll feel terrible if anything goes wrong, poor Kyaw, why isn't her mother here? Where's that sod Luke, he doesn't give a shit about her, I've seen it in his eyes for months.* Having given up with the phone, Kyaw texted Luke, *where are you? Baby's coming, need you here with me.*

The clock in the main reception area of Crowden General Hospital read 10.25 a.m. and Kyaw's phone rang. It wasn't Luke. It was Naing.

"Kyaw darling I'm leaving now. It might take five hours, don't worry and do exactly as you're told – Garuhcite par".

Kyaw held onto her friend's arm and together they walked down the main corridor with passages running off to right and left and arrows and signs everywhere – *for God's sake where is the Maternity Unit. W*ater was running down her legs and into her shoes making her feel very uncomfortable and now, for the first time since the early morning, miserable. "Sam, you will stay with me won't you? I don't want to be alone, I'm afraid". Sam didn't reply, she was frantically searching for the Maternity sign.

The Maternity reception area was surprisingly quiet. Kyaw had expected lots of women like herself all panicking and calling for attention, but no, just the one lady behind her screen asking questions, typing on her computer keyboard. Within five minutes an assistant in a blue uniform led them to a cubicle and asked Kyaw to get undressed and put on the gown. It was at this point that Kyaw realised for the first time that she really was about to have her baby, there was no going back and there was no Luke. But there was activity. A middle-aged nurse of ample proportions bustled into the cubicle, introduced herself as Claire (which, Sam whispered to Kyaw a little later, could not be a case of mistaken identity since it was emblazoned over her left and sizeable breast pocket) and proceeded to take a sample of blood before attaching Kyaw's arm to a small and wall-mounted electronic gadget which indicated that while her blood pressure was slightly raised there was nothing to worry about.

Thinking back, Sam reckoned that perhaps twenty minutes or so passed before a tall slim lady appeared. She was not sporting a name tag presumably since a badge spelling out *Senior Midwife* made such an adornment redundant. Actions speak louder than words, here enters the strong silent type and Kyaw knew instinctively she was in good hands, hands that were now feeling her abdomen for the position of the baby. She then placed a foetal stethoscope onto Kyaw's extended abdomen and put her ear to it. "I'm listening for baby's heartbeat and it's fine, your baby is strong. I see from the notes that you are four weeks early but the baby will be fully developed. Your contractions will become stronger and more frequent so I'll give you an injection of Pethidine for the pain. What I need you to do next is have a bath and afterwards (she turned to Sam) move about the room. Do not lie on the bed. It is important to stay upright and keep moving.

Time passed, Sam phoned her husband to meet the children from school, Kyaw sent two more texts to Luke, she was getting agitated, where was he? She never thought pain could be like this. Her contractions were more frequent and lasting up to a minute each. She cried out "Oh Luke, I need you here, I can't be alone, it's not fair of you to abandon me, where are you? Sam, please stay with me". Sam was saying would she feel more comfortable leaning over the edge of the bed and would it help if she rubbed her back and all Kyaw kept repeating was *where is he* and the contractions were getting more frequent, at least every five minutes. Then Kyaw's mobile pinged. It was not Luke but Naing.

"I'm within half an hour, is Luke there?"

"No, Naing he isn't, please hurry".

At five minutes past four the door opened and Naing entered accompanied by a nurse. Kyaw asked the midwife if her best friend could stay with her as she couldn't contact her husband. Sam hugged Kyaw and kissed her on the cheek.

"Now your friend is here I must go home, keep pushing, keep trying hard, it won't be long now. Soon it will be all over and you'll have a beautiful baby".

Kyaw was leaning over the bed. Her fists pummelled the mattress on each contraction. Naing had a reassuring arm around her friend's shoulder. At some point, neither could recall the time gap, Kyaw's mobile pinged. It was a text from Luke. *Phone been off during conference, leaving now.* Kyaw climbed onto the bed for the midwife to examine her, and this time the midwife could see the baby's head. The midwife was saying that as the baby is four weeks early, the birth won't take as long as if she was full term. She explained to Kyaw that as the contractions were getting stronger and more frequent, delivery was near. Kyaw was pleading for a second injection of Pethidine but the midwife refused as it could affect the baby's breathing. Instead Kyaw was offered gas and air. Naing held the mask over her friends face while she took a few breaths of gas.

"Where is my Luke?"

Naing wiped Kyaw's forehead and smoothed her hair.

"Why isn't he here?"

Kyaw started to panic and screamed with each contraction, she shouted for Luke and blamed him for the pain and agony.

"Why aren't you here? You'll miss seeing your child born – where is he Naing?"

It was early evening and Kyaw was getting very tired. The midwife said she was doing fine and was almost there. "Baby is coming. Just one big push".

"I can't I can't do it".

"Yes you can, you can do it – it won't be long now and you'll have a beautiful baby, push, push".

At just after eight on that early summer evening in that hospital so very far from Mandalay and with no mother and no husband to witness the event, a tiny baby girl entered the world.

Minutes later, Kyaw held her child and spoke to Naing in their native Burmese tongue. Roughly translated she said, "We don't need him anymore".

Seven

Aung had asked Pearl if he and Naing could visit one evening and talk about their visit to the East Midlands.

"Pearl, if we drift into our own tongue at times, I ask your forgiveness in advance, we're not being discourteous it's just that some thoughts can only be expressed that way, I'll do my best to interpret afterwards. Naing has told you about the birth and well, without wanting to appear unsympathetic, Kyaw and Luke are both adults and they'll have to sort themselves out. I don't suppose he's the first man to miss the birth of his child and won't be the last. In fact, I wasn't home when Naing was born. I want to test your reaction to an opinion I've formed about Luke, you've known him for a long time now and no doubt seen more than one side of his character. I start by asking myself this question, why was he so keen to replace Naing with Garma as a senior person in the charity? Yes, she is his sister-in-law and yes she has had administrative experience but I was quite capable of recommending a suitable person and the senior staff in his businesses comment on his ability to delegate. So, one would not expect him to interfere in the appointment of one of my key staff especially bearing in mind the language barrier. The answer is to get his own back. Although merely one trustee amongst a board, he spotted my error in giving a job to my daughter and pounced. He was gaining no obvious advantage except a psychological one. And that Pearl is my big worry".

"I do see where you're coming from but carry on".

"When I was a university lecturer I had a colleague on the humanities side who was fond of telling his students that no very wealthy man ever made his fortune by honest endeavour. He was exaggerating of course but intending to make a serious point. An entrepreneur was born to dodge and weave (Aung looked at Naing – *did I get that right?* - she nodded), defy convention, make a statement, in short be different. In the forward thrust, he or she leaves regulation, and sometimes the law, behind. As far as the go-getter is concerned, it's the powers that be and the legislators' job to catch up. I have just defined Luke Brown but there is one other ingredient. If he is beaten to the punch, it can't be left alone. He will not sit back and lick his wounds. It might take time but get even he must. I can add several examples to the replacement of Naing but one will do. The trustees of the charity agreed that our students should be paid but agreed to reimburse Luke's business. He didn't like that: they were learning and had free accommodation. So what did he do? He added a whopping so-called management fee to the re-charge. No need to seek approval of course, he just did it. So Pearl, that's my take on the character but also he's been playing fast and loose with what amounts to cheap labour. Having honed their software skills, our best students have been transferred to either the money-transfer operation or a highly secretive robotics department. Did he think I wouldn't find out or take no interest? We can add hubris to the mix.

"Another thing that one of our students picked up was the big push going on. The sales and marketing side is expanding rapidly with the CEO spending no more than a day a week at The Old Hall, most of the time she's in London and increasingly in Brussels. I just hope for Kyaw's sake that there are good business controls in place. One can't help wondering why Luke's in such a rush to make his fortune. None of my business of course but I've decided to find other UK companies and universities willing to take internees from Myanmar and I've told him so. It's for that reason I'm trying to extend my visa period. Now that Naing is back in her apartment, it's also going to be my base and we've discussed whether I might reside in the UK permanently. Pearl, I wanted you to be the first to know. I gather Marcus has a place in Brighton too. It'll be like old times – weekly reunions on the beach, all of you in your lightweight clothes and me shivering in five layers of wool. I was saying to Naing as we arrived, the only people missing from the old team will be Alice in London and the two policemen up North".

Pearl refreshed their drinks and smiled. "Dear Aung, in your precise depiction of the near future, the most important element is missing".

"Oh".

"Yes, for the very first time, Mandy and Tristan will have a grandad to hug".

Aung, removed his spectacles and asked for a tissue. Naing put her arm around his shoulder and for a while no-one spoke. Pearl broke the silence.

"You mentioned the two policemen up North well, I've a bit of news. Marcus and Neil who by the way has been promoted to Inspector, are now good friends and a bit of rivalry has developed. Marcus is convinced he'll be first to uncover any jiggery-pokery with Luke's business ventures and while Neil doesn't disagree, he says there's still a place for old-fashioned policing and their surveillance of The Old Hall will trip Luke up sooner rather than later".

"It's Scottish you know".

"Sorry, what is?"

"Jiggery-pokery".

"U Aung, go back to sleep! Actually, before you do and thinking back to the Dotcom charity, we should set up more internal controls, it's becoming a major enterprise and the last thing we want is Luke trying to take over or putting down any poison when you search for new outlets; I wouldn't put it past him. Is there merit in getting Garma over here? Perhaps a second person should be familiar with the UK set-up and wouldn't she love to see Kyaw's baby? Anyway, look at the time. I might have to throw father and daughter out to preserve my early bedtime. You may have forgotten but those two upstairs are early risers. Aung, as regards Luke's businesses, Marcus, Alice and Neil have hatched a plan. To use a bit of police language foisted on me by Marcus, *a few frighteners are imminent.* I love Neil's Yorkshire dialect as imitated by Marcus, *tha sees if pips'll squeak a bit".*

*

Luke's mobile pinged, it was a text from Jennie on reception. *Superintendent Macrae here to see you, shall I bring him in?*

"Well Superintendent, what a surprise and no appointment needed".

"Luke, hope it's OK to be informal, I was just passing, as salesmen always say, and thought I'd see if you were home – as it were. And what a home, and what an office, even blokes of my rank don't merit all this furniture and stuff – that's a framed picture of you receiving that business award isn't it? Hmm, very nice, very nice".

"Being in uniform, I take it this is no social visit".

"Afraid not, I'll come straight to the point, we're both busy men. Your uncle Adrian is dead. Judging by the ding-dong between you two at the graduation party, no tears will be shed. Am I correct?"

"Well it's a bit of a shock coming out with it just like that, obviously you don't do warm-ups. It's true we didn't get on but he was family and the last of his generation".

"Are you interested in how he died?"

"Yes of course".

"Late last night his vehicle fell into a swollen river. It was dragged out in the early hours and your uncle was inside. A forty-eight hour blackout has been imposed so the local police have a chance to gather information, find eyewitnesses and so on. The driver of the truck that hit the car is pretty shaken. Indications are that your uncle's four-wheel drive swerved into his path, but it's early days".

"Oh dear, had he been drinking?"

"Too soon to say. The forensics start today. At my level, there's an information swap on incidents like this. The first few hours are critical; running down any locals who might be involved, getting statements while the trail is hot and so on. One aspect that didn't need the white-coated crew was a very visible slash to the front off-side tyre. Fortunately, both the nearby hotel and high street have numerous camera placements so there's a good chance whoever's responsible will be spotted. You know Luke, no matter how many times one comes to someone's home to give bad news, it doesn't get easier. Normally, I'd have asked one of my constables to pop along but knowing the relationship, and I shouldn't be saying this really, your standing around these parts, it seemed the right thing to do. We often score through unintended consequences".

"Sorry?"

"Just turning over in my mind how many times things get out of control. Tyre slashing is usually a grudge thing. And look what results, a man lies in the mortuary. My colleague over in Peterborough tells me Adrian was a well-respected man, a pillar of the local community. Although not one himself, he was well known in the local Masonic Lodge. That reminds me, you were put forward here and turned down, pretty rare occurrence I'm told – being rejected. See what I mean about grudges? Still, with your business going international, who needs local contacts? Must be off, I'll get the station to keep you abreast of developments. Oh, and thanks for not offering coffee. Trying to cut down anyway. Have you heard the latest health scare? Stupid aren't they? One day red wine is good for you and the next day it makes you go blind. It's now seems that too much coffee leads to overconfidence. I'll see myself out".

*

"Hello, Miss Beatrix, that is correct isn't it? My appointment was at nine, sorry I'm a bit early, traffic this time of evening was lighter than I anticipated. I say, what a wonderfully secretive place you have here, I thought a cottage at the end of a winding lane only occurred in romantic novels. When I looked on Google Maps I assumed one would see the outline of Hardwick Hall but this vegetation blots the long view out – damson trees aren't they? My Mum used to make damson jam, I can taste it now".

"Come inside Noel, I have a cold beer waiting".

"Miss Beatrix, I have a confession to make. I'm only Noel for the purpose of my appointment. I hate false names, don't you? Most people around here know me as Detective Inspector Neil Collett and actually we have met before. Probably at a party of some sort, but you wouldn't have noticed me. Amazing what a difference clothes and a hairstyle make. Off duty I'm always low key, not jazzed up like this".

"OK Noel, Neil, whatever your name is, what do you want?"

"Not what you're offering young lady; a word to the wise. Working as a Dominatrix is legal – just. However, any lasting injuries, marks, bruises from spanking, that sort of thing is another matter entirely. Plus, the law insists on the client having what is called *an active mind to legally consent.* This statement is open to interpretation as you can imagine. The line between domination and being charged with prostitution is a thin one. Another aspect I came to advise you on is how your practice is regarded by overseas legislators. You've been travelling on business quite a lot. Australia and Belgium crop up on social media and what a Pandora's Box that can be. As you'll know all too well, what you post is one thing what a client might post quite another".

"Why are you here?"

"As I said, just a word to the wise. Hmm, no sign of a husband. Good evening Becky and give my regards to Luke".

*

The consultancy firm occupied the top floor of a newly built steel and glass office complex at the North end of Maid Marian Way, Nottingham City Centre. The most senior staff were located on the West side overlooking the Castle and it was into the large corner office that Alice was ushered by an immaculately groomed, smartly dressed, high-heeled young lady. Luke's consultant, the senior partner, was waiting.

"Good afternoon Deputy Commissioner, please take a seat. What can I do for you?"

"First an apology. Because I'm booked on the late afternoon flight from East Midlands to Heathrow, I can stay for thirty minutes at the most. I wanted a one-to-one with you about Rapidmoneyex.com".

"I see, that's Kyaw Brown's business".

"Is it? We'll let the ownership aspect pass for the time being. As you will have seen from my introductory note, I head white-collar crime at Interpol, Brussels office. Following a stream of intelligence, my staff have been looking into the trading practices of the business. The purpose of my visit is to advise you that a case is being opened and your firm should expect to be asked formally to co-operate. In the first instance this will be to answer, in writing, a series of questions".

"Deputy Commissioner, this firm acts as consultants to Rapid. We have no role in its management and take no responsibility for its actions".

"I am aware of that. However, your firm is a signatory to company formation documents and other regulatory papers. In law that makes this firm culpable should any fraud be uncovered. If you wish to challenge any assumptions made at this early stage, my advice is to make such representations without delay. I shall of course be visiting the office of Rapidmoneyex.com in the near future. Perhaps your receptionist could see me off the premises, I have a car waiting".

*

From: marcusclarke@icloud.com
To: eric@londonwall.co.uk
Subject   : screen shots

Hi Eric and hope you keep well. At least we both survived the latest virus possibly due to each of us being loners/hermits? Going through your latest screen shots and ever keen to learn, came across CFD's and buy/sell instructions. Is London Wall thinking of branching out from derivatives? Assume this was experimental work.

Fascinating stuff although far too risky for me. Interesting that my wife Alice and her team are looking into use of similar instruments and rapid trading paradigms, must be flavour of the month in fraud circles. BTW, hope you made a killing from the *Vertualteq* tip. Currently in an intensive research mode so may be a month before my next share tip. Bit of non-techie news. Leased an apartment in Brighton so why not pop down for a paddle sometime? Trust still keeping that boss of yours under control.

Kind regards MC

*

The electronic diary appointment read *5 p.m. Luke's office.* Both Becky and Eric were complaining; she in the middle of a report for an Icelandic bank and he debugging a release due out tomorrow.

"I know, I know – pressure, pressure, but your stuff is on hold for half-an-hour max, promise. Let me shoot first on a couple of things and then we'll have a war cabinet. I thought the away day went well, we all know what's on the go and at what pace. And thanks for making Siobhan welcome. Eric, it was kind of you not to interrupt when she made a couple of mistakes in her presentation, much appreciated – we all have to learn. A bit of feedback, while we had our day off, her partner got two appointments in Sydney and Siobhan changed her flight to demonstrate. She is very positive on a win with both finance houses. The second development which will help with the war effort we're coming onto, came from left field. A woman who runs the constituency office of our local MP wants him to visit us on a tour of local success stories. Apparently it was a suggestion from Dobsons on the Chesterfield Industrial Estate. You'll be amused at this. She stressed that on no account must any donation to the party be mentioned. Following the big sleaze scandal last year, strictly out of bounds. She needn't have worried. Would we give our hard-earned dosh to politicians – no sir. The thing is Becky, jump on this for all it's worth. Profile and all that. They want national cover – East Midlands Powerhouse emerges from government strategy. And, he plans a trade mission to Europe. Get you and I on that plane.

"OK, to war. I warned some time ago to expect an attack. Well, it's underway. You have both been to see me and I've had a visit. Let's decide how to respond. Arrows have been fired from four directions, I'll pick up each one as it occurred. The top cop around these parts decided to give me advance knowledge of a fatal accident. Why pick me out? Because it was my (now late) Uncle Adrian. He suspects foul play and links it to my row with Adrian during Kyaw's graduation party. Tenuous but there you go. No doubt I'm supposed to confess to driving a hundred miles to slash his tyres such that, in a drunken stupor, the old sod would drive into a river. Pathetic.

"Then, Becky has a visit from another policeman who just happens to work for top cop. Becky's private life is her own. The innuendo seems to be that she provides favours to clients who in return hand us business. Pathetic No 2.

"The next attack I take seriously. Super-top-cop Alice who, as you both know is married to the stock market genius Marcus, breaks her Friday afternoon trip from Brussels to London especially to chat to our consultant. She, of Interpol fraud fame, thinks that the consultants have broken the law by submitting paperwork to the authorities re Rapidmoney. This is almost certainly a bluff but I have to say our lady adviser is rattled. Now Becky, check on progress with signing the contracts with the two companies and you might find we need to take the work back in-house. By her visit, Alice might have made a mistake. If our methodology was flawed in transferring client money, were we merely following advice? Becky, sort it.

"The fourth foray into our affairs came from clever-boy Marcus. Eric, you made a mistake by feeding him too much. I am deadly serious now. That guy is very smart. I know for a fact he played a key part in a cold-case police review years ago. Also, of course, he sleeps with our Queen of Fraud although, as Becky knows, I have an angle on that. She and I will meet in Brussels at a time that suits me. I've given much thought to Marcus; Professor Moriarty versus Holmes one might say. The answer is to hit him in the wallet, pull a flanker in his back yard. Eric, I have a plan to get your own back and Becky we'll need help on the fake news side. OK, thanks for listening. Any other ideas on a postcard to Uncle Luke. Should either of you feel thirsty at around seven, I'll be buying in the pub. I'm meeting Murray there at six to check how his robotics stuff is progressing. I feel an expensive evening coming on and hopefully by the time I stagger home, one screaming, smelly baby will be in the Land of Nod.

*

"Hi Murray, there you are. I've got you a pint in. They've got a new barrel on, can you believe it's called Covid All Cure? How do they get away with it? Just imagine if we launched a suite of programs called Risk All Cure, we'd be ridiculed off the circuit".

"Thanks Luke, before we talk robotics I want to ask, how's the baby?"

"She's good. Kyaw says the weight has increased by twenty percent in this first month and apparently that's an excellent sign. Kyaw's doing well too, it was a difficult birth but, as they say, mother and baby are doing fine. You should come and see them, Kyaw would love that. Yesterday she was complaining that apart from her friend Sam, we've had hardly any visitors. You spent quite a lot of time with Kyaw when I was in Australia, why not start your lessons again? If she's up to it of course – which you'll soon find out. She's been a bit snappy with me since the birth but it seems that's normal, post-natal depression I've been told.

"Murray listen, I've just left a meeting with Becky and Eric, didn't invite you since it was to do with risk and money transfer. The bloody authorities are taking an interest and we have to put up defences. Anyway, I know you're pulling out the stops on the robotics software, don't need the detail. I split you off from Eric for a damn good reason. Robotics is our baby (no pun intended) and I want to keep it that way. If you pull it off, the sky's the limit, I promise you. I clued you up on how I've split the profit with my man in Mandalay. It was the only way we could get our hands on the kidney transplant code. Given the progress your team have made, I want us to get smart. Costs come off before the profit is struck and therefore the more expense the better. Work on it Murray. What's the highest rate per hour we can justify, how many hours, what licence fees have you incurred to buy in specialist stuff? Honestly, every pound you add to development cost is a pound less profit to split and, I might add, a boost to your bonus. It's likely Becky and Eric will turn up soon so mums the word. As I said, it's our baby. Incidentally, have a private word with Becky about her hobby.

*

James Salmon was feeling very pleased with himself. A text confirmed that the Stamford job went like clockwork and he had kept his promise to visit his grandfather. This second summons to Luke's private office could only be to receive the stamps or at worst to get an idea of their value.

"James, I made it perfectly clear. I wanted my uncle jolted out of his fur-lined rut or at worst done for drink-driving. What I didn't want was a visit from a senior copper telling me Uncle Adrian was dead".

"What!"

"Whoever you set on, messed up. The bloody tyre was supposed to be ruined so even a drunken ex-farm manager would realise he was driving with a flat".

James slumped in his chair.

"Oh my God, what can we do?"

"Nothing we can do, poor sod's been dragged from the bottom of a river. It'll be out on the wires tomorrow, let's hope some other major news story takes its place sooner than later. Right – action. Whatever communication you've had with knifeman gets wiped clean, and I mean at both ends and straight away. Get your mate to disappear for at least a month but with a good reason. First thing the local plods will do is sound out who of the likely lads is missing. Next, pop into Old Blackwell Church and pray".

"Luke, I don't know what to say, never expected anything like this to happen. Suppose bang goes the stamps and grandad's flat?"

"No James, when I make a promise I stick to it. But there is another little job you can do for me, and for Christ's sake when I say *you* I mean *you* – understand?"

"Yes".

"Right, listen carefully. This is what the first job should have been, a frightener not a bloody murder assignment. Got it?"

"Yes Luke, I've got it"

Eight

Pearl was saying that this was what she thought of as her *park bench of great drama*, although the single word *drama* was to understate the pain that Naing must have been going through. She and Naing had sat in exactly this spot watching Tristan at one end of the see-saw waiting for a child to sit at the other. It had seemed such an innocent remark at the time, voicing a wish that he had a brother or sister to play with. Then it all went wrong. I would want my children to have the same father; I would want to conceive naturally. Naing just erupted. She wouldn't hear of it. No, no, no. Everything that followed stemmed from those few sentences. Resigning from the dental practice, renting out her apartment and going home to Mandalay.

"Marcus are you listening to what I've been saying?"

"Yes, of course, well sort of half-listening. Have you noticed that Tristan can make that swing, which is clearly intended for older children, to go higher and higher, it looks quite dangerous to me".

"Marcus, I must be in a more philosophical mood than you this afternoon. As my daddy used to say *one learns by one's mistakes*. After he's taken a tumble, he'll be more careful".

"The philosopher with a hard shell?"

"You're right, be a knight in shining armour and slow him down, that's most likely why he's doing it anyway, anything to get your attention – the daddy who can do no wrong".

Pearl sat and watched the two of them. She started to think about mistakes and their power to change life. Marcus wouldn't be here if his grandad, all those years ago, hadn't been so sure dear Eugene was a murderer. She wouldn't be here if she'd followed her head and not her heart, pursued her career and left her daddy with a carer. Had that been a mistake? She still wasn't sure. Would a foreign correspondent from The Times have swept her off her feet instead of getting drunk with Naing? Would she now be living in a suburb of Washington DC trying to control bolshy teenagers and writing a column for The Post? Whatever mistakes we make or do not make, we are where we are. Now, aged forty-seven, she had never been happier. Why had it taken so long? And how had this lovely routine developed? She didn't mean routine in the sense of boring monotony but rather an established pattern of events, yes, that was a better way of looking at it.

Because Alice returned to Brussels on the late morning flight each Sunday, and Marcus ignored his screens and charts each Monday, he'd join Pearl and the children for Sunday lunch at the cottage and their afternoon was free. It depended on the weather. The sea front, the beach or a walk in the country or if raining or too cold then stay home and play games. On most Sundays, Naing and Aung would arrive at teatime and the family circle was complete. But, Pearl knew perfectly well that Monday morning was Marcus's favourite time. En route from his top-floor sea-view apartment in Brighton to his London base, he took Tristan to school. Before this practice started, a certain young boy wasn't awfully keen on going to school after his full-on weekend; it was different now. His school bag and water bottle were ready in good time.

Pearl emerged from her daydream. Marcus was now pulling Tristan on the zipwire and Mandy was still in her heaven – the sandpit. They'd call for an ice-cream on the way home.

*

They met at the main entrance to Parc du Cinquantenaire in the Eastern Quarter and Luke spoke first.

"Good morning Alice. It might surprise you to know that I'll soon be as familiar with Brussels as you, my sales team are breaching the barricades which surprises even me, now that the UK and Europe are supposedly financial enemies. In the finest tradition of all spy novels, I suggest we stroll along and not take a park bench and pretend to read the daily paper".

"Mr Luke Brown, this meeting is your call. What do you want?"

"First to walk and take in the morning air and secondly to ask why you felt it necessary to visit my consultant in Nottingham".

"As they say, just routine. We've picked up a bit of intelligence on how your money transfer business works. This advisory firm you're using crops up in the regulatory paperwork, thought I'd take a look, see what sort of set-up they have".

"Fine, well, I always think it's good to clear the air. There's much jealousy in the financial services industry, a lot of vested interest, a lot of old boy networks and a lot of taking Joe Public for a ride. We found a way to get funds overseas quickly and cheaply and, if it's of interest to you, I'm here as part of a UK delegation promoting our expertise to certain European laggards. I can introduce you to a senior UK minister if you have time".

"Luke, my department has little interest in what is done in any business area but rather how activity takes place and specifically examining whether it's legal. Our information is that you might be using risk management software to manipulate markets and consequently create false share prices. Be clear, this is no accusation, we are at an early stage but I will be visiting your HQ with a colleague and it's possible with a formal request to open your books".

"Oh dear Alice, I was so hoping it wouldn't come to this. I'm aware you hold a personal grudge from the past in failing to link me to that cold case business. You really should let sleeping dogs lie, the world has moved on. I give high-paid employment to over one hundred people and our sales contribute to the urgent need to boost the UK's export earnings. Aside from that I now have quite a high public profile. I do urge you to be cautious".

"None of that is of interest to me. My staff will follow the trail and see where it leads".

"You won't shake hands and let things drop?"

"No and I must get back to the office".

"Alice, before you go, can I ask a question?"

"If you must".

"How is Brendan?"

"Pardon?"

"I was wondering how your affair is progressing, have you mentioned it to Marcus yet?"

"You little piece of shit. If you think you can blackmail me, you're in bigger trouble than I thought".

"Blackmail, good God no. I wouldn't stoop so low. What goes on between man and wife is entirely their business. In any case from what I hear from Kyaw, Marcus is back with Pearl, probably finds her somewhat softer to the touch".

"Goodbye Luke, I'll see you in your office quite soon".

"Just one more thing Alice, we haven't discussed the films".

"What films?"

"You and this Brendan guy. Nice and cosy in the hotel bedroom, noisy too. I honestly didn't realise the equipment had become so sophisticated. Blackmail's not my style baby, don't want a single penny for the items or, bearing in mind your new life, a single cent. But, unless you drop the enquiries your two bosses, the one here and the one in London are in for a real erotic treat. Goodbye Alice."

*

From: eric@londonwall.co.uk
To: marcusclarke@icloud.com
Subject: Screen shots

Hi Marcus and thanks for your email. Yes, just experimenting with CFD's and related stuff. Don't suppose it'll come to anything and there won't be time now that the sales side has been ramped. Firing on all cylinders; having a job to keep up. Europe, China via our new office in Singapore and now the Australian East Coast cities.

I did score on your latest tip and many thanks. It'll go a long way to paying for my next eye operation. They're going to try a precision lens – bit nervous, any mistake will probably end my career. If it does, I'll take up your offer and tap my white stick on the Brighton prom before dipping a toe in the brine.

Marcus mate, I'd like to reciprocate with a share tip that I've picked up from a hedge fund client. All is not well with a certain quoted civil engineering contractor, something on the lines of taking profits too soon. Might be a false rumour of course, how can one tell these days with fake news lurking in the wires? Still, could be worth taking a short position. I'll send the ticker by encrypted text.

BTW, we have a new member of staff. A beautiful baby girl born of an elegant Asian lady. Luke is such a lucky bugger, I'd give my good eye to sleep with her every night, but half-blind beggars can't be choosers.

Give my regards to Alice,
Eric

Eric fired off a text to Becky. Sent you blind copy of an email to that Marcus guy. Give it a week. Then start the <u>boost to prospects</u> fake news. Just a few pence upkick will do the trick.

*

Pearl enjoyed fetching Tristan from school, she'd become friendly with a few of the mothers and a couple of grandmothers too. There was always a bit of gossip to chew over and in particular the usual complaint about one of the teachers. Most recently, a dinner lady had overstepped the mark causing Peggy, one of the regular complainers to make an appointment with the headmistress. Today was different because although the forecast was for sun later, the steady downpour meant finding whatever shelter was available and the regulars only emerged once the bell had sounded. Of the twenty-eight children in Mr Simmonds' class, Tristan was usually about third in line at the door waiting for the classroom assistant to search out Pearl. Today he must have forgotten his bag or rushed to the loo putting him at the back of the queue. After a few minutes all the children had been collected. All, that is, except Tristan. Pearl wasn't concerned, just a little annoyed at having to stand a few more minutes in the rain. Still no Tristan. With some difficulty trying to manoeuvre the pushchair as well as herself through the classroom door, all she saw was Mr Simmonds and the assistant clearing the books and papers.

"Where's Tristan?"

"You sent for him an hour or so ago".

"I did not, where is he?"

"Pearl isn't it? There must be some mistake. You sent an email asking him to be released early because his sister Mandy had an appointment at the Early Centre Nursery".

"I did not – oh my God, what's happened".

Pearl screamed and instinctively bent down to clutch Mandy. "Somebody's got him – oh my God. What about your security? You're not allowed to let my little boy out of your care. You're not allowed to do that".

Pearl was shaking, her mind went blank, she had no idea what to do. Mr Simmonds's face drained, after what seemed like an eternity he spoke to the assistant.

"Print off that email – I'll fetch the Head".

The headmistress, Mr Simmonds, the teaching assistant and Pearl all stared at the email. Pearl couldn't read a word, every single letter swam before her eyes. Mr Simmonds spoke first.

"It is from Pearl, that is her email address. She asks permission for her nephew Sam King to collect Tristan at two-fifteen and take him home to await his mother returning with Mandy from the Early Centre Nursery".

Pearl cried out that they only release Tristan to either her or Marcus and only then knowing the face matches their record. "Are you stupid or what, what have you done?"

The headmistress grabbed the printed email. "It says she knows they only have a photo record of her and Marcus but an image of Sam is attached and she needs to explain that because her nephew caught the Covid 20 virus, he was left with a weak chest and still wears a face mask. Also, she apologies for the strange headgear but he recently had an operation and needs to wear the skull cap for a further week.

"I didn't send that, it's all lies. You're only allowed to release a child to the relative matching a photo on file. My God, you've been duped. My boy has been taken. Where is my Tristan?"

The headmistress and Mr Simmonds stared at the teaching assistant.

"Ring the police on the emergency number. Mr Simmonds, go home with Pearl and her daughter and stay there till the police arrive or until I contact you. This has never happened before. We must stay calm and move fast".

Pearl took Mandy out of the pushchair and hugged her tightly. She couldn't stop shaking, her mind was in turmoil, *this can't be happening, this can't happen to me, I must be dreaming – wake up woman, wake up.* Mr Simmonds took Pearl's arm and led her gently from the classroom and steered her to the staff carpark. *I must stay alert, must not panic, must get his woman and her child home, oh my God, of all the things to happen.*

Concentrating as hard as she could, Pearl (after two failed attempts) sent a text to Naing. *Please come, Tristan is missing, call Marcus.*

*

For years to come, Pearl would look back at the entries in her diary. Mind-blowing. Fantasy - did it really happen? She couldn't be sure the stated times were correct or even the sequence of events. The day her world fell apart.

4.10 pm. Naing and Aung arrived. For a while I couldn't speak to them, couldn't stop shaking and crying. Mr Simmonds opened the toy box and started playing with Mandy. I wanted to die, what is happening to my little boy. Why has someone taken him, please don't hurt him, he's done nothing wrong. I became aware that Naing was hugging me tightly and Aung was stroking my hair. Aung went to talk to Mr Simmonds. I rushed to the kitchen and was sick. Naing told me that Marcus was on his way, he would try to contact Alice to ask if her people had any intelligence.

4.25 pm.Two police officers arrived. The woman knelt on the floor in front of me and held both my hands. The man told Mr Simmonds he could now leave but he said no, he'd stay and play with Mandy. They would go into the garden for a while. The two officers said their boss had called for reinforcements and within the next few hours all CCTV's would be scrutinised. Roadblocks were being set up and all local agencies notified. The email had been sent to the back-room guys to source the hacker. Other actions were mentioned, I was only half listening. I imagined Tristan in the corner of the playground crying and asking for his mummy. I was sick again.

5.05 pm. We all heard a screech of brakes outside and Marcus burst in. He took one look around the living room and came charging towards me, almost knocking me off the sofa. He hugged me to him for what seemed like ages. He looked at Naing and Aung and the two police officers and put his head in his hands. He was sobbing. After a while he raised his head and I wiped the tears from his face. Then he yelled, it was a sound I'd never heard before, half shout, half growl. "What bastard has done this. I'll kill him with my bare hands". He buried his head in my chest and wept uncontrollably. After a few minutes, the woman police officer suggested he go into the kitchen and throw cold water in his face, then come back to sit with me. She and her colleague needed to ask a few questions. It was very urgent, each minute counted. Had we seen anyone watching Tristan in the park or when we were out walking and especially on the beach or promenade. Could we think why Tristan didn't tell his teacher he didn't know this person who came to collect him. They fetched Mr Simmonds from the garden. The teaching assistant heard the man tell Tristan that his daddy was at home waiting to play football in the garden. The male police officer looked at me and simply said "Oh".

6.15 pm. Mandy was standing on a chair looking out towards the garden gate. It was heartbreaking. After a while she turned and said "Tristy is walking down the path". I rushed out and he was safe in my arms. I have no recollection of the next half-hour or so.

Tristan was eating his favourite tea, baked beans on toast with baby sausages. The two police officers sat at the table opposite and the woman asked if she could have one of the sausages as she hadn't had her tea and was very hungry. Pearl was astonished; he handed her one. They suggested he might like to tell them where he'd been since leaving school and what he'd done. Tristan said he had walked with his uncle Sam and before coming home they'd decided to climb the big hill and make a kite from a kit taken out of his uncle's bag. It took quite a long time because the glue had to dry and he had to paint the wings and tail. They were lucky, it was windy and the kite went up into the sky and he was allowed to hold it. Did his uncle look strange in a mask and funny hat? Tristan said no, soon after they started walking, his uncle took both off – they only had to be worn in the school. He put them away in his bag. Had he been in his uncle's car? He didn't have one, they walked. Did he need the toilet while they walked and made the kite? No, he went before he left school. Had he needed to take off any of his school uniform? No. Had his uncle needed to pick him up when they climbed the big hill? No, he did it all himself. They had one last question before going back in their police car. Had he been given any sweets? No, just the present. Could they see it please? Tristan left the table, fetched his school bag and handed a small package to the nice lady. It was still in its cellophane wrapper. I came to look at the gift as did Marcus, Naing and Aung. It was a child's reading book called *All about money*. It had four bullet points below the main title

- *How much left from my £20 note*
- *Adding up my shopping*
- *Name their currency*
- *Change one currency for another*

Luke

The male police officer asked if the gift of this book meant anything to me. Before I could answer, Marcus said "Yes".

Nine

Luke was saying that they'd agreed the last meeting was a one-off but he wanted to summarise where they stood following the attacks. He'd managed to meet up and have a chat with Alice and although there was nothing in writing, his impression was that the nascent enquiry would be put on the back burner. With the cryptocurrency scandal raging across Europe, she had bigger fish to fry. As regards the guy who had the technical knowhow to discover how the money transfer actually works, i.e. Marcus, he had a couple of things to distract him for the time being. First, his marriage was going through a bad patch and secondly his son had been involved in an upsetting incident at school. He might also be smarting from the share tip we gave him. Becky's fake news upped the price more than I thought and so smartarse Marcus would have closed his position after incurring a thumping loss.

Turning to what he called *the second division*, he'd heard no more about his uncle's accident and as regards the internees from the charity, it was likely that the supply would dry up, but the two software teams had benefitted greatly from the programme and what Eric should do now was pick out the best of the bunch and offer them permanent employment. Extending the students' visas might be an issue but he had mentioned it to the MP on the flight back from Brussels who'd promised to pass on a request – boost to the local economy and all that.

Luke thought that now they weren't having to spend time looking over their shoulder, a monetary reward was in order. He'd asked the consultant to complete the paperwork, minutes of a company meeting and such, to formalise paying the Rapidmoney preference share dividend. If they'd excuse the pun, Becky and Eric would be pleasantly surprised; money would flow rapidly into their bank account!

He wanted his two most senior executives to know that he'd taken a decision. The consultancy service would be used very little from now on. Their skill had been important during the formative stages, but it was time each business stood on its own two feet. One other not insubstantial issue was that the fees were getting out of hand and when the consultancy firm had been confronted with a piece of work that warranted defending robustly, he felt their response had been lily-livered.

Also, he'd learnt from Kyaw that U Aung was bringing Garma, Kyaw's sister, over from Myanmar to familiarise herself with the UK's work for the charity. This was at no cost to the business since the charity was paying all expenses. It was a welcome development not least because Kyaw misses her family but she can now show off her baby. He knew they would make her feel welcome and he intended to take Garma to one side and explain how much the charity had benefitted from the internship programme.

One last thing, although it didn't affect the business, old Fred Salmon was getting near the end and Kyaw had agreed with his G.P. to move him to a nursing home. It was a shame but it would come to us all eventually. Luke said if it hadn't been for his Great Uncle Harold, he'd never have met Fred and we wouldn't be in this lovely location, but instead stuck in a glass office block. Incidentally he'd promised James, Fred's grandson, use of the old man's flat. Luke mentioned that James had done a couple of jobs for him recently.

"He's a cocky little sod but I've quite taken to his rebellious nature. I've thought about taking him on as a general dogsbody giving him a grand-sounding title, something like PA to the chairman. OK Becky, Eric, that's it. We press on. There's a big world to conquer".

*

Naing was turning over in her mind what the odds might be, perhaps she should ask Marcus if they could be calculated. Three Burmese ladies sitting beside a roaring log fire in an old English country house doting over an Anglo/Burmese baby – a million to one?

She had met Kyaw's younger sister Garma at Heathrow off the early morning flight from Bangkok. The drive north had been a nightmare. A late November cloud-strewn day was not a great introduction to England but worse, it had not inhibited a flow of questions from the excited young lady that had only added to the stress of coping with a congested M25 and M1 motorway. But, by early afternoon, they had arrived safely at The Old Hall. Seeing the fond embrace of the two sisters had made the journey worthwhile and now Naing could relax and sip the, oh so English, tea and tuck into Kyaw's home-made fruitcake. Naturally, the centre of attention was Kyaw's baby. At thirteen weeks she weighed ten pounds twelve ounces and, as Kyaw proudly announced, a gain since birth of 80%. Her name had been a compromise. Obviously, Luke as the father had first choice and so the baby was Molly, after his grandmother. The second name had been suggested by Pearl. Hlaing had been Aung's wife. This name would bring back the memory of Chit and Eugene, Aung's parents. Hlaing, Kyaw loved it. *A gift of God.*

Naing had been unaware that Garma and Luke had met before but from the minute he entered the room, it was clear they had. From their spontaneous embrace it was obvious why she had been replaced at the charity by Kyaw's sister. Luke had advanced the career of an admirer. *Could there be trouble ahead?*

Although there was not much of it, Garma stroked Molly's hair and said it shone like a lantern hanging from a pagoda as it reflected the setting sun, gold turning to auburn and unlike any shade of hair she'd seen in Myanmar. She wondered if there was a legacy of blonde or ginger hair on Luke's side of the family. For the first time since releasing Garma's hand, Luke spoke.

"That's a very interesting question and not something I would have thought about. Hmm, as far as I know all my aunts and uncles had brown hair or like my Great Uncle Harold, jet black. I can now confirm that Kyaw and I have created a golden baby to complement our golden future". Kyaw handed her baby to Garma and walked over to Luke, reached for his hand and kissed him lightly on the cheek.

"Luke darling, that was a lovely thing to say".

Naing joined Garma and also stroked Molly's hair. "I tend to agree with Luke, hair colouration is an interesting subject. I know for a fact that genetic red hair is rare in Asia. I read somewhere that its origins are Moroccan. Kyaw, here's a question for you. While Luke was in Australia, did you sneak off to Marrakesh?"

Kyaw giggled. "Of course not, silly. During my pregnancy, I hardly went further than the end of the drive. Luke had me wrapped in cotton wool until, that is, I stupidly slipped on the lawn and that protection didn't help at all. Luckily my friend Sam was here to help me. Does it always happen that way? I mean, when one really needs help are the most important people always missing?"

Apart from a few gurgles from Molly, the room fell quiet until Naing broke the silence by saying she hated to break up the party but after the overnight flight and the long car journey, Garma really ought to have an early night and anyway she needed to check into the hotel. Luke thought that was sensible especially as he'd planned to take Garma to Nottingham tomorrow to go shopping for a few clothes suited to this awful November weather. It would give Naing a chance to spend quality time with Kyaw, not knowing when they'll see each other again. Would Garma like him to tuck her in? "Kyaw, my lovely, I am of course joking. Actually, thinking back to what we were talking about earlier, unless I've missed out on Becky's new recruits, the only employee we have with ginger hair is my star guy in charge of the robotics team, Murray".

*

If only to stave off boredom Marcus had, over the years, moved his office within his ground floor apartment several times, finally settling on what originally would have been the front- room parlour. It was accessed from the main living room via floor-to-ceiling double glass doors allowing him to move seamlessly from *the work space* to *the home space.* His computer screens were arranged in a semi-circle facilitating his eye scan from one to the other with minimum movement of his swivel chair and facing inwards to avoid direct daylight. This arrangement meant he had a view of the small front garden and Huddleston Road along which on this Friday morning a postman was walking. Instantly he thought of what Pearl had said all those years ago. Her surprise had come less from the solicitor's letter itself than actually receiving an item of post. He remembered her wondering when the last time that had happened. The combination of the digital age and a notice prohibiting junk mail had rendered the postman redundant. He looked to the ceiling, *Oh Pearl, thank God Tristan is safe – what would we have done?*

Marcus stared at the hand-written envelope. His heart sank. Those early days of sneaking to the cottage in Derbyshire and finding a love note on his pillow. It was the same handwriting, the same black ink.

My wonderful Marcus, the Maserati Man who swept me off my feet. How do I tell you, how do I put into words what I feel?

Marcus my darling, I have gone. To see you so happy with Tristan and Mandy has broken my heart. When I first agreed to you helping Pearl and Naing, I never for one moment envisaged the bond that could develop. I should have done, I was stupid. Stupidly drunk on my career, my ambition I suppose. You were never the kind of man who would father a child and then walk away, why oh why didn't I see that?

Marcus darling, I couldn't give you the baby we always talked of having. But I didn't know – honest to God I didn't know. I so wanted to give you a baby. When Pearl became pregnant, I realised there was something wrong with me. I had tests which showed I can't conceive. I agreed to you going with Pearl for a second child to make you happy. I needed my love to be happy – I still do.

Perhaps you guessed from that text message when we went to that wretched graduation party. If you did, you helped me by not letting on. I have been seeing a colleague named Brendan. It has been so damn easy being away in Brussels and whether due to that or not, our relationship hasn't been the same. You know that and I dreaded it getting worse, tearing each other apart. Not Alice and Marcus.

I am filling up with tears. I want you to know that he will never take your place. He is a good man and will look after me whatever the future holds, but he is not my Marcus, the only man I have ever truly loved.

I am staying in Brussels and will have my things sent for in a week or so. God bless you Marcus for making me so happy – if only things had turned out differently – if only.

All my love Alice.

Marcus folded the letter and placed it back in the envelope. For the first time he looked at the postage stamp *Belgique.* A country he hadn't been to and now never would. He closed down his work, turned off each monitor, left his office and walked through the lounge and into the hall. He reached for his camel coat, activated the alarm and locked the front door behind him. He turned up the coat collar against the bitterly cold east wind.

A few months later and in answer to Pearl's question, he couldn't say where he went. He just walked and walked. Walked into a no-Alice future.

*

"Pearl, I've put my London pad on the market. It holds too many memories and I can't visit the local pub and restaurants any more and anyway my car's stuck in its underground prison all week, the only road it knows is the M23. Given a strong broadband signal I can work anywhere, doesn't need to be Tufnell Park. I don't know why I'm trotting out all these corny excuses, the truth is I want to be down here near you and the children. You three are my life and I can't mess up again. Honestly, I won't be a nuisance. You have your place and I'll have mine".

"Marcus are you absolutely sure? They say one ought not to take a big decision soon after a life-changing event. Why not wait twelve months and see how you feel then? I shouldn't be saying this but isn't it possible you'll meet someone? I realise that right now you can't see past Alice, no-one would expect you to, but time is a great healer. I know that only too well".

"Pearl you're very sweet. You've been so good for me. I know I'm an emotional wreck. I know I'm not thinking at my best. I almost fell into a trap set by Luke's two lieutenants Eric and Becky the other day. But I didn't so the little grey cells must still be active, to a degree at least".

The two were sitting either side of the coffee table in Pearl's cottage. Mandy was in bed and Tristan was having a sleepover at Naing's. As if guided by some invisible force, Marcus slumped forward with his elbows on the table and with his head cradled in his hands. His whole body was shaking and very quietly he started to sob. Pearl moved to sit beside him and placed her arm around his shoulder, neither spoke. Slowly, Marcus raised his head and took the tissue from Pearl. After what seemed like an eternity, he looked directly at the mother of his children.

"I just want to be close to you and my children. That's all I want".

Ten

It was early evening when Naing checked into The Priory. She felt tired but it was more than that. Uncomfortable? Finding it hard to relax. She booked a table in the dining room for seven thirty, just enough time to take a shower, get changed, put on her face and maybe grab something from the chill cabinet. The meal was OK as hotel meals go, nothing exciting, nothing spicy; she chose the fish which was swamped by a white sauce destroying any delicate taste the plaice might have had. The vegetables were nicely presented but equally tasteless. Anyway, she had no appetite and decided not to prolong the agony. Could she take coffee in the lounge? Selecting a leather armchair which had been positioned to allow a view of the eighteenth green - had it not been pitch black outside - she did what she'd been aching to do since leaving the Old Hall, she phoned Pearl.

"Hi Pearl, hope I'm fine on timing, they should have gone down by now. I wanted to tell you that my room is identical to the one we shared when helping with that cold-case enquiry. We were so happy then, it made me sad thinking back and having a pre-dinner sherry exactly as we did. Do you remember how we giggled knowing that lovely senior policeman had arranged two rooms and how we couldn't save them the expense without blowing our cover? I sometimes wish …. oh well, mustn't dwell on what might have been".

"Yes Naing, I understand how you must be feeling. Times and places, they set one back. You're aching to tell me how things went and I'm dying to know".

"The most astonishing thing to me, and it brought back the doubts we have about the wisdom of persuading Kyaw to give Luke a second chance, was his casual approach. From the moment he entered the room and went into a clinch with

Kyaw's younger sister Garma, one would never have guessed he was the baby's father. As far as I could see, Luke didn't even look at Molly, never mind hold her. And when I think back to the really hard time Kyaw had giving birth and her distress at his absence, it just made my blood boil. I kept asking myself, who is this man? Do you know that at one point he even made a joke in extremely bad taste. He suggested Garma might like him to tuck her up in bed. Oh, and then he made sure we all heard of his intention to take Garma on a trip to Nottingham. Pearl, had you been Kyaw, how would you have felt? The man's a monster. There's a certain word in my language, but I won't voice it".

"Oh dear, poor Kyaw".

"I can feel myself getting all wound up again, wasn't going to bother but I'll ask for a glass of wine. I do wish you were here. I want to tell you about Molly's hair".

"That's different, didn't see that coming".

"The subject arose as a bit of light relief, eased the tense atmosphere I suppose. One of us commented on Molly's very light-coloured hair and we went round the loop of it's not Asian, no-one on Luke's side having fair hair – that sort of thing. It ended up with the name of the only person working at the Old Hall with ginger hair. It rocked me a bit because of something you once said. Trust me to add two and two to make five".

"Come on Naing, how many sherries did you have before dinner? If you're attempting to stigmatise Kyaw's honour I'll have no option but to commit you to looking after Mandy for a whole week - that'll teach you a lesson. I'll have you know there's a throw-back in every so-called British family. The Moors came north and the Vikings south. It must be a coincidence surely? I know what you're inferring but surely they didn't. It's true that Alice saw them in a slightly compromising situation towards the end of the graduation party and yes she's spent time trying to teach him some

Burmese. I expect the banter about the colour of Molly's hair will soon be forgotten".

"The thing is Pearl, I'm with Kyaw all day tomorrow. Do you think I should bring it up? If she's been playing fast and loose with this Murray guy, what will happen when Molly's features change: how on earth will they keep it secret? I mean, think of Tristan. If he isn't a miniature Marcus then, I'm not Burmese but a Dutchman. I'll ask for another glass of wine to recover my composure".

"Naing, I think you should stop talking, in fact, stop thinking and try to find your room. If you do raise the subject, for goodness sake try to make a joke – did Molly arrive because Murray rubbed up against her or something?. Then again, the Burmese race are not overly familiar with the British sense of humour – especially dentists! Actually, it might be an idea to change your drink order to a large shot of that Burmese whisky you forced down me after our boozy night in Brighton. I have some news that's just been taken off the top-secret list. Alice has left Marcus".

"What? When? Why?"

"Three weeks ago and she told him by letter, not in person. Can you believe it? As to why, she said she was heart-broken seeing him so attached to Tristan and Mandy and she'd discovered she couldn't conceive. Apparently, she didn't seek medical advice until after I became pregnant. Seems odd, not knowing her situation until then. Marcus told me the reason they got married was to have children. Of course, she did have a very successful career, maybe they left it too late"

"That's so sad, they always seemed the perfect match to me and as you've often said, they had a wonderful lifestyle. Just goes to show, that's not everything is it? I mean, she did agree to our request for a child and then you trying for a second one. What irony. It was me who got upset and now

I'm back and she's gone. Is there any chance of a reconciliation?"

"Well, who knows but she's been having an affair in Brussels and now Marcus is sort of accepting things, I doubt he'd have her back. Here's another irony; almost certainly their paths will cross over Luke's business affairs. She's opened a case on possible white-collar fraud and he's agreed to advise the police on how the computer software enables money to be moved from one country to another. One might say a meeting of minds if not bodies. By the way, Marcus seems determined to move his office to Brighton and sell up in London. It's brought home to me how profoundly the Tristan school incident has affected him and because the local police don't seem to be getting anywhere, he's spoken to Neil of the Derbyshire force. Marcus is absolutely certain that Luke was behind the kidnapping and after explaining about the reading book present, so are they. Naing, get yourself to bed – that's an order".

The following evening Naing rang Pearl again.

"Hi Pearl, just to say I'm back. I left at about three o'clock, good run really, just over four hours. Having felt I'd spent enough time with Kyaw and the baby, I cancelled a second night at the hotel. To be honest, it wasn't so much time as the atmosphere. I was really taken aback. While driving home I was thinking that on previous visits there have been groups of people to hide behind. Even yesterday one could dismiss Luke's approach as simply discourteous, but when alone with mother and baby the tension in the air is palpable".

"Naing, I'm glad you've rung and are back safely. Do you think the bad vibes were due to his Lordship taking Garma out?"

"Actually I don't, and in fact it wasn't even mentioned. Kyaw seems to accept his absence and if I wanted to be catty I might say welcomes it. Of course, her obvious antipathy towards Luke could be down to postnatal blues and yet what she said soon after Molly was born about not needing him anymore, is hard to forget. Anyway, I was relieved to leave. They might have a beautiful old mansion and lots of material wealth, but I'll take my apartment and job any day".

"Were you able to bring up *the subject?*"

"Yes, and I fear the worst. It got to late morning and Molly had fallen asleep. We were waiting for her friend Sam to arrive and quite deliberately I started speaking in our own native tongue because Kyaw recognises this as signalling a talk about our private lives. I asked if she could imagine how proud her mother would be showing off a picture of her first grandchild. Would any of her friends and neighbours have ever seen a fair-headed baby? Wasn't it remarkable that the only ginger-haired person mentioned in the rather silly conversation about race and hair colour was the guy she had been tutoring on the Burmese language and culture?"

"That sounds like the Naing I know so well. Let's lead her into a little trap – sorry, it's supposed to be a compliment, came out more as a devious manoeuvre".

"Whatever, it might have worked. It seems there was a New Year's Eve party at the Old Hall, just the senior staff plus the Burmese students who had left the charity scheme and joined the company. Outside caterers had served very nice food including Mohinga as a starter and Piquant Lobster Tails as a main dish because they reminded Luke of his very first meal after arriving in Mandalay. There was also a huge cut-glass bowl of Punch made up to Luke's own recipe. Kyaw said that after they'd welcomed in the New Year things had become a little hazy and one guest, she thought it was Becky, had too much to drink and Luke had kindly taken her home. She couldn't remember when he came back but so as not to disturb her, he'd slept in the spare room. To the amusement of all the guests, especially the students, she recalled Murray trying to give a speech thanking her and Luke for putting on such a wonderful party. It was a hoot since he spoke, or thought he had, in Burmese. The best part was afterwards when one of the students said he got a few things wrong especially in trying to say that Kyaw must have been a beautiful baby. Instead it sounded more like Kyaw must be given a beautiful baby. Pearl, I don't know what you feel but I foresee a very dangerous situation developing".

"Naing, my dear friend, you've known Kyaw almost as long as I have. Do either of us really think she would allow anyone other than her husband to make love to her? OK, hint about being under the influence, hint about mixing a few words of Burmese. I can almost hear Marcus saying *hardly Black Swan events*. The best thing we can do is keep a watching brief, granted it's difficult at this distance. Let's think. I know, her best friend Sam. Why not get a text thing going? Molly's the perfect excuse but make sure she understands we're concerned, postnatal depression will do".

"Yes, you're right, I've got myself worked up. Perhaps it's because the climate is so different here, it's like I left the South Pole in a howling gale and landed in a lounger off a tropical beach. But Pearl, I am genuinely concerned for Kyaw's welfare. You'll think this is really silly but somehow one of us needs to make her aware that she has real friends in Brighton. Should the worst happen, we can give her and the baby a home".

"I agree".

*

Robin Sedgewick had been elected as Conservative MP for the East Midlands constituency of Major Oak in 2014 following a by-election. As a dedicated Brexiteer he had, as his wife Justine put it, *backed the right horse* and after the outright majority of his party following the general election on 7th May 2015, he had entered the lower tiers of government. His political career blossomed following the election of Boris Johnson as Prime Minister in July 2019 and he was now an Under-Secretary of State for Business and Finance and a hot tip for further promotion. Becky's dealings with the local constituency office had always been with his agent Susan Reynolds and that is why she was surprised to take a call directly from Robin.

"Hi Becky and pleased to make contact again. You will have received the formal thank you letter from the office but I wanted to say personally that I was most impressed with your presentations as part of my delegation to Brussels. We have processed a few enquiries which will come your way shortly. I'm calling to alert you to clear a date in Luke Brown's diary sometime around mid-December. Following his victory in our patch last February, Luke has been short-listed for the final of UK Entrepreneur Of The Year. As usual the venue will be Grosvenor House and it falls to me to open the proceedings. I intend to stress the importance this government places on international trade and our acknowledged success in fostering the Northern Powerhouse. Oh, I trust you will be at his side and perhaps you two will join me for a drink afterwards. Good luck".

*

Kyaw had served Fried Bananas (nget pyaw gyaw) as the third course of what she hoped Garma would think of as a traditional Burmese dinner. Of course, the ingredients were not quite authentic but her friend Sam had done her best while she was still pretty much housebound. Garma said she was overwhelmed with the welcome she'd received and now this wonderful meal. Luke had bought her some lovely clothes and been most attentive when she was trying on each garment. After the meal she suggested a special fashion show for Kyaw's approval. Luke thought it best to leave the two sisters to catch up with their day and anyway he needed to spend a couple of hours in the office. But, could they do a little job for him. He wanted to set up a FaceTime session with the Rector of Yadanabon University, preferably in the morning. If they managed it, he would like Garma to stand by as interpreter even though he now realised the Rector was fluent in English.

Luke was telling the rector how pleased he was with progress on the lung robotics software. His top man, Murray, had assembled a crack team and according to the testing schedule, they expected to cut a beta version within the next four weeks. Furthermore, a competent engineering company was on standby to assemble the first group of robotics from a confirmed supply chain. Unfortunately, the software costs were running twenty percent over budget and he'd needed to sign a couple of licences for key sub-assemblies. Even so, the commercial prospects were good. The prospective manufacturer, Dobson Industries Ltd (he should visit their website and note the accreditations), had struck a provisional agreement with the NHS on price and provided there was no further escalation in Murray's costs, the royalty income should breakeven within the first year of going live. After that, the sky was the limit. If the rector wanted to visit the UK and meet the development team, he was most welcome.

Having given his progress report, was Luke in order to ask the rector's advice on two issues? First, now that his wife had obtained Anglo-Myanmar citizenship, was there any prospect of a reciprocal arrangement for himself and, perhaps dependent on that, a way he could hold funds in a Myanmar bank or other financial institution? Secondly, now that the Myanmar (Robotics) MCA Inc software had proven stability, and manufacturing the kidney transplant robotics was about to commence, would the board consider increasing his share of the equity from the present fifteen percent. He wondered if twenty to twenty-five percent might be thought more appropriate.

The rector thanked Luke for his report and he would have the question of citizenship and banking looked into. In principle, he saw no reason why the initial shareholding should not be re-examined. He was pleased that Luke's lady assistant had been invited to the UK and U Aung had mentioned that she now had a senior role in the Dotcom charity. It was gratifying that his earlier request that she be rewarded for being Luke's translator had been taken seriously and how was Garma coping with the English weather?

*

Report from The Consultant
Strictly Confidential
To Mr Luke Brown
London Wall (UK) Ltd

10th December 2023

Dear Luke,

We have agreed that our retention service will now cease. It was kind of you to place on record the value attributed to our work over the years and to emphasise that the close relationship made us feel part of your management team. In particular you highlighted our work in dealing with the regulatory aspects of Rapidmoneyex.com and helping to source the two outside companies.

Our final assignment was placing a value on your business interests.

Luke, we have worked together long enough for you to appreciate that indicating a valuation can be no more than speculative and any figure we give should not be used as a basis for raising finance or attracting a potential buyer. To list caveats would serve little purpose but obviously I can do no more than extrapolate from the present financial position and market awareness.

I deal with your interests in the order they appear on the spreadsheet I presented at our last meeting.

London Wall (UK) Ltd.
The trend line of new client wins, retention rate and rental margin indicate that in two years' time the business would sell for circa £5m. This valuation is based on a price- to-earnings ratio of five as a private company. If the shares had a free market, then this figure could double.

London Wall (Australia) Pty Ltd
The infancy of this business makes speculation difficult. However, the client wins in Sydney and the prospects from the new branches in Singapore and Brussels lead me to believe that in two years, you could envisage a valuation at least that of the UK arm. So, also in the £5m bracket as a private company

Rapidmoneyex.com
Value here is constrained by the existence of the preference shares and especially the high coupon. However, in a sale situation these would be cancelled to attract an equity investor. Margins have been cut to facilitate the third parties now playing a part in moving money. Even so, I can see a prospective buyer (think in terms of an existing player wanting you out of the market) paying in the order of £2.5 to £3.0m

Myanmar (Robotics) MCA Inc
With upwards of 15% equity, this investment could be very lucrative although extracting earnings from that country might be difficult. A colleague of mine with knowledge of both robotics and the Far Eastern tiger economies expressed a view that you could become extremely rich. But, as I said, the value may be trapped or it may have to be reinvested in Myanmar. I cannot be more specific.

LB Robotics (UK) Ltd
To value a business with no income is to court disaster. If the robotics function as intended, and if Dobsons make as good a fist at manufacture as they did for the Covid ventilators, and knowing the buying power of the NHS, you have the potential to be very successful. A figure of multiple £millions is not out of the question. Again, I cannot be more specific.

If we can help further, do not hesitate to ask. Our final invoice is attached.

Signed on behalf of TC Associates

Luke printed off the report, drew a line in red ink in the margin of the first paragraph, scanned the document and filed it on the dark web. He placed a copy in the office safe having written beneath the signature at the foot of the page *Bollocks*.

*

Pearl and Marcus were walking on the beach, happily crunching the pebbles beneath their boots. Tristan and Mandy, a few yards ahead, had almost filled the bright red plastic bucket with shells and Pearl's only care in the world was whether that small barking terrier would get too close.

"The attachment to your email took me completely by surprise. What a secretive little beaver you are. Book number two, wow! All those evenings when I couldn't stay late because you had things to do. I have yet to learn if my synopsis was of any use or did the lady wander alone into that imaginary world? You don't have to answer, the rush was to help get me out of the doldrums. I should have known. As usual I didn't".

"Marcus, this is no one-way street, no beach of pebbles leading to an impenetrable cliff face. How would I have coped without you on that awful afternoon? And, I know you and Neil will get him. I just know it. Read my sequel to Eugene, criticise, tear to shreds and condemn. I don't care".

"We can hold hands can't we. At least we can do that".

For a few minutes they walked in silence. The dog had gone.

"Pearl, I've had an idea. The leisure group with the English-weather-proof concept of children's entertainments and such have opened their fifth centre. It's on the Isle of Wight where I remember you took Kyaw when she first came over. Unfortunately, although set in a forest area called Parkhurst, it would be too soon to visit Luke in the nearby prison. Still, I looked at bookings on their website and as one would expect its crammed full at Christmas and the New Year but for the days in between it isn't. What do you think about taking the children? They have both three and two-bedroom bungalows so maybe in the larger one, a room each for we two and Tristan and Mandy in the third and then do you think Naing and Aung might stay in the smaller bungalow? We could all be a kind of family group, what in the Corvid 20 days was dubbed a bubble".

Once again they walked without speaking.

"Marcus, it's a brilliant idea, clever you. I've already invited Naing and Aung for Christmas and they'll no doubt have their own way of bringing in the New Year. Without wanting to sound selfish, let's just make a booking for you, me, and the children. Oh, and Marcus, no need for the extra expense of the larger type bungalow, two bedrooms will be fine. Let's run and tell the two seashell pickers. One last thing while I think of it. I do not, and I mean it, want you toiling over a synopsis or outline plan or anything like that for the final book of my trilogy. It has to be my own work. I need to prove to myself that I can bring the story to a logical conclusion. And this is my New Year resolution brought forward. After the trilogy, no more writing. Pearl Bennett devotes the rest of her life to being a mother".

Pearl squeezed Marcus's hand.

"And, if a certain man will have me, a wife".

Eleven

They were just over five hours into the flight to Perth and Luke was saying that as this would be her last visit, he'd like to go over what they hoped to achieve and in particular whether to continue with Siobhan's partner as a salesman, did she see merit in employing him other than on a commission-only basis?

"Luke, that's the second or third time you stressed that it's to be my last visit. That kind of approach annoys me intensely. My service agreement identifies me as Chief Executive Officer and as such I make decisions on whether business trips are necessary and their purpose".

"Hey, what's brought this on? Don't start getting stroppy with me. Becky, you've done a wonderful job with marketing and sales in Australia but I would remind you that your executive role is with London Wall UK, the Aussie side is, legally, quite separate".

"Oh, it's legals is it? Like telling Siobhan the Perth registered business would be put in her name to keep the authorities over there on side. I noticed you still own all the shares. Should I mention that to her?"

"Becky, what on Earth's got into you. Has the bubbly gone to your head?"

"No need for sarcasm, fact is, I'm thoroughly pissed off. Look, whilst there's none of the others around, let's sort a few things out".

"I'm listening, if nothing else it might take my mind off this bloody turbulence, why can't I ever get used to it?"

"Turbulence – good word that, most apposite. We could start with she who's already been mentioned, one sexy Siobhan. Luke, as the Yanks say, I've been around the block and it was obvious at first sight that you two were an item. Taking your pants down on the other side of the world is one thing, bedding her in Windsor the night dear Kyaw was in labour, quite another. Frankly, I was ashamed to be part of the *away day*. Strategy, my arse. I am perfectly aware of the two-year mission. You make your dosh, she dumps her bloke and the lovers ride off into the Gold Coast sunset. But what about us poor sods left behind? Left in the shit".

"Becky, I think you've said enough. I'll order another bottle, then sleep it off".

"Unlike some others, I don't take bribes. Let it all hang out – that's another Americanism isn't it? Listen, I did your dirty work in signing up the broker and market-maker for the rapidmoney scam. Don't you realise they now know your game? Once Marcus had rumbled Eric's little tricks, you should've closed the damn thing down. And, like a fool, I took your five pieces of silver cunningly disguised as preference shares. And I don't take bribes! We're all part of it – all sucked in".

"Christ Becky you really do have it bad. Is that it?"

"Yes, apart from the non-existent financial controls, the value of my so-called service agreement and last but not least my little hobby".

"This is getting rather tiresome. Go on".

"That lovely gentleman U Aung suggested I take a look at the checks and balances of the financial controls systems. What a farce. He's worked out how you've, what he charmingly called, *adjusted the costs* of the students sent from his charity. So I did – look at the costs that is. I found your business expenses somewhat on the high side and even worse that I was employing a few, what the accountants delightfully call *shadow employees*. The thing is Mr Chairman, you may do what you will on rapidmoney and the robotics side but you will not fiddle my risk management results. Stated simply, I will not have it. Next, in the likely event of a raid by the regulators or the police or, more likely, both, I want my employment contract paid up. I'll work out what four and a bit times my whopping annual salary and perks comes to and drop you a line. And before we start on this bottle, there's this small matter of Murray".

"What about Murray?"

"You thought he might be interested in *my hobby*. Sometimes your ability to ride roughshod over people's feelings astonishes me. Curiosity I suppose. Plus his interest in my cleavage and knickers. Why on earth would he be interested in being dominated bodily when his mind is already dominated by a certain female creature from the orient".

"Be careful Becky, be very careful".

"While the cat's away, the mice will play. While you've been cuddling Siobhan. . . I take it you've been too busy to notice the colour of Molly's hair?"

"I did notice a few spare seats further back. Becky, go and find one".

Twelve

"Ma'am, there's a call from a Marcus Clarke, will you take it?"

"Of course I'll take it – sorry, didn't mean to snap".

"Hello Alice, if I'm allowed to call you that, the girl on the switchboard asked if I'd made an appointment. A new one on me - an appointment to put through a 'phone call - thought for a second you were President of the European Council".

"I know, it's so different over here and especially at the moment due to a very big thing in play, everyone's on edge. Marcus, I would always take your call, you know that. You can get me anytime, anyplace. It's so good to hear your voice again, oh dear I'm shaking".

"Alice, I just want to ask you a question. I expect your calls are monitored – does it matter?"

"Not at all".

"Alice, would you agree to a quickie divorce?"

"Oh goodness me. Give me a minute. Oh dear".

The few seconds that passed seemed to Marcus like minutes, hours even.

"Marcus, if that's what you want. I know I've hurt you so badly but I hoped it wouldn't come to this. Despite everything I can't imagine not being your wife. Can I ask why so soon?"

"I want to marry Pearl".

"Oh dear … you'll have to give me a minute, oh, for goodness sake stop crying woman, damn, where the hell are my tissues, oh dear".

"I'm really sorry Alice but I couldn't think how else to ask you. Would it be best to leave it with you for a few days?"

"H'mm, isn't she? I mean, and the age difference".

"Alice, it's like you said in your letter to me. Pearl will never, could never, replace you. But you've gone. I don't want to be alone, always thinking of you with another man. I want to be with Tristan and Mandy. And Alice, I know it's hard to understand, and it was a first for me too, but we do have feelings for each other and I just don't care about the past. Pearl is still Naing's best friend and we all get on well together. Look, you must be very busy, but there's one more thing. We're going into business together. We want to start a publishing house. I'm winding down the day-trading and the Derbyshire police want me as a special adviser on a retention basis. Fact is with no Alice, I want a complete change of direction. And age, well, Pearl is five years older than me but what the hell. Plenty of men have older wives don't they?"

"Marcus darling. Go ahead, I owe it to you. If only …."

*

Pearl had chosen The Gingerman in Norfolk Square because it held a pleasant memory of a special evening with Naing; a memory to stow away in a top drawer. She smiled to herself: not the bottom drawer her mummy had joked she never had due to her whirlwind courtship. And she thought of the ginger biscuits nibbled with dear Eugene. It all seemed so long ago. Was she really awaiting the arrival of her prospective husband and his friend the senior police officer? The reader of novels would dismiss such a story line as pure fantasy.

Almost before he'd taken off his coat, Pearl confronted Inspector Neil Collett.

"He hasn't told you has he? I know how tongues can be loosened in the Market Inn".

"Hi Pearl, great to see you again. I have to say you look more radiant every time I come to meet this computer bloke. I don't think he's said anything apart from boring me with tales about young kids and what they get up to".

"What a relief, he promised not to but when you two get together, no secrets are safe. Neil, Marcus has asked me to marry him, or was it the other way round, I forget, but I'm so happy. Please be happy for us".

Neil grasped Pearl in a bear hug and swung her off her feet.

"It's fantastic news, you bet I'm happy for you, everyone will be. I think Marcus is the luckiest man in the world. I can't understand what Alice has done, none of us at the station can. The Super. was genuinely upset, even questioning whether he was partly responsible. He'd pushed her on. Did that lead to her high-flying career meaning more to her than the marriage? We'd all played a part in their romance and so when the news came, it was a real shock. Pearl, I shouldn't be saying these things, what's happened is past. But before I order a bottle of fizz I will make a solemn pledge. If, after all this you two mess up, I'll stitch you both up and that's a promise".

"Neil, just sit down and if you're going to be my best man, here's some advice. Start treating my bride-to-be with the respect a successful author deserves and stop trying to drink the South Coast dry. You are not in the debauched East Midlands now. We Brightonians are a sober race and you must adjust to our more refined ways".

Years later, Pearl regarded that evening as a watershed. Marcus and Neil were now true friends, she had a settled life to look forward to and her children would be in safe hands. It must have been that final thought that had prompted the question.

"Neil, pleased as we are to see you again, what is the ulterior motive for this visit?"

"Yes, you're right. We have come to an arrangement with the Sussex Police. After I've popped into Malling House in Lewes for a briefing on Monday morning I can have a poke around for a couple of days to see if I can rekindle the kidnapping enquiry. It's no reflection on their efforts but the enormous publicity and soul-searching among the school fraternity has, after a bit of pressure from on high, persuaded them to get an outsider involved. Thanks for the menu Pearl, I'll have whatever you have. Now, where was I?

"They, understandably, worked on the basis that it's a local lad and didn't buy into our theory of the story book being relevant. Any children's book would do if it was to keep the boy occupied while the kidnapper, or his accomplices, negotiated. But, as we know, the transgressor didn't. And, their theory on why there was no blackmail threat is that the young man panicked, returned Tristan and scarpered. However, we in the Derbyshire force have an advantage knowing Luke Brown and his connection to you two. Our view is that grabbing the boy had nothing to do with blackmail. It was intended as a warning - *stop digging into my software Marcus; get off my back Pearl. You both conspired to end the life of my Great Uncle Harold and now it's payback time.* Let's face it, were it not for the close interest myself and the boss take in activities centred on the Old Hall, it would have worked. Marcus, you understood the message delivered as a child's book and that's because you were intended to. Actually I'd prefer a beer to the wine if that's OK with you".

The interlude caused by the waitress not knowing whether there was any cream in the *Spicy tangy tomato and basil soup* and having to check with the chef, allowed Pearl time to think.

"Let's say we are right and Luke was behind this nasty business. Please don't take this as a criticism Neil, but surely you have to identify the young man who fooled the school into letting Tristan out, and if the local police failed to trace him, how are you going to?"

"For the two reasons we've talked about before, only this time they'll be implemented – successfully. First, Marcus is going to earn his fee. Pearl, your email was hacked. I need to find out how much technical work was done down here. By the way, and I shouldn't really be telling you this, over half our staff are now backroom. No matter what one reads in the press, it takes a lot of skill to penetrate the firewalls that are standard these days. What we know for sure is that there are some pretty smart cookies hidden away in the Old Hall. Smart enough to get into Pearl's computer? I would think so. This man sitting here sipping his overpriced white wine instead of supporting our home-grown brewers is going to tell me who hacked and how. If it's beyond even his ability, I have a budget to entice any kid he can find to do the job. Secondly, consider our much-derided non-technical detective work. Superintendent Macrae has persisted with our surveillance and, I might add, not without opposition from the bean-counters. We have some film of a young man who visits the Old Hall quite frequently. He's been identified as the grandson of the previous owner. It looks like he's preparing to move in and our snout says the staff refer to him as the chairman's personal assistant. I have some pictures to show Mr Simmonds the schoolteacher. With or without the ridiculous face and head coverings, it might spark something".

Marcus raised his wine glass and, catching the waitress's eye, rubbed his stomach purposefully with his free hand. She ignored him. "I thought this was a social visit – stupid me. I'm so hungry, think I'll take a bite out of this mahogany table".

Pearl giggled. "Should we leave and get some fish and chips, sit on the sea wall and face-up the east wind? No wait, someone's coming from the kitchen. One never knows, it might be for us".

Back at Mrs Tiggy-Winkle cottage Pearl remembered that when the WPC visited a week or so after the snatch, she said the top priority was going through the list of local lads, although of course he could have come from out of town. She said all the cameras would be checked along with reports of cars parked illegally. It hadn't helped that the school's CCTV wasn't working and that no-one had responded to the appeal for sightings of a man and boy flying a kite. She said it was like looking for a   needle in a haystack. Neil took the bottle of beer, leaned back in the armchair and stretched his legs.

"If our theory of the prime suspect is correct, this job was planned meticulously. Why use a car? Too easy to pick up, too easy to trace the owner. There are over six hundred train journeys each day between London and Brighton. Try picking one person out of that lot. And, if I was doing the scheming, I wouldn't go the full journey, I'd get off at a station earlier – I'd want to avoid the security cameras at Brighton Station. Then pick up a cab but not Uber, the calls are registered. There's still the old-fashioned taxi rank and cabbies willing to take cash. Bit more tricky on the return leg but still doable. The Sussex Police will have done their best; there's a big drug problem down here – I know where my priorities would be. Search for a local. Find a parked car. Dead end".

"So where will you start?"

"Marcus I know I've had a few beers but I couldn't possibly say. Let's lay a little bet. Fifty quid says I'll find evidence that the lad from my patch visited that school before you identify the email hacker. Pearl, you witnessed that. Best tell your man to start saving up".

*

When The Park squash club was built just over thirty years ago, the original owner had a grandiose idea. The design included a private room delightfully named The Dropshot. The indulgence facilitated entertaining important business contacts out of sight and earshot of the usual club members. Over time this space became something of a white elephant and more a source of ridicule than appreciation. But each successive club owner since those early days maintained the facade of a VIP area if only to sell the advantages of club membership. On this Saturday evening, The Dropshot, along with an outside caterer, had been booked by Luke Brown who had just the one guest, Murray.

Throughout the pre-drinks and then the fishy starter, fillet steak and pudding courses, conversation between the two men ranged over the general business climate and some of the more contentious aspects of the risk management programs. It was only when the cheese board and port arrived that Luke turned to a few specific issues he wished to air.

"I asked you to join me for dinner this evening because following an appraisal of my senior people, you have floated to the top. Obviously this must be kept between us but it means you have nudged above Eric and your salary and benefits should soon reflect that fact. I have been impressed, and I have to say pleasantly surprised, by the way you've built the robotics team and how close we are to releasing the beta version of the software. Keep piling on the development costs, once we start receiving royalties we don't want to break even too soon. Anyway, I know you understand the situation. Do take a drop more port – excellent isn't it?

"Murray, you should know that I'm doing my level best to hold the line with a very delicate situation that seems to have developed".

"Oh, what's that?"

"Comments are being made about Kyaw's, I mean our, baby. Well, not the baby as such but her hair".

"Sorry?"

"You must have noticed, it's more your colour than mine or, come to that, Kyaw's. So, man-to-man as it were, I have to ask you. Did you father the child?"

"Good God, what a question. I might have known there was a special reason for this evening, over and above the bullshit about my standing in the business".

"Murray it's no flannel. I meant every word and I'll prove it if you'll level with me. I'll ask you again, have you made love to my wife and if so, when and how. No, not how. I'm old enough to know that sort of thing. Before you answer, and I caution you to be very careful, two more rather important questions. Was she aware what was happening and are you in love with her? And listen, you may be able to continue seeing each other. Come clean, out with it".

"Pass that bottle. Oh well, here goes. Suppose this is signing my death warrant. Boss, of course I'm aware of Molly's hair, every damn member of staff is. Look, it could have been last New Year's Eve or more accurately New Year's Day. Don't think I'm trying to blame anyone else because I'm not but it might be down to that bloody punch bowl. It just about knocked my head off but I do remember putting Kyaw to bed, she was completely out of it and you had gone off with Becky. I'll be perfectly straight. I've always fancied her and being so close taking those language lessons hasn't helped. I can't believe I'm saying this, for God's sake man, she's your wife for heaven's sake. She would never have let me. Christ, did I rape her!"

"Murray, calm down. It's pretty embarrassing for me, I've heard the mutterings. Let's put our heads together, there may be a solution. What I'm about to say is absolutely confidential and I really mean that. You must promise not to divulge this to anyone".

"OK"

"I plan to sell LB Robotics. I know, I know, you'll say there's nothing there except computer code. But Murray there is, I've taken soundings. After Brexit and the two Covids there's much pent up demand for new technology to get the UK up and running again. It's amazing but no-one else seems to have thought of lung replacement as a treatment en masse for the unfortunate sods who can't be put on mechanical ventilators or where there aren't any available. And, of course, the whole world now understands how long it takes to develop an effective vaccine. The potential exists and a certain investment fund can see it. Now, here's something that will interest you. I got the consultant to put a value on my businesses and although I didn't expect much, on this one they suggested a sale value of multiple £millions. Needless to say, it's all predicated on a successful trial at Dobsons and that's where you come in. The value is in the software team modifying existing and developing new robotics. So, Murray, here's the deal. You sign a legal undertaking to stay with the business and bring each key member of your staff with you. Bear in mind the location will not be the Old Hall. If an investor spends that sort of money, you'll almost certainly be moved into a high-tech business park with room to both expand and take on other robotic applications".

"Well, I don't have any ties around here and obviously you'll want me away from Kyaw".

"Not necessarily. You'll no doubt think I'm callous but things between me and Kyaw have changed. Actually, they changed the moment she told me she was pregnant. I'll get another drink brought in. Perhaps it's just the way I'm made but after having agreed to delay starting a family, somehow a light went out. I have tried but honestly the feeling's gone. Kyaw is such a sweet loving person and she gave up her homelife and career for me. Christ, I'm getting all sentimental now".

"Luke, what do you want to happen? It's probably the drink but I'm confused."

"OK, let's cut to the chase. The perfect outcome from my perspective would be to pass some of my shares in Robotics to you so that the instant the deal is cut with an investor, you make some real money. You and the business move away. Oh, and bear in mind, it could be overseas. You do your level best to persuade Kyaw to go with you. If she sees things differently, I expect a split will mean her going back home or maybe even joining her friends near Brighton. From this point on, you can spend as much time with her as you like but for God's sake be discreet. It goes without saying that financially she'll be taken care of.

"There are a couple of other things. Remember I jokingly suggested some time ago that you asked Becky to show you her hobby, well, a little bird whispered that it was not to your taste. Fair enough but can you brief young James Salmon on what sort of things are on offer? He's got a girlfriend now and I thought it might give him some ideas. Secondly, somewhat different I might add, Becky and I have a line on the local MP. Following the trade delegation it's clear that the Government's interest is in the robotics rather than our financial work. So, I want you to meet him; probably mean a trip to London. Well, better get ourselves home now. I've an early start tomorrow agreeing a tender with my manager in Perth, looks like the salesman has pulled another prospect in Sydney".

As they entered the carpark where Luke's driver was waiting and Murray needed to wait for his Uber driver, Luke said he hoped their deal would come off. If anything went wrong, he supposed he would have little option but to file a paternity suit.

*

"Hi James, thanks for popping in. According to the feedback I've had, you're settling in well. Didn't think I'd have enough work for a full-time PA but it seems to be coming together. Before asking you to do another special job for me, I've an apology to make".

"You, apologise to me?"

"Thing is, Kyaw had a few spy cameras fitted into your grandad's apartment, just activated in the evening and during the night, so she could see he hadn't fallen out of bed. Until yesterday I forgot to remove them. Sorry but I accidentally viewed the video signals stored in the controller. We just have to be thankful Kyaw didn't beat me to it but wow, that girlfriend of yours is a real goer. If you ever fancy leasing her out for an hour or so, I'm your man. Only joking".

"I see – or rather you did. What special job?"

"You remember I had a problem with my Uncle Adrian which, granted not exactly elegantly, you dealt with, I have another issue to settle".

"Go on".

"Our dream goddess Becky has a hobby. Let's just say she likes to dominate men. Have to confess getting involved twice but on both occasions I was a bit the worse for drink and can't remember much. However, Murray will clue you up. Let's suppose you made an appointment and a mild drug was involved to help things along. Except, on her part, not so mild".

"Hang on Luke, this is heavy stuff".

"I know but then so is a man accidentally drowning in a river. And that's precisely it James, an accident. I'm not into this stuff but you lot are. Of course, you'll be named but if it's handled properly, the police will treat it for what it was; kinky sex gone wrong. It won't surprise them, she's been visited already with hints of going after her for prostitution or injuring a client. Why not take your girlfriend along and have some real fun? Tell her she's the sorcerer's apprentice. Actually, that might be one of my better ideas since she would back you up on what went wrong.

"Listen James, it's very important that you're blameless. I might as well tell you what's been on my mind for a while. There's no-one here capable of taking over when I decide to move on. I'm putting you forward for an MBA at

Imperial College. Your name is pencilled in on the succession chart".

Thirteen

An oasis by the landmark Red Canal of local folklore, just minutes from the famed Mandalay Palace and other attractions. The Hotel by the Red Canal is a convenient sanctuary, with its lush tropical greenery and calming water features. Each of the 25 suites is named after and decked in the fineries and cultural adornments of one of the four major ethnic groups.

As Pearl walked into the teak-panelled reception area, it all came flooding back; it was just as the brochure and website had promised; just as she remembered it on her first visit eight years earlier. Those eight years; never to meet dear Eugene again, exposing the evil deeds of Harold, helping Kyaw fulfil her dreams, finding and losing Naing, the birth of her children Tristan and Mandy and soon to marry Marcus. And all because an old man sought help with his library books. What would daddy have made of it? He would be happy for her, she was sure.

It had not been an easy decision. To draw a line in the sand, to give herself wholly and unconscionably to Marcus and the children, there had to be this act of redemption. Dear Eugene and Chit must have their memorial, their spirits must be together. It would be the field where Chit laid down to die. She would tell Eugene to leave that cemetery on the outskirts of Brighton. This time he would not be deceived. This time he would know Chit wanted him to return, forsaking the cold and damp of England to find the humid heat of tropical Burma. He would fly over the jungle to drop rice to the starving locals and in the evening she would be waiting for him in the little house she'd built. No butcher's yard to swill, no supermarket shelves to stock. None of that happened. Eugene and Chit together again.

"Marcus, I know this is asking a lot and I'm being a bit selfish but sometime between now and Christmas would you consider having the children for a week. I want to go back to Myanmar and I want to go alone. It's a personal quest; my piece of unfinished business. I have to set up some sort of memorial, I owe it to dear Eugene. Then we can start our lives together – do you understand?"

"Darling Pearl, of course I understand. Do it. Whether I can manage our two rascals for that long is debatable but at least I can try. We must put all this Luke business behind us and incidentally I don't know if it has any bearing on what that rogue is really up to but make time to see Garma at the charity office. Find out if she's actually working for the charity or doing Luke's bidding on some dodgy deal. You'll be interested in this, Neil has texted, he wants me up at the Derbyshire Force's HQ in early January to help with the Luke enquiry. Apparently, they expect their findings to come to a head and I'll be briefing on the money transfer software. Pearl, once my divorce comes through can we get married straight away?"

Sitting in a shady part of the garden and sipping her gin and tonic with a squeeze of fresh lime, Pearl sent a text. *Naing, help, the archivist at Madaya Town Hall, forgotten her name.* Being three a.m. UK time, Pearl saw the reply the following morning whilst eating her sliced papaya. *It's Chesa but when you arrive address her by her official title. After that fine. BTW it means Greatness so mind your Ps & Qs! I'll let her know what you want to do and ask her to help all she can.* Pearl's daddy had always insisted *business before pleasure darling* and so the boat trip would have to wait for a few days. Today it was National Highway 31 to Madaya Town.

Chesa was so pleased to see Pearl again after such a long time and she suggested paying the taxi driver for the afternoon. The Town Hall would be closed for the day. The field where Chit had died was only a short distance away and they would select a site for the memorial stone. She had contacted the owner of that small piece of land and he would be honoured to help. His ancestors lay at peace in the same cemetery as the lady to be immortalised.

Pearl selected a spot at the foot of an enormous teak tree. She remembered Eugene's story of how the lads had used teak branches to support their makeshift shelters. Could Chesa arrange for fresh bamboo leaves to be placed at the foot of the stone, perhaps changed weekly? Pearl would donate funds to the Town Hall to pay for this upkeep and what would be an appropriate sum to pay for the stone and to compensate the landowner? The stone should read, both in Burmese and in English, *In Memory of and Respect for Chit and Eugene. Together at the last.*

It was such a small field. How had Chit's family made a living from working this soil? But it was so beautiful and peaceful. Pearl understood why Chit came to this place on her days off from the hospital and after she'd retired. Where else would she want to be?

*

It was early evening and cooling slightly as the sun sank behind the Acacia trees planted round the edge of the hotel garden. Pearl sipped her glass of white wine and, on occasions, used the small wooden fork to take a slice of Mango. This was the time for reflection. It had been a long and exhausting day. The heat and humidity, but more so the emotion, had taken its toll. Chesa had promised to send images of the memorial stone. That small field was both alluring and haunting. The memory of this day would never leave her. Would she ever return?

There was an email from Naing. The channel I set up with Kyaw's friend Sam is working. She is puzzled and worried. Kyaw has told her in strict confidence that Murray is spending all his spare time with her and asking to hold and change baby Molly. Sam can tell that they like each other a lot. Murray has said that Luke may sell the robotics company and if so he would have to stay with the business even if the buyer moved his team to different premises. Sam is concerned that Kyaw might be tempted to go with him because Luke is still not paying her any attention and he's constantly on FaceTime to his manager in Perth. The girl who sorts out the travel arrangements has whispered to Kyaw that he's off to Singapore and someone from the Australian office will be demonstrating the software to several banks. The puzzle is, why doesn't Luke take his wife and leave Molly with a childminder? I hope your trip is going well. Don't forget the river cruise I recommended. Oh, be an idea to forward this to Marcus.

When the taxi pulled up on 26th Street, just one block from the US Embassy, Pearl was astonished. She was quite accustomed to the area around her hotel but this was something quite different. She was thinking it must be testament to how Mandalay had been developed over the past eight years. The Dotcom charity occupied the top floor of this huge steel and glass structure and the receptionist said her appointment had been put back ten minutes since Garma was chairing a meeting. Would she like iced tea or prefer sparkling water? In answer to Pearl's question, there were eighty-three staff on this floor and a further fifteen on the second floor used as overspill.

Pearl opened her laptop and pulled up the most recent three-month's management accounts. Even allowing for lower pay scales than the UK, the total remuneration costs shown on the accounts were far less than paying nearly one hundred people. Aside from that, she had no idea the charity had grown to this extent. Certainly the report to the trustees had not mentioned an escalation of this magnitude. After fifteen minutes, Pearl decided to act; she explained to the receptionist that having travelled such a long way and made a firm appointment on a very busy day, she could wait no longer. Perhaps Garma would prepare a report for the Board of Trustees explaining her failure to meet Pearl. The girl disappeared through a door behind her cubicle. Expressing her profound apologies, Garma emerged looking slightly flustered and ushered her guest into a small side room.

"Garma, just checking, you did get my appointment time?"

"Yes, for sure, I'm chairing a meeting on our big push into Canada and finalising the list of software houses to receive our begging literature".

"Really? Remind me, with Aung in the UK at present, who's in charge here?"

"I am".

"Really? When were you appointed and by whom?"

"Immediately Naing left and by the boss".

"And who is the boss?"

"Luke of course".

"I see. Garma, given my position as a member of the Board of Trustees of DOTCOM and as I provided the original funds, I was intending to ask for a tour of the office and speak to key members of staff but now I understand how busy you must be, we can leave that for another time. Instead, I'll ask U Aung for a report on all current activity including a list of each member of staff, their role, qualifications and details of how each was appointed. I do have one query ahead of that report".

"Yes".

"I've been looking at the management accounts and the remuneration figure seems very low considering I was told by your receptionist that almost one hundred staff are located here in Mandalay".

"Oh, that's easily explained. You get the UK figures. We produce figures for each geographical area we operate in".

"They're not consolidated for the whole of our charity work then?"

"Yes of course".

"And I hardly need to ask. Does just the *boss* receive those figures?"

"Correct".

*

Pearl was thinking she must be the only guest enjoying a pre-dinner aperitif when she was joined in the hotel garden by a lady who was not intent on maintaining the silent ambiance.

"You look English, am I correct?"

Pearl's first thought was to ask for a definition of *looking English* but with the memory of encountering Garma still fresh, she desisted.

"Indeed, yourself?"

"Every sinew, every fibre. I'm Mildred and you are?"

"Pearl".

"Nice to meet you Pearl, I expect you're the same, I'm joining a tour tomorrow and I appear to be the only one of the tour group staying in this hotel. It'll be because I paid the top price of several options. I do like nice hotels don't you? Everyone's lured here by the Burmese Death Railway and to actually see whatever's left of the Bridge over the river Kwai. I expect you're the same. Actually it's because of my grandad. He was captured by the Japanese and he perished working on the line. Well, to be honest, that's what the family thinks. *Presumed dead,* that sort of thing. Perhaps it was as well, those that returned were badly scarred you know, mentally I mean. Do you have any family connection to that terrible time?"

"Only faintly. Sorry Mildred, would've been nice to chat more but I've a table booked. Maybe see you at breakfast?"

Good God Almighty. These stupid, stupid people. If only they knew even half of it.

Pearl knew she would not be taking the boat trip. No Red Canal, no Madaya River to join the Irrawaddy. She had no feelings for it. She was not a tourist. Tomorrow she would go to the field again, this time alone. She needed to stay awhile where the stone would be. She wanted to talk to Tristan and listen in on Mandy. She wanted to tell Marcus how she felt. But it was three a.m. in the UK. She decided to cut short her stay, she wanted to go home.

*

The hand-written post-it note read *Alice, this one's for you.* The letter was embossed with the crest of Yadanabon University, Mandalay, Myanmar.

To Head of European Bureau, Interpol
Re: Mr Luke Brown, The Old Hall, UK

Dear Sir/Madam,

I bring to your attention certain matters appertaining to the above named.

For some years this gentleman has been advising my engineering faculty on the development of robotics to facilitate in vivo transplant of kidney organs. He has been paid a retainer for this consultancy work. In addition he negotiated a fifteen percent equity share in a Myanmar registered company formed to exploit any commercial benefit from this innovative work. Recently, he asked me to consider increasing this equity stake and sought my advice on obtaining dual UK/Myanmar citizenship and on placing funds in Myanmar.

My concern is his attempted use of a related matter as leverage on my position for advantageous personal gain.

The contract between this university and Mr Luke Brown stipulates that he cannot sell or pass on the software programs to any third party. Nevertheless, once the applications proved successful, he approached me to allow adaptation of the software to create robotics in the UK. In return, he offered me a share of the royalties arising from sales of the robotic application. I believe this idea was disingenuous. If a similar application was feasible in the UK, it should have been subject to cross-border discussion and regulatory approval. Furthermore, he offered to pay monies due to me in any bank of my choosing using one of his financial service companies. I took this to be an intended back-hander coercing me into allowing a breach of the spirit if not the law of our contract.

I now learn from my friend U Aung, who chairs the charity DOTCOM, that the cost of adapting our software in the UK is being manipulated to delay, reduce or prevent the payment of royalties. One final point, a young Myanmar interpreter who was party to his suggested use of the robotics software has been put in charge of the charity's activities here in Mandalay. I am wondering if that was to buy her silence.

The employment of Mr Luke Brown by this university has now ceased and I am taking advice on how to remove him from the share register of our company Myanmar (Robotics) MCA Inc.

I do not know if this gentleman has broken any UK or European law and I am aware that there is no formal diplomatic relationship between our nations. Even so, you should be cognisant of the matters I have raised.

Signed: The Rector

*

Luke was saying to Kyaw that he was really looking forward to an evening meal together once Molly had been put to bed. It seemed so long since he didn't have to go out in the evening. Luckily Murray had maintained his interest in the Burmese language and so she had adult company most evenings. He wanted her to be the first to know of an important decision he'd taken. He was closing the Rapidmoneyex.com company. He felt it had run it's course. It hadn't helped that the police had visited his consultant instilling a fear her firm might be implicated in some aspect of unlawful trading – yes, stupid, but he couldn't rely on her help anymore.

It was a shame that no dividend had been declared on the ordinary shares, especially as she held fifty-one percent but she had received her salary and he had to confess making a mistake in agreeing to the issue of preference shares and with such a high coupon. Still, it had passed a useful amount of money to Becky and Eric. First thing tomorrow he would instruct Becky to cease all sales and marketing activity and ask Eric to start extricating the money transfer code from the risk management suites of programs.

Would she be terribly upset if at some point in the evening he had to dash back to the office to receive the weekly report from the general manager in Perth?

*

Alice walked into the lobby of the Hotel Jardin Secret deliberately wearing her official uniform, showed her card to the receptionist and asked to see the manager. A young man aged perhaps thirty to thirty-five wearing a smart suit and, Alice noticed with some irony, shiny black shoes, appeared with an air of urgency that attempted to imply his life depended on meeting the tightest of tight deadlines. Alice followed him into his private office.

"Good morning Mr Maes, before I start it would be advisable to invite in a member of your security staff".

"That sounds serious. I'm personally responsible for all aspects of security. What's happened, are we in trouble?"

"That depends on how satisfied I am with your answer to my question. This can take a few minutes here or much longer back at The Bureau".

"Obviously, I'll co-operate in any way I can – we've never had any issues with our compliance with the security regulations. What's happened?"

"Mr Maes, my department is investigating a case of white-collar fraud. This work has uncovered an instance of potential blackmail. Specifically, a certain party claims to have film taken in one of your bedrooms. My question is simple, how is that possible?"

"It isn't. Since that well-reported case last year, and not involving this hotel I might add, each bedroom is swept electronically before and after each occupation".

"What about a member of your staff being paid to plant a spy camera device?"

"Any device of that sort would be picked up by the body scanner as, for example, would any items taken from a guests bedroom. The latest regulations demand we have such equipment".

"Thank you for your time Mr Maes. Should there prove to be any substance in the allegation, I'll let you know. Presumably you'd be happy to answer further questions should the need arise?"

"Of course".

Back in her office Alice called Brendan at the Lyon HQ.

"I've been to see the hotel manager who says planting a camera wouldn't get past his security systems. I'm inclined to believe him although it must be possible. Dead easy to do it himself of course, Luke slipping a few euros his way but I didn't pick up any signs. Certainly, he didn't recognise me dressed in my regalia and I doubt he ever comes front-of-house. More your invisible boss enforcing the rules. I'm now working on the basis that Luke was bluffing. In any case, now we're outed and my divorce is going through, who cares. Perhaps we should post a few bits on social media and make a few dollars – don't worry, only joking. I'll fly over on Friday evening so you'd better have those blue pills ready. To business. I'm now sending the formal request for information to the consultants in Nottingham. Usual stuff, how long have they worked for him, fees charged over time, nature of each assignment, that sort of thing. I'll offer a carrot – did they have any suspicions he was manipulating the share market – if some information is useful to us we may be able to avoid involving the firm in court proceedings.

"By the way, Marcus has been in touch. He has evidence of how the money transfer system works and I can now fire off a letter to the broker and market-maker. The net is closing and Brendan I'm over him now. Bye darling, see you on Friday".

*

James Salmon strolled into Becky's office with the air of a man who headed a company who'd just won a contested takeover battle.

"Hi Becky, she who is head of just about everything; what key client have you won today?"

"James, sweetie, whilst I fully appreciate your role as PA to the chairman, do me a favour and swiftly piss off"

"Becky, are there any listening bugs in your office? Do you record chats? Christ, I'm getting paranoid in this place".

"Of course not, what's up?"

"How to start? Becky I'm deadly serious, with the emphasis on deadly. This is not advice, it's an order. If you don't take it, he'll do it himself".

"James my lovely man, I am truly busy, what are you babbling on about?"

"Becky, you have to leave this bloody place and even quicker than instantly, you have to close down your hobby and make sure your regulars are informed and that includes me".

"Sorry?"

"Luke has asked me to dope you up so you never come round. He's got a grip on me for things I can't talk about. Becky, I'm really serious. Get that friend of yours in Aussie to offer you a job and then pitch to buy Luke's company out there. He's finished. You have to get away, leave now, leave this morning, throw a sickie, I'll cover for you. I promise on my grandad's grave, I'm telling the truth. You're the good guy around here, I've known it from the start. Just go".

Fourteen

Goodbye Maserati, welcome Chelsea Tractor having bags of space for children and all the paraphernalia. And jolly soon, goodbye police, Luke, and everything that wasn't family and friends. Hello to the kind of life he'd always wanted.

*

Inspector Neil Collett's idea of a January conference hadn't worked out. Their enquiries had spread beyond The Old Hall both geographically and commercially. It all took time, every little avenue had branched out into side streets, every person had links to others. But now they were ready. The first of April was as good a date as any.

Marcus was on edge. The top floor office of the Derbyshire Force's HQ in Ripley was unchanged from eight years earlier. The place in which Superintendent Bill Macrae brought things to a head. This room where he had so admired the work of Alice, where they had tried but failed to hide their feelings for each other. Bill spoke first.

"Marcus, Alice is aiming to join us this afternoon. If you'd rather not be here, we can get together after she's left".

"No, it's fine but thanks for thinking of it. We're divorced now and I'm with Pearl, life goes on. Not once did it ever occur to me that we would split. Our wedding, your speech. Ah well, let's get down to business, like you two, I want this lot cleared up"

"Yes, good. Neil's made this list. We'll try to stick to it, keep us on the straight and narrow – save time. Neil, kick off".

"The death of Luke's uncle Adrian. We've got the full report from the Lincolnshire Police and the inquest. The car tyre was slashed deliberately so the lad that's now owned up is in big trouble. He claims it was a favour for a mate and it's taken awhile but he's fingered a James Salmon who works for Luke, so there's the connection. Unfortunately, with no record of any payment, our colleagues over there are struggling. Still, even if it doesn't help us, at least they have their man. One thing's for certain, as if we didn't know it already, it shows just how vindictive this Luke Brown can be. His own uncle for God's sake".

"OK Neil, so far then Luke 1, Police 0. Let's move on".

"Right, the kidnapping from school of young Tristan. Marcus, am I correct, you couldn't discover who hacked Pearl on the email to the school?"

"Yes, we're into deep techie stuff now. What I can say is that it appeared to come from the same source as a hack on Alice about pictures on her mobile. Good on yer Alice, she thought I'd better know in case it got out. And who told her he had such material – Luke of course. But proof is another thing, it's like saying we suspect the Russians or the Chinese. That man is too smart for words". Bill Macrae stood up to stretch his legs.

"Smartarse is one thing, blackmail and kidnapping is quite another. But you've got your man Neil, am I right?"

"Yes, thanks to old-fashioned policing. Mind you, I damn near didn't. My trip down to Brighton was fruitless. I thought the lads at Lewes Station had done a thorough job. Fact is, there was nothing to find and my idea of the snatcher catching a train was wrong too. As well as checking all the film from the railway police, I actually caught a London train from Brighton and got off at the first stop. But again, got nowhere.

"Then we struck lucky. We got a circular from Stagebus. They had received a video of what a female passenger considered suspicious behaviour at Reading bus depot. A man wearing hideous looking headgear walked out of the ladies just ahead of her. We were in luck. The camera focused on the toilet block was working and it recorded a person of exactly the same build entering the toilet a few minutes earlier – dressed as one would expect as a female. This guy must have read too much Agatha Christie. The little runt travelled by coach in disguise.

After that it was easy. He went by coach from Nottingham to Reading but how he got to Brighton and back I don't know or care come to that. Mr Simmonds the schoolteacher has identified our man from the video and guess what, so confident was he that he didn't use his disguise on the return trip. The camera in the Nottingham bus depot shows him dumping his headgear before leaving. No reward for guessing who the kidnapper was. Thank you James Salmon for visiting The Old Hall so often and smiling at the security cameras".

"Right Neil, get your stuff to the CPS and once we get the nod, pull him in and we'll add drowning of that Adrian chap. Accessory after the fact will do. Wonder what he'll have to say about his boss Luke? Let's have a break. I'll get the sandwiches and coffee brought in. Marcus, I'd like a word in my office. Neil give us ten minutes will you".

The superintendent of police and soon-to-be head of a new publishing house, walked from the conference room, down the central corridor and into the private office.

"Marcus, I want you to know that everyone at this station is so sorry about you and Alice. It came as such a shock, you seemed so perfect together. Look, it's none of my business but I do feel partly responsible. If she'd have stayed here, and I've only twelve months left, and you'd both settled in Derbyshire; well I suppose we all should have learned by now that chocolate-box pictures never reflect real life do they? Don't answer, it's not necessary. A couple of things before we go back. Will you be available if I get mixed up in financial stuff i.e. money fiddles. Secondly, Alice is due about two o'clock with a *surprise* guest. I'd like you to stay but equally I can brief you later and we can go over it in the hotel this evening".

"Yes to the first question and I'm OK with Alice now. I'd like to see this through. I want to help put Luke Brown behind bars".

It had been reasonable to expect that the arrival of Alice would create an uneasy atmosphere, at least until the discussion of the case got underway. It didn't happen that way. Alice ignored her ex-boss and prodigy Neil, put her laptop on the desk and made straight for Marcus. The two hugged in silence. It mattered not that other people were there. It mattered not that a serious crime was to be reviewed. Two adults who once were ....

Alice introduced her guest as the management consultant who had put Luke's business on a proper footing. She had been cleared to help their enquiries and before joining the general discussion had been asked to give an opinion on the current stability of Luke's main business of risk management.

"Thank you Alice and good afternoon everyone. London Wall (UK) Ltd and its sister company registered in Australia are highly successful. They have dug deep into the market of managing financial risk and are growing rapidly. This is particularly so for the Australian arm owing to its reach into both Singapore and Europe. Because of the potential damage to reputation, the key question I have been asked is what would be the consequence of removing the chairman of each, namely Luke Brown. In our opinion the issue at this point of the growth cycle is one of management rather than leadership. In other words, each business needs to recruit a chief executive experienced in this market. This would not have been the case with the UK arm had it not been for the departure of Becky. I am told she is now in Australia and so presumably she might be attracted to head that business. London Wall UK is in a precarious position. My recommendation is for my firm to come in on a short-term contract basis to hold the fort, handle public relations and source a new chief executive. Of course, that may be seen as self-serving but we have good knowledge of the business and we withdrew from our advisory role once we were alerted to the possibility of illegal trading".

Macrae was saying that he could see commercial issues arising, there might even be political implications. If it came to it, he wondered who had the authority to appoint consultants.

"Alice, this is probably one for you. Well, it certainly is if the Financial Conduct Authority get involved. For my part, I just want to have a proper talk to this man if we think there's enough to go on. Marcus, what do we know about this money transfer business?"

"Its seed corn will go back several years. At some point possibly triggered by his trips to Perth as a young man, Luke spotted a market opportunity. Banks or specialists in this area charge a sizeable fee to move money from one country to another. Plus, there is the black hole of exchange rates; buy at one price and sell at another. A third factor is speed. As we all know, it's not just that Amazon sources stuff, the delivery is pretty much instant. Luke invented a new methodology. He could piggyback on software code he already had to alter the price of shares. Without going into the nitty-gritty, it was the profit from the increase in price that moved. The money didn't move, the data did.

"Let me talk briefly about how I picked up on what happens. Eric is the top software engineer and a good man to boot. I'll never forget how he sprang to Kyaw's defence at her graduation party. He wanted a few share tips and in return I wanted sight of some of his work. With the benefit of hindsight, I think he was tipping me off. It was that subtle I nearly missed it. He sent me a so-called shorting tip. He knew damn well I only back my own research and wouldn't buy in. My guess is that Luke asked him to, on the basis I'd get stung. Later he sent me screen shots that included interaction with third parties using a financial device not used in risk management. I could then see how it all worked. Alice, I can demonstrate to any technical party what I'm trying to put into words".

"So, it was or rather is, market manipulation?"

"Yes".

"And Eric was involved; he knew what was going on?"

"Yes". The consultant raised her hand to indicate she wanted to speak.

"Can I say something?" Macrae nodded. "This should be taken in the context of the survival or otherwise of the business. If the head of software creation is taken out, the risk management business will not survive. No company, and especially one built around technology, can lose its chairman, its CEO (who is also the driver of sales and marketing let us remember) and its top software engineer, and expect to limp along relatively unscathed. This game is too intense for that. It is not my role to comment on the legality of what these computer programs were used for but please take my view into account. One other thing, the superintendent referred to politics. However it came about, Luke Brown has been feted by the local MP and has a degree of national fame. If this affair is not handled diplomatically, forget public relations spin and the like, there will be one hell of a stink". Neil was showing signs of irritation.

"OK, OK. I get it. There are wider implications but as far as I'm concerned the goings on at The Old Hall and its tentacles can go to hell in a dustcart. This man caused the death by drowning of his own uncle. He had an innocent young child grabbed from school, which was hardly a bunch of joy for his parents, and from other intelligence we've picked up he makes a habit of shagging every eligible female within radius and, by the way, that includes twelve thousand miles to Australia. We can handle the organ grinder's monkeys with the softest of kid gloves for all I care but that man is for the high jump". Bill Macrae pushed back his chair.

"We'll take a short break and then move on to Brown's other interests. Alice, can we have five minutes in my office?" The interval lasted for over twenty minutes during which time Neil attempted to pour his charm over the lady consultant who looked dejected. Marcus joined them and asked her to send him a management fee quote saying he would do all he could. He explained that Neil hadn't meant to offend since coppers had a certain way of going about things. If she bought him a pint later she'd realise that he's as mild as a lamb. Bill and Alice returned and the conference resumed once again with the superintendent in the chair.

"There has been a somewhat surprising development. It's the early hours over there but I've taken a call from the police station in Perth. A very distraught young lady claiming to be the general manager of London Wall (Australia) Pty Ltd came in at about ten o'clock local time in floods of tears. It seems her boyfriend was drinking in a bar and one of his mates was bragging about the price his firm Tavills had secured, not only for the business she is general manager of, including its branch offices, but the head office building itself. A financial services business based in Sydney has bought the lot"."What, and Siobhan didn't even know?"

"Oh, you know her name then Marcus?"

"For sure, Pearl gets to know all the goings on from Kyaw and, latterly, her best friend Sam. In fact, Siobhan has only recently returned to Perth from Singapore where she was demonstrating the software with Luke. What else did she have to say?"

"Well, apparently she also told the desk sergeant that she and Luke had planned a future together in Australia. He was leaving his wife and she her boyfriend. It all came out when they got the man from Tavills in for a chat. Negotiations have been ongoing for nearly three months and the lawyer dealing with the sale, who it seems is also a mate, told the agent in confidence that the net proceeds have been remitted to a numbered account in Switzerland". Alice banged on the table.

"My God, he's still at it. Wait till we get hold of that legal practice". Macrae continued.

"Alice that's not all. As you'll know, Tavills is international and this bloke has said their London office had handled the same sort of instruction with the risk business here and the premises have passed to a property firm on a sale-and-leaseback basis". Neil left his chair and paced the room.

"Bloody hell, how can all this happen without anyone knowing. Christ, where is this guy?" Bill Macrae intervened saying that perhaps they should all pause and try to take in what this meant. Certainly, all this secrecy was highly suspicious but presumably he owned these two businesses and therefore was entitled to sell them. Does our consultant guest have a view?"

"Actually, not totally. Australia yes, but Luke passed some shares in the UK risk management company to Becky and Eric". Alice cut in.

"So those two have received cash for their holdings, good, that means they're implicated".

"One would think so but there are a few ways of cutting them out".

"Go on".

"He could have sold the eighty-five percent he owned leaving his two lieutenants with their minority stake in a new set-up. Or, he could have exchanged his shares for holdings in the buyer's company and then, presumably, sold those to release cash. A third more sophisticated process would be not to sell shares but merely the assets and goodwill inside the company. Luke is one smart cookie. My guess is he did a share swap".

Alice said that her flight left East Midlands at six-thirty. "Bill, shocked as we are, can we move on to the other businesses?"

"Marcus, you told us how the money transfer scam works but what's happening to the company itself?"

"Right, the Pearl intelligence trail once more. He's closed Rapidex and I might add, not before stripping out all the cash. He told his wife, who by the way held a majority stake, in a quite matter-of-fact way. She in turn checked with Becky who confirmed getting her dividends. Some sort of preference share wangle".

"I, one Superintendent Macrae, wish to make a statement. Luke Brown is a villain. Alice, anything further before you buzz off to your cushy number in Brussels?"

"Yes. Luke's thoroughly messed up in Myanmar. He underestimated the Rector of Yadanabon University, not only losing his retention fee but almost certainly his share of a company formed to make robotics. Tell you what, wherever he's bunked off to, it will not be Myanmar". The consultant raised her hand which Alice acknowledged with a nod.

"For all this man's apparent selfishness, there is one thing that might mitigate his actions, if only slightly. He told Eric's number two, Murray, that the UK robotics company was to be sold. For those who may not know, it's a pioneering process to transplant human lungs. And, a local company has signed a contract to manufacture the robotics for potential sale to the NHS. The point is, unlike what we have learned today, this company has not passed to a third party. Murray has asked my firm for advice. He has received a letter from a local solicitor saying they have been instructed to transfer half of the entire share capital to Murray and the other half to Kyaw. Like Alice, and with apologies, I must leave. If my firm can assist further, please do not hesitate to contact us".

*

Once again Aung had appeared at the school gate just as Marcus and Pearl arrived to pick up Mandy and Tristan. Of course, they both knew he hadn't just been passing but it wouldn't be mentioned and as usual both children ran to hold his hand, he was their grandad after all. As they all walked to the car, Aung was saying that his email to Garma seemed to have caused her to overreact. He thought the questions suggested by Pearl were quite straightforward. However, his follow-up text two days later had been answered by her secretary. Garma had taken a short break and was it OK if she did her best to answer the queries? He was puzzled since under the new rules she was supposed to give at least seven days' notice. He'd checked with her mother and it appeared she's taken a holiday with a friend.

*

The cruise liner Abundance had left Singapore for the Far East. Most of the three thousand passengers were booked for the whole four weeks but some were disembarking at intermediate ports. Only two were getting off at Busan in South Korea.

Garma was sunbathing by the main pool and been taken aback by the response from her friend Luke to a question from an American gentleman – or perhaps he was Canadian, she couldn't distinguish the accent. Luke had been abrupt. She was pretty sure he said he didn't talk to strangers and it was none of the man's business where he was from or what he did for a living".

Fifteen

By general consensus Sam Pembleton was a rough diamond. His business was house clearance which he'd taken over from his dad. His grandad had been a rag-and-bone man. A few of the older local people could remember the horse and cart and the distinctive cry of a*ny ragbones.* The third generation Sam lived in a large Victorian house on the edge of the village accessed via a dead-end cart track. Few went to the house, well, there was no need to. Those that had been inside spoke of a treasure trove of oil paintings, large ceramic pots, grandfather clocks and ornate carved furniture.

There was nothing unusual about the phone call. The local estate agent had a job for Sam. They had received instruction to sell the thatched Mrs Tiggy-Winkle cottage. As was routine, Sam and his two men cleared downstairs first – kitchen, living room and parlour. Sam sighed, he'd get his fee but there was nothing worth salvaging. His men were dismantling the wardrobe in the main bedroom and he started on the smaller room at the rear. Sam had seen a lot of things in his time but this took him aback. People hereabouts rarely took to books but this room was stacked with them. Each of three walls was covered in bookshelves and a few even sagged under the weight. Once more he sighed; there was no money in books – it might even cost to get rid of them. Under the window facing the back garden was a small dark-oak bureau with the writing surface still pulled down and beneath which was a genuine 18th Century Hepplewhite Camelback chair. Sam recognised it immediately. Now the morning was fine, he'd do his usual "nothing of any value – I'll get rid". He sat on the chair imagining himself back in the old days, quill pen in hand and writing instructions for the servants. The bureau would be heavy so the practice was to pull out the drawers, tip the contents into a sack and take the empty drawers first and the desk separately.

Sam found it surprisingly hard to pull out the top left-hand drawer and now he could see why; it contained foolscap pads – loads of them. He pushed the drawer back in and pulled out the lower one which was also full of pads. So was the lowest third drawer and all three on the right-hand side. He was flummoxed, how many years had he been in this game? He'd never seen anything like this before. He reopened the top left-hand drawer. The top pad had 53 written on the cover. He thought for a moment. He opened the bottom right-hand drawer and removed all the pads and saw he'd been right. The last one in the drawer was marked No1. The pads had been stowed away bottom drawer to top drawer and right to left. How strange, he felt a sense of excitement – when was the last time that had happened? Once more he was a naughty schoolboy "take your hands off me". Oh Elaine, what a girl!

Written in small and very neat blue ink, he read:- Chapter 1 – Page 1

For a Fen Tiger to be pounced upon in a land stalked by a ....

*

As he pushed open the glass-plated front door of the loacal estatate agent's office carrying the heavy box, he was met by a young man who (first impressions) looked fresh out of nappies.

"Ah, Mr Pembleton, thanks, just drop the box there please".

"Hang on young man, not so fast. Not having seen the likes of this lot before, I want these pads looked at by someone who knows what they're doing. Tell me, who lived in that cottage".

"Can't say, not on my list but thanks for bringing the box in".

"Well, take a squint at your laptop. I'm not leaving until I know".

The young man moved back to his desk and opened his laptop.

"A Miss Pollard. We were instructed by a firm of Trustees at Law".

"Name?"

"Sorry Mr Pembleton, data protection and all that".

Sam walked slowly towards the young man's desk.

"Name?"

For the first time Sam noticed a middle-aged woman sitting at the rear of the office. She left her desk and walked towards Sam, turned to the boy and nodded. He once again accessed the computer.

"Bower and Oliver".

"Phone number?"

The young man looked at his boss who once again nodded. He handed a note to Sam.

*

Ellis Crosby of Bower and Oliver was an elderly, distinguished-looking man.

"Mr Pembleton, following your call I wanted to come to your place and have a proper chat. We have taken possession of the papers as you asked and I agree they need passing to someone in the publishing world. Leave that with me. I delved into our records and uncovered a very interesting story. Many years ago there was a senior military man. I won't mention a name because I'm not sure where, as a firm, we stand on this sort of thing, but anyway he married a girl from a well-known family and they had a daughter. By all accounts this girl was, as one paper put it, *not quite normal*. What that meant is impossible to say but certainly she was sent to a special school while the parents spent years abroad due to his position in the Army. We know that when the child was quite young, her mother was involved in a fatal car accident and years later her father was killed while on active service.

"The child is shown as leaving school when she was eighteen and took a post as an assistant in a public library but the job only lasted about a year. Reading between the lines, she was dismissed, although the local authority put it somewhat more subtly. There was a report which referred to her paying insufficient attention to customers and spending most of each day browsing the books. She had lived with her father and his will left a substantial sum of money in trust for her care and maintenance. That is where we came in.

"The parental home in London was sold and some of the funds were used to purchase the cottage you have just cleared".

"So, did she live alone?"

"Yes, and all her needs were taken care of by one of our staff but actually it amounted to very little. Periodic reports from our regular visits refer to normal conversations taking place and her being clean and the cottage tidy".

"How did she get food?".

"There was a regular arrangement. She posted a list of what she needed every two weeks and we delivered. A member of our staff would go with her to the local GP and dentist as needed and it is noted that her problem seemed to be communication with people, or rather lack of it. She just seemed to be on a different wavelength somehow".

"Visitors?"

"None that we knew of although someone in the village said that about four times a year a young man called. He was noticed because he drove a *rather special car,* the make of which, apparently, was unlike any other in these parts. What's intriguing is that occasionally her food order included a particular brand of ginger biscuit and it seems she was most insistent. No other make would do".

"What on earth did she do all day?"

"Well I think you've discovered that. One of my staff has estimated that those foolscap pads contain around three hundred thousand words. No wonder she asked for specialist books to be purchased. We have invoices for books on the second world war Black Market and the Burma Campaign, various health topics and even specialist finance subjects".

"Bloody hell, what did you say her name was?"

"No-one locally seems to know her Christian name, she was referred to simply as Miss Pollard".

"But with all that family background, you must have seen her name somewhere".

"We did, it was Pearl".

The Whitby Trilogy
Part 1: Eugene
Part 2: Pearl
Part 3: Luke

Earlier works by the author

Barn door to balance sheet
Derbyshire born
Quantitative Wheezing
Poems about

For children
The adventures of Eugene

Wealth is not without its advantages, and the case to the contrary, although it has often been made, had never proved widely persuasive.

J K Galbraith

The author with his wife Julia and granddaughter Amelia

thewhitbytrilogy.co.uk

L - #0214 - 171120 - C0 - 210/148/17 - PB - DID2953668